# The Savannah Stories

# Against Their Will

# The Savannah Stories

# Against Their Will

### J.L. Lemon

This book is a work of fiction. Names, character, places and incidents are products of the author's imagination or are used fictitiously. Any resemblance to actual events or locales or persons, living or dead, is entirely coincidental.

ISBN-13: 978-0-9909589-6-3

Published 2019

"Green Eggs and Ham" ©1960  Dr. Seuss

**To Dad – My Angel on Earth**

**I am blessed to have you as my father
and my best friend.**

**To Mom – My Angel in Heaven**

**I still miss you every day of my life.**

**Courage is being scared to death...**

**and saddling up anyway.**

John Wayne

"I'll kill him," Ennis vowed.

"He's your brother," Savannah tried reasoning with her husband. "You can't kill him."

After their day she really wanted rest. Exhaustion set in from long hours in crowded planes plus layovers and the forty mile drive from Amarillo to the Rutherford Ranch outside Ennis's hometown Vega, Texas. They'd visited with family and finally retired to the guest house for the night. Now they were dressed in their pajamas and ready for bed – or so she thought.

Ennis paced in front of the bed, raking a hand through his dark hair that already looked unkempt from previous rakings. He mumbled all manner of fitting ends to his youngest brother. None of them meant for children's ears. It relieved her that their two girls, Lily (on the cusp of five) and Anna (three) slept in the bedroom next to theirs and away from his grumblings.

Her normally sedate, levelheaded spouse stopped long enough to meet her gaze. He did not appear sedate or levelheaded. For a fleeting instant she questioned if he was even her spouse because the smile crawling across his face shook a shiver down her spine. "I can't?" he repeated. "There's a lot of acreage to this ranch, sugar. I can hide a body on it somewhere." He began rattling off viable places to do just that.

Savannah gave a mental eye roll. She refused to trifle over semantics – *can't* kill him, *shouldn't* kill him, and for God's sake, *don't* kill him. It *shouldn't* require a refresher course from his thirty-nine-year-old detective sergeant wife (to a fellow homicide detective who was supposedly a mature thirty-six-year-old adult) on the drawbacks of committing murder. The long prison sentence should have been enough deterrent, not to mention that pesky Commandment stating *Thou Shalt Not Kill.* She assumed God hadn't meant it as a suggestion.

She felt safe for the night though. Considering they were a quarter mile down the road from Jake, she kinda doubted Ennis would traipse that far in his jammies to drag his brother into the night and follow through. Plus, she'd say, remember I'm six months pregnant with your son so *try reexamining the concept of "role model" before losing your mind entirely please.*

She rubbed her forehead with a sigh, her vision passing across the clock that read the unholy hour of half past midnight. Considering they crawled out of bed at four that morning, this jet lagged pregnant woman needed some sleep before talking her husband out of committing murder. "It's late and we're tired. Let's get some shuteye and plot a murder tomorrow."

To emphasize her wishes, she climbed in bed and threw the covers over her hips. Flannel PJs or not, the March nights got cold in the

Texas Panhandle – but thanks to Ennis's anger, the temperature rose to the point she nearly broke a sweat. "Come to bed, Evil Genius."

He did. Begrudgingly. Problem was he had a good point about Jake. The days of family harmony (such as they were) were kaput thanks to Jake's news. News that let hours tick by without sleep. One o'clock. Two. Two-thirty. She couldn't stop replaying the day that began innocently enough when they picked up her older sister Georgia and brother-in-law Dane (Georgia's hubby and Ennis's older brother) for their flight from Atlanta to Dallas. After a connecting flight to Amarillo in quite possibly the smallest turboprop plane known to the civilized world, Ennis's oldest brother Cal chauffeured the group to the ranch in his wife's Yukon. After greeting the family – all except Jake who was gone – they sat down to supper. When Jake finally arrived, everything went straight to hell...

2

Earlier That Afternoon

When Savannah stepped off the plane in Amarillo, an enormous weight lifted from her shoulders.

Last July she doubted she'd ever see Texas or Ennis's family again. She wasn't one to believe in miracles but surviving Jeffrey Holland's last attack changed her mind. The sadistic ex-surgeon/serial-killer tried on three occasions to claim his precious "Number 10" and came close to succeeding that past summer.

Nearly six years passed since the first two attacks. Between them they left multiple scars on her back from a brutal caning, the number "10" incised beneath her collarbone, and emotional issues that required therapy to heal from the painful memories and crippling paranoia.

A jury convicted Jeffrey of murdering nine women and attempted capital murder of a police officer. He was rewarded with a nice lengthy prison sentence – a sentence cut short thanks to Holland's lawyer. A month before Jeffrey abducted her in July, the judge granted him a new trial based on improper jury instructions. That left the killer roaming the streets and aiming straight for his obsession – Number 10. On July first Savannah came face to face with her nemesis and lost. That meeting left her clinging to life with fractured ribs, severed muscles requiring surgery (he'd refreshed the "10" above her breast with his scalpel) and one more setback she never expected to have. A heart attack. Jeffrey's coup de grâce was to drain the victim's blood while they were still alive. For Savannah the blood loss led to a heart attack and a coma. For days family and friends surrounded her bedside praying and waiting for her to regain consciousness. When she did she learned Jeffrey disappeared and no one could find him.

Once at home, growing paranoia choked out common sense and despite her family's support, she spiraled down to the days when Jeffrey's name incited panic and kneejerk reactions – checking doors and windows with gun in hand. Refusing to answer the phone or door. Savannah learned from experience that evil found cracks in a victim's peace of mind and crept in to gradually destroy it. It preyed on insecurities – the never ending "what ifs" – reducing a confident adult to a sniveling, obsessive coward. Jeffrey Holland had attacked her more than physically and emotionally. He went for her children by threatening Lily and abducting Anna. By the grace of God he hadn't hurt either one but he'd proven what Savannah maintained all along. No one was safe. Not until Jeffrey ceased to exist.

A day after her release from the hospital, a get well card arrived with a note tucked inside. The next week she received another. For weeks cards arrived in the mail from an unexpected source. Her thirteen-year-old nephew Monty in Texas. He updated her with family and local news, boosting her spirits and diverting her mind onto sunnier subjects other than where Jeffrey slithered off to since her rescue. His correspondence (and subsequent phone calls) transported her to the land of pickups, horses, cowboys, and mouthwatering BBQ. The place where agriculture, rodeos, 4H and Friday night football reigned supreme. She saved his cards and regularly reread them just to align herself with a normal existence, one without fear of Jeffrey coming back again.

Fortunately, someone ensured the killer would not make a fourth attempt. Was it wrong to say 'fortunately' in this case? If anyone considered her sentiment harsh she'd have asked if they'd had the pleasure of Jeffrey's company for oh, say, eighteen hours like she had. Or five excruciating days like one poor victim.

Jeffrey's beaten, dismembered body was discovered in a ravine – a symbolic, fitting location for him since ravines were his disposal area for his victims. Savannah offered to pin a medal on the person(s) responsible for freeing her life of evil. She hadn't been that happy since Lily and Anna were born and once she recuperated she received another joyful surprise. What she assumed might be a stomach bug turned out to be a pregnancy – or as her colleague John Mathis so eloquently stated, "Ennis slipped one past the goalie."

A lot happened since her last visit to Texas so when Georgia and Dane mentioned taking a vacation "back home" to Ennis and Dane's family ranch, she jumped at the chance to go.

As the turboprop descended to land in Amarillo, the Texas Panhandle landscape looked even more barren than normal, and flatter too if that was possible. The Panhandle was so flat, Ennis once said, a person could watch their dog run away for two weeks straight.

That part of Texas wasn't known for stands of trees, rivers, or dozens of tourist attractions. Instead it depicted the old westerns where cowboys drove herds of cattle into the breathtaking, fiery orange sunset.

John and Caroline Rutherford had four boys. Cal, Dane, Ennis and Jake, respectively. Each had their own unique personalities but they all shared four traits. Dark brown hair, rakish good looks, brawny physiques and lofty height. Jake, the shortest brother, stood an even six feet. Dane and Ennis stood two inches taller with Cal rounding out the giants at six-three.

Driving from Amarillo to Vega, the adults passed time by catching up on local and family news with Cal. Lily and Anna, however, passed the time ignoring their chit-chat and kept a sharp eye to the flat landscape for signs of their Granna's house. Lily's frustration emerged as a sigh, "Are we close, Uncle Cal?"

"Real close," he pointed off in the distance. "Look out that way. You can barely see the house." Besides Ennis, he was the only brother lacking a heavy Texas accent. Ennis's surfaced when he was upset or angry.

Lily stretched for a better view. Genetics worked in Savannah's favor with their oldest child. Blue eyes, chestnut waves and plenty of facial features safely labeled her Savannah's Mini-Me. Anna, on the other hand, inherited her daddy's overall features, his dark brown hair and warm coffee brown eyes (the perfect and frequently used weapon of persuasion).

Savannah leaned toward the window. A speck of a house rose above the horizon and she pointed, "There's Granna's house way over there."

She wasn't sure if the girls saw it or not but they reacted as if they had. Georgia took a look then whispered to her sister, "I don't see it."

"Of course not. You're old," Savannah joked, "and need glasses."

Georgia nudged her with an elbow. They shared a playful smile.

At forty-six Georgia was six years Savannah's senior and the same age as their mother when she died. Georgia aged as gracefully as their mama had and was literally her mirror image with her features, meadow green eyes and flowing brown hair. Like their mama, Georgia was soft-spoken and mild-mannered but possessed a devil of a temper when provoked.

Savannah's DNA scrounged a few of Charlene's traits for herself, namely her smile, the timbre of her voice (Ennis called Savannah's a bedroom voice), and the chestnut waves she let drape just below her shoulders.

Cal glanced at his sisters-in-law in the rearview mirror, "Hope you ladies brought your long johns. They're still forecasting eight inches of snow but you never know. It could be a lulu."

Before leaving Atlanta, they'd heard the forecast for eight inches of snow. They would be in Texas several days, plenty of time for the sun to melt off the roads. In the Texas Panhandle, eight inches amounted to child's play.

And she and Georgia weren't novices regarding Panhandle weather. They had seen it snow in April and hail in December, endured temperatures ranging from one-oh-nine on a calm summer day to minus ten degrees with winds gusting to forty in winter. An unsuspecting visitor might think he or she landed in the middle of nature's screwy experiment but one thing was certain. It took either a brave soul or complete idiot to try forecasting their weather.

"Adopted" Texans (as the Rutherfords labeled Savannah and Georgia) and savvy tourists brought overcoats and shorts for a March visit. It was the only safe thing to do.

Georgia told Cal they packed for good and bad weather then from the corner of Savannah's eye, she saw her older sister squint out the window. "Ah, there's the house," Georgia sounded like she found a missing sock. "I see it now."

"Took you long enough, Grandma," Savannah teased.

She took the ribbing well, "You're just jealous that I got a window seat on the plane."

"Yes. I am." And she was.

Cal exited the highway onto a parallel road. Savannah's back was grateful they were close. They spent all day sitting, either on a plane or waiting to board one.

Lily's eyes brightened when she spied the ranch entrance. Two sturdy metal poles anchored the black metal sign arching overhead. In big black letters it spelled "Rutherford". Both girls knew the sign by heart. It meant one last jaunt down another road and one last turn, this one into the driveway.

"Hurry, Uncle Cal," Lily prodded. "I wanna see Granna."

Anna echoed the sentiment with an enthusiastic *me too*.

Cal chuckled, "Wait another minute, girls. Granna's anxious to see you too."

The house in the near distance stood alone, surrounded by shade trees in the front and fruit and pecan trees in back. The rest was acres and acres of ranchland. The first time Savannah saw the Texas Panhandle, she compared it (privately, of course) to another planet. Deathly quiet surroundings, no one within shouting range (like their neighbors back home), low humidity (not exactly a drawback for native Georgians) and for some reason God saw fit to leave the area flat as a board and virtually without trees. She guessed He ran out of them.

Ennis's childhood home seemed to invite visitors. The sizeable two story home with a large porch and white railings had two towering maples in the front yard that gleamed crimson in fall.

Mama Rutherford's pampered rose bushes lined the flowerbeds in front of the house. In spring the full blooms and sweet perfume reminded Savannah of her mama who cherished her flowers and rose bushes.

The family drove up to the less picturesque winter version of the property. Bony, leafless branches swayed in the wind (it *always* blew there), the roses just began budding out and a brittle yellow carpet replaced the soft, rich green grass.

In the distance Jake's house came into view. He, along with Cal and Bobbi, built homes on the ranch and both sat "yonder ways down the road" as Mama Rutherford put it. Another house, this one a smaller, ranch-style (originally a guest house) sat near Jake's place. Mama handed Ennis the key and christened it his and Savannah's (it held a special place in Savannah's heart from her first visit to Texas) and later Mama added a separate bedroom for the girls. At the rate the kids kept coming, Savannah reflected, his mother should have kept the builders on speed dial.

Dane and Georgia preferred to stay at the main house. Georgia enjoyed watching Texas sunrises, unwinding in the peaceful rural setting and helping Mama prepare breakfast early every morning.

Over the years the ranch became a second home, full of love, laughter and family. This marked Savannah's first visit since her encounter with Jeffrey Holland. She drew a deep breath and sighed. Texas would be good for her, good for them all.

Cal wheeled the Yukon onto the semi-circle drive in front of the house.

Savannah barely released her seatbelt when both girls squirmed to get out so to avoid a mutiny, she freed them from the safety seats. Ennis helped Lily down while Georgia took care of Anna. Savannah, meanwhile, stretched her back. Her posterior spent the trip from Dallas to Amarillo in relative numbness so she stood a moment for the blood to circulate to her legs. She hated traveling during pregnancy. Women suffered enough indignities with the condition anyway but airplane bathrooms, small seats and her claustrophobia really didn't encourage a relaxed atmosphere. But they were there now. Finally.

"I remember the first time you set foot here," Ennis told her. He raised the SUV's liftgate for their luggage. "You wanted to run away when you saw everyone piling out the door."

Dane grabbed his and Georgia's suitcases, "Looked like a deer in the headlights.”

Cal pitched in to help unload, “You did look a little green.”

A bemused smile curled Georgia’s lips, “You never told me that.”

Savannah frowned at her spouse’s airing what she considered her dirty laundry, “And I think you know why.”  She explained to the guys, “I was overwhelmed by the multitudes crowding the porch and the fact every male in the family is twenty feet tall.”

Dane prodded, “C’mon.  You were scared to death.  Admit it.”

“Okay, I was,” she capitulated, “but you people don’t scare me anymore.  So there.”

Cal laughed, “That’s because you’re one of us now.”

The girls raced up the porch steps and knocked on the front door. “Granna, we’re here!” Lily shouted.

A short moment passed when the door opened and an elderly woman resembling a plump Ellie Ewing stepped out.  Mama Rutherford wore a sky blue pantsuit covered with an apron bearing a chicken motif. She wore her silver hair in a bob reminiscent of Mrs. Ewing and possessed a voice as soft and friendly as her features.  She beamed at the sight of her granddaughters stretching for a hug then bent to one knee and invited them both into her arms.  Savannah loved coming to Texas. A person just felt at home at the Rutherford Ranch, where life slowed to a simple, gentle pace and the familial surroundings encouraged kicking back and enjoying each other’s company.

Delight filled Mama Rutherford’s voice, “My goodness how you two have grown!  And so adorable in your pink sweaters too!”

Mama began making the rounds with her boys then turned to

Georgia and Savannah. She'd always treated them like daughters and that day she eagerly hugged them at the same time as she had Lily and Anna. "My girls are home again. It's so good to see you."

The sweetest smile crossed Mama's face when she laid a hand on Savannah's belly. "How's my newest grandson? Have you chosen a middle name yet?"

"Not yet. I hope this kid ends up with one. We just can't make up our minds." They chose Ennis's middle name Daniel for their son but afterward drew a blank. Daniel What? Daniel No Name Rutherford, that's what, at least so far. They stayed up late bouncing suggestions back and forth like an endless tennis match. Nothing sounded right. Of course family members, friends and colleagues offered suggestions, Dane first and foremost. Not a week went by without a reminder that "Dane" was a strong, masculine name and guaranteed not to get the boy's butt kicked at recess like Gaylord or Phinnaeus. Ennis nixed the idea saying he and Savannah risked developing a stutter from saying Daniel Dane for the rest of their lives.

Mama leaned down to address Daniel Whoever personally, "We'll find you a name that fits, won't we, young man?"

Cal's wife Bobbi, a young, trim forty-four and no sissy about helping around the ranch, emerged from the house looking chic in jeans and colorful Aztec print blouse. She bounded down the porch stairs arms wide open for hugs from their guests.

The redhead's spunk never ceased to amaze Savannah. Always energetic, always in good spirits. Savannah had yet to see Bobbi truly angry but figured deep down that iconic redhead temper blew higher than Vesuvius if provoked just right.

Bobbi made quick hellos to everyone then excused herself to tend supper.   Before disappearing into the house, she called out, "We're having butter beans so bring your appetites!"

The mention of supper inspired a Pavlovian response from Savannah whose mouth watered that the thought of Mama's butter beans seasoned with bacon and a touch of onion.

The door opened again.   Savannah's three nephews stood aside for their mother hurrying back into the house.   Thirteen-year-old Monty, the oldest, experienced such a growth spurt, Savannah barely recognized him.   The three wore jeans and the standard attire in that part of the world.   Dallas Cowboys and Texas Rangers t-shirts.   Ten-year-old Tyler and seven-year-old Zach raced down the stairs to greet their uncles then hugged the aunts.   Savannah noticed Georgia's eyes bugged at Zach's surprisingly stout hold.

In a sea of brown-headed, brown-eyed Rutherford men, Zach stood out with his mama's coppery red hair and sparkling blue eyes. He inherited her bubbly personality but also his daddy's strength. When he embraced Savannah, he wrung her dry.

Tyler and Monty took after Cal, Monty especially. Dark wavy hair and warm, kind eyes that probably made several girls swoon.  He shook hands with the men then gave Georgia a good tight hug. Savannah opened her arms to her young nephew who wasn't so young or small anymore.  He stood within mere inches of her five nine.  She remembered when they met – he stood eye level to her waist.  Back then the shy six-year-old toed the dirt, unsure of how to interact with "Uncle

Ennis's girlfriend".

A blizzard brought the two closer during that visit. The boy ventured alone into the storm, trying to return home from a friend's house. No one knew where he was or which route he'd taken, the road in front of the house or the dirt road at the back of the ranch. The family took off on horseback. Savannah and Ennis headed out to the dirt road while Dane, Cal and Jake searched along the front. Savannah had found Monty. He'd taken a tumble into the gully beside the road and hurt himself, unable to continue on. While waiting for the cavalry to arrive (and against Ennis's wishes), she carefully made her way down the cliff-like ravine to hold and shield Monty from the bitter wind and snow. She and her nephew shared a special bond ever since.

She and Monty wrapped each other in a warm, snug embrace. In a way it felt like a son welcoming her home. They parted and she gave him a once over, "You get more handsome every year. Next time we see each other you'll be a foot taller too."

Monty glanced down, blushing. A lock of hair fell across his forehead. For an instant it took her back to the little six-year-old toeing the dirt. "How ya been, kid?" she asked.

Looking up, he broke into a lopsided grin, "Fine. How've you been?"

The two parted and she pointed to her stomach, "Inflating like a balloon. A few more months and you're a cousin again."

"You're not showing much with Daniel, not like you did with Anna," he held his hand out to her six-to-seven month appearance with Anna Rose.

He was right. For some reason she lacked the six month girth with Daniel that she'd had with either of her girls. "Then he must be too skinny. While I'm here, I'll try to fatten him up."

"Is he moving yet?"

"Sure is. He's been squirming since we landed." She placed his hand to the right of her navel, "Give him a minute and maybe he'll say hi."

Her nephew waited. Daniel finally tapped at his hand. "That feels so weird," Monty said. Weird or not, he held his hand there until the baby bumped his palm again. Apparently the teen used the wait to gather his courage regarding a sensitive subject. "So you're really doing alright after last summer?"

"Monty," Cal scolded as if his son uttered a sailor-worthy expletive. "We discussed this. That subject's off-limits."

Monty hung his head, apologizing. He meant well by asking, but she'd never tell him the truth. Memories and nightmares plagued her too often to say she'd actually recovered. "Alright" was as far as she would stretch it. "It's okay, Cal," she said. "We just try to avoid that topic around the girls, especially saying his name." Since July, hearing Jeffrey's name launched Lily into crying fits while Anna withdrew into silence. Like their mother, neither of the kids coped well with those memories. Difference was Savannah could kind of compartmentalize them and temporarily tuck them away. At the girls' ages, they couldn't.

She tipped the teen's chin up until making eye contact, "Monty, you deserve to know. Your cards and phone calls kept my spirits up during my recovery. To answer your question, I'm doing alright and," she kissed his cheek, "seeing you and the family is the best medicine for me."

O   O   O

A person felt at home in Mama's house from the moment they stepped in. The living room had a rustic appearance with pine ceiling beams, dark paneled walls and beige carpet. A long leather couch faced the fireplace and TV (mounted above the mantel) while another smaller one sat beneath the picture window. A formal family portrait hung behind the longer couch. The four boys (Ennis was a sophomore in high school) stood behind their parents in a neat, stair-stepped row. It was the last family picture taken before John passed away.

His and Caroline's harmonious marriage extended to the home's blended furnishings – his preferences for rich wood and earthy colors mixed well with her brighter and more feminine touches including paintings of birds and flowers hanging in the bedrooms. Caroline's most prized piece of furniture sat in front of the bookcase. A rocking chair John built for relaxing, knitting and rocking babies. She'd done a lot more of the latter two, knitting her way through sweaters, blankets, and baby items and when it came to babies, she'd rocked four sons and five grandchildren to sleep in the dependable old chair.

Mama pulled back the dining room drapes to let in the natural light. A large pot of creamy butter beans sat in the middle of the table, along with the side dishes she and Bobbi prepared, including fried potatoes, cornbread and a pan of mac and cheese for the children (including Dane and Ennis).

The family took their places at their respective tables – adults at the long hardwood table that seated twelve and the "under twelve crowd" settled at a smaller table nearby.

Jake's usual roost remained empty because he was out with "his lady friend", Cal said. For months the rumor mill worked overtime about this "lady friend" who apparently was a local gal. From day one Ennis questioned who in their right mind would marry his temperamental brother and tolerate his wishy-washy moods. Jake did have a quick trigger on his anger, Savannah admitted that, so she looked forward to meeting this extraordinary female.

They joined hands for the prayer then dug into the delicious meal. Savannah liberally sprinkled Tabasco sauce over her butter beans and at Lily's behest gave hers a little squirt too. The beans, fried potatoes and cornbread served as a fine reward for exhausted souls after a long, grueling day of travel.

Halfway through the meal, the front door opened. "I'm home!" Jake bellowed.

No one actually stopped eating because number one, they were tired and hungry and number two, the food was just too damn good to let get cold.

Jake stood in the dining room doorway looking sharp in his black button-down shirt, blue jeans and boots. No one mistook a Rutherford boy. They all took after their father and favored enough a blind fool noticed the family resemblance. One surprising accessory that changed his whole appearance – and not for the better, in Savannah's opinion – a new mustache so full and thick (plus a patch beneath his lower lip) that visions of Doc Holliday came to mind.

Ennis thought along the same lines when he snickered, "Leave your six-shooters with Wyatt, Mr. Holliday?"

Jake was the least tolerant brother when teased and Savannah expected him to blow his top. He smirked instead.

Dane pointed to his brother's whiskers, "What's with the lip wig?"

Jake stroked the object of attention, "Just wanted a change. Plus my girl likes it."

"You missed a spot under your lip," Ennis prodded.

Savannah prodded back with a nudge for him to hush. He leaned back in the chair, "So who is this girl we've heard so little about? According to Ma, you're attached at the hip."

Jake's smile spread from ear to ear. Somehow it looked odd on the normally grumpy brother. He leaned his broad shoulders against the doorjamb then hooked his thumbs in his belt adorned with a silver oval buckle. The light glinted off the gold "JR" in the buckle's center.

One Christmas their daddy gifted each son with their own special belt buckle. All but Cal's had their initials. Cal wore a silver buckle similar to Jake's except instead of his initials it bore the ranch's brand – a backwards "R" with a second forward facing "R" with their spines aligned back to back.

Jake ignored his brother and looked at Savannah, "Y'all have a good flight?"

She replied the trip was long but fine. She declined to expound that she didn't recommend flying to expectant mothers who had to be shoe-spooned into those ridiculously tiny plane seats. Her arse still felt squeezed into ninety degree angles. Everything she owned gradually swelled too large to fit anywhere and kept growing by the month. Feet, thighs, boobs – even the plane's seat belt was a tad snug across her fatter than normal belly and she was only six months into her last (she hoped) pregnancy.

"So you're feeling alright? Baby doing well and all?" he wanted to know.

The question gave her pause. Jake never cared that much about her, much less her comfort level. She nodded with a thumbs-up. The question pricked Ennis's suspicion, "Why are you asking her that?"

"Geez, Ennis," Jake groused, "can't a brother-in-law care once in a while?"

"Yes," he said, "but not you. You never ask how she's feeling."

"I can ignore her if you want but I don't reckon that would be polite, would it?"

"Boys," Mama's brusqueness silenced the budding argument. She lifted a brow at Jake. Nothing need be said.

"Sorry, Mama," Jake apologized.

"Pull up a chair and join us, Jake," Savannah motioned to his usual seat, "Mama and Bobbi made a delicious supper."

"Does that include me too, Jakie?" a female voice lilted.

Savannah's fork clattered to her plate. Oh no... It couldn't be. That twang. That back-woodsy, over-accentuated Texas drawl belonged to only one person. A quick survey of Mama's and Bobbi's faces revealed the ugly truth. The Rutherfords knew. They *knew* this woman might show up and muscle in on their butter beans and cornbread.

Georgia noticed her sister's distress, "What's wrong? Is the baby kicking?"

"Indigestion, I think," Savannah whispered back. "And it's not because of the food."

Jake stretched the ridiculous mustache to its limit. The smirk alone freaked her out but this huge Cheshire Cat thing? Uh-uh. Something was wrong and it revolved around the hinges-on-a-rusty-gate voice hiding behind Jake. He asked, "We got enough food for another guest?"

Cal pushed an empty chair out with his boot, "Better start now 'cause it's going fast."

Jake reached behind him, tugged the not-so-mystery guest into view. Four jaws – not spoons or forks – dropped from utter shock. Dane, Ennis, Georgia and Savannah.

Stephen King was right, Savannah bemoaned inside. Sometimes they come back.

Jake eased his arm around Jenny Lee Crawford's waist to draw her closer. She hadn't changed much over the last few years. Still annoyingly pretty with her black hair and dark eyes that she batted quicker than a Southern Belle could say *bless your heart*. Her flamboyant attire, though, could cripple a person with an unbearable migraine. Sequins embellished an eye-watering fuschia blouse, formfitting faded jeans and rounding off the ensemble – multicolored western boots. She looked like a reject from the Grand Ole Opry. A little too heavy on the makeup, a little too front heavy in the boobs and a little too bottom heavy in the butt and a whole lot heavy on the hate for Savannah. That was Jenny Lee. Not that Savannah stood in judgment, not in her expanding condition – and an expanding condition that around Jenny Lee, tweaked Savannah's insecurities.

Make no mistake, Savannah told Georgia years ago. Jenny Lee Crawford's features and shiny jet-black hair were weapons any married woman should guard against. Especially the woman married to Ennis.

Georgia gently patted her sister's leg in a nervous tempo. It'll be okay, she whispered.

Had she lost her mind? Yes, Georgia and Jenny Lee's acquaintanceship fared far better than Savannah and Jenny's. The former pair actually conversed in friendly tones, smiled and got along. The latter? Staying in the same room spurred malicious remarks from Jenny and barely restrained civility from Savannah. The reason? Ennis slipped a ring on Savannah's finger, not hers. Whenever possible Jenny turned her animosity on her and let the insults fly. So Georgia's Mary Poppins's attitude of *it'll be okay* sounded utterly stupid. Savannah's expression conveyed as much.

Jenny Lee scanned their audience for reactions – specifically Savannah whose better half huffed up, ready to explode. Jenny shifted to her nemesis with a subtle arrogant tilt of her chin and tiny sneer. Savannah soon discovered why.

"Everyone," Jake proudly announced, "Jenny Lee and I have some good news."

And he said it with a straight face, Savannah marveled. *Jenny Lee and I have some good news.* A sudden nasty headache panged at her temple. Another nifty headache caused by none other than Jenny Lee. Still, she held out hope that *you're shipping Jenny Lee to a remote island and stealing the boats and coconuts?* Savannah wasn't that lucky of course. Judging by their goofy grins and amorous embrace, she had an ominous feeling her future danced on the precipice of abysmal misery.

"You've been dating *her?*" Ennis was furious.

Ignoring his brother's tone, Jake replied, "Yeah, since fall."

Ennis scanned the faces at the table, accusing, "Y'all knew about it?"

Bobbi glanced away. Cal settled for an uncomfortable nod. Mama replied, "We didn't want to upset you but we also didn't expect him to bring her here during your visit."

Savannah's hubby stewed beside her, scowling at them. She understood his feelings. No one expected to walk into *this* minefield.

Armed with that unnatural (and unnerving) grin, Jake handed down the family's sentence, "Jenny and I are engaged for a fall wedding!"

Ennis bolted to his feet, threw his napkin in his plate. He stormed out grumbling something akin to *get me outta this circus,* only he embellished it with a colorful R-rated word or two in between.

Everyone else turned to Savannah. What did they expect? That she would pitch a hissy fit? Faint? Or perhaps lose her supper right then and there? The last option edged out the others but only by a nose. And it was such a good supper too, she lamented.

She tried Georgia's approach by putting a Doris Day "Que Sera Sera" spin on it. Did she really care who the raucous raven-haired monster married?  Did it matter that if Jenny married a Rutherford, she and Savannah would spend holidays together?  And reunions?  And summer barbecues?  And God only knew how many other occasions?  Did Savannah really care about it?  *Hell yes. Screw Doris Day's happy-go-lucky shit. This is one of my worst nightmares come true. The beast has come to roost in my family nest.*

Jenny Lee thrust her newly adorned left hand toward Savannah who pressed back in her chair.

Dane finally regained use of his faculties, "I never took my brother for being an easy mark.  Jake, you've been conned–"

"Dane," Mama Rutherford called him down, "mind your tongue and your manners."

Meanwhile Jenny Lee kept pushing the ring closer to Savannah, silently daring her to expound on Dane's sentiments.  She would have except Mama already sounded fed up with the group's lack of enthusiasm for Jake's news.

"This is quite a surprise but it's wonderful news."  Mama sounded way happier than anyone else looked.  She said one thing but her eyes conveyed the truth.  Today represented a scant taste of future family get-togethers.

Jenny fanned her fingers, showing off the ring until the light glinted off the little diamond.

Georgia's anxious patting switched to a firm grasp on her sister's thigh while congratulating the bride-to-be, "I know you and Jake will be happy."

The same could not be said for Daniel.  He reacted to his

mother's rising stress. A tightening in her belly signaled bumpy roads ahead if she didn't settle down or Jenny refused to back off.

Jenny Lee tilted her chin a tad higher with a haughty, "Thank you, Georgia. At least *some* people have manners."

The meager remains of Savannah's graciousness emerged as a tense, "*Some* people are still trying to digest the news."

Jenny cozied so snug against Jake they practically shared the same skin. The two appeared sickeningly in love. Doomed, Savannah bemoaned. The family's future was flat-out doomed.

Apparently Ennis remembered he had a pregnant wife that he'd abandoned in the heat of battle. He returned to his seat and took Savannah's hand in a show of solidarity. They had spent from morning until late afternoon in airports or on a plane, sitting in a seat as roomy and cozy as a relic from the Inquisition. She was tired. Her back ached and her unborn son practiced his aerobics on and off throughout the trip. If he took after his sisters, he would soon throw the switch on his mama's central nervous system, throwing her into a fit worthy of the Exorcist. Oh, the pleasures of pregnancy. Toss in a grenade called Jenny Lee and let the party begin.

Ennis sneered at Jake and his betrothed, "Is this a marriage of convenience?"

"Jake and I have been in love for months," Jenny smooched "Jakie" on the cheek. "I can't believe I didn't fall for him sooner." Then she charged at Ennis, threw her arms around him and squeezed until his eyes bugged, "We're gonna be family, Sugarbear!"

Savannah felt reasonably sure Jenny said Sugarbear but with her drawl it emerged Sugarbayer. Either way, cutsie names were the privilege of the spouse, not the ex-girlfriend. Protocol dictated Savannah rise from her seat and slap the ever-loving shit out of the bold offender but a cramp seized her. And seeing Jenny's octopus-like embrace on Ennis – and the fact his face was smashed into those enormous boobs – did not help.

It took effort for Ennis to shrug free of Jenny Lee's smothering hold. Once his face faded from plum to cherry red, he asked Savannah if she was okay.

A little rub here and there convinced Daniel to relax. She blew out a gradual breath as Jenny Lee rolled her eyes, "Geez, it's just a baby."

Savannah snapped around to confront Jenny but Georgia put a firm hand to her sister's arm. She put words to Savannah's drop-dead glare, "Jenny, it's been a long day for us. Please keep that in mind."

…And the cramp crept back in all its painful glory.

"Of course," Jenny Lee pouted, "but you'd think she'd be a *little* happy for me an' Jake."

Savannah hated contending with a cramp and a brat. Jenny's ridiculous statement just doubled her aggravation, "I'm absolutely rapturous over your news but my son is stretching his legs at the current time. After today, bearing these moments with grace takes effort."

She waved off the comment, "Well, you should be used to it by now. You've already had two kids."

Savannah tensed. Georgia's grip dug into her sister's arm. The resulting pain turned her ire on the older sibling with an order to let go. Georgia reluctantly did.

The females at the table – and Ennis – turned their attention to

Savannah's growing angst, effectively pushing Jenny aside. Dane centered on Jake. Savannah interpreted the former's expression as *why did you bring this intruder into our midst and threaten to marry it?* Cal looked none too pleased either. She wondered why. He had to realize this confrontation was coming eventually.

Mama rose from her seat, "Savannah, honey, try walking if Daniel will let you. Here, let me help you."

Great idea. Plus it would put some mileage between her and the jealous brat. Savannah didn't carry the baby six months just to spend her life behind bars for killing Jenny Lee Crawford.

"Daniel? That's his name?" Jenny Lee sounded surprised.

When Ennis replied "yes" she smiled, "Oh, Ennis, it's perfect. I'm so happy for you. A namesake."

Georgia and Mama rounded the table to Savannah. Mama gave a subtle nod to Bobbi who then motioned Monty over and whispered in his ear.

Ennis stared after his wife baby-stepping out of the room. He was more concerned with her than with Jenny's gushing enthusiasm. He told Jake's new fiancée, "It was Savannah's idea to name him after me."

"Oh." The word dropped like a rock. "What's his middle name?"

Savannah opted to continue the trek to the living room. Ennis could field this question – which he did, "We're still tossing names around." He called after his wife, "Are you gonna be okay, babe?"

"I'll be fine in a little while." After lots of peace and quiet...

Bobbi took Jenny's hand, "Let's go talk nuptials." She said it so convincingly even Savannah believed her sincerity.  Monty joined in by asking to be an usher at the wedding.  Jenny Lee giggled with glee, "Why surely, you sweet thing.  I was gonna ask if you would."

Once they had the room to themselves, Mama sighed out a pent-up breath.  Savannah shook her head for the same reason.  One confrontation down, a billion more to go.

## 3

A big silvery moon hung overhead by the time Ennis, Savannah and the girls retired to their ranch house down the way. The few hours with Jenny sapped their energy, not to mention put a damper on their vacation. All Savannah wanted was to climb between the covers, throw them over her head and pretend the day never happened.

They drove Dane's F-150, his most prized possession until marrying Georgia and moving to Atlanta. Savannah relaxed when the headlights illuminated their sanctuary up ahead. White with a slate colored roof, nothing looked so close to heaven, especially that night.

Ennis parked in front of the house. The warm glow from the porch light beckoned her back to the good old days when she and Ennis sat at the bistro set on the front porch drinking coffee and watching the Texas sunrise. She looked longingly at that charming table and pair of chairs and wished for those dreamy days of peace and quiet, just her and Ennis (with the kids asleep inside), and no thought or mention of Jenny Lee during their visit.

Lily and Anna sleepily blinked awake when Mama and Daddy

carried them inside to bed. Ennis restrained from mentioning Jenny until they'd tucked the girls in and shut the bedroom door, effectively closing them off from Daddy's seething.

Conversation trickled between husband and wife as they undressed. She concentrated on the family and food. When he did speak, Ennis brooded over Jake and Jenny Lee.

The two moved in harmony together around the small bathroom. Living in a small house years ago trained them to synchronize each task so as not to tangle up or crowd each other. Neither accidently elbowed the other while brushing their teeth or squeezing past to use the toilet. The bed was a different story though. No matter how quaint the ranch house was, the charm failed to translate to the full size bed awaiting them – and cramming into a bed that size became problematic for comfort and space, especially for a pregnant woman. Savannah thanked God her six month belly didn't pooch out as far with Daniel as it had with Anna.

But at the rate Ennis paced the floor, Savannah needn't worry about space. She had the whole bed to herself. More pacing answered her prods to get some sleep for the big cookout planned the next day.

While he stewed she let her vision wander to the picture gallery Mama hung on the opposite wall. Pictures of Ennis's parents, Dane and Georgia, Cal and Bobbi, one of Monty, Tyler and Zach and lastly a photo of Jake encircled a portrait of Ennis, Savannah and the girls. Lily sat in her daddy's lap and Anna in her mother's. In a few years they would update the portrait to include their son. For now four happy, oblivious faces smiled back at Savannah. She'd bet her life whoever said "ignorance is bliss" ran across a Crawford in their lifetime. That morning when they boarded the plane to Dallas, snowfall totals and scheduling vacation days remained the biggest logistics issues. Now the mere idea of logistics sounded laughable. Forget blizzards. They had Hurricane Jenny to contend with. Forever.

"...I'll kill him. That's what I'll do. I'll kill him."

Ennis's outburst drew her attention back to him. In the process her vision skimmed across a cross-stitched Bible verse Mama framed and placed on the wall that began *Love is patient, love is kind...* Savannah skipped to the part reading *it is not easily angered, it keeps no record of wrongs* and asked God to hold that thought while her husband went berserk. "He's your brother. You can't kill him," she said. When they left that evening, however, the entire family might have voted to run Jake – and his choice of mate – out of town.

Ennis stopped mid-stride. He sounded like a mob boss bent on revenge, "There's a lot of acreage to this ranch, sugar. I can hide a body on it somewhere." He stepped to the window, fingered the blue curtains aside. He glared hard toward the main house where Jake stayed the night, "I can always dump him in that gully where Monty fell years ago. I doubt anyone would find his sorry carcass there."

"Except me since you just mentioned it."

"You wouldn't testify against me. You're my wife."

"For the record, I'd appreciate not being put in that position at all. Ennis, come to bed. It's after midnight. Let's get some shut-eye and plot a murder tomorrow."

Calming down an irate spouse equated to sneezing with your eyes open – at least with Ennis. The man took forever to accept the truth.

Come hell or high water, Jake and Jenny were getting hitched.  Ennis had taken an over-the-counter sleep aid after they put the girls to bed but at that rate, he'd need two just to yawn.

Since their marriage he'd adjusted to the noise of city life, the traffic, the horns and sirens but when they visited the ranch, the silence kept him awake.  It required a day or two to adjust before the quiet of the country – or "Hicksville" as fellow detective John Mathis called it – allowed for sleep.  Traffic was scarce down the road in front of the ranch. Maybe twenty or thirty vehicles a day and a person had to strain to hear the whisper of tires on pavement or a rumbling muffler passing by. However on calm, hot summer nights, a perspiring insomniac heard the roar and whine of eighteen wheelers charging down I-40 in the distance.

She patted the bed, "Come to bed, Evil Genius."

Ennis finally climbed in, kissed her then slipped his hand beneath her top.  His cool touch settled on her baby bump.  Moments passed when Daniel tapped ever-so-softly against his palm.

Ennis grinned.  Finally.  Savannah nearly sighed.  They actually stood a chance of getting some sleep that night.

"He's active," Ennis said.

"He's had a big day since it's his first time on a plane.  He's telling you about it."

"That's my boy," my husband crowed with pride.

"Yep," she agreed.  "A regular Superman at six months.  Already able to dent Mama's spine with a single kick."  Her mind drifted to spending future holidays around Jenny Lee.  Chowing down on juicy, tender turkey and the sumptuous trimmings while resisting the urge to club the brat with a nice, fat drumstick.

"...buy you a Cowboys jersey with your name stamped across the back and a little football for you to play with," Ennis said to her navel.

Seeing her handsome hunk speaking to her belly was priceless and endearing. Her fingers threaded his hair, tickled his ear, "Is Sugarbear cooing to his wittle boy?"

Warm lips pressed to her bare stomach. Ennis teased, "Mama's playing with fire tonight."

"Sugarbayerrrrrr," she drawled in her best Texas accent, "how could you treat me this way? I'm carryin' yore child. The frewt of yore loins."

"You're pushin' it, babe," he propped his chin on the highest point of her six month Everest. "And your accent sucks."

His fingers skimmed along her belly then feather-touched along her side. When she shivered, his mouth lifted in a tiny mischievous grin.

Her hand grasped his. The scamp knew how she hated tickling. "Okay, okay. I won't tease you about her anymore. Truce?"

"Truce." His hand returned to her stomach, tapped at Daniel's condo. Nothing.

Maybe he didn't appreciate tickling either, she thought.

"I know you've told me with Lily and Anna but remind me what it feels like when the baby moves."

Pregnancy both fascinated and confused him which inspired the strangest questions – some of which were beyond her experience or knowledge. Ennis possessed the curiosity of a child, the sexual appetite of a teenager and a surprising maturity that many men never seem to acquire. How many husbands asked that question? How many really cared? "It kinda feels like popcorn popping. Sometimes like butterflies fluttering around."

His eyes closed, the corners of his mouth still faintly lifted as if picturing her description. When Daniel poked at his palm, Ennis's smile eased into a leisure one she instantly recognized and loved. It was the very smile that sent her head over heels for Ennis Rutherford. Savannah called the feeling "stupid-happy", and she recommended it to anyone willing to listen – even a bratty woman who easily held a grudge and a temperamental, brooding rancher with peculiar preferences in a fiancée.

Reality encroached on Ennis's good mood. Jenny Lee had that effect on them both, like their own personal black cat always crossing their paths.

He moved up as she turned on her side to face him. He propped his arm on her waist. Fingertips caressed the small of her back. Ennis's height and build gave him an intimidating appearance. Broad shoulders, trim waist and muscular in all the right places. He treated Savannah as delicate as a porcelain doll, his touch inspiring smiles, wiping tears or bringing pleasure. And he was all hers. That was why Jenny Lee Crawford hated her.

"My brother is a fool," he declared. "He actually believes she loves him."

"Maybe Jake's lonely. His brothers are married and having kids. Maybe he wants companionship too." Though dealing with Jake required a forgiving female heart, tolerant soul, and ability to disarm a tricky disposition. Three qualities that, in Savannah's opinion, Jenny lacked so far.

"Then buy a goldfish. That way when its mouth moves, nothing comes out."

She frowned at him.

"Or he could get a dog. They're more loyal, they provide good companionship and God knows their barking doesn't compare to her jabbering."

She tried reasoning with him, "Ennis, the wedding may not happen. Fall is several months away."

"Well, if Jake's desperate for a wife, there's nothing to be done about it, I guess. He's not noted for being receptive to logic."

"So you believe Jake's marrying for convenience and that he doesn't love her?"

"He told me and Dane this was the only way to shut down the nagging over his single status."

That sounded more like a "Jake" answer to two pushy siblings breathing down his neck, not necessarily the truth. He wasn't a receptive person, Ennis was right, but growing up with three older brothers couldn't have been easy.

Ennis continued, "I figure Jenny Lee poured on the charm so he either *thinks* he's in love or he's settled for the first female who showed serious interest." He rolled his eyes, "And my brothers call *me* dense at times."

"Maybe he is in love." Stranger things happened... but nothing quite as strange as the expression Ennis gave her.

"Then I don't know who to pity more, him or her, 'cause I sure as hell pity us. We have to deal with Jenny every time we visit. You especially."

Yes, there was that. But what could she say? Like most situations, there were good points and bad ones. Good for Jake that he found love (if he had). Not so good for the Ennis Rutherford family when they landed in Texas from now on. Ennis felt betrayed by Jake for dating her and also by his family for not forewarning him of the relationship. He felt shafted by Jenny Lee for "reeling in" his brother. As for Savannah, the joy of holidays cooled to tepid hope. Instead of laughing and having fun with everyone, she'd be dodging Jenny's snide remarks and sharp insults.

For now, though, Ennis needed a pep talk. She pressed a kiss to his lips, assuring, "We'll make it, babe. Just because she's marrying Jake doesn't mean we're living with her. Remember, she has to deal with me too and she'll learn my boundaries. Don't worry."

"You're either a blind optimist or flat-out delusional." Ennis's vision passed over her shoulder to the nightstand, "Hey, Ma framed our picture from last Christmas."

And enlarged it to a five by seven too. She'd placed it on Savannah's nightstand in prominent view. She wagered a five by seven of Georgia and Dane graced her sister and brother-in-law's nightstand as well. Mama's love of snapping holiday pictures rivaled a fashion photographer at a photo shoot. A hundred poses meant a hundred pictures.

Savannah nodded behind him, "She also updated the girls' photos on your nightstand. She's always busy with something. Pictures, knitting, preserves, gardening."

"She'd go crazy if her hands sat still. You two remind me of each other."

"I plant flowers and pray they live. I don't knit and I don't can tomatoes. They're already in cans at Kroger," she joked.

"Yeah but you stay busy with us, work and church. You love to cook and play golf. And you garden, too."

"Only because your membership as a Steel Magnolia is revoked if you're a Southern woman and don't garden."

He smiled at that. "Nobody'd have the nerve to revoke your membership, not with your grit. You're the only woman I ever met that fought against accepting a *first date*, much less getting involved."

True, but his persistence, charm and good looks chipped away at her stubborn streak. She stood no chance anyway because any woman with two eyes, a brain and an ounce of libido would have surrendered the battle. He'd never believe her inner struggle back then, or the extra miles she ran and cool showers she endured to keep that stubborn streak intact.

She shrugged, "For the record I fought the whole idea because of work. Nothing creates more hell than co-workers who break up after being involved. That and except for Roy Carlson, I hadn't had great luck with the men in my life."

He slowly traced the scars of her childhood through the flannel fabric. Her father R.J.'s handiwork crisscrossed her back and bottom in a roadmap of abuse. Over the years he'd memorized the marks left by belts and willow branches. His soft stroking, odd as it sounded, seemed apologetic for her painful youth.

She felt his temper rising with her last statement. She'd not only suffered at the hands of her father but also a possessive boyfriend who used his fists more than his mouth to communicate.

Savannah veered the conversation back to Jenny before anger got the better of him. "I assume Jenny had a better experience with the male population since she clings to them."

He nodded, "Her folks and brothers spoiled her rotten and they had the money to do it. She grew up believing she should have whatever or whoever she desired."

Well, that explained things better. A spoiled little rich girl. Daddy's angel. Savannah's daddy called her his "baby girl" but didn't blink an eye about flogging the shit out of her if she looked at him wrong. Suffering beatings altered a person's outlook on life but so did the other extreme. No matter her upbringing, "I can't fault Jenny Lee for one thing."

Ennis's brow lifted. Coming from Savannah, those words not only intrigued but confused him. She faulted Jenny for plenty since knowing her and Ms. Crawford reciprocated in kind. Savannah touched his cheek, "She wanted a good man in her life. One who'd protect her, love her, and cherish her. You're a fine man, Ennis. I'm just glad you're my husband and not hers."

4

Cal's truck rumbled past the ranch house shortly after four that morning. Farmers and ranchers shared a lot in common, one being that certain tasks required attention before sunrise – before heat, cold or moisture affected their livelihoods. At the Rutherford Ranch four o'clock was the routine wake-up call year-round but summertime demanded it when the day's heat set in early and fried everyone's decent moods (including the cattle's).

The deep throb of Cal's Dodge woke Savannah that morning, bringing consciousness to an unwilling brain and sore body. She swore she took a beating the day before, both physical and emotional. Then she remembered they'd fought Round One with Jenny Lee and the flouncy, flamboyant twerp won.

Bleary-eyed and stretching stiff, achy muscles, she and Ennis stumbled to the bathroom, shouldering past each other to brush their teeth and grab a quick shower.

Before endeavoring to roust their two tired children at such an outrageous hour, they fortified themselves with a cup of Savannah's coffee.  Strong enough to lift weights, or as Ennis accused, "strong enough to kill weeds".

By five o'clock the brood headed to the main house in Dane's Ford.  Savannah took advantage of the ranch's breathtaking view overhead.  Few places provided such beauty at night, free of smog, trees and blaring city lights.  Sunset was her favorite in Texas.  Nighttime rated a close second.

While Ennis drove, she leaned to the window for a peek at the sky.  Stars sparkled like diamonds on black velvet.  A curtain of midnight hung over the landscape with only a soft glow from the town's street lights.  There was no traffic, no birds, no airplanes overhead, no distractions.  Just pristine silence and a beautiful night sky.

The rich smoky aroma of bacon caressed Savannah's senses when they stepped in the back door.  Bobbi stood at the stove frying the luscious smelling delicacy.  Mama wore her red and white "Mama Hen" apron while cracking eggs to scramble.  Savannah wanted to get busy preparing the biscuits since everyone raved about them the last several years.

She and Ennis carried the girls to the living room couch to sleep out the morning, leaving Savannah free to join the ladies while Ennis stayed with the kids and Dane who busied himself monitoring the weather reports on TV.  He'd left Georgia to sleep in, he said, and for once she hadn't argued with the idea.

Mama's roomy kitchen comfortably accommodated four busy cooks plus a couple of hungry males stepping in to check the meal's progress.  Sometimes the inviting ambiance invited too many hungry men and kids, creating traffic jams around the marble-topped island and roadblocks to the stained cabinets stocked with dishes or pots and pans.

Savannah donned an apron and approached Mama's rooster canister set. Accessing the flour meant removing the rooster's head (she felt a little odd beheading a chicken for flour) but the whole kitchen reflected Mama's love for the feathered foul from plump white hens and proud roosters with azure tails. She prized her "family" of foul clucking away in their nearby coop and chose only the most trusted individuals to collect their precious eggs.

Savannah gathered the other biscuit ingredients, fully expecting to see Georgia at the door soon. Owning a bakery back home demanded early hours so her sister's inner alarm clock might soon curtail Dane's suggestion of sleeping in.

Savannah collected the heavy cream and half and half when Bobbi stopped her. "Better make four or five batches," she said. "'Member last time the boys dug right in and left us girls wishin' for more."

She had a point. Rutherford appetites bordered on astounding. "You're right," Savannah reached for an extra cream. "Ennis will probably eat three of them himself."

"And my boys could eat a dozen apiece. You've seen how they plow through a meal."

Savannah worked relatively fast for a zombie. By the time she filled the fourth pan she checked the clock. It crept close to six-thirty and no sign of Georgia. Her sister, also a popular author, attended two book signings the day before they left for Texas – one in Atlanta, the other in Athens about seventy miles away so Savannah sympathized with her. Spending all day on the road then the next day battling crowded airports *and* the clock to catch their flights wore anyone out. Georgia was dog-tired but without her the kitchen missed the last piece to its puzzle.

Mama continued working on eggs for scrambling. Bobbi fried enough bacon to feed a small army and afterward proceeded to prepare the gravy. Delicious aromas filled the kitchen, tempting Dane and Ennis to lean in, inquiring when the meal would be ready.

Once Cal and Jake returned, Ennis popped in long enough to say he and Jake were headed to the basement to gather things for that afternoon's cookout. She heard Cal before she saw him. Cowboy boots had a distinct sound but she could tell Cal from Jake just by his stride. The tallest Rutherford sauntered in, greeted Savannah then moseyed up to his wife, kissed her cheek then leaned down to sniff the gravy. She received a five-star rating. He went from Bobbi to Mama whose eggs got a thumbs-up, then to Savannah.

His smile said it all, "Those, Mrs. Ennis, are officially Texas-sized biscuits. You have learned well over the years."

She chuckled her thanks. He winked, "We'll make a genuine Texan outta you yet," then wandered into the living room.

Savannah still basked in his approval when Jenny Lee rounded the corner. Why was *she* still there? She had a home, right? A bed of her own and food to eat? She wasn't exactly a stray.

"Mornin', y'all," Jenny beamed. "Fine day, isn't it?"

It certainly *was,* Savannah bemoaned but playing nice, she forced a genial greeting. Her hands squeezed the dough harder than necessary while Mama and Bobbi returned Jenny Lee's salutation. Savannah guessed God had a reason for Jenny's presence. *He's testing my patience with another infant. A short, busty one dressed in skin tight jeans, boots and eye-watering fuchsia blouse – the same clothes she wore yesterday.*

Savannah hated to be nosy (and obvious) but, "You stayed the night?" Her knuckles sank into the dough pretending it was Jenny's face.

"I fell asleep on the couch last night. Jakie was worried about me going home alone so he volunteered his old bedroom."

How thoughtful. Conscientious Jakie worried about his sweetheart's safety – in Vega, the bustling metropolis boasting nine hundred fifty people. The town with a crime rate as high as Mayberry. "That was sweet of him."

"He pampers me," she bragged. "What can I say?"

*That you're leaving and never coming back...*

Jenny supervised Savannah's kneading for long, excruciating seconds. "Where's Georgia?"

"Sleeping in." And like oxygen, Savannah needed her soon or she'd faint and expire – which was probably why Jenny hovered like a human helicopter. Oh, the alluring temptation of mashing a gob of dough in that yap of hers... But Savannah's mother whispered two words from the heavens. Be nice. "She had book signings day before yesterday so she's tired."

"Hmm," Jenny Lee's nose wrinkled at the partially filled pan. "I'd hoped she'd make the biscuits. After all, she's the cook in your family, right?"

*If we're getting snotty about it, the technical term is baker, not cook, and no, she's not the only baker or cook in the family.* She implored her sister to appear at the door and save her. No Georgia yet so she debated over running upstairs and while shaking her sister awake, she'd lecture her about leaving Baby Sis alone to deal with the crazy person.

Bobbi stepped up instead. She paused stirring gravy, clamped her hands to her hips, "Jenny, I'll have you know those biscuits are wonderful. I prefer them over any other *and* Ennis eats five or six of them in one sitting. Savannah's a first-rate cook in her own right."

A hot flush warmed Savannah's cheeks. Bobbi's compliment went straight to her heart, plus the feisty redhead assumed Georgia's job only with more vigor – and a dash of venom. Jenny drew back at the dressing down. Meanwhile Savannah and Bobbi exchanged a look, the former's of thanks, the latter's of acknowledgement. The two resumed their duties, leaving Jenny to recoup the pieces of her pride. It didn't take long.

"Five or six?" Jenny sounded amazed. "Well, I betcha Ennis'd eat *every one* of mine. Why don't we try a contest sometime?"

Savannah rolled her eyes, answering with absolute certainty, "Because you'll lose."

Dane strode in then froze upon sight of Jenny Lee. "Oh, for the love of God," he groaned. "It's too early for her," he spun on his heel and traipsed out again.

"I doubt I'd lose," Jenny pressed. "Ennis loves my cooking."

"He *adores* mine," Savannah backed off the kneading. If she continued, the biscuits would be harder than Jenny's head.

Bobbi sighed, "Jenny Lee, don't fuss. Savannah and Georgia have won actual competitions and money with their culinary fare."

The brat's temper flared, "I'm tired of hearin' about her and how wonderful she is. Why you'd think she was born and bred of royalty the way ever'one goes on about her."

*"Her" is standing right here and that rolling pin is looking mighty inviting...*

"Jenny, darlin'," Mama called, "why don't you set the table? You need something to do."

*Yeah, besides causing trouble.* Savannah dusted the flour off her hands and pointed to an upper cabinet beside the sink, "The plates are in there."

"*I know where the plates are,*" Jenny Lee huffed then stomped her way toward the cabinet.

"Mama," Lily called from the doorway. She rubbed her eyes and yawned, "can I help?"

It wasn't Georgia but perhaps a small child might bridle the runaway mouth on Jake's fiancée. "Sure, honey. Ask Granna what you can do."

Mama Rutherford waved her over to help with the eggs. Jenny Lee wound up for Round Two but Savannah cut her off by reminding Lily, "Sweetie, wash your hands before helping."

Lily pushed a nearby stool to the sink, stepped up and proceeded to wash.

China plates clattered loud enough everyone winced. Jenny Lee cradled them in the crook of her arm then stomped past Savannah to the dining room while mocking *the plates are in there*. She doled out plates around the table, making sure the whole family heard her, "I mean, we hear about every detail in your life. The cases you investigate, your pregnancies, every sneeze. Ennis never gets his due and he was born here–"

During Jenny's rant, Bobbi marched to the doorway between the kitchen and dining room. "Hush up, Jenny Lee."

The redhead's scolding should have stopped the madness, but Jenny plowed on, "Why I thought we'd never hear the end of you and that Jeffrey Holland boy. Every week for months. Read like a soap opera."

Savannah flinched. Jenny blindsided her with that one. Her phrasing and accusing tone left the impression Savannah acted scandalously with Jeffrey, not been the victim of his brutality. Savannah held her temper – by a thread – but it soon unraveled when Lily ran past, her eyes brimming with tears.

Jaw clenched, Savannah trapped a plethora of scathing words behind pursed lips. The traumatic event was still very raw and real for Lily. She was well aware of his name, face and the physical damage he inflicted on her mother. It took months for the nightmares to fade enough Savannah and Ennis shared the bed without her. One mention of Jeffrey's name rekindled the nightmares. Here we go again, Savannah seethed. All thanks to Jenny Lee's jealous streak.

Amid Mama and Bobbi calling Jenny Lee down, Savannah hurried to wash the flour off her hands and found herself scrubbing so hard the skin bloomed blood red. It took a few seconds to calm down enough to avoid screaming – or throttling Jake's betrothed. She would tend to Lily but not before setting a thirty-something-year-old bully straight.

She finished drying her hands then slammed the dish towel on the cabinet. When Jenny turned, Savannah hoped she sensed the murder in her eyes, "I have to settle my daughter down right now but when I'm done doing that, you and I are having a long chat."

O   O   O

No matter what Jenny may have believed, Savannah's ordeal in July made the weekly local paper twice. After an initial front page write-up, the editor dedicated a modest sized space the following week for Bobbi's updates via Mama who remained by Savannah's bedside at the hospital. Those updates highlighted Savannah's shoulder surgery, the heart attack, her emergence from the coma, a sunny account of her reunion with the girls at the hospital and finally, the continued search for Jeffrey Holland. Despite Jenny's claim, not a single sneeze of Savannah's was reported.

Jenny's cavalier attitude reminded her of her malicious cousins on Charlene's side. Nothing mattered except them and the joy they received from spewing detestable, hurtful words. They and Jenny perfected verbal cruelty but Savannah could handle it. What she wouldn't tolerate? Anyone hurting her children. She lived by the adage "Hurt me and you're gonna feel pain. Hurt my best friend and you'll need an ambulance. Hurt my family and I'm gonna need a shovel."

She marched through the living room toward the location of her daughter's crying. The bathroom. Dane was already on his way to find Lily, "She upset about Jeffrey?"

Savannah nodded as she passed by. She was too angry to speak.

Lily's weeping spilled into the hallway. The sound closed a fist around Savannah's heart until it ached. Her little girl didn't deserve to be a casualty in Jenny's war.

Lily bounded into her arms. Savannah held her, softly shushing her to no avail. Tears dampened her sweater as Lily squeezed her tight. "Sweetie," her mama kissed her hair, "it's okay. We're all okay. Calm down."

"Why is she... so mean... to you?"

Now wasn't the time for brutal honesty so she opted to detour around it and put it in terms her daughter might understand, "She's my Brittany." Brittany Stone, the class bully, a rich girl who teased anyone who wore anything other than designer clothes. She'd centered on Lily because her parents were "just cops" and ridiculed her for wearing "cheap" clothes. The last one stung Savannah. Lily's outfits were anything but cheap, just ask their bank account. Brittany sank her teeth in and refused to let it go – until Lily pulled those fangs by defending herself. Since then Brittany pretty much left Lily alone. In a moment of folly, Savannah entertained siccing Lily on Jenny Lee.

She parted from the embrace, "And, like you do with Brittany, I try to ignore Jenny when she upsets me." She kissed her daughter's cheek, "But I won't let her upset my baby. That's where I draw the line."

Lily's red-rimmed eyes blinked, sending two more tears down her cheeks. Savannah swept them away, "The important thing to remember is Jeffrey's gone. He's never coming back."

Lily nodded, "I remember."

"There's nothing to worry about or get upset about." She chanced a tiny smile, "So what do you say? Let's enjoy our time with Granna and the family and ignore Jenny?"

Lily swiped the backs of her hands across her cheeks with an *okay*.

The door opened without the courtesy of a knock. Savannah rounded on the intruder thinking Jenny not only had gall but also a death wish. The sight of Ennis slackened her posture.

"What happened?" he asked. "Dane said Jenny upset Lily."

A thunderous storm brewed behind his eyes by the time she finished explaining the situation. There'd be a maiming, that expression said, and he didn't give a diddly-shit who witnessed it.

Before he bolted out the door, Savannah reminded, "We don't have enough vacation time for a murder trial. Jenny's not worth it."

"Daddy, that lady's being mean to Mama," Lily informed him. "She said *his* name."

He clenched his fists, "I promise she won't say it again."

"Ennis," Savannah warned, "Jenny and I will have a talk. I don't want you involved."

"No," he argued. "She's upset my family for the last time. I'm straightening her out."

Nice thought but, "Unless you have a jackhammer that'll penetrate her concrete skull, I doubt it'll work but you can try."

"Sugar, I *am* the jackhammer," he about-faced and left her debating over hiring a defense lawyer for him. Mere seconds elapsed when his baritone voice, fuming and verging on shouting, drowned out the TV.

Lily stared wide-eyed up at her mother. Savannah hoped her nervousness didn't show when she patted Lily's back, "Daddy really means business."

While he wiped the floor with Ms. Crawford, Lily dried the rest of her tears. Savannah counted off one minute of silence after his tirade concluded. She decided to check out the crime scene (if there was one) when Jenny Lee appeared at the door.

An unexpected meekness replaced the arrogance in her features. Ennis cut her down to size to the point she reluctantly spoke when she did it was hushed, "Savannah, I need to say something."

Lily spun to face her, "Leave my mama alone."

That's my girl, Savannah reflected with pride. Lily positioned herself between her mother and Jenny Lee, feet planted, fists clenched at her sides like her daddy's moment earlier. She was ready for battle. In her youth Savannah did and said the same thing to her aunts when they pecked at Charlene. And like Jenny Lee, they recoiled at the bold youth defending her mama.

Ms. Crawford hesitated before cautiously proceeding, "I want to apologize to both of you. I'm sorry for mentioning J–" she stopped before uttering the name. "For mentioning *him*."

Jenny glanced down at Lily then back to Savannah, "Ennis and Caroline explained what happened. I didn't know about the..." she tapped between her breasts to, Savannah assumed, signify a heart attack.

This from the woman who professed to scouring the local paper closer than a scientist watching microbes multiply. Claiming ignorance didn't fly however to prevent Lily from pouncing on Jenny, she dialed down the resentment. "Lily knows about the heart attack, but *he* is a very sensitive subject with our family. Think what you want about me, Jenny, but leave my children out of this."

Lily crossed her arms, "And leave my mama out of it too."

The corners of Jenny's mouth curled slightly at the girl's bravado. "She takes after you in every way, doesn't she?"

"I like to think so."

Savannah's nemesis offered a small olive branch before leaving, "For what it's worth, I'm sorry for upsetting you and Lily."

Savannah and Lily trekked through the living room. Cal, Dane and the nephews still lounged in front of the TV. Jenny was nowhere in sight. Savannah pictured her in a desperate search for Jake, charging into his arms and sobbing for sympathy after Ennis's verbal reaming out.

Cal raised his coffee cup in tribute, "Here's to Lily. You've got spunk, kiddo. You're the youngest Rutherford to ever corral Jenny."

Well, since Lily yelled every word, Savannah figured the whole house had a front row seat.

Lily glanced up at her mama, confused. No one congratulated her for shouting at an adult before. Savannah and Ennis taught their girls the Do Unto Others principle but also added a caveat to the Golden Rule: people can be pushed to their limit so be kind but don't be abused.

She patted Lily's shoulder, "It's okay to thank Uncle Cal. He knows what he's talking about."

She politely did so. Ennis descended the stairs still grim-faced and edgy from confronting Jenny. Apparently he'd taken a time-out for himself afterward. Judging from his stance, he needed to take a few extra minutes. "That's not spunk," he corrected Cal. "That's her mother's fire."

Why did that sound like criticism? Yes, Savannah had a temper but so did he as Jenny found out. She pondered his statement's meaning while his brothers belly-laughed. Ennis found no humor in their revelry, "What's so funny?"

Cal volunteered, "You were no even-tempered lamb as a child, no matter what you led your wife and kids to believe. You're responsible for at least half of Ma's gray hair."

"Ma already had gray hair before I was six," he shot back. "I'm not responsible for it. You and Dane are. You added a few more when you stole Ma's nail polish remover and painted the shower soap. She wasn't happy about that."

Cal waved it off, "Boys will be boys."

Cal's three sons traded looks then giggles. Monty's vision settled on his baby brother. Savannah saw devious ideas germinating in that gaze and wondered if Cal's "boys will be boys" mantra might apply if *he* ended up washing with lather-less soap.

"Ennis, quit whining," Dane sighed. "Brothers pull pranks. That's what brothers do."

Cal laughed at him, "You didn't exercise that tolerant attitude when Ennis put food coloring on your toothbrush."

Savannah resisted running her tongue over her teeth. Instead, she and Lily gave Ennis sidelong glances of disbelief.

"Daddy…" Lily's admonition trailed to silence.

Ennis blushed redder than a boiled lobster.

Cal continued his story, "Dane refused to smile – or talk much – for days. Kind of a nice respite."

Dane levered from his chair with a scowl, "I'm finding my wife. *She* loves me."

Savannah still couldn't fathom Ennis doing such a thing but just in case, "I'm hiding the food coloring when we get home."

She and Lily went to the kitchen and left Ennis staring daggers at Cal.

"Good to see you two back," Mama greeted her two returning helpers. "Savannah, honey, would you see to the gravy? I can't turn loose from these eggs."

"I'll be right there." Savannah noticed how she avoided the word *stir.* There'd already been enough stirring things up that morning.

Lily tugged at Mama Rutherford's apron, "What can I do, Granna?"

"Darlin', I saved the most important job for you. We need napkins on yours and Anna's table or breakfast won't be complete."

The "most important" status brought a smile to Savannah and a bounce back to Lily's step. Jenny Lee bailed after setting the plates out. Savannah prayed if Georgia ever woke up, she'd place the silverware. Trusting Jenny with knives or forks probably wasn't prudent right then.

Bobbi sidled up beside Savannah, "What's the family DEFCON

status?"

"Three for now but it can jump to One in an instant."

She seemed relieved, "If Ennis can't calm her down, Mama will."

And if Jenny jumped the tracks after those two finished with her, Savannah planned to step in – and no one wanted that. Of the Rutherfords, only Ennis and Dane ever witnessed the scope of her temper (the latter when she confronted the man who nearly killed Ennis) but she had a feeling the rest of the family heard about it.

She commenced "seeing to" the gravy and keeping it free of lumps. The repeated action gave her a chance to reclaim her calm from the earlier row with Jenny. Mama was no fool. She understood the benefits of "seeing to" the gravy. In general it provided a respite for the cook and opportunity to breathe despite the chaos surrounding them whether it be a whining toddler clinging to the mother's leg, a blaring TV or, in this case, a moron who enjoyed inflaming old wounds or creating new ones...

"Good morning," said a bubbly, well-rested Georgia greeted.

Morning? Yes. Good? That was a matter of opinion. But Savannah behaved herself and responded in kind, minus the ever-so-cheerful inflection.

Très chic in jeans and a green sweater matching her eyes, Georgia also took time to apply makeup and wash and comb her hair. Savannah's was combed. Period. Thankfully she passed jealous about twenty biscuits ago.

Georgia scooped up the silverware to set the tables. She tossed a cautious glance to the door then whispered to her sister, "Dane said

Jenny acted out again.  What did I miss?"

Now *this* was more like it.  Savannah smiled, "Well, since you asked…"

## 5

Grandma Culberson prided herself on proper etiquette and demanded no less from her three daughters. From social graces to handling a five course meal, she schooled Katherine, Emma and Charlene until they rivaled high society. And God help them if they slacked on place settings and table manners, Charlene told her own daughters years later.

In some cases Charlene took a less rigid approach by teaching Georgia and Savannah the basics on protocol and proper table manners. "No elbows on the table – you weren't raised in a barn", "chew with your mouth closed", "never, never, *never* divorce the salt and pepper – pass them as a pair" and "no stretching across the table to pass dishes". When it came to table settings, however, things got complicated. At five years old Savannah learned how to set a basic table. By age six, she noticed the table sprouted extra silverware, china and glasses during her lessons. Who in the world used all this stuff, she asked her mama. *You might someday* Charlene replied then proceeded to quiz her on each item's name and purpose. At seven years old, Savannah knew how to arrange a formal and informal place setting and could remember the "rest" and "finished" positions for the fork and knife, both Continental and American style.

Meals at the Rutherford house fell far short of formal dining, much less extra forks, knives and plates. But the other basic rules applied, especially the "no stretching to pass dishes". When a table seated twelve, it took coordination or else they risked utter chaos. Enter Jenny Lee Crawford, Chaos Expert Extraordinaire.

At some point in life, most people learned like the wheels on a bus, the food normally went round and round in one direction, from person to person, or the whole thing went to hell quickly. Most people, that was, except Jenny. That morning at breakfast she confused the issue by passing the eggs left to Monty instead of right to Jake, thus setting off an obstruction that backed up four people long. Monty, bless his young sweet heart, remedied the situation by hurriedly scooping eggs into his plate and freeing up traffic.

Dane waited for the eggs, drumming his fingers on the table until giving up with an impatient sigh, "Jenny, if you're gonna be part of the clan, learn to pass food to the right."

Sitting beside Georgia, Savannah felt her move slightly. She recognized the gesture from her childhood. She'd tapped Dane's foot as a warning to hush. Just a gentle rap, nothing compared to what she'd lay on her baby sister when they were kids. Savannah often thought Georgia should have played soccer or auditioned for an NFL kicker. The woman packed a bruising kick when she chose to. In all fairness, Georgia only laid one on her when she sensed trouble brewing between Savannah and their father. Better to suffer a bruised calf from me, she told Savannah back then, than a beating from Daddy.

This time Georgia fired a mild warning at Dane, telling her sweetheart that meals weren't the time or place to take potshots. Savannah only wished Jenny Lee abided by that rule. While waiting her turn for the eggs, she reflected how Jenny would have driven Charlene to the nuthouse by passing to the left.

"These biscuits are kinda tough," said Jake's bride-to-be. "Good thing there's gravy." She punctuated the statement by ladling two spoonfuls of Bobbi's white cream gravy on top of her biscuit.

Georgia turned her attention from Dane to Savannah who whispered to her *kick me and I'll hurt ya.*

"I think they're good." Cal reached for another, "Fluffy too. Tell me again, Jenny Lee, what was your contribution to the meal? I forgot."

The group went quiet. All eyes shifted to the troublemaker who flushed beet red, her mouth working like a fish out of water. "Well, I – I didn't… I couldn't…"

Savannah figured she struggled for a suitable excuse for her lapse in manners. Every female over three years old offered their help with the meal. Every female except her.

Jenny stammered, "I didn't want to crowd the kitchen."

Dane nudged Georgia, mumbling *yeah, right.* The eggs finally arrived to his delight so he indulged in two scoops. Georgia seemed relieved, "I heard the men discussing pranks this morning. I never told Ennis what kind of shenanigans Savannah on me and our brother Seth."

Savannah slowly swiveled to her. Georgia tried – at her sister's expense – changing the subject to lower the tension among the crowd.

Savannah leveled a look accusing her common sense of jumping off the plane without a parachute, "Funny. I never noticed your forked tongue before. Georgia, find another topic. No one wants to hear about my misspent youth." Because she'd been hell to live with, especially when Georgia or Seth pissed her off...

"Yes, we do!" Lily and Anna bubbled with glee. Unfortunately Monty and his brothers seemed just as enthralled.

"No, we don't." Finally Jenny Lee said something Savannah agreed with.

Cal grinned at his now fidgeting sister-in-law, "So you were a terror too, eh?"

Well, yes but, "Nothing like food coloring on a toothbrush."

Ennis shrank from Mama's frown and Dane's evil eye.

"That's debatable," Georgia replied. "She could either make her point or make you miserable, whichever mood struck her." With that, she looked directly at Jenny Lee.

Ah... Now Savannah understood. Her sister provided a heads-up to the brat. *Don't push Savannah too far or things might get ugly.*

Georgia honed the skill of warning a person in the most tasteful manner. She refined it to such an art that Charlene once commented that her oldest girl could tell someone to go to hell in such a pleasant manner, they'd look forward to the trip.

"Just keep it G-rated," Savannah grumbled then turned to her girls, "And you two don't listen."

"She dropped two raisins in Seth's coffee once. That sent him into orbit because he thought they were bugs."

For some reason Savannah felt the need to explain, "He shouldn't have chased off my boyfriend."

Lily gasped, "He chased Daddy off?"

Uh-oh.  Before Uncle Seth lost a member of his fan club, Savannah clarified, "This was before I met Daddy.  I had to kiss a few frogs before finding my prince."

That amused Georgia, "You were eight."

"I started my quest early."

"Tell us more, Aunt Georgia," Tyler said.

Except Jenny Lee and Savannah, every warm body at the table sat fascinated with Georgia's anecdotes.  As for Savannah, she considered it duplicitous conduct to expose a person's embarrassing misdeeds.

Georgia proceeded, oblivious to (or ignoring) her sister's scowl, "I think I was eleven.  My friends and I planned to see a movie one Saturday."

"Oh no."  Savannah buried her face in her napkin then debated over just stuffing it in her sister's mouth and being done with it.  "Georgia, don't.  I was a child – okay, a brat.  Don't give my kids leverage for later.  They might use it."

Of course Georgia went on her merry way.  That's what sisters did.  "Savannah wanted to go but we didn't want a kid tagging along.  When I got home, I always read before going to bed so when I opened my Hardy Boys paperback, imagine my surprise when I found–"

"She scribbled on the pages," Monty blurted.

No, Savannah groaned to herself.  It was worse than that.  Much worse.  She hung her head in shame.

"No," Georgia said, "she very carefully tore out the last five pages and stole them."

The group went silent. Except Cal who chuckled and Lily who berated her mother, "Mama, you were mean."

Savannah hoped her sister was pleased with herself. "Gee, thanks for tarnishing my image with the kids."

Ennis shot Dane a dirty glare, "That's what older siblings are good for."

Struggling to salvage a shred of self-esteem, she asked Lily, "I'm not mean *now*, am I?"

"No, Mama, you're not mean now."

"Lily," Georgia called, "she gave me the pages later that night. She was very young and she apologized. And I don't recommend you or Anna do those things to each other. Your mother will kill me if you do."

Oh, so she hadn't *completely* lost her mind.

"She also salted my orange juice once," Georgia revealed as an afterthought – or was it? "Never figured out how she slipped it in without me noticing."

Savannah just sighed.

## 6

Savannah and Lily climbed into Dane's F-150 and drove to the local market for chips, sodas and other extras for the afternoon cookout.

One thing about Vega: To newbies, locating a business turned into a perverse Easter egg hunt since street signs were scarce in places. Learning the layout was easy enough but until then one might take a few extra turns getting to their destination.

Until that week the area experienced an unseasonably warm winter however a bank of purple clouds loomed low on the horizon – a portent of the forthcoming bitter winds and blizzard conditions. They would barely wrap up their cookout before winter blew in.

An approaching driver gave her a quick finger wave. Ennis called it the Texas Howdy, a gesture country folk learned early in life – probably when they transitioned from liquid to solid food, she figured. There were other variations to the Howdy but Savannah got lost in the details and settled on raising her forefinger for the general How-Ya-Doin' type greeting.

Being from a city of three million people, it incensed Savannah the first time a Texan lifted his finger at her while driving, only because she mistook which finger he'd used. People in Atlanta who offered hand gestures involving a finger did not mean it in a nice way and it could never be misconstrued as a friendly wave.

The market sat across from the two story revival style Oldham County courthouse. Surrounded by mature trees, the red brick structure built in the early nineteen hundreds possessed a dash of Old South Savannah found charming. If nothing else it served as a landmark to guide any perplexed driver toward the market and courthouse square, with or without street signs.

Fields stretched hundreds of yards beside and behind the market. The closest businesses were located in a strip mall constructed when angle parking, sturdy brick buildings and wood shingled awnings were the norm. Lined in a neat row were a bakery, florist, coffee shop, an insurance company and City Hall.

Savannah pulled in beside a white Chevy sedan in the market's parking lot. The driver, a woman around the same age, sat inside chatting on her phone. She did a doubletake at Savannah but returned the nod of acknowledgment.

A handful of people roamed the sidewalks around the courthouse square, either enjoying the nice day or tending to last minute business before the storm. Eight cars sat in angle parking in front of the coffee shop, insurance company and City Hall. The coffee shop had folks lingering around vehicles and shooting the breeze. At City Hall a man dressed in typical cowboy attire had his arm propped on a Jeep Cherokee's open window, chatting up the driver. The man – she estimated his age at thirty-nine or forty like her – gave Savannah a brief wave.    She waved back.    Since they'd never met, she figured he recognized Dane's Ford and offered the gesture from habit.

Helping Lily out of the truck, she saw the Cherokee's driver climb out and hand the keys to the cowboy. They shook hands and the driver proceeded into City Hall.

The Vega market fell between Kroger and a mom and pop operation that carried an impressive variety of items.  In many ways the town exemplified small town life where porch sitting, Sunday suppers with family and women's quilting clubs were as routine as traffic jams in big cities.  Men tipped their caps (whether a Stetson or tried-and-true John Deere green and white) and addressed Savannah with a polite "ma'am" and Lily with a smile and hello.  These men grew up opening doors for a woman, pulling out her chair to seat her at meals and standing when she entered the room.    Savannah loved visiting but actually residing there posed a problem since she loathed every resident knowing her business before she did…   Grandma Culberson lived in a small community and news traveled faster than a chicken chased by Colonel Sanders.

She and Lily pushed a squeaky-wheeled cart around narrow, claustrophobic (for Savannah anyway) aisles, collecting items on a list assembled by Mama, Georgia and Bobbi.  Jenny Lee conveniently got lost in another part of the house when the other four women planned the menu. Savannah guessed Jenny opted not to "crowd the kitchen" again, except this time the cooking would be held outside on the grill. Kind of hard to crowd the outdoors…

Chips, veggies, soft drinks and ingredients for desserts went into the basket. Georgia planned the dessert menu which meant multiple goodies to choose from. For the cookout she decided on chocolate pies, brownies, and a couple of fruit pies. Once they returned home, Savannah promised to lend a hand like she did on her free Saturdays at Georgia's bakery.

She turned to load a six pack of Sprite into the basket only to see Lily holding a six pack of Dr. Pepper (Dane's obsession). She stared up at Savannah with big, pleading blue eyes. *Yeah. Nice try kid.* "Honey, that's not on the list. Put it back."

She hefted it toward the basket anyway, "Uncle Dane wants it."

Yes. As if Savannah hadn't seen Uncle Dane pull her daughter aside for a private huddle before they left. He was the sneakiness of the brothers by far.

The Chevy sedan driver rounded the corner carrying a handheld basket. She faltered upon sight of Savannah but opted to forge ahead to the soft drink display. The Dr. Pepper dustup took a back seat to the hesitant stranger who, for an instant, considered relocating to a different aisle altogether for some reason. Savannah patted Lily's back, "Hon, Granna said he had plenty."

"But he asked me to get some," Lily whined as if Dane's very existence depended on the sodas.

"Uncle Dane knows you're susceptible to his charms, that's why."

Her brow wrinkled, "What's that mean?"

A side glance revealed the woman ventured closer. The fact she kept sneaking covert glimpses of her and Lily set Savannah on edge.

After Jeffrey Holland she'd never take anything for granted, even sweet, sleepy rural towns. Sure Vega boasted nine hundred fifty residents but how many were kooks? To be safe, Savannah casually positioned herself between the woman and Lily. While doing so, she committed her basic appearance to memory. Trim, petite, five-six, brown shoulder length hair, blue shirt, red plaid coat, jeans and steel toe work boots.

"Susceptible," Savannah repeated while keeping a subtle eye on Red Plaid's whereabouts. "In your case it means you'll do what he asks because you love him."

"Please, Mama, he really wants 'em..."

To remove the distraction of Lily's crusade, she caved in and placed the Dr. Pepper in the basket. "Polish your charm until it shines, kid," she told her daughter, "because *you're* telling Granna why we brought it home. She's more *susceptible* to your charm than she is mine."

Pleased with her success, Lily grinned, "Mama, you're funny."

"No, I'm supposed to be the parent but those sad blue eyes of yours are my kryptonite." She stepped closer to Lily since the mystery woman approached them – slow and casual but still enough to concern Savannah. Slow and casual meant nothing. Jeffrey had been casual too.

"Forgive me for staring but aren't you Ennis Rutherford's wife?"

Savannah faced the woman while nonchalantly blocking Lily from her, "Yes, I'm Savannah Rutherford."

The stranger offered her hand and after a snug handshake, Red Plaid introduced herself, "Gina Sutton. I recognized you by your picture in the paper last summer. How are you doing?"

"Much better. Been back at work for some time now."

Lily peeked around her mother's hip, "Mama's a sergeant with the police. I helped her study for the test." She told anyone who would listen that she helped her mama study for the exam. She felt a great sense of pride and in Savannah's opinion she deserved to.

Gina seemed appropriately impressed for Lily's sake, "I'll bet your mom appreciated that help too. Sergeant is a very important job. I know you're proud of her."

Savannah still felt uneasy about the encounter because it seemed as if Gina was uneasy too. Lily insisted on interacting so her mama stepped aside to introduce the two – and to watch Gina closely.

The slender woman crouched to Lily's level and shook her hand, "Nice to meet you, Lily. You look so much like your mother you could be twins."

Bingo. Instant friend. A giant grin spread across Lily's face, "I got a little sister named Anna. She looks like Daddy. I'm gettin' a baby brother too. His name is Daniel."

Gina's gaze shifted to Savannah's baby bump. Her cheeks paled. The smile faded a degree then seemed to struggle back again when she stood to congratulate Savannah.

For some reason the pregnancy unsettled Gina so Savannah changed the subject. "So how do you know Ennis?"

"We worked together years ago." She hesitated a second, "I left for Albuquerque but came back after my sister was diagnosed with cancer. Since it coincided with my divorce, I moved in with my sister and took care of her until she died."

Savannah expressed her condolences.    She had firsthand experience caring for a loved one dying of cancer.   Gina lost her sister. Savannah lost her mother.

Gina dabbed her eyes, "Thank you.  I still miss her very much." And, as Savannah had a minute earlier, Gina changed the subject.  She pointed to the shopping cart, "The Rutherfords having another barbecue?"

"We're having hamburgers!" Lily interjected a bit too loud. "Granna makes the best.  You should have one."

Gina appreciated the offer, she said but, "I'm going to Amarillo for some things then I'm visiting a friend before the storm hits."

Savannah shrugged a shoulder, "If you have time, drop by. There'll be plenty and I'm sure Ennis would like to see you."

Lily rubbed her tummy, "Mama and Aunt Georgia are making chocolate pie."

"Well," Savannah told her kid, "Mama and Aunt Georgia can't make it without chocolate so we'd better get home."

They parted ways with Gina and headed for the checkout.

Mother and daughter netted three paper sacks brimming with supplies including Lily's biggest treasure, Uncle Dane's Dr. Pepper. Savannah carried the two heavier sacks and handed Lily the lighter one. Dane's Ford was a big blue monster but not as big as Ennis's Ram back home.  Her hubby preferred size over speed these days and that was fine with her.  She'd rather ride in a tractor than a rocket.

On the way to the truck she fished out the truck key while listening to Lily talk nonstop about the cookout and lending a hand with desserts. "Yes," Savannah said, "I'm sure Aunt Georgia will let you help with the pies. But you have to promise to keep quiet about me sneaking a bite or two of peach pie filling. You keep her busy while I do that and I'll throw in another scoop of ice cream for you at dessert." She winked at her daughter.

Lily's smile evaporated. Her eyes opened so wide Savannah feared they'd fall out. Someone approached her from behind, that expression said, and that someone scared the bejesus out of Lily.

Savannah started to turn as a man's voice presumed, "I'll be a monkey's uncle if that's not Mrs. Savannah Rutherford."

She intended to meet the man eye to eye. She missed by a good six to seven inches. Six to seven inches *up*. The cowboy standing between the fenders of Dane's pickup and the neighboring Silverado came from the land of giants. He was also the guy who accepted the Cherokee keys from his friend. Funny, she thought, he hadn't looked that tall from a distance.

He rubbed the black stubble along his jaw, "Yep, that's you alright." He stepped closer but not too close – yet. Still, considering his height, the breadth of his shoulders and overall brawn – not to mention that roguish smile, she felt plenty uncomfortable. He'd caught her, hands full, and basically fumbling with the truck keys. Lily made matters worse by voluntarily shifting behind her, thus blocking their only available exit. Savannah tilted back as he neared, keeping eye contact while wondering how this man knew her and why he felt chummy enough to hem them in and lean against the passenger door.

She put the heaviest sack down, freeing the hand holding the keys, just in case she needed a weapon. Once she took a second to really look at him, though, his features and the midnight black hair curling from beneath the Stetson tickled the haven't-I-seen-you-before nerve. "I'm sorry but have we met?" she asked.

He extended his hand, "No ma'am, not officially." His warm, rough hand slid around hers for a firm, cordial shake. "I'm Joe Bob Crawford and I can sure see why you spark my sister's jealous streak."

*Dear God, there's more of them.* How many Crawfords infested this town anyway? *How about saying something, stupid?* "You're Jenny Lee's brother?" *No, not* how about saying something <u>stupid</u> *but* how about saying <u>something</u>, stupid – *oh, nevermind.*

That wily smile widened across his whiskered cheeks, "Yup. I'll say Ennis did well for himself with you." His gaze shifted to Lily then to Savannah's belly, "Been busy too, according to my envious sister. Two fillies in the pasture and a colt on the way." He peeped around her hip and eased his hand out to Lily, "What's your name, kiddo?"

Owl-eyed at the large hand, she reached out as if it might bite, "Lily."

His grasp swallowed hers. He gave it a gentle shake, "A pretty name for a pretty little lady. You're the spittin' image of your ma."

For a kid who refused to budge a moment ago, Lily sure emerged like a butterfly breaking free of a cocoon. Savannah moved aside as much as possible for her smiling daughter who thanked Joe Bob for his compliment.

Despite his daunting appearance, at least Joe Bob inherited charisma and kindness that apparently skipped his sister in the gene pool.

He nodded to Savannah's baby bump, "How far along?"

"Six months."

Joe Bob relieved her of the grocery sack cradled in her arm, "I know Ennis's ma is on top of the world.  The more grandkids, the better."  He tried opening the truck door.  It was locked.  "You got the keys handy?"

He sounded amused that she bothered securing the truck.  She dangled the keys between her thumb and forefinger then opened the door.

Joe Bob teased, "Clearly you're a city girl.  Everything stays locked."  He placed both sacks on the passenger floorboard then loaded Lily's sack.  "But I understand.  In the city it pays to be cautious, especially after what happened to you."  He leaned onto his knees, "And what're you doing today, Miss Lily?"

She burst at the seams to tell him, "We're having hamburgers, brownies and ice cream today!"

"That's sounds yummy to me.  Eat a bowl of that ice cream for me and don't forget the chocolate syrup on top.  That makes it even better."  He straightened to full height.  Five-nine never felt so short but it did that day.  Against his towering frame she felt about as tall as her daughter.

He apologized for his earlier comment, "Sorry for bringing up bad times.  I kept track of everything through Bobbi's updates in the paper.  Glad to see you're okay."

"Thanks."  God help her.  She actually *liked* a Crawford.  So where had the saner relatives been hiding all these years?  She put a more diplomatic spin on that question before actually asking.

"I worked on a ranch in Oklahoma the past several years," he said. "Moved back here last summer. Think I'll stay now. Kinda missed this place."

A blue Malibu and black Dodge Ram pulled into the market's parking lot. An elderly couple exited the sedan while a younger family of three climbed out of the pickup. The younger husband sported that same glazed boredom that plenty of men developed on grocery shopping day. In contrast the older gentleman walked hand in hand with his wife as they offered a cheery *good afternoon* to the trio around Dane's truck. The husband reminded Savannah of her friend Peter Thompson back home in Atlanta.

Savannah, Lily and Joe Bob responded in kind with Lily's being the most enthusiastic greeting. She must have noticed the similarity to Mr. Thompson too.

"I'm glad you're staying," Savannah told Joe Bob with complete sincerity. Since he'd worked on a ranch, he'd bridled plenty of unruly animals so perhaps he could try his hand at shoving a bit in his half-cocked sister's mouth. Well, it never hurt to hope, right? "Why don't you drop by for a burger this afternoon? Supper's around five." She nodded to the sacks nestled together in the passenger floorboard, "We'll have plenty."

"Thanks for the offer but I gotta help a friend with fence work before that storm hits."

The experts forecasted eight inches. No big deal for most people in those parts. Throw another log on the fire, snuggle in and wait for the sun to shine again. Firewood and provisions were paramount for comfort and peace of mind – and some, like Mama, also installed a generator in case of prolonged power outages during heavier storms. Ranchers stayed busy during those times, taking extra measures to protect their livelihood by watching weather reports the way stockbrokers tracked market trends. They planned and prepared for worse weather than forecasted so their cattle didn't suffer.

Savannah asked Joe Bob about updated snow totals.

"They're still saying eight but I bet there'll be a foot. My shoulder's cranky today."

She sympathized with that. Since she arrived, her shoulder gave her fits too. The impending snowstorm affected the surgery site more than cold fronts or rain. She knew her own inventory of wounds and scars but, "What happened to your shoulder?"

"Broke it bull riding fifteen years ago. Got Uncle Arthur in it now. Doc prescribed ibuprofen for it. Most of the time it works. Not today though."

"Bull riding, huh?" She was tempted to expound on engaging in dangerous activities but considering her occupation, she thought better of it.

Lily tugged on her mother's jacket, "Mama, can we go?"

"Yes, honey, we can go." She gave Joe Bob a sheepish shrug, "Sorry. She's been excited all morning about the cookout."

Lily's face lit up, "Monty said he'll let me chase pigs today!"

*Over my dead body.* Since when did Mama bring pigs back to the ranch anyway? Lily still wore diapers the last time an oinker called the ranch home.

It confused Joe Bob too, "Mrs. Rutherford have hogs again?"

She shook her head, "It's news to me just like this chasing business." Now to set her eager child straight on one thing, "Unless you enjoy bathing twice today, young lady, there'll be no pig chasing." She would have a chat with Monty upon their return. First she'd ask him if he'd lost his mind. Then she'd tell him if he actually tried the stunt, *he* would be the pig and *she* would do the chasing. He might be surprised, she would conclude, how fast an angry mother could run.

Joe Bob smiled in a way that convinced Savannah the single Panhandle ladies swooned with regularity when he aimed those pearly whites in their direction. God sure put extra oomph into Texas men and their looks. It made her even more thankful she met Ennis who possessed his own dazzling, knee-weakening smile. The treasured diamond ring on her left hand proved it.

"Your ma's right, Lily. They don't call 'em stinkers for nothing. Best get Monty to teach you horseshoes. Now that's a fun game." His vision switched to Savannah, "And much cleaner."

She mouthed *thank you* to him. He chuckled, "Gotta watch Cal's kids. They find trouble or make it." He extended his hand to Lily, "Here. I'll give you a boost in the truck."

Lily kind of shied from his reaching hand. Ennis's hands weren't small either but his lacked calluses and a rough texture like Joe Bob's. After a short mental debate (and her mother's nod), she let him lift her inside and belt her in.

Savannah thanked him then hesitated a beat before mentioning the obvious, "You don't seem to be anything like Jenny Lee."

He actually laughed, "I hope not. Honestly, none of us brothers did her any favors. She was the only girl so between us and Ma and Pa, we spoiled her rotten. She's a handful alright."

*That's not what I'd call her but hey, potayto, potahto, it's all semantics.*

He checked his watch, "I'd better hit the road. That fence ain't fixing itself and Murray's down in his back and can't do it." He tipped his hat to each of them, "Nice to meet you, Mrs. Ennis Rutherford and pretty Miss Lily."

"It was a pleasure to meet you, Joe Bob." And it had been.

Savannah climbed in the truck and latched the seatbelt. Lily watched quietly as Joe Bob ambled off with one last wave. She finally spoke, "Mama?"

The Ford rumbled to life when Savannah turned the key. "What, honey?" she asked.

"Who's Uncle Arthur and how did he get in that man's shoulder?"

O  O  O

The smell of fresh baked brownies greeted Savannah and Lily when they stepped into the house. That and a semi-heated discussion in the kitchen revolving around Bobbi's cooking. Cal married an adventurous woman. She enjoyed experimenting with flavors and ingredients then test driving them on the family. Sometimes it succeeded, other times it backfired.

None of the brothers went for her butternut squash lasagna.  Ditto for the Hawaiian BBQ Chicken Pizza.  In Dane's words "it's heresy to put chicken or pineapple on a pizza" and as for the lasagna, Jake demanded an answer to *what the hell is a butternut squash anyway?*

But one meal remained sacred.  The cookout.  No one fooled around with those beef patties grilled over aromatic mesquite wood, at least not anymore.  After Bobbi's sausage and beef concoction caused an absolute uprising, Ennis decreed that anything involving a grill was off limits to Bobbi's "Frankenfood".  Only when Georgia and Savannah found coleslaw tucked between the hybrid patty and the sesame seed bun did they concur (but in a more tactful fashion).  They loved cole slaw but as a side dish, not on a hamburger.

So when Bobbi volunteered to prepare the patties for grilling, Savannah expected stout opposition to arise.  Within seconds every male except Cal objected.

"No," Dane said with surprising brusqueness, "we're not turning Bobbi loose with the meat anymore.  I trust Ma, Georgia and Savannah."

"I'm with Dane," Ennis agreed.  "Bobbi has too many bizarre ideas."

Savannah slowed down, waiting out Bobbi's reply.  Nothing provoked a woman's ire like being pecked at regarding her housekeeping or cooking.

As expected, Bobbi bowed up, "Bizarre?  Name one *bizarre* thing I've done to a burger."

Enter Jake who voiced mild irritation, "Okay.  The last cookout we had.  What was that ugly green thing I found on mine?  An old horse apple?"

"For your information," she said, "those were slices of avocado, not horse apple. I was tryin' to class things up a bit. This family is stuck in a culinary rut."

Jake snorted, "I like my rut. Let's take a vote. I nominate Ma, Georgia and Savannah to make the burgers and Cal to grill 'em."

"I second," Ennis replied.

"Count me in," Dane added.

"Fine," Bobbi huffed. "All you men, have it your way. My husband and boys like my cooking, that's what matters. Personally though, I think it's rude to pile the work on our guests. They're already making the desserts."

Jake pushed a person's buttons the way Mozart played a concerto, "Oh, now don't get upset. No one's stopping you from chopping alfalfa and slicing horse apples for your own burger."

The sacks outweighed the heavy conversation so Savannah and Lily resumed their trek to the kitchen.

Meanwhile Bobbi blustered something about Neanderthals. An outsider might assume their raw sentiments were genuine. Truth was Jake enjoyed poking his family's egos but no one held a serious grudge (at least as far as Savannah knew). She figured Bobbi deliberately exaggerated her offense. After all, she'd get a day off from flattening and shaping dozens of patties *and* standing over a smoky grill. Plus it gave Cal a chance to showcase his grilling talents. Bobbi shot one last volley for good measure, "I can help Georgia and Savannah with the desserts – if that pleases Their Majesties."

"Only if they supervise you," Jake zinged back.

Lily and her mother braved the kitchen. Except for Cal's boys and Jenny, the entire family crowded the room. Mama, Georgia and Bobbi prepared vegetables for the burgers. Cal and Jake leaned a hip against the marble island while Dane propped his elbows on the countertop. The instant Georgia turned her back, her hubby snuck a few chopped walnuts from the bowl meant for another batch of brownies. She glanced back and playfully swatted his hand away. Savannah found out early that her sister not only possessed a strong sixth sense but had eyes in the back of her head. To that day, she couldn't swipe a taste of peach pie filling without Georgia knowing it.

Ennis watched the ladies work while holding a very contented Anna on his hip. Both brightened the second they saw Savannah and Lily. "Hey, you're back," Ennis gifted both with a kiss.

She sat the bags on the counter then pecked a kiss to Anna's chubby cheek. Anna's grin widened.

"Thank goodness you are too," Mama sighed. "We were afraid something happened to you two. Ennis was on his head with worry."

Savannah slid her husband an incredulous look, "Did you think we got lost in downtown or stuck in traffic?"

Lily giggled. Ennis just blushed. He wasn't too concerned since her cell phone never rang – but it sounded good.

Bobbi sliced an onion with a tad too much vigor, "A word to the wise, Savannah. Don't even try to introduce a little culture to these galoots. They refuse any attempt to broaden their palates."

Unlike Jake, Ennis and Dane tried new dishes, especially if

Georgia prepared them. Nothing against Bobbi but Georgia's ability to blend flavors far surpassed hers.

Jake glanced inside each sack for a cursory inventory, "You didn't buy anything weird, did you? No avocados, Brussels sprouts, tofu or anything that grows in Hawaii?"

"I heard that, Jacob," Bobbi snapped.

"We bought the mundane usual," Savannah assured Jake. "Nothing more adventurous than jalapeños."

Ennis's brow puckered, "You *were* gone a while. What took so long?"

Aww, how sweet of him to be so concerned. Just for that she stole another kiss. "We ran across two folks we'd never met before. One was Joe Bob—"

"My brother?" Jenny Lee inquired from the doorway.

Savannah gave her a quizzical look. Curiosity tempted her to ask *how many men answer to Joe Bob in this town anyway?* "He claimed to be your brother, yes." Though she wondered why he'd do such a thing.

"How is he?" Cal asked.

"Fine but busy. Helping someone fix a fence before the storm."

Dane nodded to the clock, "He'll have to hurry. It's supposed to be here before seven tonight."

"My brother spoke to you?"

Poor Joe Bob, Savannah thought. He introduced himself to the wrong Rutherford today and now he's in deep doo-doo. "Yes, Jenny Lee. Sought me out and spoke to me." Then she mumbled, "Imagine that."

Ennis repositioned Anna to his other hip. He flashed a frown at

Jenny to shut up then asked, "Who else did you see?"

"A former colleague of yours. A woman about my age. Gina…" The last name escaped her – probably because of Jenny's spur-of-the-moment interrogation.

The room's temperature dropped. If Jenny considered exchanging hellos with Joe Bob verboten, the entire clan viewed speaking to Gina What's-Her-Name a hanging offense.

Mama dried her hands with a dishtowel then turned to Savannah, "Gina Sutton?"

Sutton. *That* was her name. "Yes," she cautiously drew the word out, wondering when one of them might start hunting for a rope and a suitable tree.

Ennis lowered Anna to the floor, told her and Lily to find their cousins in the living room. Cal rubbed the back of his neck. Dane cursed under his breath which caught Georgia's attention. She stopped unloading grocery sacks. "Who's Gina Sutton?" she asked.

That's what Savannah wanted to know but Jenny interrupted her by shouting, "*Why did you talk to Gina Sutton?*"

Now *that* sounded threatening. If Jenny wanted to test drive Savannah's temper (again), this time she'd give her the full ride, "Because, like Joe Bob, Gina Sutton approached me, not vise versa. It would have been rude to ignore her. Jenny, I basically exchanged hellos with her. It's not as if we discovered we're long lost sisters."

"Jenny, settle down," Mama said. She used her kinder, gentler voice for her confused daughter-in-law, "It's okay, honey. Don't feel bad but so you know, Gina is short for Regina." As if that name should explain everything.

Ennis elaborated, "Her maiden name was Regina Gibson."

Regina Gibson. Reggie Gibson. Oh boy. Yes, Savannah recognized *that* name and her knees went weak when it registered. She'd been chatting up the enemy and not realized it. "Oh my God, Ennis. I'm so sorry." Not sorry for talking to Gina as such, but for what she'd done during that conversation.

"Don't be sorry." Ennis kissed her, "You were being polite. As for the past, I'm tired of reliving it. I've got a wonderful life now. That's what matters."

Jaws plummeted. Who replaced Ennis with this imposter? For years he lost his civility and religion at the mere mention of Reggie Gibson so had he suddenly found forgiveness for his former partner? Savannah doubted it.

Jenny wobbled from a sudden sinking spell and braced against the counter, "Ennis, after what Reggie did to you, I can't–"

"That doesn't mean *I'll* acknowledge her but Savannah can." The bitterness everyone expected crept into his voice, "It's *my* grudge against Reggie and it'll always be there."

Bobbi heaved a sigh of resignation, "We should have forewarned Savannah that Gina moved back. Just never guessed they'd meet up."

Gina Sutton – or Regina Gibson – hadn't lied. She and Ennis had worked together as deputy sheriffs (Gibson was the senior officer) and one traffic stop changed their professional and personal lives forever.

One evening Regina (or Reggie as Ennis called her) and Ennis stopped a car reported stolen. The pregnant driver, Kelly Roberts, fidgeted in the seat, moving her hands in wild gestures while demanding an explanation as to why they'd pulled her over. They explained the car was reported stolen and she'd been speeding. She claimed harassment and added they had no right to stop her. She was trying to leave her abusive husband, she said, and it figured he'd convinced every cop in the county to stop her if she tried.

Ennis assured her they weren't "paid off" as she accused and didn't even know her husband. He'd only angered her by saying it. She refused to show her license and insurance because she'd "done nothing wrong" and repeatedly told them – in the most colorful language – what she thought of cops.

Roberts continually ignored orders to keep her hands on the steering wheel. Deputy Rutherford (new on the job) grew nervous with the constant movement but it angered Reggie. Both unholstered their weapons as a precaution. No problem with their actions thus far – except seeing the guns (despite the weapons being pointed at the ground) stoked the woman's belligerence. Her hand dove beneath the seat. This marked the beginning of Ennis's nightmare with Reggie. In a matter of seconds, Gibson shouted *gun* and fired. Ennis fired. He'd seen Roberts grasping a small black object but was unable to identify it as a gun. His shot hit woman in the side. Reggie's hit square in the woman's belly. What Gibson thought was a gun turned out to be a purse. When she realized her mistake, Ennis said, she ordered the ambulance delayed so she could "think this through" he heard her mumble. He made the call anyway. Gibson flew mad that he'd disobeyed her and vowed to have him dismissed. She was fired. Ennis resigned. Kelly Roberts survived but her baby didn't.

Roberts sued for an unimaginable amount of money. The only good thing to emerge from the disaster was she dropped her lawsuit against Ennis for whatever reason, but not Reggie. Since the incident, not one word passed between Ennis and Reggie.

The encounter that afternoon at the store made sense now. Gina's hesitation when she first saw Savannah. Her blanched complexion once noticing Savannah's pregnancy. Her declining the invitation to supper. Perhaps Gina did have business in Amarillo before the storm. Either way had she showed, the family *would've* fetched a rope and found a tree. Maybe two. One for Gina, the other for Savannah. Now she felt obligated to confess her sin of inviting the enemy to break bread with them.

Ennis stood there, a mix of emotions passing across his features. Anger. Pain. Embarrassment.

Savannah wrapped her arms around him, "I'm so sorry for what I did."

He returned the embrace, "It's okay, babe. You didn't know."

"Keep that in mind because I hope you forgive me for this. I hope you all do." She nervously cleared her throat and, judging by the evolving expressions around her, she would've considered running for the hills – if there *were* any in the Panhandle, "I, um… invited her to the cookout."

The women groaned in unison, the men grumbled under their breath. Everyone except Georgia flinched as if Savannah slapped them. Ennis just looked shell-shocked. She hastily amended, "But she declined.

Said she was going to Amarillo to visit a friend."

Dane muttered, "You mean she *has* a friend?"

Otherwise total silence. She stepped back a step. Then another. The temperature in the room plummeted again so she volunteered, "I'll go peacefully, just don't excommunicate Lily. She had nothing to do with it. I'll thumb it to the airport." She hoped she was joking.

A smile cracked Mama's stern frown, "Oh, honey, you just surprised us that's all. Gina wouldn't have come anyway so no need to flee the state."

Cal swiped a walnut unbeknownst to Georgia, "Nah, we'll keep you around a while. You keep things interesting."

Ennis finally snapped from his daze. Savannah was grateful the family forgave her. Well, except for You-Know-Who. Arms crossed, Jenny Lee harrumphed Cal's softball approach and lobbed a fastball right between the eyes, "Are ya sure you and Reggie *aren't* long lost sisters?"

## 7

Any woman who enjoyed baking or canning would have envied Mama's massive backyard. On one side cherry, peach, plum and several pecan trees lined the yard. On the other and within close walking distance stretched Mama's sizeable vegetable garden. Well, *sizeable* didn't do it justice. *Enormous* described it better. It sprawled half a football field long and equally as wide. Summer saw bountiful harvests of corn, onions, black-eyed peas, green beans, tomatoes and potatoes. Between canning and freezing, Mama's chest freezer and basement stayed well supplied.

The huge backyard regularly played host to parties and saw its share of weddings including Savannah and Ennis's and later Georgia and Dane's. A couple of wicker chairs on the porch provided welcome respite from the blistering summer sun and made cooler spring and fall days a joy to watch the horizon transform from blue to tangerine and magenta. Nothing beat sitting with family, sipping sweet tea and listening to melodic choir of mockingbirds serenading an appreciative audience.

In hours those chipper birds and their appreciative audience would retreat to their respective nests to ride out the storm. The false spring fooled only flowers, grass, trees and tourists — not Texas Panhandle residents. They knew better. In March, they realized the green sprigs sprouting from their lawns and tree buds peeking from branches would soon freeze or be covered in winter's last hurrah. Twenty-seven hours earlier Savannah's family landed in Amarillo to sixty degree weather. Today forecasters expected temperatures to top seventy-five before Old Man Winter buried spring's hopes in eight inches of snow.

For now family, friends and neighbors basked in the warmth and chatted while indulging in the first cookout of the season. Fragrant smoke drifted in the slight breeze. Cal stood at the grill, tending burgers dressed like a cowboy chef in boots, jeans, blue checked shirt — and an apron declaring him "Grill Master", a title he lived up to.

Savannah and Georgia kept watch on the ominous dark clouds inching closer. The ache in Savannah's shoulder deepened the last few hours. She waved off the change, blaming everything from sleeping on it wrong to a simple strain. Until now. Maybe the storm explained the strange nagging sensation in the pit of her gut. That uneasy premonition that something bad lurked on the horizon — and not just a snowstorm. Stop worrying and enjoy today, she finally told herself, and keep an eye out for children mingling with pigs.

During the meal she kept an eye out for Joe Bob, hoping he'd have a chance to drop by — if for nothing else than to offset his sister's cuckoo personality. Jenny Lee flitted from person to person interrupting conversations and wagging her engagement ring at guests. Lord, Savannah needed a dose of normal from a Crawford.

The girls and their cousins wolfed down their meals long before the adults settled in for theirs. Savannah balanced the time between eating and tracking their movements. If they left her sight, she would pursue. Instead of fulfilling the promise of chasing pigs, so far Cal's boys busied the girls playing slop-free games such as tag, hide and seek, and even introduced them to horseshoes as Joe Bob suggested. Lily seemed to enjoy it. Anna yawned.

Halfway through Savannah's meal, the five of them went MIA. It was time to hunt the girls down and fast. She hadn't seen a single pig on the ranch in years but remembered where to find the previous residents' old pen.

As feared, the boys led the girls in that direction. A single two-fingered whistle (she was forever in Georgia's debt for teaching her that trick) stopped the wanderers. She waved Monty over.

At thirteen, he not only developed manliness in his features but shot up in height so the two practically stood eye to eye. Manliness and height aside, she planned to lay down the law since he wasn't the poor sap forced to scrub filth and muck off her kids if they wallowed in pig poo. "You boys cut it out. The girls don't need to catch a pig. And where exactly are these pigs anyway? I thought your grandma got rid of them."

He shrugged a shoulder, "They're around here somewhere." He kinda laughed, "C'mon, Aunt Savannah, the girls are having fun."

She, however, was less than amused. She exercised her *last straw* smile because one stinky, muddy child *would be* the last straw, especially with her aching shoulder. "They won't think it's fun when I'm done with them. Don't make me come after you too."

He realized her threat held merit but he also knew she wouldn't lay a hand on him or yell at him. No, if her stern warning failed to sway him, she'd tattle to Bobbi and Cal and let them handle the situation. "If you're this bored, young man, there are dishes waiting to be washed. Between the three of you, you'd be done in time to clean the yard before the storm rolls in."

The boy tested her patience by laughing again. This didn't bode well for her future with Daniel. If a nephew blew her off, what would her son do? He asked, "You really want us to stop?"

"Don't I look like I do?"

Well, that snuffed his amusement. Most of it, at least. Instead of laughing he smirked, "I'll call 'em off on one condition."

Savannah's brow shot up. So he resorted to *conditions*, did he? She slung an arm across his shoulders, pulling him close. "Why, Mr. Montgomery," she drawled, "are you trying to blackmail a police officer?"

"Give me a prank to pull on Tyler and I'll tell them to stop. No one has to know you helped me so stop frowning. I won't say a word."

That seemed cheap enough except she'd have a bulls-eye on her back with his parents if she followed through. "Listen, kid, I barely escaped being tarred and feathered today because of an innocent mistake. What would happen if I purposefully volunteered new ways to wreak havoc in your family?" She teasingly snorted, "I thought you and I were friends."

"We are but c'mon. Just one? I won't tell anyone." He lifted his hand, "Scout's Honor."

She countered it with the Girl Scout sign, "I don't know about the Boy Scouts but the Girl Scout Law mentions nothing about aiding and abetting practical jokes. It does mention something about respecting others and being responsible for what I say and do, though."

"Aunt Savannah–"

"Say I do this for you. When your mama and daddy have you in a room with the bright lights and begin their relentless interrogation *then* they sentence you to a month of shoveling horse pucky as punishment for pranking your brother, you don't think you'd cave under pressure and squeal on me?"

He went silent then frowned as if picturing his parents in that situation. No bright lights but the threat of cleaning the horse stalls seemed to resonate with him.

"Monty, I'm asking nicely. Please keep my girls out of the slop, okay?"

His broad shoulders drooped, "We'll take 'em to pet the horses."

"Savannah!" Cal leaned out the back door. "Phone call for you!"

Her first thought was her brother. Seth volunteered to check theirs and Georgia and Dane's houses and pick up the mail in their absence. Hopefully the call was a general update on things back home – but for him to single her out, something must have gone wrong. She left Monty with a reminder to play nice with Aunt Savannah then headed for the house at a leisure jog.

Cal, Dane and Jake huddled together in the mudroom, speculating on the mystery phone call. The whispers and low tones ceased the instant she stepped inside. Jake and Dane crossed their arms.

Their expressions said it all. She was in the soup again. What the hell had she done now besides try to eat supper and save her kids from a malodorous fate?

Cal clamped a hand over the phone's mouthpiece, "You get caught jaywalking or speeding?"

She took a wild guess it wasn't Seth on the phone. "Of course not," she replied. She reached for the phone but he refused to relinquish custody of it. "Double parking?" he asked.

In Vega, Texas? Was he serious? Hell, not even the angle parking was full most of the time. "No. Why the questions?"

He waggled the receiver in his hand, "It's the sheriff. He's asking Mrs. Savannah Rutherford to beat it down to his office ASAP."

"Fess up, Peach," Dane prompted. "What'd you do?"

She waited for Jake's contribution. He wisely kept quiet but his mouth quirked. Yes, yes, she caught the irony of the situation. A cop in trouble with the law. Except, "I don't know why the sheriff wants to talk and I won't know unless Cal surrenders the phone."

Just because a person married into the family didn't exempt them from jokes, needling or outright annoyances. Cal handed the phone over but no one left the room. She appraised the curious faces around her then cleared her throat before addressing the caller, "Hello."

"Savannah Rutherford?" a deep, resonant drawl inquired. It sounded like God summoning her. And of course God was a native Texan, everyone knew that.

"Yes." She shooed the three eavesdroppers angling for better positions to hear. They retreated a half-step. And men called women nosy.

"Mrs. Rutherford, this is Sheriff Frank Guthrie. Would you mind coming to my office for a minute? I need to ask you some questions."

She did a mental eye roll. The brothers sounded as if Guthrie sent out a posse to hunt her down. "Questions about what, Sheriff?"

"It's in regards to Joe Bob Crawford. I'm holding him for theft."

She nearly swallowed her tongue, "Theft?" The three men in front of her simultaneously dropped their jaws. They whispered among each other until Cal shushed them.

"Yes, ma'am," Sheriff Guthrie replied. "I realize this is an inconvenience but it won't take long."

The clock on the wall read six-thirty. "I'll be there around seven, Sheriff." When she ended the call, the brothers surrounded her, wanting answers.

"Peach," Dane looked on the verge of a smile, "did you get caught slipping spuds in your pockets at the market? Because if you did the least you coulda done was throw in another Dr. Pepper or two. Woulda made it worthwhile."

"Sorry," she played along, "but I only wanted a fast getaway at the time. Maybe Georgia will hijack a Dr. Pepper truck for you. Then you'll have two jailbirds in the family."

Jake pressed, "Who's in trouble? Whoever it is they're probably innocent. Guthrie's a hard-nosed old codger. Tickets you for one lousy U-turn."

"Not to defend him or anything," she said, "but aren't those illegal in Texas?"

"Jakie!" Jenny Lee cried from the backyard.   She sounded distraught so Savannah assumed Joe Bob used his one phone call for her. Savannah patted Jake's arm with a sympathetic, "I think you're about to be enlightened to the situation."

She went to the kitchen, asking a favor along the way, "Please keep the girls away from the pigs while I'm gone."

Cal frowned, "What pigs?"

Oh boy.  Why did she suddenly feel stupid?  So Mr. Monty tried his hand at pranking her and the girls.  Little did the boy realize – this officially meant war.

"We don't have hogs anymore," Jake replied.  "Haven't for a couple of years, remember?  Ma couldn't stand the cost or smell of 'em."

Dane was confused too, "Who told you she had hogs?"

"I think I know."  Cal marched to the back door and hollered for the culprit, "Monty, front and center!"

This wasn't over, she hated to tell her clever young nephew. He'd begged her to educate him on "just one" prank.  Oh, she'd school him, alright.  He'd learn quite a lesson at that time too.

After Cal had a word with his son, she caught Monty alone, "Nice trick, kid, but I've got an arsenal of them so watch your back." She winked, "Day *and* night."

o  o  o

During her years as an official Rutherford, she'd yet to meet longtime sheriff Frank Guthrie. She'd seen the "hard-nosed" lawman's picture in the paper and likened him to Wilford Brimley in a beige uniform. Mid-sixties, Santa Claus gut and an equally expansive walrus mustache. Dane and Jake belly-laughed at the Wilford Brimley comparison. Jake "doubted" the real Wilford would "ticket someone for making that blasted U-turn." Then Dane accused, "What heartless mongrel cites a person for their God-given right to drive fifteen little ol' miles per hour over the speed limit?"

"This heartless mongrel," Savannah replied, "and I crowed about it every day when I patrolled the streets."

They sneered but shut up.

Though it was unfounded, she felt slightly nervous about meeting Guthrie since he was sheriff during the whole Ennis/Reggie Gibson/Kelly Roberts fiasco years ago. He'd treated Ennis with respect during the investigation, Mama had said, and after Ennis resigned, Guthrie and his former deputy continued to be friends. The same could not be said of Guthrie and Reggie Gibson.

Savannah borrowed Dane's truck for the drive. The squatty one-story sheriff's office – added later to the south side of the courthouse – looked rather puny against the massive building but the man inside, according to the Rutherford brothers, made up for that misconception.

One white patrol car (a Charger) sat in the meager three slot parking area. She pulled in beside the Charger. A brief glance at the sky and increasingly chilly breeze forewarned of the storm's imminent arrival. The advancing steel gray cloud bank swallowed the retreating sun and hung directly overhead. She estimated less than thirty minutes and the bitter winds would move in along with a few snowflakes.

She grabbed small two paper sacks in the passenger seat. She and Mama prepared a meal each for Guthrie and Joe Bob, complete with hamburgers, brownies and sodas. They never met a man that refused a hamburger, they said, and after a day's work either "sheriffing" or repairing a fence, it might hit the spot.

She stepped inside to a tidy yet utilitarian interior complete with fluorescent overhead lighting, polished floors and beige walls. Bright light and the faint sound of Alex Trebek's voice spilled from a doorway down the hall. Guthrie's office.

He'd settled in for a slow, uneventful evening of TV viewing. Kicked back with feet propped on a cabinet behind his desk, he appeared fully engrossed in watching the portable TV sitting beside a fax machine. Because of his position he was unaware of her arrival – and she knew better than to interrupt a Jeopardy fiend during Final Jeopardy. Savannah waited for the question but didn't pay attention to it. She checked her watch instead.

"Fokker," Guthrie blurted with confidence.

Savannah nearly dropped the sacks thinking he cut loose with something bawdy. That twang, she lamented. A strong Texas twang (like a thick Georgia drawl) could mangle any normal word depending on the person saying it.

He bragged to the empty room, "Yessiree, that's who made the Red Baron's plane. Knock me over with a feather if I'm wrong."

Savannah took that moment to knock, "Sheriff?"

The rotund man might have been in his mid-sixties but he was literally fast on his feet. In two seconds, he stood, chagrined, while lowering the TV volume, "Mrs. Rutherford, Frank Guthrie. Pleasure to meet you."

In person, he sounded thisclose to Sam Elliott's – only with a heavy Texas accent. She gave his hand a solid shake, "Nice to finally meet you, Sheriff. I've heard a lot about you."

"Don't believe half of what you heard if it came from your brothers-in-law – Dane and Jake in partic'lar. Those two invented the reason for speed limits." He offered her a chair then nodded to her baby bump, "Looks like Ennis'll be a daddy again soon."

After standing all day, her feet needed a rest. She eased into the seat. "He's excited to have a boy this time, yes."

"I'll make this quick so you can get on the road. Thanks for taking time out of your evening." He zeroed in on the paper sacks still in her hand. The aroma was hard to miss but he said nothing.

No one except Dane asked why she and Mama packed the portable suppers. When he found out why, he jokingly accused Savannah of paying Guthrie off with food to drop the charges against her. She replied he could thank his mother for the bribe. Then she kindly requested two Dr. Peppers from Dane because a person risked life and limb if they filched one without him knowing it. He kept track of those drinks the way King Midas counted his gold.

She extended a bag to Guthrie, "Caroline sent this for you. Thought you might be hungry."

Guthrie seemed genuinely touched by the sentiment and eagerly peeked in the sack. He approved. Nose poised over the aroma wafting out, his thick, graying mustache broadened in a smile, "She's always thinking of others. I'll give her a call and thank her." He eyed the other bag as he said this.

"I brought one for Joe Bob too."

Disbelief furrowed Guthrie's serene features, "Since when do you get along with the Crawfords?"

"Jenny Lee and I don't get along but Joe Bob seems nor–" her mouth snapped shut. *Way to go. Alienate the only Crawford you get along with. Calling him normal implies Jenny Lee isn't (which is true) but to actually say it?*

"Shifty, that's what," Guthrie said. "He's shifty."

She wondered if he covered her Freudian slip with a joke or if he truly meant it. She'd spent a scant ten minutes conversing with Joe Bob that afternoon, hardly enough time to construct a true measure of his character but her gut said he was a good man and not shifty at all.

"I hope she was gonna say *normal!*" Joe Bob shouted from somewhere in the back.

"I was going to say normal, yes." At least he hadn't taken exception to her goof. "Can I have my supper now please?" Joe Bob asked. "She brought me one special so don't be lifting it for yourself, Guthrie."

"Simmer down in there. Business first then you can eat." He grumbled about impatient jailbirds rushing him along. "What's he in such an all-fired hurry for? He's not going anywhere." Guthrie shuffled a couple of papers on his desk until settling on one, "Ma'am, 'bout what time did you and Joe Bob talk today?"

"It was around noon. My daughter and I came to town for groceries."

"I told you, Guthrie!" Joe Bob shouted. "I met Savannah and her daughter Lily! Now do you believe me?"

"Be quiet," Guthrie barked. His attention gravitated to the paper sack before making eye contact with her again.

Joe Bob needn't have worried. If nothing else, hunger would expedite Guthrie's questioning. He proved her right. "Was he on foot?"

It finally hit her why Joe Bob sat behind bars, "Is he accused of stealing a Jeep Grand Cherokee?"

He nodded, "Got a call from Andy Beck's wife Kelsey about two o'clock saying she saw Joe Bob driving her Cherokee along a county road. I couldn't reach Andy on his phone so I picked Crawford up. Took me forever to find him. He was hiding out at the Murray place."

"Hidin' out, my eye," Joe Bob argued. "I was fixing his fence and you know yourself Kelsey's never cottoned to me. She thinks I drag Andy away from his honey-dos too much."

A strong wind gust hit the building. Sleet pelted against the window screen. Great, she thought. And I'm listening to these guys argue.

"I'll believe her over you any day," he shot back. "At least I've never arrested *her.*"

"I was fifteen!" Joe Bob's incredulity verged on offense. Guthrie's tone did sound semi-judgmental. "For the record," Guthrie's jailbird said, "it was teenage mischief and I worked to pay off the damage. Guthrie, don't make Savannah think I'm a felon."

While the two bickered, the TV's radar map held Savannah's attention. The blizzard's leading edge passed through Vega and behind it, a giant white blob closed in on the city. As the meteorologist pointed to Vega, a steady wind cranked up outside and drove sleet in sheets against the windows. The storm hit with a vengeance.

Her cell phone chimed with a message from Ennis. She squinted to read *Sleet's here. Bout done?* She texted back: *Bout. See you soon. Love U.*

"Ennis?" Guthrie nodded to her phone.

It chimed again. Ennis texted a heart with U2 beside it. She couldn't help but smile. "Yes. He updated me on the weather." She needed to get home so she volunteered, "Sheriff, is Andy Beck tall, thin, and got a long face?"

Joe Bob's hopes renewed, "A horse face, that's right!"

Guthrie fired a baleful glare through the wall behind her– toward the jail, she guessed. "That pretty much describes him, yes."

"I saw him hand the keys to Joe Bob before Lily and I went in the market. Joe Bob waved at me, I waved back. That's when I saw Beck hand over the keys then shake Joe Bob's hand and walk into City Hall."

"Thank you, Savannah. See, Sheriff? I told you the truth."

Guthrie still didn't seem happy, "Why did you need Kelsey's car anyway? You have that old Silverado."

"Because *that old Silverado* is being repaired in Amarillo. Be there another two days. Can I have my supper now?"

Savannah gave a little shrug and pleading smile, "It *is* getting cold."

Guthrie waved her in the direction of the jail. Joe Bob sat on the cell's bottom bunk, elbows on knees, his fingers shoved through his hair in frustration.

The lines between Joe Bob's brows smoothed upon casting eyes on his newfound friend and the sack she held. He met her at the jail door, "I owe you big time. Thank you for springing me from this nasty situation and for the supper."

"Don't mention it. Enjoy the meal and from now on make sure to tell Andy's wife you're borrowing the car – and probably let the sheriff know too, just to avoid a mix-up." She slid the paper sack between the bars, "Hope you like lettuce and tomato. Just pick 'em off if you don't."

A rapturous smile brightened his features when he sniffed the contents, "I don't care if it's got a Buick on it. It smells great and I'm starving. Thanks for thinking of me. This is a dream compared to stale bologna between two slices of concrete Guthrie passes off as a sandwich."

He sat down, tucked the napkin in the V of his shirt, unfolded the wax paper wrapper and took a healthy bite of the burger. The moan he released reminded her of her own reaction to peach pie. Pure bliss. Even his eyes rolled back, "This is the best burger I've had in years." He reached in to find dessert, "A big, fat brownie too. It sure pays to call you for help."

When he pulled the Dr. Pepper from the sack, he reacted as if she brought him a stack of money, "You do have serious clout, don't you? How'd you wheedle this from Dane? He's real stingy with these."

Yes, he was. When he discovered the intended recipient, he fussed (sort of) but she reminded him of the stash Lily successfully campaigned for at the store. "Oh," she replied, "I just asked nicely."

Another gust of wind buffeted the building. It was way past time to leave. They chatted a little longer then she went to bid farewell to Guthrie, if he was done questioning her. By then he'd devoured half the burger. He placed the remainder aside then swiped the napkin over his mouth and that grandiose mustache. "I appreciate you coming down here to clear this up," he said. "Soon as he finishes eating he can go home."

He patted his stomach, "Thank you for the supper too. Mighty good indeed. I'll call Caroline after you leave, let her know you're on your way back. I do have one last question before you go. Y'all heard about those five that escaped the prison down south this morning?"

She peeked at the radar. The white blob swallowed Vega and churned toward Amarillo. "'Fraid not. Been too busy with the cookout to have the TV on. The guys mainly keep up with the weather."

The phone chimed with another text from Ennis. *Hurry up. Roads getting slick. 60 mph winds moving in.*

*Leaving soon*, she texted back.

Guthrie swiveled to the computer. Keys clacked with impressive speed. He rose from his seat, offered it to her, "Take a quick read."

She fished her glasses from her purse then sat down. He'd accessed a website that posted the escapees' mugshots and details.

Trey Mason, twenty-eight, African American, originally from Louisiana. Ultra ebony skin, round faced and hefty, Mason not only kept in shape at the dinner table but also carried the weight on a bulky, imposing six foot frame. Not quite big ol' John Coffey from the Green

Mile but close. Mason was sentenced to fifteen years for drug dealing and escaped with three years left to serve.

Luis Muñoz. Twenty-nine years old. Hispanic with piercing ice blue eyes, angular jaw and a thorny vine tattoo ringing his neck. Proud defiance stared at her from the screen. She'd seen that expression on killers before. The one warning *screw with me and die.* Convicted of multiple murders (one a cop) and sentenced to life without parole after his death sentence was overturned. The write-up listed one delightful bonus to any future law enforcement unlucky enough to cross his path. A tattoo spanning the width of his chest showed a cop getting shot between the eyes. Inked above the crude masterpiece was "F*CK THE POLICE", only the phrase was spelled in all its shocking glory.

She clicked the "Next" button at the bottom of the page. Manuel Sanchez, thirty-two. A skinny Hispanic with a low brow, dark burred off hair and a scar running down the side of a face that seemed a shade this side of crazy. The bulletin listed several gang tattoos. Convicted and sentenced to life for shooting up a pawn shop and killing four people.

The third pillar of society was Scott Hadley, the oldest of the bunch at thirty-four. His friendly, almost boyish features presented a deceptive outer façade to his true nature. A jury saw through that façade and sent him away for breaking into an elderly woman's home, beating and raping her then leaving her to die. The victim managed to pull herself to the phone to call 911 and give police a description of her attacker. He was caught the next day trailing another elderly woman from a grocery store. He'd offered to carry her bags home for her just before the cops arrested him.

And last but not least, the next mouse click brought up Alan Brozek, thirty years old. He favored a younger Pat Boone, only this Pat Boone smiled a disarming, boy-next-door grin in his mugshot. That boy-next-door served a life sentence until escaping that morning. She read on, trying not to seem impatient. When she delved into his details, she forgot the clock, the phone, and the pelting sleet outside.

The innocuous boyish features and stupid grin provided a convincing veneer concealing Brozek's unspeakable crime. The luckier parents testified that they caught him trying to lure their young daughters (around Lily's age) to his van. The unluckiest suffered through forensics evidence and the coroner's testimony of how Brozek violated their baby girl and silenced her cries by strangling her. He then crammed the child into a duffel bag, added some bricks and threw her body in a lake.

Savannah leaned back, releasing a long, unsteady breath. Her phone chimed again. Why was Ennis so antsy? It was wind and a little sleet. No need for the National Guard and helicopters. It surprised her to see not Ennis but Georgia's name on the text. *Please be on your way.*

In other words either Ennis or the girls were driving everyone crazy. *Leaving now,* she texted back.

Savannah vacated the chair on slightly weakened knees. Five convicted felons roamed free and while Texas was impressively huge, what if they headed north toward Amarillo? Toward Vega? Toward her family? Chances were slim but she always heeded her gut feelings. After Jake kicked off the visit with his engagement announcement to Jenny Lee, Savannah refused to believe the trip's unpleasant surprises were over.

8

A shiver shuddered through her the moment she stepped out of the sheriff's office. A cold, stiff gust knocked her sideways forcing her to grab the stair railing. Now she understood Ennis's concern. Wind-driven sleet stung her cheeks. Enough sleet fell that the sidewalks and street glistened in white. She gathered her jacket (which felt more than inadequate now) and took care descending the steps and walking to Dane's truck.

Gales punched at the Ford on the way home, battering it hard enough she fought to keep it on the road. *60 mph my eye*, she sneered. *These gusts are at least 70.* By the time she arrived at the house, her hands and arms felt like she'd wrestled with a suspect twice her size.

Ennis and the girls greeted her at the back door with warm hugs. Georgia wrapped her arms around her with a whispered thanks for the speedy return. Ennis stood vigil at the front window the last twenty minutes, Georgia said, alternating between staring at his watch and debating over calling her instead of texting. Ennis rarely showed a clingy nature but she understood after becoming a human pinball in that wind.

She shook off the initial chill then went to the kitchen for a cup of coffee. Half a spoonful of sugar, two of cream, stir and voilà! – instant heaven. She lifted the cup to her lips when Dane strode in, "Did that thief enjoy my Dr. Pepper?"

His feigned disgust amused her. He and Joe Bob had been friends since childhood but besides Georgia, Dr. Pepper was truly the love of his life. Savannah patted his arm with a consoling, "His incarceration was a misunderstanding and yes, your Dr. Pepper went to a good cause. Joe Bob appreciated your sacrifice."

He ambled off with a snort, "Ennis, your wife stretches the truth longer than the Great Wall of China."

Ennis flashed him a dirty look then sidled up behind Savannah to embrace her. She relaxed in his snug embrace. He swept her hair aside, pressed a lingering kiss to her nape, his voice smooth as silk, "I missed you."

A slow, thoughtful smile curved her lips, "I can tell."

"You're still cold." He cuddled closer, "I have a surefire way to warm you up."

His inviting proposal delivered with that sexy lilt was difficult to resist. She placed her hand atop his resting on her six month proof of, "That's how we got in this shape if you recall."

He nibbled at her earlobe, murmuring, "And it was fun getting in that shape too."

"Savannah," Jenny Lee called from the doorway. It jerked Savannah back from fond memories of "getting in that shape" to the present where an unwelcome intruder spoiled hers and Ennis's private moment.

Ennis sighed. His warm breath caressed her ear which didn't exactly help her horniness either.

Savannah cleared her throat before speaking. No need to alert the universe to hers and Ennis's passionate plight. Savannah wished he'd back off a little but felt his erection pressing against her. Both desire and embarrassment darkened her complexion. "Yes, Jenny Lee?"

And of course Jenny hemmed and hawed, dragging the moment into an excruciating eternity. Whatever lingered on her tongue either tasted mighty bitter or mighty inappropriate. She surprised them both with, "Thanks for defendin' Joe Bob. He called and told me what you did."

Through her haze of lust, it occurred to Savannah that Jenny offered thanks, not an insult. No matter what the saying said, she just proved it *was* possible to squeeze blood from a stone... "I don't want anyone wrongly accused. Did he make it home okay?"

Jenny nodded, apparently oblivious to or just ignoring the awkward scene in front of her, "Sheriff Guthrie gave him a lift."

"Good. Maybe he can weather the snowstorm in comfort now."

"Thanks again. I didn't expect that from you."

*Why doesn't that surprise me?* "No problem." It took serious effort to sound pleasant without impatience creeping into her voice. Hers and Ennis's predicament was embarrassing enough without the wrong person laying eyes on them. Had Dane or Jake seen the two, the moment would be recited at family gatherings until the end of time.

Savannah and Ennis watched her exit the kitchen then they

relaxed, verging on collapse.  She whispered, "How about asking your soldier to retreat?"

"Easier said than done when I'm around you."  He hugged her tighter, kissed her ear, "You reckon the girls might stay here tonight and give us one night alone?"

Probably, she told him.  Lily and Anna considered Georgia and Dane their second set of parents anyway so it wouldn't be a hard sell.  For now though, she needed to change conversational channels before someone more observant popped in.  She found the perfect subject to tame their carnal uprisings.  "Five prisoners escaped from maximum security in Gatesville, or *Gatesvull* as Guthrie called it."

She turned in his embrace.  He smirked, probably at her "Gatesvull" comment.  City and town names became verbal land mines in every state but in the South they were regular as potholes and deep as canyons.  While New Yorkers said Awl-buh-nee, Georgians pronounced their own Albany Ail-binny.  They threw many a tourist into a tizzy by saying Mack-donna, which read McDonough to any unsuspecting visitor.  Duluth had been Dew-looth before the city built their mall and adopted the Yankee pronunciation of Duh-looth.

But good ol' Texas had Miami.  Not to be mistaken for the Florida metropolis pronunciation.  No way.  Somehow Texans screwed it around into My-am-uh.  To annoy the outsiders they also rerouted other names off the beaten path.  Mexia was Muh-hay-uh, and Waxahatchie was Woks-uh-hat-chee so God only knew about simple, nondescript Gatesville.

"We saw it on the news while you were gone," Ennis said.

"You're not worried about them, are you?"

"It's not often a cop killer, pedophile and three other felons escape a maximum security prison."

He dismissed the comment by kissing the tip of her nose, "Sugar, they'd be stupid to come north with this weather moving through."

"Yes, if they've heard about the weather.  Still, I'm bringing my .38 in the morning.  Can't hurt to have it available in case the run-of-the-mill gang of criminals or encyclopedia salesman drops by."

Ennis's expression accused her of being reality impaired.  "Your .38?  Don't you think you're overreacting?  No escaped convict will risk traveling this far north and if they do, they'll cruise by us on I-40 and head to New Mexico."

"Stranger things have happened.  No one suspected a charming surgeon to be a serial killer either and look at Jeffrey."  Yes, the old paranoia breached the fortress of common sense.  Crazy killers did that to her, especially when one of the crazy killers murdered kids.  Ennis should have expected the "overreaction", she thought.  He'd lived with her long enough.

Dane sauntered in to examine the selection in Mama's fruit bowl on the counter.  He polished an apple on his shirt, "Peach, we've got so much firepower in this house you don't need your little ol' .38.  Stop worrying."

Oh really?  She leaned against the cabinet, crossed her arms, "When you have children, I'll see if you still maintain this cavalier attitude.  These guys are murderers and perverts and their crimes span every age group from kids to elderly."

"This ranch is off the beaten path," he reasoned. "They'd have to make one heckuva wrong turn to get here. Seriously, settle down."

As Ennis said moments earlier – easier said than done. He'd not read the gory details of their crimes.

Cal's voice carried from living room, "They revised the forecast. We've got twelve to sixteen inches of snow on the way. I need volunteers for feed duty. Dane, Ennis, front and center."

Savannah groaned. The storm graduated from inconvenient to ludicrous. God really had a sense of humor, she lamented. Sixteen inches of snow? In Texas? *Don't get me wrong, Lord. I like Texas but I don't want to grow old here.*

"Look on the bright side, Peach," Dane crunched into the apple, "All that snow'll keep those five fellas from driving through here, for sure."

Cal leaned in, "Saddle up, brothers. We've got a long night."

Severe winter weather called for two feedings – morning and night – and a change to higher nutrient feed. Cows grew a thicker winter coat to bear the colder months but even so, around eighteen degrees was a critical temperature for them. To help maintain body temperature the men added a feeding at night. Between the extra feeding, checking water tanks for frozen water (and chopping ice with an ax when it did) *and* checking windbreaks protecting cattle from bitter winds, the men stayed busy during those times.

As always Savannah and Georgia joined the troops. They took turns driving the truck or tractor while the men did the heavy work. Savannah's eager sister already donned her coat but Cal annoyingly blocked Savannah from hers.

"Sorry," he said, "but you're staying here."

*Excuse me?* "I always help with the livestock."

Cal tipped his Stetson back, pulled on his work gloves while opting for a more diplomatic approach, "No offense, little lady, but you've always helped when you weren't great with child. Georgia can handle the truck but you and the baby shouldn't be bouncing around pastures and dirt roads."

She nearly scoffed at the "little lady" comment. Anyone who watched her six month transformation realized how *not* little she grew day by day. And a lady? Yeah, right.

Cal's refusal kinda stung but she understood. Georgia offered a sympathetic, "Maybe next trip, hon." She and Dane rushed out the door like teenagers who'd finagled the car keys for the night. Next trip. Right. By then she and Ennis would be up to their eyeballs in formula, diapers and baby wipes again.

Far less enthusiastic than Georgia, Ennis bid Savannah goodbye with a kiss and promise to see her soon. After they left, she gathered the girls and settled in for an evening with the ladies – and Jenny Lee.

## 9

A blanket of snow eight inches thick greeted Savannah early the next morning. Judging by the current heavy snowfall, their revision of sixteen seemed tame. Her heart sank at the forecast. The Alps got sixteen inches of snow, not Texas. That amount forced roads and airports to close which meant rescheduling flights and using more vacation days. Not exactly what they'd planned.

While Ennis caught up on sleep, she showered and dressed in jeans and a wine and gray argyle sweater Georgia and Dane bought her for Christmas. Might as well be fashionable during the blizzard, she thought.

The coffee brewed slower than usual or maybe she imagined it. After pouring a cup she took a minute to recall the last blizzard she weathered in Texas. It snowed until delaying flights, preventing travel and generally crippling the area for a day or two – and that storm paled in comparison to sixteen frustrating, obstructive inches.

Drawing the kitchen curtain aside, she sighed at the disheartening scene. By the time they arrived in Atlanta, she and Georgia would owe

Seth a truckload of favors.

Lily bounded from the other bedroom, "I wanna build a snowman today. A big one!"

Savannah shushed her, pointing to Lily's yawning, listless daddy hunched on the side of the bed. "Keep it down, hon," she told the cheerful youngster. "Daddy's trying to wake up."

He rose to his feet with a groan. Physically he looked rather sad. Bleary-eyed, feet shuffling along and a comical bed head that caused Lily to point and giggle. Not amused, he nodded to the bathroom, "I'm going in there."

Lily followed behind, "Can we make a snowman? Please, Daddy?"

His mouth stretched into another cavernous yawn. He then put great effort into raking his fingers through his unruly hair. Before shutting himself away in the bathroom, he did what any self-respecting parent did. He deflected the question, "Ask your mother."

Lily's enthusiasm dimmed a few watts, "Can we, Mama? Daddy doesn't want to. He's grumpy."

"Once the wind dies down and the snow stops, I promise you and Anna can make a snowman. Right now it's too cold and windy and there's more snow on the way." Damn it.

Lily considered objecting until a gust slammed against the front door. A couple of rafters popped overhead. The strange noises unsettled her enough she didn't argue.

Yes, the weather killed a lot of nice plans, Savannah wanted to say. Porch sitting, snowman building, and getting home on time.

Someone needed a pep talk and not just the pint-sized someone either. "Cheer up, sweetie. The storm can't last forever," she said for both their sakes. "And Daddy's grumpy because he's tired. He stayed up past his bedtime feeding cows. He'll be in a better mood once he wakes up."

They'd not just fed livestock she discovered when the brood dragged in hours later. They also added heaters to the water tanks and checked the windbreaks while battling snow and bitter wind. After breakfast the men planned to make the rounds again.

Savannah reminded, "We're moving to Granna's during the storm so why don't you get dressed and pack everything you brought?"

Lily hurried back to the bedroom at the mention of moving to Granna's house. Lily adored Ennis's mother. Savannah allowed herself to imagine how Lily and Anna would have loved their Grandma Charlene whose love, generosity and kindness equaled Granna's.

She shook free of wistful ponderings to unlock the suitcase and retrieve her .38 before Lily returned. Seeing the weapon might raise questions from the girls – questions she preferred to avoid so she covered it with her sweater. She already expected Ennis to call her paranoid since reports of the "Gatesville Five" slowed to a trickle the night before.

While Ennis showered and Lily dressed, Savannah assessed the weather from the front window. Sloping snow drifts swept to the tops of Dane's truck tires already equipped with snow chains. The pastures – what she could see of them in the dark – disappeared beneath a blanket of snow. In the near distance, almost obscured by a wall of white, Mama's fruit trees already began sagging beneath a layer of the clingy white stuff. With enough accumulation it would test the heartiest of branches throughout the region, weighing them down until they snapped – and fell on power lines and knocking out electricity. Savannah gained a new respect for Mama's forethought of installing a generator.

At her mother-in-law's request, Savannah began packing their luggage for the move to the main house. Mama wanted everyone under one roof during the storm and thankfully her house could just barely accommodate the whole family. For Cal's boys, she converted her husband's study into a makeshift bedroom. One thing large families planned for: large gatherings. That meant extra sheets, blankets, pillows and folding beds.

Cal and Jake stayed up to the wee hours equipping the tractor with chains and a snowplow blade. But don't worry, they told the two fretting females from Georgia, it's rarely required. Rarely or not, at the rate the snow fell, she expected that decision might pay off soon.

She gathered up hand lotion she left on the nightstand and tucked it in the train case. The book she'd been reading went in the suitcase just as Lily entered the room. She wore her jeans and a maroon and gray argyle sweater nearly identical to her mother's. Savannah couldn't resist, "Grandma Charlene would call you pretty as a peach. And you are."

Lily leaned onto the bed, "What was Gramma Charlene like?"

Savannah smiled, touched at Lily's interest in a grandma who cherished the idea of spoiling grandchildren and looked forward to the day the house rang with their laughter. If only cancer hadn't cheated her out of her dream, Savannah reflected sadly.

Someday she planned to show her daughters video of Christmases long ago – but even now she found it difficult to watch them without getting depressed. "She was a lot like Granna. She loved children, going to church, cooking and spent her spare time in her flower garden. Know what her favorite flower was?"

Lily shook her head. Savannah bent to kiss her cheek, "The lily."

Lily's mouth dropped open. "Really?"

"M-hmm. We named you after Grandma Charlene's favorite flower. Oh, and by the way, Cinderella was her favorite Disney Princess."

Lily's eyes brightened, "Gramma loved Cinderella?"

"Yep. And Sleeping Beauty and Snow White too but Cinderella was tops with her." Charlene probably sympathized with the character since she had two snaky sisters of her own. "Someday we'll watch videos of Grandma at Christmas – that was her most favorite holiday, you know. She would sit in the floor and play dolls or games with us when we were little." Sudden, overwhelming sorrow tightened her throat. Before her mood plummeted and tears choked her voice, she zipped the suitcase shut and changed the subject, "Did you pack your things?"

"U-huh," Lily dutifully returned to the bedroom. Savannah heard a *thunk* then a dragging noise. Before leaving Atlanta, she packed Lily's suitcase. At some point Lily rearranged the contents, removed a few clothes (who needed those boring things anyway?) and replaced them with important items including toys and books. Savannah demanded the clothes take priority and they had, but the child still managed to squirrel toys and books around them, utilizing every available inch of space – and more. Since Savannah and Ennis served as her personal valets, Lily hadn't had a chance to test the suitcase's weight. Lugging that thing through the maze of airports was no job for a pantywaist. Now Lily reaped the benefits of her overzealousness. Those precious books and toys (and boring clothes) weighed a ton for a kid her size. Both hands white-knuckled the handle as she strained and wrestled the suitcase to her mother, "This is heavy."

"Well, Daddy and I told you not to pack so many books and toys." Savannah relieved her of the "heavy" luggage, hoisted it on the bed and opened it, "Are you sure you got everything? We probably won't be back here for days."

Despite Lily's confident nod, Savannah still planned to check the bedroom before leaving. There would be no opportunity to return, at least easily, for a day or two and nothing disrupted family harmony like a child crying about a missing doll.

Ennis shut off the shower. There'd be just enough time to wake Anna, get her dressed and pack her things before he began fidgeting to leave. Cal wanted an early morning for feeding cattle.

Anna cocooned herself by curling up and tucking the covers under her chin. It seemed rude to interrupt such angelic slumber. Savannah kissed her, greeted her with a *good morning.* Anna barely stirred.

"Wake up, baby. We're staying at Granna's a few days, remember?"

Dark eyes opened to slits. Anna mumbled a complaint.

"Honey, we're all tired," Savannah replied.

"'Specially Daddy," Lily sulked. "He's in a bad mood."

Ennis leaned in, "Rise and shine.  We gotta go so I can help Uncle Cal."  The shave and shower improved his appearance but not necessarily his mood.  Anna decided dressing wasn't such a bad idea.

In the meantime Ennis indulged in a cup of coffee and waited impatiently for Savannah to check the place over for forgotten items.

With Ennis behind the wheel, the truck handled the snow better than she imagined.  The road disappeared hours ago but he kept driving as if by memory, keeping the truck moving smooth and steady, the chains churning into drifts she felt sure should have left them stranded.  The girls spent the trip in round-eyed awe at the overnight transformation.  Savannah just wanted to get there, help with breakfast and wait for the sun to come out again, whenever that might be.

The jaunt from the truck to the back door was a weather war zone.  Icy nettles stung their faces and hands.  Squalls stole their breath and buffeted them on the slick patio and porch, threatening their balance as they carried their precious cargo.

She and Ennis cradled the girls close and shielded them from wind and snow.  They both sighed with relief once stepping in the calm warmth and safety of the house.

Women's laughter and the rich, smoky smell of bacon frying beckoned her toward the kitchen.  The cheerful atmosphere (and prospect of food) also drew the girls.  They began shedding winter wear.  Lily unwrapped in record time.  Anna's haste trying to unzip her coat resulted in frustration and a plea to her mother for help.

Shrugging off her coat, Savannah concentrated on the weather report coming from the living room TV.  *Amarillo airport closed.*

*Impassable roads by evening.  Potential record-breaking snowfall.*  She prayed the forecast was exaggerated.  She really liked her home and wanted to see it again before her fortieth birthday.

The mudroom had a long bench lining a row of alcoves behind it.  Each alcove contained a coat hook and an upper cubby for hats and gloves and a floor level cubby for storing boots.  When the whole family gathered, couples doubled up to claim one alcove for two people.  She and Ennis took the last empty one.  Boots, Sherpa-lined rancher coats, and Stetsons occupied most of the others.

Savannah unburdened their youngest of her coat and scarf (Anna had managed to remove her hat and gloves before the coat thwarted her).  Meanwhile Lily handed off her winter accessories to Ennis then stowed her boots beside the back door.  She promptly headed off to greet the masses, leaving Anna squirming and begging her sister to wait for her.

Then she shifted those dark, judging eyes on her mother – the slowest schlub on Earth in her estimation – who fumbled to remove small boots off the restless three-year-old.

"Hold still," Savannah told her, "I'm about done."  At that hour of the morning the kid was lucky her mama remembered what Velcro was, much less how to unfasten it.

"Huwwy, Mama."

Their baby hadn't mastered her "R's" yet and as cute as she sounded, the stare meant business.  So hurrying – or huwwying – was tops on Mama's list.  "Believe me, hon, I'm trying."  Anything to release the fidgeting kid into the wild to seek out her sibling.

The moment she finished unwrapping Anna, the girl took off

faster than a racehorse out of the gate to catch up with Lily. The child reminded Savannah of herself at times, especially regarding an older sister. Always underfoot, wanting to be close to Big Sis.

"I'll unload the luggage and get it upstairs," Ennis said. He dreaded staying at the main house. Too much "togetherness" he called it. Everywhere they turned someone would be there.

His already low spirits scraped bottom the moment they stepped in the house. Savannah tried cheering him up, "Staying here might actually be fun. Like a party." Hearing it out loud she realized how ridiculous that sounded.

And yes, he stared at her like her marbles fell out, "Fun, eh? Jenny Lee didn't go home, remember? She stayed here last night. Still sound like fun?"

Oh. She forgot that part. Her shoulders sagged with the realization she'd endorsed her own nightmare.

"Yeah," Ennis zipped his coat again. "I didn't think so."

"Don't forget to tell me our room number. I'd hate to walk in on Georgia and Dane – or Jake and Jenny Lee." She gradually lost her appetite with that last image.

"Jake's sleeping in Daddy's study with the boys. Ma's keeping Jenny in Jake's bedroom, the furthest from us. We're on the other end of the hall next to Dane and Georgia. The last bedroom."

He'd said "the last bedroom" as if it represented their personal Waterloo. She pecked a kiss to his lips, "I knew your mother was smart."

He nearly smiled, "She just knows it's difficult to clean blood out of carpet."

When Savannah left him, he seemed calmer or maybe just resigned to their new digs.

On the way to the kitchen she passed by the dining room. The person doling out silverware on the tables was the reason the family required such delicate and strategic arrangement. Or simply, the reason staying there would probably *not* be fun. She greeted Jenny Lee anyway. Jenny ignored her.

The world could count on a number of things. The sun rising and setting each day, politicians lying, babies crying and Jenny Lee holding a grudge tighter than an alligator with lock jaw. Apparently the previous night's truce – thanks to Joe Bob – lasted five whole minutes and the war commenced again.

Jenny sat the forks on the right side of the plates, the spoons and knives on the left. Savannah tried saving her from another berating from Dane, "The forks go on the left, Jenny Lee."

She shot Savannah the evil eye, snatched up the last fork and commenced reorganizing the utensils. She grumbled something ending with *I don't need some know-it-all telling me what to do.*

Savannah resisted sharing Charlene's helpful table setting hints. *L-E-F-T and F-O-R-K have four letters. R-I-G-H-T, K-N-I-F-E and S-P-O-O-N have five.*

Jenny wouldn't appreciate the hints especially if they came from her, Savannah decided, so she moved on to the kitchen where the less contentious people hung out. Bobbi fried bacon, Mama tended gravy and Georgia gathered eggs from the fridge for scrambling later.

Savannah's sister raised a brow, teasing, "Look who's fashionably late.  Get your beauty sleep?"

She snorted, "It wasn't me who needed it as you'll soon discover.
My husband is gloomier than this infernal weather."  She shivered, "It's
brutal out there."

"Reminds me of the fifties," Mama said.  "Had two storms blow
through, one in February of fifty-six, the other in March of fifty-seven.
We had snow to the rooftops – and the drifts?  Thirty feet tall."

Yeah, right.   Texans and their "everything's bigger in Texas"
philosophy.  Savannah couldn't help it.  She rolled her eyes, laughing,
"Good one, Mama, but a shade overboard on the theatrics.  Drifts thirty
feet tall?"

Mama halfway smiled, "I'm not embellishin', honey.  I've got the
pictures and newspaper clippings to prove it.  I'll show you after
breakfast."

Talk about reality crashing in.  Savannah's throat worked as if the
words were physical things lodged in there.  Meanwhile her stomach and
jaw plummeted as well as her hopes of ever getting home again.  Then,
"*Thirty feet tall?*"

Somehow Georgia and Bobbi found humor in the outburst.
Mama continued as if reciting a recipe for lasagna, not one for disaster,
"Oh yes, both storms were record breakers.  In fifty-seven, we got twenty
inches but fifty-six was the worst.  Vega holds the record of most snowfall
in state history.  It snowed for ninety-two hours straight.  Gave us forty-
three inches, killed a lot of Daddy's cattle and what cattle survived they
airlifted feed in for them.  My brother tunneled out the front door and
climbed on the roof to shovel snow off of it.  Daddy was afraid the roof

might collapse."

Potential record-breaking snowfall, the weatherman had said. That meant between twenty-one and forty-three inches for Vega. Or, she trembled to think, did it mean *more* than forty-three?

Mama's dissertation quelled Georgia's chipper disposition. Her complexion paled. Savannah felt vindicated. *Not funny anymore is it, sis? When did reality dawn on you – before or after 'shoveling snow off a roof'?*

Bobbi abandoned her skillet, set it aside then herded her sisters-in-law toward a couple of chairs.

Savannah waved it off, thanking her. She wanted to remain upright in case her seed of nausea bloomed into a full-fledged problem. "I'm just trying to fathom forty-three inches of snow. Texas weather is so neurotic."

Mama chuckled, "My lands, honey, those type storms are rare birds around here. We've seen numerous blizzards like this one and they don't shut us down for long. When they do it's just a day or two, like that storm years ago when you found Monty in the gully. Stop fretting."

Cal appeared at the kitchen doorway, began to speak then stopped short when viewing Savannah's complexion, "What happened? You're as pale as a pearl."

Thirty foot drifts and tunneling out of a house, that's what happened, she wanted to say.

He pulled a chair closer, "Sit down." When she hesitated, he urged her down with a hand on her shoulder. His insistence worried her and she soon discovered why.

"Ladies," he announced, "the forecast has changed. Instead of sixteen inches, we're preparing for twenty-four."

*Yep, glad I'm sitting down.*

Georgia's eyes glazed over and she swayed. Savannah pointed to a neighboring chair, "Better grab one now. They'll be going fast with this news."

"Twenty-four inches," her older sister repeated in disbelief. "And the storm in fifty-seven was twenty?"

Mama shrugged it off, "Girls, we've survived these things before. We'll get through this one too. We've got plenty of food and supplies, plenty of wood for the fireplace along with a generator if the power gives out. We'll be fine."

Then someone should tell your face, Savannah wanted to say. Because with each word, Mama's brow sank a tad deeper and a hint of trepidation burdened her voice. Georgia noticed it too. Whether she admitted it or not, the latest forecast rattled Ennis's mother, a veteran of battling such storms.

Georgia and Savannah lived through flooding rains, an ice storm or two and a close shave with a tornado once or twice. But twenty-four inches of snow? For "two little Georgia girls" as Dane called them, that amount didn't just worry them, it downright freaked them out. And seeing ripples on the surface of his mother's once calm waters didn't exactly help.

Dane stepped in the kitchen, "Hey, is breakfast about r…" He surveyed the shell-shocked expressions on his wife and sister-in-law. "Oh," he told Cal. "You told them."

Georgia stared into oblivion, "Twenty-four inches?" Astronomical amounts of snow would fall on the Rutherford Ranch, trapping them for days, maybe even a week or more depending on local roads, the interstate, and the road at the ranch. For a painful instant Savannah envisioned herself sitting in that very chair, singing Happy Birthday to Lily – in April – because the snow only melted past the window frames.

Dane's carefree demeanor chose that moment to shine. He bent down to smack a kiss on his wife's cheek, "Cheer up, darlin'. We can keep each other warm at night if the heat goes off."

She gifted him the same incredulous frown Ennis gave Savannah when she assumed this Walton family closeness might be "fun".

Cal's stomach growled. He motioned Dane to the stove, "You do the eggs and I'll finish the bacon. Seems as though half our womenfolk are out of commission."

Mama shooed her boys off, "Go back to your TV. Everything's fine. Breakfast'll be ready when it's ready."

It took several seconds before Bobbi and the "two little Georgia girls" snapped free of their dazes. Placing the iron skillet back to the burner, Bobbi resumed frying bacon. Georgia followed suit shortly after, cracking eggs in a bowl. Savannah collected the heavy cream, half and half and other ingredients for the biscuits. A quick perusal at the dining table had Savannah shaking her head.

"What's wrong?" Georgia asked.

Savannah told her about Jenny's silverware snafu. She seemed surprised, "Really? Did you tell her the 'L-E-F-T and F-O-R-K have four letters' trick?"

What, and be stabbed in the eye with the shiniest F-O-R-K on the T-A-B-L-E? "Are you kidding? I'd like to leave here alive."

Georgia peered around the corner. Jenny took her sweet time positioning plates just so. "Well, one thing's for sure," the older sister replied. "Breakfast ought to be interesting."

o   o   o

When the family sat down to eat, everyone noticed a little something different with the place settings. The women ignored it (because they halfway expected it) but the men looked thoroughly confused. Cal centered on Jenny, "Why are the utensils backwards?"

"Because that's her nature," Dane mumbled under his breath.

Apparently Jenny Lee misinterpreted Savannah's earlier prompt regarding forks as malicious criticism and reset the table to her liking.

Savannah noticed Anna, sitting at the children's table, eyed the family, probably wondering what the hold-up was on eating. Lily, sitting beside her sister, lifted her fork in a questioning manner. Yes, it's backwards, her mama's expression said, but follow my lead. She, along with the others, moved their silverware to their proper positions.

"Geez, Jenny Lee," Dane complained, "didn't you take home economics in school?"

She bowed up, "Yes."

"I'da thought they'd teach you how to set a table. I mean that's like taking shop and not learning how to hammer."

Jake flared mad. Savannah wasn't sure if he kept quiet for Mama's benefit or was just too infuriated to speak. The latter rarely occurred.

Ennis turned to his wife, taunting, "This feeling like a party yet?"

*Smartass.* "I'd tell you how it feels but there are children present."

Across the table, Jake tossed his napkin in his empty plate. "Dane, that's my fiancée you're talking to."

"Yeah, and good luck eating your soup with a fork when you're married."

"Hush," Georgia muttered to her husband. She glanced at Mama whose mouth tightened due to her son's incessant ribbing.

Meanwhile, Jenny Lee attempted to preserve her pride, "Who cares what side the fork is on?" She glared across at Savannah, daring her to speak up which she did not. They were destined to spend days locked up together in the house so she refused to throw gasoline on a fire she never intended to start in the first place.

Dane, though, couldn't resist dumping a truckload of fuel on it. "*Who cares what side the fork is on?* People who can't stab their steak with a spoon, that's who."

"*Dane,*" Georgia reinforced the stronger admonition with a cautionary scowl.

Monty and his brothers snickered. That was the last straw for Jenny. "It's just silverware. You act like I replaced everything with shovels and shears." She jabbed a finger at Savannah, "B'sides, she started it when she—"

"Dearest Heavenly Father," Mama's disgruntlement carried over the crowd. She gently clasped Ennis and Bobbi's hands then nodded to the rest. The family abided almost in unison, taking their neighbor's hands and bowing heads as Mama Rutherford offered the blessing in the old Southern Baptist Preacher Way – with passion and a little bit of fire and brimstone warning that there'd be hell to pay if anyone stepped too far out of line.

Serving dishes passed around without a word spoken. The only noises were sounds of spoons clanking into serving dishes and silverware at work on plates. When Mama bared her claws, the adults retreated into tense silence while the children shyly withdrew as if God Himself scolded the group.

Savannah decided to lighten things up. Monty provided the perfect opportunity when he reached for his orange juice glass. She casually made eye contact then focused on the juice.

He stopped in mid-reach. The question so clear in his eyes went unspoken. Did you monkey with my orange juice?

Time for her best poker face. *Maybe. Maybe not. Try it and see...*

His daddy noticed his hand suspended over the glass, looked at Monty then back to Savannah. Georgia watched Monty and her sister stare each other down as did Dane and Ennis. Jenny Lee sat oblivious and still steaming over the earlier argument.

Monty broke the visual standoff by stealing his brother's orange juice.

"Hey!" Tyler protested. "Gimme back my glass."

"Take mine," Monty plunked his glass in front of his brother. He sipped from Tyler's glass then tossed a smug grin at his aunt.

Monty watched Tyler grab the glass given to him and glug down a swallow. The boy sat the glass down and resumed eating.

By then the tension in the room waned to chuckles and smiles – except for Monty who appeared puzzled.

A sly smile curved Savannah's lips. "In due time, young man. The master prankster will strike in due time."

## 10

By noon, knee deep drifts hugged the corners of Mama's house. Roads were difficult to travel throughout the area except the southeastern part of the Panhandle. Authorities closed I-40 at the New Mexico state line due to whiteout conditions and snow accumulation. Amarillo's mayor and police chief flat-out told people to stay home. Do not pass Go, do not collect two hundred dollars, but just stay home.

The men left after breakfast to tend to the livestock. The ladies congregated in the dining room for coffee and conversation. Savannah retreated to the living room with the crackling fire to keep her warm and to watch weather updates by Amarillo's self-appointed "snowologist" Bill Bowman, or "Breezy Bill" as the locals called him.

She stood at the large picture window. High winds drove the snow in horizontal sheets. Rafters creaked and popped from gusts slamming into the two story house. Savannah couldn't imagine anyone surviving the storm if it stranded them between towns. Hiking miles for help in that weather meant certain death. The worst part – their men (and Cal's boys) braved that weather to save the family's livelihood.

For the last several minutes, an odd, anxious gnawing settled in the pit of her belly. The sixth sense kind warning something wasn't right. Had something bad happened? Her gut said yes and it revolved around Ennis.

Why had he left that morning with Cal and the others? He was bone-tired from the night before and even a little clumsy when dressing to leave. He stumbled pulling on his jeans and got overbalanced putting on his work boots. The latter nearly resulted in him taking a header into the wall. It seemed humorous at the time but what if he'd truly hurt himself out there in that dangerous storm?

Savannah hurried to the back door, squinted into the storm. A wall of white blocked all but the faint shadow of Dane's pickup parked several yards away. Seeing out to the barn was hopeless, much less into the pastures where the men were.

She blew out a frustrated sigh while meandering back to the living room. Until the men returned home safe she'd teeter on the edge of claustrophobia *and* insanity.

One thing was certain. Texas was a whole other country than Georgia. At any given time the sun could turn Atlanta into a Turkish bath. Hot, humid and more uncomfortable than plenty of people cared to admit. Summer in the Texas Panhandle meant the sun brutalized residents with a dry, searing heat and winter meant a colder, snowier climate suited to dressing in layers and wearing coats and gloves. Throw a native Atlantan in a snowstorm and the world ended. Venturing outside meant making complete fools of themselves either by slipping on ice-sheeted sidewalks or wrecking their cars (one storm saw over a thousand wrecks in twelve hours – and that was only three counties out of Atlanta's nine). Smarter residents burrowed in their homes until the safety of the sun burned away the white plague. Her home state was no stranger to cold and snow but residents just didn't confront the mess unless an emergency arose. Scarlett had the right idea, she thought. *I'll think about it tomorrow.* Enough *tomorrows* and the snow would be gone.

She gave Texas credit for two things. Their men were undoubtedly more handsome and sometimes the "everything's bigger" panned out, especially regarding snow. When it snowed in the Panhandle, it *dumped*.

Two arms wrapped around her from behind. Georgia hugged her close, "Try not to worry. They'll be back soon."

Savannah welcomed the embrace, "It's so treacherous out there. I feel like something's wrong."

"You're just nervous because of the weather. We're not used to this back home." Georgia's palms flattened against Daniel's hangout, "How's my nephew holding up in this blizzard?"

"Better than his mother. He's like Ennis. This doesn't seem to bother him." The baby poked at Georgia's hand. Savannah envisioned him giving his aunt a thumbs-up.

Daniel's interaction delighted Auntie, "Good morning, Daniel."

Another tap, this one stronger. Savannah said, "He's telling you he wanted to go with Daddy."

"You're safer and warmer in there, little one," Georgia told him. "There's plenty of time to brave blizzards later in life."

Blizzards, Savannah huffed. She prayed the horrible storm abated before it buried them alive.

The noon news detailed the massive storm's havoc and devastation. After dumping record snow amounts in the Northwest, Colorado, and northern New Mexico, it mowed through Texas then dropped in for an unwelcome visit in Oklahoma, stunning residents with an ice storm, slicking streets and causing numerous accidents. The local newscaster told of stranded motorists, wrecks, and rescues and deaths spanning nine states. The blizzard caused everything from roof collapses, broken water pipes flooding homes to unattended electric heaters sparking house fires.

The behemoth storm affected millions of people except for a handful of elusive fugitives. If traveling west, east or south from Gatesville they'd encounter violent thunderstorms capable of baseball-sized hail and tornadoes. Tornado watches covered the state's lower half and overlapped into Louisiana. Abilene and Tyler already reported large hail and wall clouds. Traveling north, torrential rains in Dallas and Denton awaited the felons. Veering northwest via U.S. 287 brought them to the leading edge of the North Pole with sleet at Wichita Falls, snow around Chillicothe and the blizzard in Amarillo.

Neither bars, concrete walls or dangerous weather discouraged the five inmates. They got busy after gaining their freedom. They stole a pickup in Gatesville, drove east to Waco where they robbed a gun store of anything with a trigger and stocked up on ammunition. A block from the gun store they carjacked a fresh ride from a single mother who barely had time to save her infant son from the car seat in the back.

After the local update Savannah switched to CNN. Though not her favorite news channel, it was the first one she came across. She started tracking the inmates' movements on her phone's map application the night before. The Rutherford brothers (including her hubby) thought she'd lost her mind by doing so but what else was there to do in this lousy storm? Watch the Weather Channel and commiserate with half the country?

From Waco, the five inmates drove to Fort Worth, pulled into a 7-Eleven, robbed the register and patrons and made off with money, food for their stomachs and gas for their shanghaied Chevy. In the process they killed a cop trying to stop the robbery – but not before he expedited big ol' Creole Trey Mason to God's office for a one-on-one chat.

Video footage revealed investigators and lab techs swarming the scene. Sunlight gleamed off dozens of shell casings on the convenience store's sidewalk. A sheet covered the officer's bullet-riddled body – shot at least fifteen times, CNN said.

The network mentioned no other sightings but the evidence pointed toward her original fear. Gatesville to Waco to Fort Worth. The Rutherford men could pooh-pooh her paranoia all they wanted. The four felons headed north, not south. They ventured exactly opposite of what people expected and that's what made her nervous. The highways going north funneled into Oklahoma City or toward Amarillo through highway 287. She admitted Vega was a stretch considering the weather and isolated area but the "isolated" part bothered her most. If she were on the lam, she wouldn't exactly trek down major highways or risk moseying through many large cities, not after the Fort Worth fiasco. Too many alert residents might recognize her, not to mention law enforcement officers would have her picture and be out for blood since she murdered one of their own. "They still haven't captured those guys yet," she told Georgia.

Her sister hesitated. When she spoke it was a mixture of sadness and unease, "I know. I heard about the police officer in Fort Worth. He killed one before he died, they said. Mason, right?"

"Yes, Trey Mason. The only one not put away for murder. Did you notice the general direction they're headed? North."

"Hon, stop worrying about them. They know law enforcement's looking for them."

Savannah appreciated the efforts to allay her concern however the simple truth boiled down to, "Yes, they do and they don't care." She sternly met Georgia's gaze, "They shot that cop at least fifteen times. *Fifteen.* So no, they don't care who gets in their way and the ones who do will pay with their lives. These guys have nothing to lose because they know they'll either get away or die trying."

A breaking news banner drew their attention. The screen split into four sections reminding Savannah of the old Brady Bunch intro. Instead of Mike, Carol, Alice and the kids, these pictures showed four mugshots. In the upper left, Luis Muñoz. Manual Sanchez occupied the upper right while the lower left revealed Scott Hadley and shameless degenerate Alan Brozek smiled at viewers from the last square.

The photos faded to a solemn brunette sitting at the news desk, "We have sad news to report this hour. The four inmates who escaped a Texas prison struck again early this morning. This is footage taken three hours ago in Decatur, Texas." The image switched to a helicopter shot of a home surrounded by plentiful acreage. Smoke billowed from a large two story home. Red, amber and bright orange flames roiled from shattered windows, curled from beneath eaves and stretched to the heavens. They licked and lapped like an angry dragon consuming the structure from the inside out.

Fire trucks lined the road. Firefighters wielded bulky hoses snaked across a soggy, trampled lawn. They struggled to contain the blaze against the gusty wind.

"The bodies of two adults and two children were later found inside the home. Police have confirmed the four inmates stayed overnight after killing the family then later setting fire to the home and taking their car. A Chevy Cobalt found in the garage has been identified as the vehicle carjacked from a mother in Waco yesterday afternoon. Authorities are now asking the public's help locating a late model silver Toyota 4Runner missing from the home's garage. That license plate is–"

Savannah looked away. That poor family. The four bastards killed them and their children then threw a match to the place – or had the monsters left the ill-fated family alive when they set it ablaze?

Georgia was talking but Savannah descended into darker images. Finally the sound of a child's voice brought her back. Jimmy Tate, the sole survivor of the fire, the CNN banner read. The boy around seven or eight, his face sooty and tear-streaked, recounted how the four men broke into the house during the night, tied everyone up and rode out a violent storm ravaging the area. They had "a lot of guns" and shot his father for trying to tackle one of them. "The man with creepy blue eyes" the boy called him.

Savannah shivered as Luis Muñoz's image flashed in her mind.

Long before the sun rose, the four poured gasoline on walls and floors, set the house ablaze then left – but not before taking the boy's six-year-old sister Andrea. "The children's aunt provided Andrea's photo to authorities who issued an Amber Alert this morning." The reporter continued with a description of Andrea as the screen switched from the traumatized, weeping boy to a family photo taken at Easter. The Tate family looked fresh from Sunday services. Andrea dressed in a cute pink dress trimmed in lace and accessorized with a sweet, dimpled smile.

The little girl presented a tempting morsel for perverts like Brozek with her long, silky brown hair, sparkling blue eyes the color of afternoon sky, and a slight tilt of her head suggesting a shy, thoughtful nature.

Tears blurred Savannah's vision. God only knew what that pervert Alan Brozek did – or was still doing – to the child.

"Sweetie," Georgia hugged her sister tight, "stop watching this."

"...I tried to help them," the girl's brother sobbed. A police officer put a hand to his shoulder for a show of support but nothing anyone did or said would ease such heartache or soften the cruel truth. Four monsters murdered the boy's family, abducted his sister and left him alone in the world save for his aunt. He dissolved in tears, "I hid in the basement all night and when I heard them screaming and smelled smoke, I *tried* to save them but the fire spread so fast."

Georgia thumbed a button on the remote until landing on ESPN, "Stop watching the news. The storm's depressing enough."

"A little help here!" Cal hollered from the back door. "Ennis is out of commission."

"I knew something was wrong," Savannah told Georgia as they hurried to the mudroom. Her worries shifted from burning houses, abducted children and ruthless killers to dredging up various dangerous scenarios associated with ranch life – falls, cuts, broken bones, equipment accidents, animals stepping on people or kicking them. Include the hazardous weather and the risks multiplied. Sometimes an injury was minor while others required medical attention by a family doctor or worse, a ride to the ER which was a joke in that weather.

The four brothers plus Monty left that morning dressed in so many layers of clothes it was a wonder they could move. For the finishing touches they pulled on Carhartt overalls and heavy duty coats with hoodies, not to mention the usual winter attire.

The men pushed their hoodies back to reveal bright red cheeks and foreheads. Stubborn snow clung to their coats, overalls and boots. They'd gone out suited up for war with the blizzard but their weary postures told who currently won the battle.

Dane had his arm around Ennis's waist for support while Ennis kept the weight off his right leg.

"What happened?" Savannah asked the men finding places to lean, either the wall or on their knees.

Jake drew his arm across his forehead, "He slipped on some ice outside the barn. Landed on his knee."

Ennis grimaced against the pain. A groaned curse fell from his lips, "You can't see a damn thing out there. Not even ten feet in front of you. A gust caught me and I went down. I feel stupid."

Savannah sympathized. Not only his knee took a beating but his pride had too. It wouldn't soothe either one but, "It could've happened to anyone, babe. You're home now so let's get these wet clothes off and park you somewhere comfortable."

Between her and Georgia they managed to strip the outer layers down to his flannel shirt and jeans. He eased onto the bench with another miserable groan. The room fell silent when Savannah approached the biggest obstacle of all. His work boots. When she removed them Savannah expected a shit storm of cussing that turned the air blue so she sent Georgia to occupy the girls in the living room. Sure enough, the first sign of pressure produced a colorful (yet thankfully subdued) string of profanities. The painful process inspired groans and hostile glares from her hubby that reminded her of her own during the throes of labor.

Once free of the boots, Ennis wiped a shaky hand down his pale, glistening face. He reached for Dane, "Help me to the couch before I pass out." He looked to his wife, "I could really use something for pain."

Ice and ibuprofen. He'd try both but he'd want a slug of hooch to wash the pills down, she knew that. Her hubby's intelligence stretched far and wide on most subjects except dealing with pain. She steeled herself for reminding him why mixing alcohol and pain meds was dangerous *and* also not happening. He'd get mad but better mad than dead, she'd say.

Cal clapped Jake on the shoulder, "C'mon. We still got work to do." He stopped long enough to tell Savannah, "Dane's staying here to cart Ennis around. He'll get him upstairs for you."

Savannah thanked him but fell short of asking if Dane could knock him out for her too because Ennis reverted thirty-five years when he hurt himself. Mama and Bobbi filed out of the kitchen at the sight of Dane helping Hopalong to the couch. Their questions went unanswered by Ennis, leaving Dane to give an update. Savannah suspected Ennis didn't trust himself to utter sentences without blistering the walls.

Georgia put her arm around her sister, tugged her close. She probably felt equally sorry for Savannah and Ennis. Ennis for obvious reasons and Savannah because neither of their husbands coped well when hurt.

Jenny Lee stepped in the room as Dane explained what happened. Georgia squeezed Savannah a shade tighter after feeling her tense up. As feared, the gregarious hillbilly (Savannah was past thinking generous thoughts at that point) converged on Ennis faster than an overzealous teenager who laid eyes on Elvis, "Oh darlin', just look at you!"

Ennis shrugged away from her. Not one to be deterred, she stroked his back, "Poor thing, you can barely walk. Let me grab a blanket so you can warm up. Then I'll bring you a good stiff drink to ease the ache."

"Jenny," Dane snapped, "stop hanging on him like a cheap suit. He don't need you or a drink. Whatever he needs Savannah'll get it for him."

He might as well have called her ugly. "I'm just trying to help."

"As if this day needed more drama," Savannah mumbled under

her breath. "Now we've got Florence Nightingale muscling in on my husband."

Georgia chuckled. Savannah lifted a brow, questioning what part of that statement said *laugh*. To set her older sister straight, she proposed, "If she drags out the bandages and alcohol, you wrap her mouth with one and I'll soak her head in the other. Deal?"

Georgia toned her humor down to a smile, "Hon, if she takes over your job as nurse, I suspect Ennis will save us the trouble and do both."

O   O   O

Cal's boys high-fived each other when a Spurs player sank a three pointer against Oklahoma City. San Antonio led by twelve and the larger the lead, the louder the three boys cheered.

Rutherfords and sports went together like mashed potatoes and gravy. Obsessions changed with the seasons. Most of the nation called them fall, winter, spring and summer. To Cal, Jake, Dane, Ennis and the boys (any blood relative it seemed) they associated seasons with sports – football, basketball, baseball and NASCAR. They considered those sports the desserts of the entertainment "food pyramid". Soccer, tennis and golf, as Savannah learned long ago, represented the cauliflower, beets and broccoli.

Once, long, long ago, she made the mistake of flipping the channel to a golf game and they all stared at her as if she'd landed from Mars. Golf was *okay* they said, but didn't really mean it. The TV magically turned back to the lifeblood of Texans in spring. Tried and true, red white and blue Rangers baseball. Savannah fell asleep in the third inning.

And basketball? Well, the glow dimmed for her and Ennis when their kids came along. They'd watch an occasional game and keep track of the Finals but otherwise they had enough noise in the house without hearing a bouncing ball or sneakers squeaking on the basketball court, thank you. Infants took exception to anything interrupting their sleep and shared their discontent in the loudest possible way. And sometimes toddlers weren't any better.

That evening Savannah added one more baby to that list. Ennis. When Monty, Tyler and Zach cheered the Spurs to a fifteen point lead, Ennis gave them the stink eye. He'd been in a lousy mood since his accident and it only deteriorated throughout the day. No one interacted with him unless forced to.

Lazily rocking in her trusty rocking chair, Mama resumed knitting. The rest halfway paid attention to the game as they quietly conversed among themselves. Cal, Bobbi, Jake and Jenny parked on the couch near the picture window while Dane, Georgia, Ennis and Savannah chose the couch facing the fireplace and TV. The girls lounged in the floor with the boys, cheering when they cheered which added to Ennis's upset.

He reached to rub his knee then thought better of it. He winced instead. Late that afternoon Savannah also did a fair amount of wincing after seeing the swollen knob connecting his calf to his thigh. She dreaded to see it the next morning.

Earlier Mama fetched her husband's walking stick for him. For the first time since he fell Ennis smiled upon seeing his daddy's treasured cane. He ran his hand along the gold horse's head atop the wooden cane, stroked the mane smoothed out from years of use. Savannah swore for a few moments, pain surrendered to welcome memories.

He'd quieted down since his and Savannah's squabble that afternoon. Once downing ibuprofen and using an ice pack, Ennis fumed at the lack of pain relief and suggested a stronger remedy. Two shots of Wild Turkey. A discussion began that ended in an argument. Savannah refused to pour a drop of it for him. That's when Ennis escalated to fussy and settled out at thorny. An hour later when various family members told him to shut up (Jake offered him a belt alright – of his fist, not whiskey), she regrettably caved to Ennis's demand – but only to save bloodshed between the brothers.

Before handing over the first drink (she poured a third of a shot, not a full one), she geared up for a lecture on mixing booze and medicine. He countered with a furious scowl. She backed off reminding *you know the risks*. He wanted relief, he said, not a public service announcement. Savannah pursed her lips but shut up. He criticized the two "miserly" shots then complained when she announced her retirement as bartender. Once her *miserly* efforts took effect, he drifted into a light, fitful sleep. Everyone breathed a sigh of relief.

Mama and Georgia threw together Sloppy Joes for a quick meal. Savannah noticed how they'd absconded to the kitchen like their feet were on fire, all to escape his snoring. She joined them for a welcome break from her cranky spouse.

Ennis roused in time to eat but getting him to ingest food proved much harder, of course, than getting him to swill the Wild Turkey.

Savannah told him if he *ever* wanted another drop of Kickin' Chicken, get busy chewing.  He reluctantly did.

"If he was my husband," Jenny Lee chastised, "I'd give him anything he wanted, even a snort of hooch.  He's injured."

*You will be too if you don't shut your yap.*  Savannah shot a withering, "He needs to eat, not drink," back at her.

"She's right, Jenny," Ennis held a hand to his gut.  "Feels like I drank battery acid."

Why had he slightly slurred that sentence?  The two shots she served him shouldn't have affected his speech.

He dutifully ate his supper, choosing to ignore the weather report.  According to the weatherman, so far Vega received thirteen inches.  Earlier the radar looked encouraging that the blizzard wound down.  Now Breezy Bill (more like Windbag Willy, she groused) – the one who'd tempted fate by joking about a "Snowpocalypse" – chagrined his way through the "unexpected" momentum the storm gained during the last couple of hours.  Mother Nature changed her mind, Windbag chuckled.  It intensified around Tucumcari, New Mexico, a town about eighty miles west of Vega and barreled toward the Texas Panhandle, packing a brutal amount of snow.  The area "could" see a total of twenty-eight inches.

While the rest of the family shook their heads or sighed, Georgia and Savannah stared dumbly at the TV.  An unbelievable twenty-eight inches.  Twenty-eight.  Inches.  Plus drifting.  And Windbag smiled when he said it.

"So what?" Jake shrugged. "It's only fifteen more than what's there already."

Some situations deserved optimism or even silly jokes. Others begged for a hard glare. This fell into yet another category – *slap the ever-loving shit* out of the person cracking wise about becoming the North Pole. "Yes," she replied to Ennis's knucklehead brother, "fifteen inches and four more days of isolation. Sounds lovely."

Mama's rocking chair halted its faint rhythmic squeak. The steady clicking of knitting needles at work ceased their progress on a project that looked suspiciously like blue baby booties. She declared a confident, "We'll make it, honey. Don't you worry," then resumed knitting again.

"Start worrying when Ma runs low on yarn," Dane said. "If she runs out of that, *then* the world ends."

Mama's mouth tilted in a small smile but she never denied his claim. Knitting was her stress reliever the way working crosswords was Savannah's. Mama's only irritation (and it was mild at that) reared up when her yarn snagged on the rocker's armrest, making her pluck it free to continue working.

On the other sofa, Jenny Lee held her fiancé's hand, whispered in his ear then grinned. Jake nodded. Bobbi snuggled against Cal's side, his arm curled around her while the youngsters waited for Windbag Willy to conclude lying about expected snow totals. Monty took the opportunity to grab a snack from the kitchen. Before long he reappeared holding a glass of milk and a saucer of Oreos. He settled beside his brothers and dunked a cookie, "Can we change it back to the game yet?"

"Yes, darlin'," Bobbi rolled her eyes, feigning exasperation, "though I can't imagine what we might have missed."

"The Spurs hafta make the playoffs." Tyler delivered the statement with the direst gravity.

Bobbi played along, "Well, time's a'wastin'. Change the channel or they might–"

"Yuck," Monty wrinkled his nose. He forced himself to swallow the bite then eyeballed the other Oreos. He zeroed in on the culprit – Aunt Savannah. "*Toothpaste?*"

The adults restrained their laughter. The kids didn't even try.

"Pigs?" Savannah reminded.

"Where'd you learn that–" he gulped a swallow of milk to wash down the chalky texture.

Georgia replied, "Monty, she's got many, many years of experience you don't."

Savannah took slight offense, "I'm not that old, Georgia. I didn't exactly tote God's Commandments down the mountain."

Several quick knocks on the front door silenced the family. They glanced at each other wondering the same thing. Who managed to plow *thirteen inches of snow plus drifting* to get there?

Mama paused knitting, "Who in the world could that be in this weather?"

The impatient visitor thumbed the doorbell three times. With a heavy sigh, Cal levered to his feet, "Best find out before they freeze to death."

"I'm breaking their fingers if they don't lay off the doorbell," Jake grumbled.

No one expressed genuine concern about the visitor's identity. Savannah, on the other hand, eased her hand back to her holster. She tracked the Gatesville inmates' movements in a generally northern track. In their haste, snow in the Texas Panhandle might have sounded easier to traverse than ice in Oklahoma. If they diverted northwest to Amarillo, maneuvering through the city's eight inches of snow was easier than pulling Vega's thirteen. What happened if that stolen 4Runner became stranded in those thirteen inches of snow? Or had they heard 1-40 shut down at the New Mexico state line? Maybe to avoid confrontation with law enforcement, they detoured off the interstate and found a nice, cozy, out-of-the-way house to wait out the storm? Then they'd kill the family, set the place on fire and leave. Why not? They'd done it in Decatur.

Ennis wrinkled his nose at her hand poised over the .38. "You gonna shoot 'em after Jake breaks their fingers? It's just a stranded driver."

Those two "chintzy" shots of whiskey (as he later reclassified them) sure loosened his tongue. Syllables halfway blended together. S's stretched longer while her patience grew shorter by the insult. She would worry about all that shortly. For now, she braced for whoever sought shelter from the storm and prayed it wasn't a gang of escaped murderers.

Cal pulled the door open. Ghostlike shrieks of wind pushed and wailed against the glass screen door. Hand on her gun, Savannah prepared to act fast since Cal's posture turned rigid. He said nothing nor did he offer refuge to the visitor or visitors.

Jake bolted upright at the sight outside. His shoulders squared and fists clenched.

"Goodness gracious," Mama put away her knitting then padded to the door. "You boys act like the devil himself is outside." Then *she* drew up short upon once seeing their uninvited guest or guests.

Savannah began pulling the .38 free when a voice said, "My car's stuck down the road. It's taken twenty minutes to walk here and I'm freezing."

Savannah's hand retreated. The unexpected company wasn't four crazy convicts but a woman sounding on the verge of exhaustion. Her plea failed to persuade Cal who fumed, "You *do* realize whose residence this is."

The brusque question shocked Savannah. Cal Rutherford exemplified courtesy, particularly around women.

"Yes," the unknown female's voice shivered, "and if there'd been another house within walking distance I'd have gone there instead. Please, Cal…"

Mama rubbed her forehead as if stricken by a sudden headache. She uttered a resigned, "Let her in."

Jake wheeled to his mother, "You're kidding, Ma."

Upon seeing the mystery guest's identity, Jenny Lee let her feelings fly, "No way. Not *her*. She can go to he…" the word "hell" seized on the tip of her tongue. She rephrased, "She can go to Eldon Killibrew's farm. He'll take her in."

"Jenny," Mama replied, "she's here and we'll make the best of it."

Who was this pariah that Jenny sentenced to trudge two extra miles in such inclement weather?

Savannah leaned aside to find out who Jenny Lee hated as much as her. Jenny usually reserved such venom for their exchanges.

"I said let her in," Mama commanded. "It's the Christian thing to do. Can't let her freeze to death."

"Says who?" Jake blurted then recoiled at his mother's surly frown.

Ennis struggled to separate the words, "Who is it?" The question blended vaguely into *whozit.*

Cal turned to Savannah, "You might want to hold him down for this." He thumbed the door latch, stepped aside.

Gina Sutton – née Reggie Gibson – hugged her arms tight around her midriff. She'd brushed off the bulk of the snow but a clinging layer remained plastered to her jeans, red and black plaid coat and red knit hat.

It took less than two seconds for Ennis to react to the person invading his beloved childhood home. Through the haze of Wild Turkey, his vision narrowed into a glare more frigid than the wind outside. "Get her outta here. Jenny's right. Eldon's farm isn't that far away. Let her go there."

Gina would collapse and likely die trying to forge ahead two more miles to the Killibrew farm, not that Ennis cared right then. Taking stock of the men's demeanors, none of them did.

Mama countered, "Now Ennis, the Bible says–"

"Did she screw with anyone's lives in the Bible? No. Get her out." He leaned forward to stand then grabbed his knee, groaning.

Anger, frustration and the whiskey fueled his little tantrum – a tantrum that escalated when he shoved his hand between his and Savannah's hips.

She felt him grope for her .38. She wrapped her hand tight around the weapon, keeping it safely holstered, "Don't be foolish, Ennis. Calm down." She understood his rage but he'd lost his marbles and the only times he lost those marbles? When he ingested alcohol – and more than two "chintzy" shots of it. His knee prevented him from walking without assistance and only one individual would grant any wish or request he made. If Jenny Lee interfered one more time, Savannah planned to have a *Come to Jesus Meeting* with her.

Ennis crammed his hand deeper around her hip. He tried slipping the holster off her belt. "Gimme that thing. That's why you have it. To shoot criminals."

She slapped his hand. Hard. Ennis retreated to rub the sting out. She'd do it again, her expression warned, so don't push it.

Jenny Lee stabbed a finger at Savannah, "This is all *your* fault. This traitor hasn't set foot on Rutherford land in years until *you* chatted her up."

There it was. The blame. It surprised her when Ennis leveled his anger at Jenny, "Leave Savannah outta this. It's not her fault the car got stuck." He instructed his mother, "Throw Gibson a blanket and let her bed down in the garage. Otherwise she leaves, storm or no storm."

His mother seemed as fed up as Savannah, "This is my house. I say who stays and who doesn't."

Meanwhile Gina quietly shrugged from her wool coat and another flannel jacket. She hung them on the coat rack by the door,

"Thank you for your kindness, Caroline. I'm sorry to impose on you." She removed her hat and snow boots, and placed those and her gloves neatly in the entry corner.  She turned and surveyed the group like a trapped mouse eyeing a roomful of cats.

Mama's mouth, like Cal's, thinned to a tense line, "Well, we try to live by the Golden Rule."  She put the family on notice, "That goes for all of us."

Understandably, Ennis didn't feel very charitable toward his former colleague.  None of them did.  Not even Mama.  By her features it was clear no matter what she said, this act of kindness grated on her. "Gina, go change out of your wet clothes.  I'll fetch you a robe and something to wear while they dry."  She headed to the stairs, "You remember where the bathroom is."

Jake followed behind his mother, "Ma, come on.  After what she did?"

"Jacob, not another word," she cautioned in a manner Savannah certainly would have heeded.  "Gina, you can sleep on the couch tonight. I'll be back with your clothes and bedding."

Gina stayed put, "Thank you again, Caroline.  I'll try to stay out of the way."

"Try real hard," Jenny Lee said.

Before venturing upstairs, Mama made eye contact with every person over thirteen, "I won't say it again.  If you're in this house, 'do unto others' is the rule.  In simpler terms, if you can't say anything nice, keep quiet."

Despite the lecture being aimed at the adults, Monty, his

brothers, Lily and Anna listened up. Savannah heard Lily gulp.

"In that case, I'll need another slug," Ennis proclaimed. "Sugar, grab me a refill. A big one."

She shook her head, "You don't need any more booze."

Gina walk past them toward the bathroom. Ennis's jaw clenched tight. If looks could kill, Savannah thought. Then he directed the prickly mood at his wife, "I'll get it myself." He gripped the cane until his knuckles blanched.

She placed a hand to his arm. The muscles flexed beneath her touch. She chanced a gentle caution, "Ennis, don't. You'll only suffer later."

His free hand braced on the sofa's edge and he tried pushing to his feet. He fell back with a disgruntled groan, "One swallow, Savannah. You want me to beg?"

"Of course not. I'll bring you another ibuprofen but no more whiskey for you tonight." Since someone named Jenny Lee "helped out" enough.

Jenny Lee jumped from her seat, "I'll get it for you, Ennis."

Savannah stood to oppose her, "No, you won't. He's had plenty or can't you tell by his slurred sp–"

"Who wants pie?" Georgia butted in.

Savannah rounded on her sister who clutched her elbow in a parental fashion. She tried shaking it off. Georgia reinforced the grip until her sister shot her a glare. Georgia ruined the pivotal moment for her. She intended on reading Jenny Lee the riot act for "helping" Ennis right into Happyland then she planned to enumerate the repercussions of

trying it again.   Now she looked like a petulant child about to be
disciplined by her mother.

Georgia crooked her finger at Dane, whispered in his ear.   When
he nodded, she recited the dessert menu as if everything was fine and she
hadn't saved Jenny Lee from being pounded to a pulp, "We made two
each of apple, cherry, peach and chocolate.   Let's bring Ennis something
sweet.   Apple with ice cream?"

Savannah responded with a terse nod but conferred with Grumpy
to be sure.

A cheerless smile verged on a sneer.   He slurred the tiniest bit,
"Annd don't forget to–"

"Nuke the pie in the microwave first," Savannah finished.   No,
no more booze for him that night.   The earlier indulgences already
affected his behavior in a negative way.   She knew by experience he only
got nastier the more he drank.

She motioned Lily and Anna to the kitchen while she told
Georgia, "You can let go now."

She did.   "I asked Dane to police Jenny.   That should hopefully
prevent bloodshed."

Savannah's shoulders sagged, "Thank you.   Anytime he drinks the
hard stuff he loses his mind.   Georgia," she dropped to a whisper, "he
went for my gun."

"I saw it," her sister flinched.   Years ago Georgia saw firsthand
how whiskey changed Ennis.   It was never pretty.   It robbed him of
inhibitions, loosened his tongue and provoked ridiculous, malicious
behavior.   Of course Savannah had the right to judge.   Back in the bad

old days she wore a worse title among her mother's family. Alcoholic. Accurate or not, it still took tremendous self-control not to indulge when life put its foot on her neck. A little like now, she thought, but she'd drown her troubles in Georgia's luscious peach pie, not liquid courage. Gina's arrival not only complicated issues but sapped Savannah. That, compounded with Jenny Lee's demeanor, would make life as joyous as a root canal.

A tugging on her sweater broke up hers and Georgia's one-on-one. Lily and Anna stared up at their mother. "Can we have chocolate pie and ice cream?" Lily asked.

Leave it to those sweet little faces to diffuse a temper. "You sure can, baby."

She and Georgia joined Bobbi in the kitchen. The women sidestepped youngsters from three to thirteen that blocked counters, drawers and the microwave, all waiting anxiously for their desserts. The women looked frazzled by the time the under-twenty crowd left the room.

The peace and quiet lasted a brief minute (too brief in Savannah's opinion) when the phone rang. Bobbi answered the call, "Georgia, for you. It's Seth."

Savannah took the opportunity to slice herself a modest piece of peach pie then grabbed a bowl for Ennis's apple and side of ice cream.

Judging by Georgia's end of the conversation their brother called to update everyone on their mail and catch up on news.

The kitchen's peaceful atmosphere concerned Savannah. Where was Jenny Lee? Tending bar for Ennis and ignoring the apple pie her fiancé requested? No, she reminded herself, Dane's watching her so stop worrying.

Georgia tapped her on the shoulder, "Your turn," then passed her the phone. Seth relayed the important mail they received then said their abode remained squared away. Before ending the conversation, they discussed weather. He bragged about Atlanta's cool, dry weather (he mastered the art of aggravation years ago) and since he despised complaining she retaliated by sulking about Texas snow.

The women took turns slicing pies, nuking them then scooping ice cream for the men and themselves. Bobbi threw a scoop of strawberry ice cream on Cal's cherry pie. Savannah just stared.

"I know," Bobbi conceded. "He's weird. But try serving him cherry without strawberry ice cream and he'll go on a hunger strike until it's fixed."

"Hey, y'all," a perky Jenny Lee greeted. "Any pie left?"

Bobbi waved her over. Jenny passed by, beaming from ear to ear – at Savannah.

That smile set her on edge but Jenny Lee's wink set off alarms. Prudent folks in Ms. Crawford's crosshairs needed to buckle in for a bumpy ride when she smiled *and* winked at them. Savannah knew she faced a long evening fighting Jenny away from the hooch and a longer night with Ennis's bellyaching. Her patience already ran thin with both.

Savannah scooped a piece of apple pie into the bowl and popped it in the microwave. She asked Georgia who patiently waited her turn at the nuke box, "How many pies did you get delivered before the snow got too deep?"

"Only had time for two. Eldon and Jackie were very gracious and said they'd bring over some milk and eggs in the morning if the weather allowed."

The timer beeped. Savannah removed the pie and stepped in line behind Bobbi for ice cream, "I don't think it'll allow."

Bobbi offered her two cents, "True but Eldon might surprise you. He's one determined man."

"Savannah," a woman softly summoned from the doorway. Gina. She scanned the kitchen's occupants as if expecting them to hold whips and broadswords, not saucers and spoons. Never one to disappoint, Jenny Lee huffed an about-face into the living room. She marched past Savannah muttering the same title she'd bestowed on Gina. *Traitor.*

Gina wore a pair of Mama's slippers, a long flannel nightgown and fluffy sky blue robe. Gathering the robe's collar together, she padded to Savannah but kept a keen eye (and nervous smile) toward Bobbi and Georgia. Her voice remained a hushed whisper, "I'm guessing they told you what happened between me and Ennis."

Savannah nodded, cutting a glance at Georgia who appeared equally uneasy. Yes, Ennis informed his missus of the incident many years ago. That wasn't her problem. What bothered her was she felt duped by a stranger who brought Ennis to his knees professionally as wholly as Jeffrey Holland physically brought her to hers.

Bobbi overheard Gina's comment and before Savannah knew it she'd stabbed the spoon back into the ice cream carton, "Next." The normally dauntless redhead gathered hers and Cal's desserts and fled the room.

Savannah scooped a dollop onto Ennis's pie then one on hers. This was a conversation she did not want to have so to take the pressure off, she introduced Gina and Georgia. They exchanged a courteous hello. Say something else, she silently implored her older sister. *Please, help me out here...*

But Georgia excused herself to the other side of the room, avoiding the two like they had leprosy.

With Georgia out of earshot Gina relaxed somewhat, "At the time I really thought I saw a gun."

"Okay," was all she said. Gina failed to mention (Savannah noticed the woman had a bad habit of that) delaying the ambulance call for Kelly Roberts. Savannah assumed she reserved that tidbit to squirrel away a shred of dignity.

"I never wanted to hurt Ennis or his career. I also didn't intend to mislead you at the market. I apologize for not explaining who I was."

Spending the night in a lion's den probably inspired the apology. Since the family sharpened their claws, Savannah saw no reason to join the mauling. They'd be together a while so she'd play nice. "No apology necessary. As for the past, I like to keep things there if I can. Let's just concentrate on riding out this storm. In the meantime," she motioned to the pies lining the counter, "grab a snack. There are brownies and plenty of pies to choose from. Apple, cherry, peach and chocolate."

For the first time since arriving, Gina truly smiled, "Thank you. I think I will." She went straight to the peach pie, "How'd Ennis hurt himself?"

"Slipped on some ice." That reminded her to get another ibuprofen for him.

"That's awful. You're both having a bad day, especially since I showed up. Him for obvious reasons and now you have to battle his temper and Jenny Lee." She rolled her eyes, "She'll always carry that torch for him."

"Yes. A torch for him and a baseball bat for me."

The two shared a covert chuckle. It was nice to commiserate with another victim of the brat's hatred.

Georgia turned, amused yet surprised at the soft laughter.

Gina nudged Savannah, "You're lucky. She'd flatten me with a Mack truck – if she could drive a stick."

The two shared another subdued giggle then the women gathered their desserts and returned to the living room.

Savannah held two bowls and Georgia somehow successfully and gracefully carried three – Dane's in one hand, hers balanced behind it on her wrist and Mama's in her other hand. The show-off.

The sisters paused halfway in the room. Ennis was fast asleep, his head tilted back and mouth wide open. The noises rattling from his throat mimicked a stubborn lawnmower engine struggling to start. Earlier Savannah left an aching, surly husband behind. Now nothing roused him, not a basketball game, conversation, or spoons scraping bowls. She was glad he finally got rest.

Mama stacked Gina's blankets and pillow beside the couch then eased into her rocker. She accepted the bowl of apple pie and ice cream from Georgia with a soft thanks. The genial, soft-spoken lady they knew and loved replaced the hellfire and brimstone version of Mama Rutherford.

Ennis drew a deep breath. The stubborn lawnmower engine rattled to life then transformed to the ripping chainsaw Savannah heard every night in bed. All five kids looked at Ennis then each other, probably wondering how the hell a person could generate such a raucous noise. Monty's remedy? Raise the TV's volume.

Dane and Cal rounded the corner. Both froze in dismay to stare at their brother.

"Sandman came early," Georgia joked then eased down on the couch, careful not to disturb Ennis. She nudged Dane when he reached across to poke his brother.

"We can't even hear the TV," he griped. He looked at Savannah in disbelief, "How do you sleep with that racket?"

To be honest, "Sometimes I don't."

Ennis snuffled, snorted then awoke with a start. Savannah sympathized, "Do you want apple pie or an early bedtime?"

Ennis accepted the pie. She took her place beside him, noticing he stared through, not at, the pie.

Jake piped up, "Eat the pie, Ennis. Keep your mouth busy with anything 'cept making that God-awful noise."

Dane agreed, "You belong on a track with an engineer and a caboose."

"You snore tooo," Ennis slurred, "so shut uup."

Well, someone stayed busy while she was gone, Savannah thought. His thick, elongated syllables gave taffy a run for its money.

He smelled like a brewery and someone was about to pay.

"I don't snore," Dane said.

"I sslept in the top bunk for years lisstening to you knock shingles off the house."

Oh yeah. He was drunk to the nines. Texans spoke slowly anyway but someone dialed down his speech to the extra slow setting. When she left he sounded semi-coherent. Now he was so stewed he'd bleed bourbon, not blood. "*What happened to you?*" she accused. More to the point, *who happened to you?* And why the hell hadn't Dane stopped Jenny Lee?

Ennis's eyes tightened, "Don't look at me that way." Then the glassy-eyed stare fixated on Gina who'd settled in an out of the way chair near the corner, "If I'm expected to be Christian to her, I need more booze. Jenny's a fanntastic bartennner."

Savannah assumed he meant to say *bartender,* and she agreed with one thing. Jenny was a generous "bartennner" if nothing else. She imagined Ennis slamming back shots of Wild Turkey while Jenny kept the refills coming. His condition certainly explained why Jenny Lee gleefully pranced into the kitchen and Savannah fought the urge to break her in half for it too. Ms. Crawford seemed pleased with herself but did she care that he'd wobble to bed on one good leg and wake up with a blinding hangover? No.

Georgia climbed all over Dane, "You said you'd watch Jenny."

Dane shrank back, "Nature called. I can't be in two places at once. I'm sorry."

Ennis's bowl tilted at a dangerous angle so Savannah placed it on the end table beside him. She clenched her teeth, trapping a scathing (and R-rated) berating behind them when he wagged the glass at Jenny requesting a top-up.

Again Jenny Lee jumped to her feet, happy to oblige. Savannah pointed to the couch, "Sit down. You've done enough."

"Jenny," Mama called without glancing up from her bowl, "it's not your concern."

"Well, *she* doesn't care if he's hurting," Ms. Crawford assumed.

"Said the woman who fubarred him," Savannah mumbled. *He can't even feel his tongue, much less pain.* Her temper strained at the leash anyway but Jenny, chin thrust in a defiant gesture, strutted toward the liquor cabinet.

Savannah shoved her bowl at Georgia who fumbled to take it before accidentally dumping her own dessert in her lap. Bolting upright, Savannah's long strides overtook Jenny's swaggering gait. Before Ennis's "bartennner" realized it, Savannah snatched the bourbon from the counter and placed it inside the cabinet. "Mama? The key."

"Third shelf behind you, honey," she said. Calm and casual as if Savannah asked which drawer to find a spoon. "Keep the key with you."

"Yes, ma'am. I will." In seconds the liquor cabinet stood locked tight, inaccessible to everyone except herself.

Jenny's brow plummeted, her hands curled into fists. The two visually squared off. Jenny wanted to knock Savannah sideways and Savannah dared her to try.

Her bravado struck Savannah as comical but laughing was the last thing on her mind. "You don't want to tangle with me, Jenny. Not tonight."

"Jenny Lee," Mama said, "either sit down or go fetch yours and Jake's desserts." The authoritarian in Mama left no room for argument. Heaving an angry sigh, Jenny did as she was told and sat down – much to Jake's disgust.

"Well, Lord," he huffed. "Guess it's up to me to get *my* pie."

Dane couldn't help but chuckle, "Jenny has the attention span of a hyperactive poodle. You're lucky she remembered to–"

"Son," Mama massaged her temple, "shut up."

Meanwhile, Ennis wormed on the couch, "Damn it, Savannah, don't make me come after that key. You'll regret it."

Yeah, right. Number one, he wasn't inclined to violence and number two, he'd be lucky to take one step before landing on his nose.

The family – and Gina – seemed glued to the drama unfolding in their midst. Lily and Anna watched but tiffs weren't new at their house. They'd seen their parents quarrel over stupid things before.

For Savannah, the trip felt doomed from the start. Too many bizarre things happened. Jake and Jenny Lee announcing their engagement. A mountainous snowfall trapping them inside the house and crippling every means of travel. And a drunk Ennis Rutherford threatening his pregnant wife when she refused to plunge him into the happy-water and let him drink his way out. He felt picked on since the engagement announcement. The knee injury plus Gina's arrival just added more fuel to his pity party. But his wife's apparent "duplicity" polished off any remaining civility.

"Gonna wrestle the key from me, are you?" she asked her hubby.

Cal's boys giggled.

If need be, Ennis answered.

Savannah patted her pocket, "Gotta catch me first, dear, and that idea doesn't seem plausible at the moment."

"Oh, shut up, Your Highness," he griped. "I wanted a sip, that's it."

Jaws dropped. Cal's boys looked at each other then at Savannah, waiting for her reaction.

"My brothers are morons," Cal declared with disgust.

As for Savannah, the song said it all. Thank God for Kids. They believed in Santa, lit the room with the sunshine in their smiles, they had a million questions beginning in *where* and *why* – and on that evening with snow piled to the heavens, two little angels prevented their mother from tying their drunk daddy in a knot.

But the two little angels didn't prevent Granna from setting her son straight. She put her bowl aside, "Ennis, do you remember how I deal with an unruly child? Unless you apologize, I'll sic the Board of Education on you."

Now stifled giggles rose from Lily and Anna. Monty, Tyler and Zach shared a chuckle. Yes, imagining that sweet older lady paddling her thirty-six-year-old son prompted a spark of hilarity but her expression quashed any doubt that she'd damn well do it and make her efforts memorable.

The Board of Education held legendary status in the Rutherford household. For years the four brothers debated over who received the worst paddling from their daddy's homemade disciplinary implement.

The cedar plank measured an impressive fifteen inches in length, its breadth wide enough to serve its purpose but still remain aerodynamic. Mr. Rutherford painted one side forest green and labeled it "Mild". The other side he painted fire engine red with "Wild" written on it. When wielded by their daddy, Ennis said, it could convert a nonbeliever to beg God's forgiveness for past *and* future sins. Savannah expected their mother could ring a person's bell with it too.

Mama's reference to the Board sobered Ennis slightly. Alcohol reduced him to a testy, petulant boy and Savannah realized his mother stood the best chance of penetrating the haze of booze. "What'll it be?" Mama was halfway to her feet, "An apology or a meeting with the Board?"

"I'm sorry," he said, but didn't really mean it. By morning, the Ennis Savannah knew and loved would return and offer a genuine apology. For now, the family would bear the brunt of Bratty Ennis and wait it out.

Mama took up her knitting, shaking her head and asking the Lord for help.

Ennis glared at Gina, "But I've got good reason for being grumpy."

Mama stopped in the middle of a knit one or purl two. She and Savannah exchanged a look that pretty much deemed Ennis a card-carrying idiot. "Son," she said, "it'll be a long night for you but don't make it any longer for the rest of us. Go on to bed."

Bed? What a laugh. Neither he nor Savannah would see much of one once the Kickin' Chicken kicked back in full force. Ennis would live to regret every drop he consumed.  She remembered the rollercoaster ride trying to pilot the bed while keeping her cookies down.  It never worked for her and it certainly wouldn't for a novice bourbon drinker like Ennis.

## 11

Dane and Jake lugged Ennis up the stairs to bed. Well, Dane lugged and Jake supervised from the bottom stair. Dane used the human crutch method until Ennis lost his backbone somewhere along the way, leaving his older brother to bear the brunt of his weight while physically hauling him up the narrow staircase. All Savannah could do was watch his struggle from the landing.

Dane channeled his strength into pulling Ennis up another step, "You're feeding him too well, Peach. He's heavier than ol' Gert when she's full up with milk."

"Keep moving," Jake directed from below. "You're nearly there."

Dane scowled. "You should be toting him to bed. It was your fiancée who sloshed him up."

"You're the one who answered nature's call that let her get him sloshed. Georgia's still sore at you for that."

It bothered Savannah to leave the heavy lifting (so to speak) to her brother-in-law but when she stepped down to help, Dane shooed her back. So she offered what she could. Her thanks. Then she suggested –

in her nicest way – that Jake could pitch in and give Dane a breather. He begrudgingly did so and hauled her semi-conscious hubby to their bedroom. Ennis grunted when he flopped flat on the mattress.

"I hope you packed a parachute for this flight," Savannah told her pickled spouse.

Dane stretched his neck and back, "And I hope Jenny Lee didn't pack it for him."

The name inflamed her anew. She felt positively thunderous but abstained from speaking her mind since Jake stood nearby. Jenny's behavior appalled him enough he apologized on her behalf but truth was nothing could help Ennis now, least of all words. She offered a benign, "What's done is done."

Jake propped Ennis's legs onto the bed, "He'll feel worse once he's reminded he told you to shut up."

For a guy who chose to marry a weirdo, Jake delivered some real dandies on occasion. She did not argue his point.

The clock read ten. Savannah planned on crawling in and maybe getting two or three hours of sleep before all hell broke loose. Once getting Ennis horizontal (which he mostly accomplished himself), Jake saddled her and Dane with the strenuous chore of wrestling drunken "ol' Gert" around to undress him – while avoiding pulling a muscle or losing their religion.

The challenging task soon grew increasingly arduous when her limp-as-a-noodle husband couldn't sit up or hold his head steady. Despite his inebriated condition, his mouth functioned fine. He complained the whole time, accusing them of manhandling him and making him nauseous.  She and Dane looked downright ridiculous, she imagined, rolling a grown man hither and yon to remove his shirt then lifting his hips to slide his jeans off.  The next comedy of errors began when they dressed him in PJ's.  Ennis was solid brawn and formidable anyway but the dead weight of his muscular arms and heavy legs made the task excessively laborious.

The two stood back to appraise their work.  Ennis passed out after they finished.  Savannah and Dane looked close to joining him.  She sighed onto the bed, thanking Dane for his help.  Hands on hips, he stared hopelessly at his brother, "Anytime.  Listen, you'll have your hands full tonight so if you need help with him, I'm right next door."

She thanked him again and let him join Georgia.  Because of the bedroom's location, Ennis wouldn't have time to run to the bathroom once the ugliness set in.  Savannah employed a trick from her drinking days to aid in his plight.  She placed a liner in the wastebasket and set it beside the bed.

She shook her head at her "ol' Gert", lamenting what lay ahead of him.  All because Jenny Lee Crawford wanted to please him.

At midnight, the backlash hit.  He tossed back the covers so violently the blanket slapped her in the face.  She switched on the bedside lamp and bailed out to retrieve the trash can for him.  He scrambled to climb out of bed only to singe the quiet nighttime with cuss words so hot they would scorch the most seasoned sailor.  Somewhere in his string of obscenities she heard the words "my damn knee".

He hugged the trash can to him and cut loose.  Each heave began down deep, dredging his depths until unleashing bone-jarring results that made him wilt over the blue bin. She winced in sympathy. The Wild Turkey exacted revenge and forced Ennis to pay for his sins with interest.

Savannah hurried to the bathroom for cold, wet washcloths. For an instant she seriously entertained dragging that do-gooder Jenny Lee out of her nice, cozy bed to witness his hellacious misery. His guttural groans changed her mind. Ennis needed her worse. In the morning Jenny Lee could see the results of being a great "bartennner".

Savannah mopped his face and neck with the washcloths until he shivered and held her off, his body sagging. Both hands death-gripped the wastebasket.

Another round shuddered through him. She held the cloth to his throat hoping to curb yet another surge of sickness.

"God, I'm stiff and sore everywhere. And I'm–" he shoved her hand away to battle a heave. He barely won, "I'm sorry for ignoring you earlier. I–" His stomach lurched but nothing came up. Ennis braced a hand on the nightstand for stability, "I should have listened."

Nothing humbled a person like a raging hangover. No need for an apology, she assured.

He pressed the cloth to his forehead, "My head is gonna split open and this hurling's killin' me. What the hell was I thinkin'?"

"You wanted relief and Jenny offered it."

"I am *so, so* sorry for what I said to you. You were trying to help–" another wave of sickness cut his statement short.

He dove for the wastebasket again. Savannah flinched when his forehead banged the rim. She wanted to say something positive. Any shred of hope that his nightmare might run its course soon. Truth was whatever she said would be a lie and he'd know it since this counted as the third binge since their marriage – but she had to admit, he really made this hangover count.

A knock tapped at the door. Georgia cracked the door open far enough to see the two sitting together on the side of the bed. Dane peered over her shoulder. "Need help?" Georgia asked. Her sister's expression conveyed a compassion Savannah recalled from her own drunken benders – until they became a habit, that was.

Savannah shook her head, "Unless you can bring me that space cadet's head on a platter, no, but thanks for checking."

Before closing the door they reminded, "Call if you need us."

The Kickin' Chicken kicked back until three o'clock when he collapsed on the bed miserable and exhausted, his arm slung over his eyes and a cold cloth draped across this throat and a second across his forehead. Savannah wanted to kill Jenny Lee.

O   O   O

The alarm blared her awake at seven that morning. A sluggish slap shut it off. She stretched the stiffness from her back, pushed herself upright and rubbed the blurriness from her eyes. The four hours raced by. Somewhere between The Chicken's Last Stand of the night and the alarm, she recalled movement in the hallway. Quiet voices, children posing questions and Georgia's gentle assurances. What time had that been? Savannah never bothered looking at the clock. Sweet, precious slumber beckoned her back because seven o'clock would arrive mighty early. And it had.

Savannah gathered the train case and change of clothes. Trudging to the bathroom she marveled at the quiet downstairs. No activity in the kitchen (or luscious bacon aroma wafting upstairs) and no conversation from the men usually parked in the living room. Strange – but not as strange as her hair's condition upon glancing in the mirror. It looked like it was styled by a stun gun. One of the joys of staying up late. She spruced up, changed into her jeans and an argyle sweater then returned to the trickiest task of all. Waking Ennis.

Savannah stood at the foot of the bed debating over waking him or leaving him to sleep. Ennis seemed to rest better after the three o'clock siege and regaining consciousness after a drunken rampage was a drinker's version of hell. If one managed to push themselves upright and stand steady enough, they counted themselves lucky to kneel at the throne just before they puked up their kidneys. They did this while praying their brains didn't shoot out their ears in the process. The unfortunate victim realized the impossibility of it (or by that time, *hoped* it was impossible) – but only because their brain felt three times the size of their head and it risked exploding before actually being ejected.

Ennis's chest rose and fell in long, deep breaths, his open mouth trying but not quite succeeding in snoring. Nasal squeaks eked past his throat with each inhalation. At least he'd rested for a few hours. She considered that a success.

She put a hand to his arm, kissed his cheek. His skin felt cool thanks to the washcloths he positioned in strategic places. Sprigs of hair splayed out in front like wild weeds. He looked worse for wear but that paled in comparison to what awaited him.

She kissed him again. This time the eyes moved beneath the eyelids. His mouth closed and opened once then twice. His tongue shifted inside until sticking to the roof of his mouth. He didn't seem all that interested in prying it loose either.

Jenny Lee would call her cruel for waking him. Savannah knew from past experience to get up and moving or the hangover lasted longer – or seemed to. "Mornin'," she said. She wasn't stupid enough to add the "good" to "morning", and made sure to use the gentlest voice or else he might accuse her of shouting at him.

Ennis's bleary gaze struggled to focus. He immediately squinted against the light, muttering a disappointed, "I'm not dead?"

"No, honey, you're not dead."

"Might as well be. Can't I sleep–" he flailed and fought the covers, throwing them back until they spilled to the floor. He kicked his feet off the bed and instantly groaned about his knee.

She handed him the wastebasket and leaned away in case his aim was off. Ennis may have resembled a crazed muppet from Sesame Street with his wild hair but the man's reflexes were second to none. He clutched the wastebasket close to up-chuck in it. The muscles in his neck and back bunched tight so she gave them a light massage. Ennis thanked her "for taking pity on a brainless idiot's soul" then slung his arms across the wastebasket's rim. He left his head hanging halfway inside and when he spoke he sounded stuck in a small cave, "I'll never touch bourbon again. If this hangover doesn't kill me, shoot me and put me out of my misery."

Don't be silly, she said.  "If I can survive the morning after getting blitzed, you can too."

"No offense but you had more practice at it."

Yes, she certainly did.  "No offense taken."

It took several minutes to help him dress considering he alternated between clothing himself and bowing over the bin.

Before venturing downstairs, Savannah equipped her snubnose and pulled the sweater over it.

Ennis stared at her like she'd lost her mind, "Really?  Fifty feet of snow, traffic's at a standstill, and you still insist on that?"

Well, at least he felt decent enough to carp at her.  "Boy Scouts aren't the only ones who believe in being prepared."

He rubbed his face, "Girls Scouts in Georgia must have one hell of an oath."

A smile tugged at her lips.  His attempt at wit buoyed hope for the rest of the day.  He'd feel like a dung heap for most of it but he clung to his sense of humor.  So far.

As for Savannah, she'd listen to her husband accuse her of being a few clowns short of a circus.  All her clowns were present and accounted for, thank you very much, so the gun stayed on her hip.  Forewarned was forearmed.  The four escapees remained at large as of bedtime the night before.  Authorities shut down I-40 at the state lines, narrowing the escapees' avenues of travel.  Maybe they diverted back southwest toward El Paso or south to Laredo.  The family bet on that scenario rather than Savannah's "cockeyed" idea of them traveling I-40 through Amarillo.  Last night's updated snow totals listed Amarillo with twelve inches and

Mother Nature dumping sixteen on Vega. This from a storm predicted to last an additional twenty-four hours. Why travel north into a blizzard, the family maintained, when Mexico boasted clear skies and sunshine?

She and Ennis paused at the stairway's landing. Hungover or not, Ennis noticed the same thing she had earlier. For a house full of people, it never stayed quiet except during the night. "What's going on?" he mumbled.

She whispered, "It was like this when I got up." That old foreboding returned. Nothing she could pinpoint right away but no breakfast, no voices or noises and the kids climbing out of bed before seven? Two and two added up to five.

Ennis led the way downstairs, white-knuckling his daddy's cane in one hand while the other kept a death grip on the railing. The knee throbbed pretty hard judging by his careful, measured steps.

The living room came into view as they descended the stairs. The bar sat close to the corner and Mama's rocker sat beside it. Seeing her in that rocker at such an early hour set off Savannah's inner alarm that something truly was wrong. How wrong, she wasn't sure but Mama Rutherford *never* sat down before breakfast – and that morning she sat uncomfortably stiff and erect, not at all like her usual relaxed posture.

Savannah leaned a tad over the railing for a better view of her mother-in-law. Mama's wrists were tied.

Ennis saw it too. "Go back quick," he whispered.

Savannah wheeled toward the upstairs landing. It was too late.

## 12

He spanned most of the upstairs landing. From her point of view he looked like a giant. His shoulders and arms bulged with muscle beneath the red flannel shirt. Jeans stretched over powerful thighs and buttoned at a lean waist. Thick-soled work boots stood shoulder-width apart blocking Savannah's escape.

Luis Muñoz smiled down at her. He aimed a gun straight at the cornered husband and wife. She dared not press a hand to her queasy stomach. He might misconstrue the movement and pull the trigger. Two things fueled her nausea. Muñoz's presence but also the fact he'd probably been upstairs during hers and Ennis's discussion regarding her .38. Had they mentioned the weapon specifically? She couldn't remember but didn't think so. No, they hadn't, she decided. So the secret secured at her hip remained just that. A secret – for now at least.

Muñoz looked considerably more imposing than his mugshot. The powerhouse body refined in a prison yard, the black stubble sprouting from his jaw that clenched when her gaze lingered too long – and those ice blue eyes narrowing at her as if she flipped him off.

"Don't get ideas, Señora," he warned in a thick Hispanic accent. "Just do as you're told." He flicked his wrist, using the gun to convey his message. Downstairs now.

She turned back to see Manuel Sanchez at the bottom stair, same attire as his partner, only he wielded an assault rifle instead of a .45.

Muñoz's feet pounded down the stairs behind her. She stiffened when he pressed the gun barrel to the back of her head. "You two go join the others. I expect good manners from you both." He put a firm hand to her shoulder, "Move."

Slumped on a barstool beside Mama, Scott Hadley yawned. The oak cabinet Savannah locked the night before had been pried open, leaving the door hanging askew. Hadley helped himself to the Wild Turkey by filling a shot glass to the rim. Beside the bottle lay a .45, a collection of cell phones, purses and billfolds.

Alan Brozek stood guard over the group. He may have dressed like his compadres and been equipped with his own firepower but unlike Muñoz, he let the .45 hang by his side.

The four assembled the family into two groups. Male and female. The men took the couch in front of the picture window with Monty, Tyler and Zach remaining in the floor. The women were assigned the couch facing the fireplace and TV. Georgia held Lily and Anna sat with Bobbi. Everyone's hands including the children's were tied. Both girls cried and reached for their parents. Before the noise literally triggered a disaster for them, Ennis and Savannah tried to assure them everything would be okay. Both despised lying to their kids.

Ennis hobbled to the men's assigned couch where he settled

between Cal and Dane.

Muñoz guided Savannah to Georgia and Gina who'd scooted apart to make room.

Sanchez and Muñoz huddled in a powwow. Hadley leaned down to inspect the bar's selections. Savannah watched Brozek. He approached his two conferring partners, leaving all four intruders' backs turned.

Savannah slipped her holster off and shoved it deep between the cushions. Gina and the family saw it but Jenny Lee, parked beside Gina, hadn't.

Muñoz pushed Brozek away, "Keep an eye on them. Anyone gives you trouble, shoot 'em."

Brozek appraised their two newest additions. Considering Ennis's condition, Brozek seemed to assess his threat as low. Then he turned to Savannah and smiled. Not a threatening one but something he probably believed pleasant. Her internet trolling gave her basic insight into the five (now four) escaped inmates. Brozek was so deceivingly charming he chatted with one victim's family before later currying their daughter off to molest her. At the trial her parents noted how at ease they felt with him as they spoke. They called him the last person they'd ever peg as a pervert. After reading that, only a fool let their guard down around any of them, particularly "Mr. Nice Guy".

Muñoz sent Sanchez for more cord then settled on Savannah. She fought the urge to recoil when he stalked closer. "I could easily take that expression personally. You don't want that." He told Brozek, "Watch her."

"Don't worry," Mr. Nice Guy said. He seemed confident that, "The others, especially her kids, will keep her in line."

She hoped he hadn't banked his life on it. "How'd they get in?" she asked her sister.

"They knocked on the door a little after six-thirty." Georgia kept a keen eye to the foursome while whispering, "Mama opened the door thinking it might be stranded travelers. They stormed inside and made us bring the kids down. They waylaid Jenny earlier when she came downstairs then you and Ennis just now."

Sanchez returned with two lengths of cord. He bound Savannah's wrists together then headed to Ennis. Muñoz grabbed her left hand. He wanted her ring.

She jerked her hand back and locked the diamond wedding ring in her fist. The back of his hand landed across her cheek, sending her sideways against Gina. Nerves screamed to life. Tears blurred her vision. In that time, Muñoz pried her fingers open and yanked the cherished ring off. He gave it a brief appraisal before pocketing it.

She held a cool palm to the hot, stinging flesh to soothe it while scowling at Muñoz for stealing the symbol of her husband's love. It only represented fast money to him but it meant the world to her.

"Where's your wallet and phone?" Sanchez asked Ennis. He'd already stripped Ennis of his gold wedding band and tossed it to Muñoz who dropped it in his pocket with an apathy reserved for loose change.

Ennis refused to speak. He swallowed once, twice then three times in forewarning of an impending upheaval. He'd puked himself dry overnight but the foursome didn't know that. Sanchez stepped back just in case.

Muñoz scoffed at his skittish companion then turned to brace Savannah, "Where's your purse and phone?"

While Ennis's stomach battled the urge to barf, hers dropped into free fall. The ebbing pain in her face and ear took a backseat to his question – or more to the point, the consequences of answering it. Her clutch contained her cell phone, and like Ennis's billfold, money and a police ID. She sensed the timer on their two lives ticking down and neither of them stood a chance of stopping it.

Muñoz shoved the .45 at her. Sanchez warded off Ennis's attempt to stand. It didn't prevent Ennis from chewing Muñoz out and telling him to leave his wife alone. Savannah and Ennis exchanged a glance. He nodded. "Upstairs," she said, resigned.

Georgia's wide-eyed stare accused her of cutting ties with sanity. I know, I know, Savannah wanted to say. *We know our IDs and badges are in the billfold and purse. We know we risk getting killed because we're cops but what choice do we have?*

Displeased with the simple yet truthful answer, Muñoz bent toward her. Base fear pressed her back into the cushions, away from his aggression – and that sharp, ghostly stare.

"Do not screw with me." He chose to overlook the *or else*. "Where *upstairs* are the purse, wallet and cell phones?"

"Upstairs, turn right, the bedroom at the end of the hall. The purse and billfold are on the dresser."

"And the phones?"

"On the nightstands."

The corners of his mouth lifted in a taunting grin, "See? It's not so hard to cooperate. Brozek, go get 'em."

Alan Brozek stowed the .45 in his waistband, marched up the stairs with sluggish, heavy footfalls. A pause. "Which way again?" he called from above.

Muñoz rolled his eyes, "Right, you idiot. It's the last bedroom. Can you find it or will you get lost?"

There was no answer. The ceiling creaked as he lumbered around upstairs. Brozek finally returned holding Savannah's clutch in one hand and Ennis's billfold and both cell phones in the other. He looked pretty unhappy over being ridiculed.

"Everything there?" Muñoz asked.

Lips pursed tight, Brozek nodded. The blue-eyed Hispanic slid the gun in his waistband, pocketed Ennis's billfold then took the purse. He underhanded the phones to Hadley who placed them in the pile of other personal effects.

Muñoz eyed Savannah as he unsnapped the purse's catch. Another look passed between her and Ennis. He'd gone pale and swallowed hard, still curbing a heave. Both realized what came next.

Plunging his hand inside, Muñoz's brow raised. "You got lots of money in here, don't you? That's a fat wallet." He withdrew his hand, tucked the purse under his arm to investigate his find.

Savannah swore her heart stopped. She recognized the item he held. Georgia recognized it. Ennis did too. It represented her death sentence. The instant Muñoz opened it he'd realize it wasn't a "fat wallet". It was her Atlanta Police ID and badge. Muñoz briefly studied then opened it. Acid crept up her throat, forcing her to swallow it back. *This is it. Ennis, Daniel and I will die right here in front of our family.*

Muñoz's jaw clenched and released. His eyes narrowed and when their vision met, the intrinsic urge to flee flooded her.

"Detective Sergeant Savannah Prince, Atlanta Police." He flipped the ID around so each person in the room got a good look at the picture and badge.

Fifteen bullets, was her mind's morbid reminder. They pumped at least fifteen shots into the last cop they encountered.

Hadley, tossing back another shot of whiskey, slammed the glass down. The report jolted Savannah from the dark thoughts. A clear-cut, unanimous sentiment crossed his cohorts' faces. Kill the bitch. Muñoz stepped closer, "You know what I've done for the last ten years?"

According to his features, that question really didn't require an answer but even as he closed in, she squared her shoulders and returned his bold gaze. If she was dying today she would die with dignity because according to his face and posture, changing his mind was impossible.

He tossed the ID in her lap, "I've dreamed of getting my hands on a cop." He flung her purse across the room. As it frisbeed through the air, a handful of items including her car and house keys jangled out and sailed between Hadley's shoulder and Mama's head then slammed into the bookcase behind them.

Brozek collected and returned the scattered things to the purse. Everything except the keys. He studied the key ring a moment. A decorative metal frame bordered the little photo of Lily and Anna embracing each other. The fact Brozek laid eyes on the picture – and touched it – made Savannah squirm, as if somehow he'd violated them by doing so.    Brozek glanced back at her then the girls in Georgia and Bobbi's laps.  He placed the keys in the purse and added it to the other belongings on the bar.

Muñoz retrieved Ennis's billfold.  Savannah expected the sight of another badge to drive Muñoz over the edge and start spraying bullets.  It didn't.  His fingers gripped the billfold so hard it shook in his grasp. "Imagine that. We got ourselves *two* cops."  This time he underhanded the billfold to Hadley.

The bulk of his rage seemed to abate.  Instead he appeared to mull something over.  Sanchez barged past him, the assault rifle aimed straight at Savannah, "Leave 'em to me."

Muñoz pushed the barrel toward the floor, "I'm not ready to kill 'em yet."

Savannah breathed a quiet sigh of relief but only for a second.

Muñoz's fingers fisted in her sweater, pulled her to her feet. "Hands up, Sergeant Prince."

She obeyed.  His hands started from her shoulders and worked down.  She winced at the rough treatment of her breasts and the unnecessary forceful search at her waist.  Only when he reached her calves and ankles did she chance a breath.  The breath died in her throat when he centered on her belly.  He pressed a hand to the baby bump, smiling, "Pregnant.  How pregnant are you, Sergeant?"

"Six months."  She cursed at her quivering voice.  The wicked slant of his mouth taunted her that one decent punch would kill her baby – that's all it would take – and that smile conveyed just how much he'd enjoy doing it.

"Wanna keep that kid alive a little longer?"

"Yes." She slowly lowered her hands. Nothing short of a brick wall could protect Daniel if Muñoz hauled off and punched her but she had to try.

"Then tell me where your gun is. Yours and your husband's. If you refuse," his hand balled into a fist, "I'll get it outta you somehow, even if that baby has to die."

Sanchez leveled the same basic threat to Ennis who sounded out-and-out miserable, "We're on vacation. We never take our weapons on vacation."

Panic rioted inside her. Where the hell had he dredged that lie from? Cops *always* brought their guns with them. It was, she assumed, common knowledge among humankind. She focused on the battering ram on the end of Muñoz's arm, cocked and ready to launch. Then forced herself to make Ennis's lie sound believable, "He's right. Neither of us do."

By his tone, she failed. "You sure about that?" he asked. "Are you real sure?"

*Lily saw me. She saw me hide the gun between the couch cushions. She might point right to it to back Muñoz off.*

Ice water coursed through her heart. *What do I do?* Surrendering the gun might buy more time if not for her and Ennis, perhaps for everyone else. But they needed the insurance that gun provided. That small glimmer of hope. "We left them home. We left our guns at home." *Forgive me, little one,* she pleaded to her baby, *if I've made the wrong decision.  Please forgive me…*

He jerked the .45 from his waistband.  The barrel pressed between her eyes, sending her back a step.  "You must think I'm stupid." His finger tightened on the trigger.

Anna's crying ramped up to full-fledged bawling.  Bobbi shielded her from the scene and tried to settle her down.  From the corner of her eye Savannah saw Lily bury her sobs in Georgia's bosom, unable to watch.  Savannah was grateful.

"You're not stupid," she told Muñoz.  *But you're mean as hell.* "But we left the guns at home."  She tried to maintain eye contact.  Lose it and lose your life, the cop manual said.  Well, what chapter covered staring down a killer holding a gun to your head while your children, spouse and family were present?  None.

Lily's weeping escalated into a storm of tears.  *Please don't hurt Mama*, she pleaded.

Muñoz shifted his attention – but not the gun – to Lily, "Then tell me where her gun is."

Savannah's breath caught in her throat.  *Don't say a word, baby. Daddy and I won't live another minute if you do.*  The seconds dragged on, extending each one into a lifetime of agonizing waiting.

In her usual composed style (and thick Southern brogue), Georgia tried to diffuse the situation – and get Lily off the hook, "She knows nothing about the guns.  She's a child.  Why would she?"  She drew her niece closer, whispered to her.  Savannah prayed she told the girl to keep quiet about Mama's friend "Mr. Smith" tucked between the cushions.

Brozek rounded behind Muñoz to approach Lily. There was that damn Mr. Rogers smile again. The one that stoked Savannah's homicidal urge. He crouched eye level with Lily, laid his hand on her knee. Savannah flinched.

"What's your name, honey?" Brozek inquired. "Mine's Alan."

Lily drew her legs into Georgia's lap to escape his bold touch. Georgia came to the rescue again, "Her name is Lily. She doesn't like strangers so don't touch her. She'll be okay once her mother sits down with her."

He stood up, "Lily, everything'll be alright. Once your mom does what Luis says she can sit down with you."

"Back off." Savannah told Brozek. She left off *pervert* for obvious reasons.

A smartass grin tilted Muñoz's mouth. "She won't be if we don't get those guns you claim not to have. Brozek," he summoned, "take Mommy upstairs to check their luggage. I have a feeling we might find those elusive guns there. While you're gone I'll keep her kid company. And you, Sergeant Savannah Prince, if you lied about the guns," pointed to Lily, "that kid dies."

Her shiver amused him. Oh yes. She got the message. She and Ennis gambled their daughter's life over two revolvers. Hers sat safely tucked away (she hoped) but his wasn't. At least she didn't think so.

Brozek grasped her arm. Unlike Muñoz who topped out around six feet to her five nine, she and the child molester stood eye to eye.

He kept his hold gentle and his .45 pointed toward the floor while tendering a stern caution, "I won't hesitate to shoot if you try anything stupid."

Savannah merely nodded. She was too busy trying to remember if Ennis moved his .38 from the suitcase. They locked their weapons in their own combination cases for traveling and also to discourage snoopy kids. They discussed moving them from their suitcases to a top shelf in the closet for added protection. She'd moved hers after removing the .38 but had Ennis remembered to move his before he slipped on the ice and hurt himself?

Brozek motioned her up the stairs. He fell in behind, close enough she felt the pressure of the gun at her back.

For the most part the bedroom looked neat as a pin. The bed, though, rivaled a disaster. Savannah tried straightening the bed covers after Ennis crawled out that morning but beneath Mama's now wrinkled hand-sewn quilt laid rumpled sheets. Savannah could almost see her mother shaking her head in disapproval.

"Get your suitcase," Brozek directed.

They lined their luggage beside the closet. The only piece out of place was the case containing medications. That sat on the dresser. She hefted her suitcase on the bed then nodded across the room, "My heart medication's in the case over there. I'd like to take those before we go downstairs."

Brozek focused on the locking case, not her request. The small black briefcase with a three tumbler lock resembled a handgun case only this one contained her heart medication and their over-the-counter supplements. However Brozek's expression said it all. He'd stumbled onto the Holy Grail. Proof that she'd lied about the guns.

Brozek opted to fetch that little piece of luggage himself. He laid it on the bed, pointed to it with the gun, "Open it then step aside."

The man represented the epitome of daft or desperate if he assumed she'd hand over their weapons so easily. Savannah pretty much lumped him into both categories. She discreetly rolled the tumblers one by one then lifted the lid.

Brozek pulled the case closer, visibly disappointed at what he saw, "Just pills." He rummaged the bottles, digging to the bottom, jumbling prescription bottles with supplements in search of something that was never there. A gun. Disbelief replaced the fading disappointment, "That's it? Pills?"

"I told you it was medication." *You nitwit.*

Brozek cherry picked the bottles bearing her name. He examined them long enough that she worried he'd deny her. A most effective way to keep a heart patient in line – dangle their meds like a carrot. When Brozek spoke, though, it wasn't on whether she'd be allowed to take the pills. It was a question and it proved he wasn't exactly the sharpest knife in the drawer, "Savannah Rutherford? I thought your name was Prince."

Savannah's thumb instinctively stroked the base of her ring finger, longing to feel the ring there. "Rutherford is my married name. I use my maiden name at work." *Satisfied, Sherlock?*

He studied the bottles, settling on one, "Tell me what these are for."

Savannah wanted to slap him. What difference did it make? She needed them but for whatever reason he wanted to know their function. She pointed to the first bottle, "That's a beta blocker," then to the second and third bottles, "a blood thinner and the other one is nitroglycerin. As I said, considering the situation I'd like to take those meds."

To her relief he handed over the bottles, "You can take 'em after we check the luggage."

She shoved the lot in her pockets then took a bottle of aspirin from the case, showed it to him for his approval. Brozek gave an impatient nod and checked the clock on the nightstand, "Open the suitcase before Muñoz gets upset again."

Again? Since they went upstairs Muñoz constantly kvetched about one thing or another. Telling the girls to shut up. Ordering Hadley to escort "the boy" (Zach, she assumed) outside to collect firewood. Between it all, he and Sanchez volleyed back and forth, ramping each other's tempers regarding the storm and when they could leave.

Savannah unzipped the Samsonite, flopped the top back. Brozek took the liberty of thrusting his hand inside, rooting through her nicely folded clothes like a feral hog nosing for food. He left no piece of clothing undefiled, no nook, cranny or pocket unsearched. His confidence dwindled when he found no gun.

Muñoz shouted from downstairs, "You find the guns yet?"

Brozek hollered back, "I don't think they brought 'em!"

"*You don't think?* Who asked you to *think?* Find 'em or I will."

Brozek's mood darkened. He resented being told what to do. "Get the rest of your luggage."

Another trip, this one for Ennis's suitcase. Another violent rifling. No gun. Ennis apparently moved it the day before. She was never so relieved to see the dejection on Alan Brozek's face.

He leaned in the closet then went to tiptoe. He'd need a stool and a longer reach to find the gun cases, if he could see them at all. The closet had recesses and convenient hideaways to save space. They'd planned to use a spot within a tall adult's reach but also concealed the cases with other items. Their girls, though well-behaved, still exhibited a fair amount of curiosity and as every parent knew, never underestimate a child's determination to investigate new or verboten things.

"This is all your luggage?" he asked.

She pointed to the case beside the corner chair, "Just the train case is left. It has makeup and our toiletries in it."

A quick search yielded the same dismal results. His shoulders slackened. No Holy Grail which meant no peace from Muñoz. He motioned her to the door, "Take your medication and we'll head downstairs."

He escorted her to the bathroom. Before he changed his mind (or Muñoz caught her) she fished out the blood thinner and beta blocker, popped them in her mouth and cupped her hands beneath the faucet.

"Your daughters are pretty."

She choked in mid-swallow, groped for the cobalt blue towel hanging nearby. She used it to muffle her coughing and also keep the pills down. *'Your daughters are pretty?' Mention how pretty my daughters are again and I'll tear your throat out, pervert.*

"How old are they?" He leaned against the door, the gun's trajectory lazily angled away from her.

For a moment she ran a scenario of knocking him off balance to claim the gun but realized his three buddies downstairs would mow through her family before she could save them. "Three and nearly five," she answered.

"What's the holdup!?" Muñoz thundered from the stairway.

Brozek nodded toward the medicine bottles on the counter, "Get 'em and let's go."

His hand closed around her elbow firm enough to mean business. They exited the bathroom just as Muñoz hoofed it down the hall to meet them. He was not happy, "You find those guns?"

"I went through the luggage myself," Brozek replied, "They're telling the truth."

Muñoz's blue gaze settled on her. His brow sank. The fight or flight instinct kicked into high gear. She wanted, *needed*, to run. He'd kill her, she feared, merely for *thinking* she lied to him.

"Where are the guns, bitch? Tell me or I start beating you."

To her surprise, Brozek backed her up, "They're not here. I searched every piece of luggage."

Well, nearly every piece, she thought but kept it to herself.

Muñoz advanced on him, "Are you really that stupid? Name one cop that leaves their gun at home on vacation."

Brozek struggled for an answer. His silence reinforced Muñoz's aggravation, "That's right, you can't. Now find something to keep her kids busy instead of crying their asses off."

Savannah tensed, corralling her tongue behind pursed lips. Muñoz saw it, "You got something to say?"

"No, she doesn't," Brozek answered. His fingers clamped down on her elbow until bone met bone. He dragged her back, away from Muñoz. Be quiet, he whispered.

"No, no," the cop killer stalked closer, pressed the .45 against her belly. "By all means, Sergeant, speak your mind."

She did not. Brozek towed her backward and Savannah blindly retreated, letting his grasp lead the way. They abruptly stopped. She backed against his chest, pushing for more space between her and Muñoz. She glanced behind her. They were trapped against the wall.

When she faced Muñoz his fist crashed into her jaw, snapping her head sideways. The lights dimmed. Her knees folded, forcing her to rely on Brozek's hold to stop her descent. Blood coated her tongue. Through blurred vision and spinning senses she fought to regain her composure in case Muñoz struck again. She learned from experience that, like Noah's animals, punches came in twos – at least for her.

Muñoz stood within inches of her, "Much as I want to pull the trigger, I want you alive right now." He started toward the stairway, telling Brozek, "Bring her downstairs. I'm putting the bitch to work."

Brozek waited until Muñoz's heavy footfalls receded down the stairs. Even then he feared being overheard so he mumbled, "He's insane in case you haven't noticed. He *will* shoot either you or your kids if you don't settle down. He did it in Decatur. Cut their throats *in front of the parents* so no one's off limits."

They descended the stairs. Savannah worked her jaw hoping the lump she'd swallowed wasn't the tip of her tongue. She gingerly wiped blood away with the back of her hand but missed enough it incited an uproar among the family. Afraid he'd turn his ire on them, Savannah assured the group she was okay.  She realized how idiotic she sounded.

Muñoz met them at the bottom stair, "Hadley will find a shovel and your job will be clearing off the porches and sidewalks."

If she hadn't swallowed her tongue, she came close with that announcement.  He might as well have sentenced her to digging holes in sand dunes.

Hadley asked the obvious question, "Why?  It's still snowing and there's more forecast."

"Yes, genius, I know but the sergeant needs to work off some energy.  Isn't that right, Sarge?  Exercise is good for the baby.  Keeps it healthy and alive."

She refused to comment on that ridiculous spiel while Hadley, resigned, sighed to the group, "Where are the shovels?"

Ennis panicked, "For God's sake, she's pregnant and takes heart medicine."  He grimaced his way to the couch's edge, "Let me shovel instead."

Muñoz and Sanchez laughed.

Cal, Dane and Jake joined their wounded brother's campaign.  Dane said, "We'll get it done ten times faster than Savannah can alone."

"Let the rest of us do the work," Georgia implored.  The room erupted in voices clamoring to help.  The whole family from Mama to Lily – even Gina – offered to shoulder her penance.  The show of support brought tears to Savannah's eyes.

Muñoz's short, penetrating whistle silenced the room, "Only Sarge is qualified for this job."

It had been ages since Savannah saw Georgia or Ennis so angry.

Before Muñoz set his sights on those two (*I could easily take that expression personally*, he'd said), she thanked everyone for volunteering. Well, everyone minus Jenny Lee who proved she *could* be quiet on occasion.

A look passed between Savannah, her sister and husband. One acknowledging the gravity of Muñoz's demand. Shoveling snow presented its own hazards but shoveling in bitter, high winds? Savannah bolstered her poker face to reassure Georgia and Ennis she'd be okay out there in the arctic. She hoped she hadn't lied.

Hadley struck out to find a shovel. The basement door slammed. Well, he'd sure find a shovel there, she thought. Two of them to be exact.

He returned with two tools. A snow shovel and a trowel. "Thought I'd give you a choice," he smirked at Muñoz.

Savannah rolled her eyes. *Oh goody. A comedian.*

The joke also fell flat with Muñoz who fished in his pocket, "Unless you're helping her shovel with that dinky thing, shove it up your ass. We want out of here don't we?" One flick of the wrist opened the hunting knife in Muñoz's hand. He cut her wrists free while telling Brozek, "Make sure she stays busy. If I see you coddling her, we'll be one man short when we leave this place. Understand?"

Brozek nodded, took her by the arm, "Let's go. I'll get you a coat."

Muñoz stopped him, "They're our coats now."

"C'mon, Luis," Brozek complained. "Shoveling snow in that weather without a coat?"

"No coat. She goes as is. If she works hard she can come inside." He looked at Savannah, "Start with the back porch. Thirty minutes outside earns you ten inside. You slack off and you'll work until you die out there. And with all the people in this room, you *are* expendable."

Brozek tugged at her, probably sensing her desire to slug a certain blue-eyed bully.

Hadley thrust the shovel at her, "Have fun, sweetheart."

*Drop dead, idiot,* she scowled.

Brozek urged her along with a grip refusing argument. She'd had no chance to bid her family farewell, either a temporary one or the other basically saying *been nice knowing ya.*

Overnight the wind buffeted the house and snowflakes pelted window screens like gravel. By morning the gales died down but still blew at a speed she feared working in, especially with no coat, hat or gloves.

Brozek opened the back door. The two stared into the blinding white squalls. It obscured any view past Dane's pickup buried in a drift. Savannah shook her head. *I'm so screwed.*

He leaned closer to whisper, "I'll try to sneak you inside in ten minutes. No promises though. Wait a minute." He reached into Cal's alcove for a fleece-lined hat with ear flaps. To her surprise he handed it to her, "Maybe this'll help."

Oh it would help but it countermanded Muñoz's edict of "she goes as is". No way would she remind him either. The hat fit a tad loose – not that Cal had a big head –but a hard gust would tear that sucker right off her head.

Brozek grabbed a long brown and beige wool scarf from a shelf in the nearest alcove. Ennis's scarf. "Wear this too. Muñoz'll never know."

Somehow she doubted that. Satan saw everything. For the last several minutes Brozek buddied up to her, went out of his way to be warm, understanding and sympathetic. She knew the truth. He wanted her girls as payment and that price was too steep to pay for his false kindness. To ease the anguish of her assigned task, though, she'd accept whatever goodwill he offered because she couldn't protect her kids if she died out there.

She wrapped the long scarf over her head to secure the hat then around her nose and mouth. She breathed in the clean fresh scent of Irish Spring and Ennis, she sought comfort in that smell. It provided focus for the task ahead. *My family depends on me. No giving up and no letting them down.*

Nice thought except the daunting white fury outside whittled away at her confidence. Fortitude was swell but Mother Nature packed one hell of a punch – like Muñoz. In addition to the hat and scarf she needed a coat and gloves. How long could a person stay alive before their body succumbed to bitter temperatures? And her biggest concern: What if overexertion triggered a heart attack? If she needed help, would anyone bother or would Brozek leave her outside to die then help himself to her "pretty" daughters?

He glanced down the hall. For Muñoz, she assumed. He quickly reached into Cal's alcove for a pair of gloves, "And these."

She pulled them on before he changed his mind. Since he felt so generous, she pulled the scarf down to ask, "How about a coat too?"

"Sorry. That's the one thing he'll nail me on." His hand at the small of her back nudged her to the door. Eyes closed, she drew in one last deep breath before forging ahead. *Ennis and the kids. Georgia, Dane, Mama and the others. Think while you work. Find a way to save them before–*

A brutal, unforgiving tempest hit like a saw blade, sucking the warm breath from her lungs and shoving her back against Brozek when he opened the door.

He pushed her onto the steps – into a two foot high drift – and shut the door behind her.

The backyard and landscape transformed into a sea of snow and drifts rivaling her height in places. One of those mammoth drifts (at least waist high) swept across the back yard and curved around the side of the house close to the generator room.

Standing in the dense two foot drift and seeing the deeper snow awaiting her on the porch and sidewalk, her hope fell away. *I'm not just screwed, I'm screwed to China.*

Back hunched against the stinging snow she stabbed the shovel into the drift to begin clearing it from around her legs. Savannah had shoveled snow before but apparently Atlanta snow was different from Texas snow. Everything was bigger in Texas the natives touted. They forgot to mention wind blew harder and snow turned to snowcrete. The first attempt to pitch a shovelful aside resulted in half of the snow clinging to the shovel. Worse, the snow deepened the further down she shoveled until the porch confirmed her worst fears. She really *was* screwed to China and she'd have to dig her way there. When the shovel finally scraped concrete she took a step and nearly slipped on the icy sheen of sleet beneath. As if there aren't enough obstacles already, she griped.

Her vision strayed in the direction of the ranch house down the way. Mama kept two rifles there, plus the little house had its own phone connection to the outside world. She stared longingly down the road. Sheriff Guthrie was one phone call away. Winning the lottery held better odds than traipsing a quarter mile in that weather and since Brozek stationed himself at the kitchen window to watch her, she'd barely get twenty feet before someone shot her.

The muscles in her back and shoulders knotted the longer she shoveled. Perspiration dampened her back and chest beneath her snow covered sweater. The old ticker revved into high gear, pounding hard and fast. And the snow kept getting deeper.

She shoveled in layers. Six laborious inches at a time because a person didn't start a marathon at a sprint. They paced themselves for the long haul.

By the time she cleaned off the bottom stair, she faced a three foot drift. At that rate it would take forever to scoop a small trail on the porch. Time for a break and re-evaluation of her goals.

The back door jerked open. Had ten minutes passed because she swore it seemed like thirty. She spun to see not Brozek but Muñoz who held Anna on his hip. The red-faced, wailing child held on for dear life as Muñoz leaned out the door. She reached for her mother, calling her, begging Savannah to take her.

Muñoz surveyed her work, "Not good enough. If you want this

kid to live, work harder and faster. I want results. I don't see 'em, she's dead." He extended his hand, "Take the hat, scarf and gloves off now. Did you ask for 'em?"

Savannah removed the precious winter wear, handed them over, "No."

"But you remember what I said, right?"

"Yes."

"Then you get another fifteen minutes for not reminding *him*." He slammed the door.

A gust buffeted her, tousling her hair, chilling her to the bone. For all its bluster the storm failed to drown out Anna's hysterical crying. The sound sank into Savannah's heart like talons. It also fueled her rage at the black-hearted asshole holding her sweet, terrified baby hostage – just to ensure "Sarge" didn't slack off. Savannah vowed to show that blue-eyed son of a bitch how determined a mother could be. And if given a chance, she'd bash that shovel against his nose and beat him into oblivion.

Again and again she plunged the shovel into the drift, paring it down and heaving the weight aside. More often than not half of it froze to the shovel and nearly threw her off balance. Exhaustion set in. Muscles weakened. Numb fingers refused to grasp as tight. The parts that hadn't lost feeling ached from the cold and exertion.

The inevitable truth dawned after several more turns. The assigned task was insurmountable, no matter her strength, strategy, speed or contempt for Muñoz. Snow kept falling and covering her efforts.

She allowed herself few breaks since every minute wasted valuable time. Rest was a luxury for people whose children weren't held hostage by a killer. The memory of Anna's cries motivated Savannah to redouble her efforts. Arms straining, teeth clenched and back aching, she tossed another shovel full and groaned when the majority of it stuck.

A new low-level ache joined the chorus. One that spread across her upper back. The ache eventually crept into her jaw and across her throat. If this was a warning sign, she didn't have time to fall face-first into a drift and die of a heart attack. *Not now, you weak little bastard,* she berated the racing internal organ. *My baby girl needs me…*

She glanced back at the kitchen window. Brozek stood guard, watching. Work harder, faster – no slacking, Muñoz warned. And something told her as nice as Mr. Brozek treated her, he'd rat her out in a New York Minute.

He motioned for her to keep working. M-hmm. Her new best friend just let his cards show. After all, he and his companions burned down a home with the family tied up and alive inside. They weren't exactly candidates for sainthood.

How long had she been outside anyway? Thirty minutes? An hour? Or a measly ten minutes?

*It's muscle strain and the result of Muñoz's punch earlier,* she assured. *That's why your back and jaw hurt. To be safe take a nitroglycerin and aspirin during your next break. It'll be okay.* But after a heart attack it was difficult to trust that vital organ again, especially in such a strenuous situation.

Weatherman Breezy Bill's caution soared to the forefront. *Shoveling snow is more dangerous than exercising full throttle on a treadmill. The strain causes a sudden increase in blood pressure... Cold air restricts blood vessels and decreases oxygen to the heart...*

A hot molten band anchored across her back and shoulders. The dull pain in her jaw and throat gradually closed in a fist. Instead of dwelling on the current symptoms, she checked off the ones she didn't have. No shortness of breath, well, nothing abnormal for such activity. No nausea or dizziness and the biggie – no chest pain or pressure.

*Keep working until that perverted Neolithic asshole opens the door for you.*

In the police academy (many years and two and a half kids ago), Savannah scaled walls, lifted weights, ran miles at a time and battled instructors acting as suspects fighting to grab her gun. Now she worked out by jogging the neighborhood and doing weight training, the latter mostly by lifting two kids and toting them around on her hips or in her arms. She was no pansy. But that snow... That God-awful, two-ton snow... Each load weighed ten or fifteen pounds, she'd have bet her pension on it – *if* she stood a chance of collecting that pension. If Muñoz got his way, she wouldn't see her next paycheck, much less retirement.

She paused to wipe her brow and take a moment to assess her physical· condition again. Pain in shoulders, back and jaw – all present and slowly intensifying. Exhaustion sank to the bone. Fighting though the pain grew harder. The situation digressed fast and she'd have very little to show for her efforts. *How long have I been out here? Seems like a lifetime.*

Wiping the back of her hand across her runny nose, the pain set like a branding iron across her back. The severity pushed away any fanciful possibility of muscle strain. She leaned onto the shovel while snow whipped and swirled around her. It was the most laborious work she'd done with a compromised heart and now it appeared it might fail her.

The back door opened and Brozek waved her inside. "Take a break."

Hot tears stung her eyes. Finally. A chance to really rest. Savannah trudged up the porch stairs on legs liquid from fatigue and arms so tired and weak they shook like leaves. Brushing snow from her hair and clothes sapped the last of her strength. She dared a glance at her previous work. The wind covered the once visible concrete with a fresh layer of snow and adding insult to injury, it reconstructed part of the drift she'd struggled to remove. She dreaded to see Muñoz's reaction and prayed her lack of success hadn't signed Anna's death warrant.

A strained groan eked past the uncomfortable feeling in her throat – but she noticed she wasn't the only one grimacing. Since they last saw each other an impressive knot began sprouting beneath Brozek's eye. Muñoz's doing, no doubt. Payment for lending her the hat, scarf and gloves.

Brozek shushed her as she stepped inside, whispering, "Sit down over there."

*Yes, let's have our heart attack in privacy. By the way, Mr. Benevolent, exactly how long have I been outside?* A narrow glance at the clock revealed forty, not thirty minutes passed. "I'll try to sneak you inside in ten," he'd said. *Yeah, right. I'll bet you tried real hard.*

If her hands hadn't basically frozen into claws, she'd have reached for the .45 in his waistband, yanked it out and shot him. Instead she wanted to know about Anna and Lily. "My girls," she managed between labored breaths. "Are they okay? Has he hurt them?"

He shook his head, "They're fine and judging by your progress, they'll stay that way."

Hey, look who's an optimist, she sneered. They weren't his kids so what did he care?

Brozek pointed to the bench lining the row of alcoves, "Sit down. I'll be back."

Once he left the room, she eased her hand in her pocket for the nitroglycerin and aspirin. She needed that dose ASAP. Her fingers struggled to open the nitro. They fumbled to grip the bottle then slipped off the lid. She tried focusing past the radiating pain between her shoulders and tried again to no avail. Why, she despaired, when you needed something so badly did everything go wrong? In her condition the childproof lid might as well have been a bank vault.

"I'll take those." Brozek was back with a steaming cup of coffee and a glass of water.

Trembling hands clasped the bottle to her chest. Like hell she'd surrender her only means of relief.

He countered her glare, "Take it easy, Mom. I'll help if you'll hand me the bottles." Brozek sat the beverages aside and held his hand out.

Swiping them from her would've been a breeze. To her surprise he waited her out. What a choice. Trust him or keep the pills and risk dropping them. She extended the bottles to him.

He shook an aspirin and nitroglycerin in his hand. She chewed the aspirin and chased it with water, clasping the glass between both hands the way Anna occasionally drank her juice. Now for the nitro which presented more of a challenge because of its small size.

Savannah reached for the tiny pill in Brozek's palm but his fingers closed around it. Her vision snapped up to his with an accusing, "Is there a problem?"

He stared at her trembling hands, listened to her short, pained breaths. Was he debating over helping her now? Afraid Muñoz might belt him again? Or was "Mom" too great a threat to his getting chummy with her daughters?

He pinched the pill between his thumb and forefinger, "Lift your tongue."

Ah, yes. Brozek the Benevolent was back. Before he changed his mind, she reached for it herself, "Let me try."

"No. You'll drop it and there aren't a lot of pills here. Those precious angels shouldn't lose their mother over pride, should they? Open your mouth."

She groaned again. His comment, apparently intended to comfort her, only intensified the pain. *Dear God, if he utters one more cutesy name regarding my girls, I'm going to strangle this pervert – if I don't keel over first.*

Desperation, fear and overall misery convinced her to comply. He dropped it in and she leaned back leaving him staring at the wall clock. One minute elapsed. Anticipation got the best of Nervous Nellie.

"Feeling better yet?"

*Why do you care?* Why *had* he been kind to her? Nothing stopped him from letting her die. One less obstacle to those pretty girls, she thought. She answered by shaking her head.

He sat the bottles beside her. The clock became his new obsession. Another minute down. "Any change?"

Again she shook her head, "Give it a chance. It takes time." But she too began doubting whether the pill would work.

Four long minutes dragged on. To divert his attention from the clock she reached for the hot coffee to warm her hands. Mr. Molester interpreted it as an encouraging sign. He smiled, "You're doing great out there."

Great huh? Another forty minutes and she'd need paramedics or an undertaker. One trembling finger looped through the handle. She cradled a palm beneath the cup but when she lifted it, muscles in her arms quivered. She debated the risk of drinking the coveted hot liquid and possibly chipping a tooth. She sat the cup down.

A shiver raked from head to toe. She hugged herself to settle the shakes. Brozek glanced behind him for prying ears then to her surprise, lifted a Sherpa lined rancher's coat from the alcove behind her. "Here," he whispered. "Maybe this will knock the chill off."

If it felt any closer to heaven, she'd have been breaking bread with Jesus. Savannah snuggled deep into its warmth. When the ice in her veins thawed, it set her feet, hands and face ablaze in throbbing heat. A small price to pay for being out of the storm.

"Why are you being so nice?" As if she didn't know.

"Unlike Muñoz I have no interest in killing a cop unless I'm forced to.  Plus the second I saw you, I thought about a girlfriend I had years ago."  He smiled wistfully, "She was really sweet and had pretty blue eyes like yours."

*Pretty blue eyes like Lily's you mean because we share the same shade of blue.*  Just another reason she needed to stay alive – hint, hint, nitroglycerin.  She had to keep Brozek away from her kids.

The coffee's aroma drew her vision to the cup beside her.  Brozek handed it to her.  Despite the shakes, she carefully lifted the ceramic mug to her lips and sipped.  A relieved sigh emptied her tired lungs.  Not only did the stout liquid provide long-awaited warmth to her insides, the nitroglycerin relieved the burning sensation across her back and released the invisible fist gripping her throat.  She sat the cup down before she spilled it.

Brozek's eyes flared, "Muñoz is coming."  He stripped the coat away.  She ducked for him to return it to the alcove behind her.  In that brief instant the gun in his waistband leaned temptingly close to her.  Less than two feet separated her and the .45.  One swift movement.  One second and she'd have it in her hand.

Savannah reached just as Muñoz rounded the corner.  Her hand dropped to her lap.  Brozek never saw her try for the gun and his body blocked Muñoz's view of her attempt.  The sudden rush of adrenaline sent her heart racing and another ache shooting across her back.

Muñoz eyeballed their positions and their close proximity to each other.  Yes, the sight could've been misconstrued in a slutty sort of way.  Brozek straddling her knees and his crotch so close to her face.  The blue-eyed taskmaster had other things on his mind though. He glanced around Brozek's shoulder to ask her, "You learned your lesson or do you need another shift outside? This time'll be an hour."

*I'm sorry, do I look stupid to you?* "I'd like to stay inside."

"You step out of line again, you go outside for good." He turned to Brozek, "Put her with the others." He about-faced and left for the living room.

She stuffed the medicine in her pocket as Brozek escorted her back to the family.

O  O  O

The family's welcome brought back memories of Seth's return after wartime deployment. Everyone's joy, the many hugs and even more tears. He'd fought for freedom, his country and his family. Savannah remembered the relief of seeing her brother home and finally safe from danger.

She couldn't claim fighting for freedom or her country but she sure as hell fought like a dog for her family. Her foes had different names too. Instead of terrorists abroad, dust storms and sand fleas, she stood her ground against four escaped killers, a hellacious blizzard and a bum heart. So being the recipient of cheers, elation and tearful greetings, she understood how grateful her brother felt to see his family again.

Brozek led her back to her seat between Georgia and Gina and handed her a blanket that she snuggled beneath. Lily and Anna climbed across Bobbi and Georgia's laps to join their mother.

Savannah hugged her babies to her and pressed lingering kisses to their hair. She'd not failed sweet Anna who cuddled as close as possible. Neither girl cared about their mother's wet hair or icky, damp sweater. They just wanted their mama and frankly their mama wanted them too.

The fire across the way crackled and snapped. It would require more wood soon. Savannah dreaded to see who got "volunteered" to fetch more logs. She just prayed it would be a quick trip and not another forty minute banishment.

Mama's antique mantel clock read nine-thirty. Two and a half hours passed since she and Ennis descended the stairs into the nightmare.

Georgia clasped her hand, gave it a gentle squeeze. "I'm so glad you're okay."

Me too, she said and left it at that. She'd sit on a cactus before before telling the Queen of Concern about the aspirin and nitro pill.

Georgia leaned closer, whispering that during her absence Sanchez and Hadley ransacked the house for valuables and weapons. They cleaned out Mama's jewelry box then complained about the lack of loot. A modest pair of diamond earrings, two broaches, a cameo, a diamond and amethyst necklace and a string of pearls.

The guns they collected compensated for the small amount of jewelry, Georgia continued. Sanchez combed the house for weapons she said, and found two shotguns, two rifles and a .22, most of which belonged to Mama's husband. Georgia hadn't mentioned Ennis's .38 which was not only encouraging but amazing. Maybe they figured since Brozek rummaged the suitcases, it was useless to search the room. Or, Savannah suspected, they were a little on the dense side and somehow managed to overlook it.

Sanchez shushed the family's subdued conversations. Windbag Willy (or Breezy Bill to the people still talking to him at that point) and his colleagues returned for an update. Sanchez laughed because it seemed America couldn't recognize four escaped inmates if their lives depended on it. For years Savannah wished people paid better attention but as a rookie she learned how unobservant the public was.

That day citizens called in false sightings throughout the state. Police pulled over citizens to verify identities and ended up delaying (and embarrassing) not only drivers and passengers but themselves as well. Some reports had the four driving east toward Louisiana and others mentioned Kansas. One eyewitness reported seeing four men matching their description driving along 1-20 outside Abilene.

The update included footage of the burning home in Decatur. The upbeat mood of Savannah's safe return gave way to a somber silence around the room. They all knew what lay ahead of them if they didn't gain the upper hand soon.

The newscaster switched topics to Amarillo and area school cancellations. Business and church closings followed. Dozens of closings scrolled across the bottom of the screen from various cities and communities. When Vega's closings rolled around, Savannah figured it might read "Don't bother. The whole town is closed."

She yawned from the newscaster's constant droning. Ten minutes of jabbering boiled down to *more snow, more wind, no roads or airports open and no sign of the inmates.*

The aches plaguing Savannah's back and throat subsided enough her eyelids drooped and allowed her mind to let go of morbid thoughts of heart attacks and shoveling snow. She drifted into a light sleep with her girls nestled in beside her and her arms draped around them both.

## 13

Plates clattering woke her up. Sanchez stood guard armed with the assault rifle perched on his hip like some modern day Jesse James daring someone to challenge him. Missing in action were Hadley, Brozek and Muñoz who, by the sound of it, raided the fridge and cupboards then toted their brimming plates into the living room for everyone to see and smell. Brozek and Muñoz chose to chow down on roasted chicken while Hadley gorged on Mama's honey-glazed ham. The sight added insult to injury since Savannah went to bed obsessing over the luscious smoked ham with a sweet caramelized glaze. Obsessing over it when she wasn't obsessing over her hungover husband, that was. In her mind she considered the sandwich a reward for tolerating her husband's childish behavior but most of all Jenny Lee's interference. Once in bed she drifted off planning the perfect sandwich. Bread slathered in creamy mayonnaise then piling on two, maybe three slices of ham and bringing lettuce, tomato and cheese to the party. Now some jerk wolfed down the succulent fare so fast he probably never tasted it.

After his eating orgy, Brozek returned from the kitchen holding a hammered copper bowl. The girls perked up. They recognized it as "Granna's candy bowl". Mama kept a variety of miniature fun size bars in the bowl, all kinds for all tastes.

Lily and Anna sat straighter, their eager vision tracking his movements from person to person as he handed out candy – one each. Thanks to the men's gluttonous spree, the once brimming bowl shrank to a sparse number of Snickers, Milky Way and Crunch.

Lily chose a Crunch while Anna grabbed up two Snickers. Lily protested the two bars. Brozek shushed her then slipped her another Crunch bar with a wink and a hushed *it'll be our little secret...*

None of the felonious four instilled a warm fuzzy, feeling but Brozek put Savannah on constant edge around the girls. He'd begun cozying up to them already but his "little secrets" stopped with an extra candy bar – or she'd stop him from breathing.

Smiling, Brozek handed Savannah a Snickers. *Go ahead and smile, pervert. That "old girlfriend" bullshit was just that. You think if you treat "Mom" well then her kids might drop their guard.* The problem was it could happen. Lily and Anna were smart but they were also very young. Thankfully for now they were terrified of the intruders but the longer Muñoz threatened everyone while Brozek played Mr. Nice Guy, Savannah worried they might fall for his act.

Savannah accepted the candy bar then tightened her embrace around the girls – the unspoken warning: *Touch our kids and their father and I will tear you apart. Whatever you did to Andrea Tate will not happen to these girls. Period.*

"Hey, wait." Sanchez zeroed in on Lily's extra Crunch bar, "That kid got two?"

"They're kids, Manuel," Brozek answered as if that should suffice. "Kids are always hungry."

Muñoz grabbed the bowl from his comrade, "Then the parents go without." He swiped the Snickers bar from Savannah, threw it in the bowl that he shoved into Brozek's gut, "Give the others one candy bar. *One.* You understand?"

For a murderer, Alan Brozek sure cowered from his colleague's dressing-down. The mouse of a man rarely made eye contact with overbearing Muñoz. Savannah figured Brozek's prison mates taught him a lesson or two during his stay. Not even hardcore convicts liked bastards who molested and killed the most vulnerable and trusting people on the planet.

Brozek resumed passing out a single bar to everyone except Ennis and Savannah. Meanwhile, Anna devoured her first Snickers and Lily carefully unwrapped one Crunch bar. She offered it to her mother. Savannah shook her head, touched at the sweet gesture, "I'm okay, baby, but thank you." Lily turned to Ennis who mustered a smile and shook his head with a *thank you.*

The children ate their meager meal. The family and Gina offered theirs to Savannah and Ennis but they declined. Jenny Lee, on the other hand, barely took time to chew hers before swallowing it down.

## 14

Mama's clock played through the Westminster Chime then struck the noon hour. Muñoz flipped the channel from CNN's incessant political drivel. Nothing like politics to dull a person's interest. He settled on a local Amarillo station. Good ol' Breezy Bill's channel. She wondered who produced the most hot air – CNN or him.

Since eating her snack Anna stretched across Gina and Savannah's laps for a nap. Lily stayed awake and focused on Muñoz who paced like a caged animal and blamed his cohorts for the "wrong turn" north toward Colorado instead of south to Mexico. He wanted a way out of the house, out of Vega and out of Texas and the weather reports gave no hope of that anytime soon.

In a way Savannah understood his aggravation. The meteorologist waltzed across the radar screen without the common decency to show the slightest chagrin or remorse. No, he flashed a toothy grin to duped viewers instead. The grin widened when he updated snow totals and drift heights. Once again nature crowned Vega King of the Blizzard. The deepest snow and the tallest drifts. Savannah wanted to maim the man grinning his ass off and cracking cutesy jokes. *He* wasn't the one Muñoz would recruit to dig out. *She* was. And the cop killer already eyed Savannah after a quick peek outside. She expected he'd soon summon her back to work.

Brozek tried his hand at assuring his buddy, "Luis, stop worrying. Everyone's stranded and the car's probably buried in snow so we're safe here. It's a small town anyway which means maybe a sheriff and one deputy and they're stuck too."

As if they'd been stranded in Hicksville where Sheriff Simpleton and Deputy Dunce enforced the law. Guthrie employed more than one deputy but Brozek was right about one thing. They were probably unable to motivate since Texas lawmen probably lacked vehicles equipped to handle snowstorms on steroids.

Sanchez switched back to CNN in time to hear a recap of their escape and murderous rampage across Texas. The video changed to the 7-11 and the dead cop on the sidewalk. The camera zoomed in on the covered body and the blood pooling from beneath the sheet. Then the video changed to the burning home in Decatur.

Sanchez cut loose in a sadistic laugh, "Burn, baby, burn." He turned to the family, "You shoulda heard their screams. Priceless."

Bobbi and Georgia squirmed at the sight. Others averted their eyes. Savannah and Ennis stole a glance at each other. If they didn't do something soon the images on TV might as well say Vega, Texas.

Muñoz's temper already ran on rims and Sanchez's psychopathic side went from bad to worse during the day. How long before they started shooting people out of anger, impatience or simple boredom?

Anna stirred awake. She yawned then tucked herself safely between Savannah and Gina. A minute passed when she crooked her finger at her mother. Savannah leaned closer to hear her whisper, "I gotta peepee."

"Me too," Lily joined in.

Brozek overheard them. He held out his hands, one to Anna, the other to Lily, "Here. I'll take you."

Like hell you will, Savannah literally bit her tongue before lashing out with that gem. Now wasn't the time to destroy that flimsy bridge she and Brozek built. The fact both girls physically retreated from him added credence to her reply, "They want me to take them."

Brozek stepped back to allow the girls down and Savannah to stand. He followed the trio to the bathroom. The girls clamored inside for first dibs, Lily using the "I'm older" reasoning and Anna arguing she spoke up first. Savannah sided with Anna. She used that opportunity to casually shut the door and lock it just as Brozek tried muscling in. A smile crossed her face. The slow bastard. "We'll be out in a few minutes," she assured him.

When she opened the door, he blocked the exit, holding the .45 at his side but nonetheless agitated. "Do that again and I'll take 'em myself – without Mom along." He let his threat sink in before stepping aside.

They returned to their seats. Savannah handed her blanket to a stewing Brozek who snatched it from her grasp. Anna stared at the bookcase behind Hadley and Mama. Once again she cupped her hand around her mama's ear. This time she whispered, "Would you read me

'Green Eggs & Ham'?"

Savannah doubted the four men would vote to hear "Green Eggs & Ham" but she'd ask for the book anyway. Perhaps His Highness Brozek wouldn't crawl up her keister for asking the question.

Muñoz beat him to the punch, "What's that brat want now?"

Instinctively she drew both girls closer while keeping a calm voice, "She wants me to read to her." *And she's not a brat, you son of a bitch.*

Sanchez protested, "I wanna hear the news, not 'Twinkle, Twinkle, Little Star'."

*That's a song, you idiot, not a story.* She forced a sweet, "Please?"

Brozek went to the bookshelves. Mama's collection of authors ranged from classics to modern. Zane Gray, Louis L'Amour (her husband John's favorites) and Debbie Macomber, Mary Higgins Clark and Georgia's books (for herself). The bottom shelf offered a generous selection of children's books from Dr. Seuss and A.A. Milne to Roald Dahl and Laura Ingalls Wilder.

Brozek perused the selections until finding "Green Eggs & Ham". "Luis, the kids have been good."

He swiveled to Brozek. His expression screamed *so what?*

"C'mon," the pervert said. "Let her read to 'em. It'll keep 'em quiet."

Sanchez sighed, realizing he might lose the battle. Muñoz put Savannah on notice, "When I say stop, you better stop, because I hate kids *and* their books."

Brozek offered her the book in a friendlier fashion than he'd grabbed the blanket earlier.  Evidently, he was over his snit.

Lily mentioned in a quiet, meek voice, "Mama needs her reading glasses."

Muñoz's mouth tightened while a beaming grin brightened Brozek's face.  He leaned onto his knees, his voice soft – perfect for interacting with skittish kids, "Do you know where her glasses are?"

Savannah answered for her, "Upstairs on my nightstand."

His smile lasted the trip up the stairs.  That grin put her on edge. He prided himself on that brief conversation with Lily, like he'd gained ground in scaling her defensive wall.  Lily wasn't dumb.  She just wanted normalcy around her and to maintain a fraction of it, Mama needed her glasses to read.

Brozek bounded down the stairway.  Dropping to one knee, he handed the glasses to Lily with a sugary, "Here are her glasses, sweetheart. If you want anything else, let me know."

Lily leaned away from him and into Savannah.  That one subtle move pushed him off her defensive wall, leaving him crestfallen.

Curbing a satisfied smile, Savannah slid her glasses on, "Lily's fine.  Thanks for my glasses."  *Don't get cute with my daughter, sleazeball.  She's not stupid and I'm not dead yet so watch it.*

The girls leaned back and relaxed when she opened the book's orange cover.  She cleared her throat and began reading.  Partway through the book Sanchez mimicked the lines in a silly childlike voice, "'I do not like them in a house, I do not like them with a mouse,'" then improvised, "I do not like them on the grass so everyone can kiss my a–"

"*I do not like them here or there*," Savannah projected loud enough to drown out the profanity. Muñoz scowled at her but she carried on anyway, "'*I do not like them anywhere*'."

Muñoz's narrow gaze dropped to the book, "Brozek, pick something less annoying."

But he chose Laura Ingalls Wilder, a book Lily might enjoy but would undoubtedly make Anna antsy. Not good in their situation. "It's a little advanced for Anna," Savannah said. "How about the Berenstain Bears or 'Pooh Goes Visiting'?"

Brozek returned to the shelf, fingered a few books aside until settling on one, "'The Berenstain Bears and the Golden Rule'? Good enough?"

"That will work." She opened the book and began reading. The girls listened intently while she tailored her voice for each character, Papa Bear, Mama Bear and Brother and Sister Bear.

Anna tapped a drawing of Papa Bear, "That's Daddy."

Savannah smiled, "That's right, sweetheart." Both glanced across the room to Ennis. Anna waved. He braved his own smile and waved back.

Anna mashed her finger on Mama then Sister Bear, "And that's you and me!"

"Shut up, brat," Sanchez barked from the picture window. "Bad enough I gotta hear crap like," his voice rose to the same mocking childlike tone, 'the Golden Rule is the most important rule there is'," then it returned to normal, "but your screaming is too much."

Both Anna and Lily recoiled from his scolding. Savannah fired a withering glare at him. She'd managed to briefly divert the girls' attention just for Sanchez to plunge them back into unfettered fear. She hugged them tighter, kept her voice soft and even, "It's okay, girls. He wouldn't know the Golden Rule if it hit him in the nose."

Brozek crouched in front of Anna, put a hand on her knee, "It's okay, Anna. He's a grumpy grouch like Oscar on Sesame Street."

Peering over her glasses, Savannah focused on his hand, fighting the instinct to slap it away. He patted Anna's thigh, but once his vision locked on "Mom's", he stood and backed up a step. Message received.

The girls leaned in closer as Muñoz approached. Savannah laid the book in her lap, removed her specs to make solid eye contact with him. He struck with snakelike speed grabbing the book and flinging it against the wall. It nearly dented Brozek's head as it flew by. "Sanchez has a point," Muñoz said to Savannah. "What's this Golden Rule bullshit anyway? Your idea of a moral guilt trip for us?"

Before he reached the point of tossing her outside again, she replied truthfully, "I'm reading the book Brozek chose."

Georgia nudged her sister. Her brow sank. Don't goad him, the expression said.

Muñoz placed the gun barrel against her jaw and redirected her vision from Georgia to him. "You put too much emphasis on those words you read, like you're preaching to us," he said. "The only Golden Rule around here is 'do what Muñoz says'." He mumbled a string of profanity that probably gave God a migraine then turned his ire on Brozek, "Find another damn book."

Sanchez's posture stiffened, "We got company."

Hope kindled among the family. Savannah prayed the visitor

turned out to be Sheriff Guthrie, even if he used snowshoes, a dog sled or rubbed a genie lamp to get there.

"*Everyone's stranded inside*," Muñoz grumbled. "Isn't that what you said, Brozek?"

Sanchez stood in disbelief, "Who gets out in this weather? I mean who *can* get out in this weather?"

The four readied their weapons. Hadley stirred for the first time since gifting Savannah with a snow shovel. No more heavy-lidded, apathetic yawns for him. Eyes sharp and alert, he grabbed the .45 on the bar, "Cops. That's who."

Muñoz eyeballed the family in silent accusation. He stalked toward Savannah, "You're the only one who's left the room."

She pressed back into the cushion, "To take my kids to pee, not to call the police. There's no phone in there and you took my cell phone."

Sanchez peeked out again, "It's a tractor. A green one."

Muñoz turned to Mama. "You. You live here, right?"

Mama seethed behind pursed lips. She nodded.

"See who it is then get rid of 'em quick. One sign that anything's wrong and I'll shoot every kid in this place then work my way through the rest of you."

Mama came to her feet and met Sanchez at the window. "It's our neighbor Eldon Killibrew," she said. "He's probably bringing a basket of eggs, maybe some milk."

"Why would he do that?" Muñoz. Always the skeptic.

One thing could be said of Caroline Rutherford. She backed

down to no one. Not the U.S. government when they tried reneging on disaster relief funds the summer after Ennis's daddy passed away. Not Savannah's daddy who came to the hospital drunk when Savannah had breast cancer surgery – and Mama confronted him in a roomful of witnesses. Now she faced four dangerous criminals who had nothing to lose and killing a nervy elderly lady meant nothing to them. The Steel Magnolia stood five feet two and faced a man over a foot taller yet she refused to yield.

Mama Rutherford squared her shoulders before replying with that same grit, "Because he and his wife Jackie know my kids are home for a visit and we run through those two items quick around here. Georgia and Savannah baked pies yesterday and we gave the Killibrews a couple for their family. They are being neighborly and repaying their kindness."

"Listen, old lady," he fumed, "you and that one over there," his .45 gestured to Savannah, "you both got big mouths. Use them too much and you won't live long. You're gonna take the eggs and milk and tell him to get lost. Understand? Otherwise, Elroy's joining our party."

"*Eldon*," she corrected. "I'll do what I can if you stop pointing that gun willy-nilly at my family."

His right eye narrowed. Savannah watched his hand tighten on the weapon. She held her breath, praying Mama hadn't tempted fate once too often.

He aimed at Savannah instead, "Sergeant. Over here. Now."

A shiver strafed down her back. *Me? What did I do?* She swallowed back the question and got to her feet. The girls clutched at her hands and sweater, desperate to hold her back.  Their pleas for her to stay got on Muñoz's nerves so Savannah assured them it would be okay. Once more she prayed it wasn't a lie.

The tractor's engine rumbled nearer, alternately slowed in an obvious struggle then gained speed as Eldon Killibrew churned the John Deere's tire chains and plow blade through the snow.  Unbeknownst to Eldon, a genial, good-hearted farmer in his late forties, he drove into a nightmare he might not drive away from.

Muñoz grabbed Savannah's arm and nudged the gun against her belly, "Plain enough for you, Grandma?  Screw up and she and the baby die." He motioned to Sanchez, "Cut her free."

Sanchez dug a folding knife from his pocket and cut the rope binding Mama's wrists.

The John Deere's deep rumble wound down to a low idle.  The cab door closed.  Seconds later Eldon banged on the door shouting, "Caroline!  It's Eldon!"

Anyone who met Mr. Killibrew might assume he was hearing impaired because of his loud manner of speaking.  Vega residents recognized him by his volume, not necessarily his face since a person heard him before actually seeing him.  Years ago Savannah discovered it was just his nature.  Loud.  All the time.  "Caroline!" he tried again. "Unless y'all went to the Bahamas, open up!"

Mama gave her daughter-in-law a reassuring glance to say *don't worry*.  Muñoz guided Savannah back against the wall out of Eldon's sight.  His hand clamped around her left arm and kept the gun nestled at her belly.

Mama opened the door to Eldon's enthusiastic, "Afternoon, Caroline. Meant to drop these off before the storm kicked in but Darcy went into labor. Lasted most of the night."

Sanchez and Brozek stared at each other, stunned. They must have assumed Darcy was a woman. The family, however, knew she was a cow and a cranky one at that.

"Is she okay?" Mama asked as if everything on the Rutherford side of the road was just fine, thank you very much.

"Yeah, had some troubles," Eldon replied over the howling wind that didn't stand a chance against his boisterous nature. "She wouldn't dilate then she tired out. Me an' Joe Bob stayed the night in the barn but Darcy and the calf are fine."

"That's a relief."

Sanchez sneered at the word *calf.* He nodded to Muñoz as if to say *put the babbling bastard out of his misery already.*

"Yup," Eldon sounded proud as a peacock. "It was a struggle but she made it thanks to Joe Bob. Say, he's been trying to get hold of Jenny. Have y'all heard from her?"

Too often actually, Savannah rolled her eyes.

"She stayed here last night," Mama answered. "The storm must have taken the phones out. I'll tell her he tried to call."

"He'll appreciate that."

Muñoz shifted his weight. The gun poked a shade harder. He wanted Mama to get rid of Eldon and quick.

"Eldon, I'd invite you in but a couple of us are under the weather today. I don't want them sharing it with you if it's contagious. I guess the snow didn't agree with them."

Eldon downplayed it in his usual laidback style, "No problem. Gotta get back anyway. I'm gonna try to check around for anyone needing help, at least as long as my tractor can handle the snow. It took a while to get here. Had to dig out a few times. Those Yankees can say what they want about tractors bein' slow but they motivate places their highfalutin' Jaggywars and Beemers can't."

"So true. Be careful out there, Eldon, and be mindful who you pick up. Never know who you might encounter."

No shit, Savannah thought.

Ferocious, bitter gusts billowed a fine cloud of snow inside. A stronger gust followed, blowing hard enough Mama turned from the storm of flakes swirling in. An involuntary shiver shook Savannah. How the hell did Eldon tolerate such inclement weather? The answer: Eldon was a Texan and it never paid to underestimate or question their abilities, resolve or sanity.

"Aw, I'm not worried. I've had good luck all my life. I got Jackie, the kids, my health and my farm. I'm the luckiest fella alive."

*You are if you leave now.* Savannah wished he would leave, just to save himself.

"Move it along," Muñoz whispered to Mama.

Whether she heard him or not, she followed his orders, "Well, don't stay out too long or Jackie will get concerned." She glanced back at her shivering daughter-in-law, "Savannah, honey, could you help me carry this? Eldon needs to get back before the storm gets worse."

Which by then one additional inch of snow mattered as much as another raindrop in a flood. Twenty, thirty or forty inches. It was all insurmountable.

Muñoz pressed harder on the gun. The pressure rousted Daniel to kick back. Savannah's heart went in her throat. Muñoz hadn't noticed since he whispered in her ear, "One wrong move."

Yes, yes, her nod acknowledged. One wrong move and she and her son were toast. She scraped together a convincing smile and joined Mama at the door to greet Eldon.

Muñoz whispered *Sarge* then pointed to her jaw. Since Eldon arrived, fear overrode pain. Savannah forgot about the swelling and turned it just out of Eldon's view. She probably looked ridiculous in that position but breathing sounded more appealing than his judging her stance.

By then, Eldon hunched against the wind and snow. He carried two gallons of milk in one hand and cradled a bowl of eggs in the crook of the other. He cracked a grin at her, "Ma'am, you and your sister saved the day with those pies, what with Darcy calving last night. Between us, the kids and Joe Bob, both of 'em are history."

"Glad you enjoyed them, Eldon–"

"Oh yes, ma'am. I'd be obliged if you'd pass our thanks along to your sister as well. Her bakery must be the talk of the town 'cause those were larrupin' good. No wonder Dane's getting fat."

An offended Dane made his indignation known – albeit quietly, "*Fat?* I'm not getting fat." A pause then, "Am I?"

"No, sweetheart," Georgia appeased him, "you're not."

"Just fluffy," Ennis retorted.

Eldon overheard the exchange. He leaned to see in. Savannah casually stepped closer to Mama, blocking his view. She held her breath. Felt her heart racing. If Eldon noticed anything wrong, Muñoz and his men would kill him then the family. She cleared her throat as a sign for the group to pipe down, "Georgia will be happy to hear the pies were a success." She reached for the milk but Eldon shook his head, "No ma'am, that's no job for a lady who's expectin'. I'll take 'em in for you." Then his brow sank.

*Stay calm*, she pleaded with herself. *Now's not the time to lose your composure. Act casual.* But it was too late. Her one meager thread of control began fraying… *He's staring at my jaw. He knows.*

Eldon's gaze zeroed in like a laser, "Looks like someone whomped you good. How'd it happen?"

Savannah's mind went blank. Mama's eyes flared. For once she offered no easy, believable answer. Muñoz loomed in Savannah's peripheral vision, the .45 aimed at her belly. *Make it good. Everyone's lives depend on it.* She scrounged for an acceptable lie, "I… I'm embarrassed to say, Eldon." *Come on, stop tripping over your tongue. Wait. Tripping.* "Consequences of tripping into the dresser. I stumbled over the train case. I feel silly but there it is." *Good job, idiot. That was the lamest excuse this side of "I walked into a door".* Lying about injuries had never been a strong suit. She learned that years ago when her boyfriend Toby Jackson kept clobbering her and Georgia interrogated her over the bruises. That had been to save her pride, though. This lie she hoped saved her family.

Surprisingly Eldon bought the explanation. He shook his head,

"Gotta be more careful. Got a baby on board, remember."

Hard to forget that, Eldon, especially now, she thought.

Mama's impatience emerged, "Accidents happen. We're grateful it wasn't worse." She hurriedly transferred the bowl of eggs to Savannah who felt too dumb to do anything past nod at Eldon. "Here, honey," Mama told her mute daughter-in-law, "you take the eggs and I'll get the milk." She gathered the two gallons in one hand, offered another thanks to Eldon and told him to say hi to his family and Joe Bob for them.

"Will do." He squinted against another wind gust, "Well, gotta make my rounds for stranded folks then get back home. Jackie's got a hundred things for me to do. I'm captive until this mess clears up."

Mama's shoulders slumped, she shook her head with a truthful, "Aren't we all?"

He tipped his cap to the ladies, "Y'all have a good visit and if you need anything, give us a holler on one of your cell phones – if the towers still work, that is. I'll let Ma Bell know your landline's out. It'll take days for 'em to get out here though."

"Thanks, Eldon, but we'll take care of it," Mama said. "Right now the peace and quiet from solicitors is nice."

The two bid farewell to their only chance for help. Mama heaved a sigh when she closed the door. Savannah's knees went weak.

She and Mama turned to tote Eldon's delivery to the kitchen. Muñoz blocked their path, told them to sit down. Mama argued, "I refuse to let this food spoil. Allow us to put this away properly before you bully us back to our seats."

Savannah clenched in places that made her wince. The faces

around the room collectively flinched at Mama's boldness. Muñoz's light brown complexion darkened. Savannah could almost hear him say *I'm not taking this shit from some old lady* then aim and fire.

"She's right." Hadley reclaimed his roost at the bar. "We need the food."

Muñoz despised Hadley's statement however true it might be. He told Mama, "Both of you put the food away and get your asses back in here. You got thirty seconds. Thirty-one and someone in this room dies. Go."

Savannah took off at a sprint with Mama close behind. Savannah mentally counted off seconds while throwing open the fridge and shoving food aside to make room for the large bowl of eggs. It evolved into a hellacious Food Tetris where none of the pieces fit quite right. The previous day's casserole – stored from table to fridge in a long, foil covered baking dish might as well have been an elephant sitting on the shelf. Her vision darted from one shelf to another, searching for a solution before time ran out. *Ten... eleven... twelve...*

*Three more inches is all I need to fit this bastard on that shelf. Three little inches stands between life or death for my family.* Another quick search for anything to push, tilt, stack or wedge items. *Fifteen, sixteen, seventeen...*

"Ten seconds left!" Ennis shouted from the living room. "Hurry!"

Panic set in. Somewhere between debating elephants and spelunking for precious inches, her timing fell behind. She changed her plan to milk first, then eggs.

The side of the Minute Maid carton suffered the brunt of her haste when she shoved a gallon of milk beside it in the door. She pushed ketchup, mustard and soda aside to fit the other gallon in the opposite door. Now the eggs. One sweep of her arm sent everything from butter, cheese and veggies to the side. The casserole went beside them. *Twenty-three... twenty-four...*

"Savannah," Ennis prodded with stern urgency, "hurry up!"

"I am," she replied, grabbing the egg bowl from the counter and crammed it in the remaining space. The snug fit left the bowl cocked partially onto the casserole dish.

Door closed, she rushed to Mama, grabbed her hand and raced back to the living room. She leaned on her knees to catch her breath and calm down. Eggs and milk. She never imagined putting away groceries could endanger her family.

Mama laid a hand to her back and praised her efforts.

Muñoz's gaze centered on the clock, "You cut things short, don't you, Sergeant? Two seconds to spare." He waved to Hadley, "Tie 'em up."

Hadley rolled his eyes as if the request was not only boring but beneath him, "Brozek, you do it."

Alan Brozek pulled a formidable folding knife from his jeans. He cut two lengths of cord with the four inch blade then approached Mama.

Chin thrust out in defiance, she refused to comply. Brozek expressed a courteous warning to obey or face Muñoz. Sanchez would have already tackled her and tied her up. Muñoz would be minus one bullet after shooting her. But not Alan Brozek, good buddy to all.

Mama capitulated once Muñoz got involved. Brozek approached Savannah. When she hesitated he prompted, "Your hands, Mom."

"Savannah, just do it," Ennis advised from across the room. He realized she tested Brozek and wasn't thrilled about the idea.

Hers and Brozek's gazes held steady. He answered with a subtle brow drop and a gentle warning, "Listen to your husband."

Something small and solid nestled at the small of her back. Muñoz's .45. He leaned to her ear and spoke in a tone that sent a nasty tingle along her spine, "Brozek's too easy on you." He snapped the cord from Brozek's grasp, "But I'll tie this around your wrists or your neck. You decide which one your kids see."

The gun's pressure vanished. In her mind she saw him winding the cord around his hands, preparing to strangle her.

Wrists crossed, she extended her hands as a sign of surrender.

"Savannah, *do it now.*" Ennis's urgency implored her to comply – and she had. From his vantage point he just couldn't see it.

Muñoz's hands came from above. She had enough time to see the cord stretched taut between them before Bobbi cried out to Monty. The terrified scream sent Savannah's heart in her throat.

"Monty, stop!" Cal yelled. She imagined if God used that tone with all His children, people might think twice before committing the smallest of sins.

The world slowed to a crawl. A hundred things seemed to happen in those brief seconds. Muñoz's forearm – not the cord – cinched across her throat. He slung the cord away to retrieve the .45 in his waistband. A wrenching turn toward the men's couch made her stumble to gain her footing but the muscular arm across her throat held her upright.

More panicked appeals to Monty, these from family and Gina, jumbled together but they all meant the same thing. *Stop. Go back.*

Footfalls pounded the floor toward Savannah and Muñoz. For thirteen, nature gifted Monty with the broad Rutherford shoulders. From top to bottom those young muscles developed strong and solid from years of ranch work.

Savannah waved him back, echoing the group's sentiment. The courageous teenager ignored the plea. He bulled toward the killer like a linebacker rushing a quarterback.

"Monty, stop!" Savannah echoed the others. In her mind, the teen reverted to a child. Back then the cherub-cheeked, bashful boy a little older than Lily toed the dirt when Ennis introduced them. For days he'd shied from "the girl with the funny name". Less than a week later, the girl with the funny name found him in a blizzard, alone and unconscious. She'd held him in her arms to warm and shield him until help came. She saved him, he'd said. Now that little boy tried returning the gesture, only he would pay with his life.

"You are one dead bastard," Muñoz vowed. With one arm clamped across Savannah's throat, he aimed the gun at the boy.

Her viewpoint shrank to Monty charging toward a premature death. She vaguely saw Cal come to his feet and rush at Monty in hopes of pulling him to safety. He'd never make it.

She threw her hand against Muñoz's wrist the instant before he pulled the trigger. The deafening blast echoed off walls and speared her brain. Women's screams, crying children and raging men faded to the background. Savannah waited for her cherished nephew to either fall dead on the floor or retreat.

He did neither. Hints of that timid tyke surfaced in the teenager. He froze, wide-eyed, much as he had when she first met him.

Tears trembled in her eyes. She literally felt sick and weak from fear. "Monty, please…" A wave of her hand finished the thought. *Go sit down.* The bullet came so close to nailing the sweet boy between the eyes. Her efforts barely deflected the shot into the ceiling.

Muñoz pushed her aside, the gun still fisted in his hand. "You wanna be a hero?" he asked Monty.

Cal stepped forward until Sanchez stopped him. He reached in hopes of retrieving his son, "I'm right here, Monty. Come on back."

Muñoz struck with lightning speed. The impact of his backhanded swing drove the gun butt into Monty's cheek, sending him to the floor, dazed. Blood trickled from his mouth but his vision never strayed from the gun.

"Get your boy," Muñoz told Cal then spun to Gina who hugged a hysterical Anna in an attempt to quiet her. "Shut that kid up."

Ennis's ex-partner tightened her embrace, "I'm trying but it takes time with frightened children."

Cal brought Monty to his feet. Defeated, Monty hung his head and took his daddy's lead back to the couch, a hand cradling his cheek.

Savannah joined the others in consoling him. Guilt settled like a stone in her stomach. It was her fault Monty risked his life and suffered a hell of a blow for his efforts.

Muñoz wheeled then launched his fist into her temple. Fireworks of every color exploded behind her eyes. The floor met her knees – or vise versa she wasn't sure which – and she collapsed with a whimper near Jenny Lee.

Jenny drew back until her knees practically tucked beneath her chin. Savannah figured Jenny realized she won a front row seat to her bane's demise.

Muñoz advanced with the gun aimed straight at her. She scrambled back, away from him. He quickly closed the distance. In a feeble attempt to protect Daniel, one hand shielded her unborn baby while her other extended to Muñoz in a shaky "stop" gesture.

Behind him, the men were on their feet and headed toward Muñoz. Ennis led the charge until Sanchez drove the butt of the assault rifle into his stomach. Ennis dropped at Georgia's feet with a groan. Sanchez hustled the others back by threatening to mow down Zach, Tyler and Monty.

Across the room Muñoz's expression handed down Savannah's sentence. He wanted revenge for her disobedience – and for embarrassing him.

Her brain raced for something to say before he killed her in front of everyone. Anything to stop the runaway chaos she'd started by defying him. But what did she and Muñoz have in common? *Think.* "I was protecting my family," she stammered. "You'd do the same if our roles were reversed." At least she hoped he would.

His blue eyes narrowed. Not only had she dug her own grave by helping Monty but somehow her last comment pushed her in.

His tone described the depth of shit she was in and it was rising by the second, "Yeah, if I had any family left."

Her stomach dropped like an elevator in free fall. *What have I done? By testing that gutless wonder Brozek, Daniel and I will die right here, right now...*

"My mother was all I had." The finger on the trigger seemed to squeeze down ever so slightly – or was that her imagination? The tear in his eye, however, was as real as her fear.

"She died three months ago trying to get me a new trial. You cops always bitch that the system works against you. Try having one detective make it her life's goal to see you rot and die in prison. All because she wanted one more conviction before retiring. I got a life sentence in a concrete hole and my mother got a grave but that bitch cop got a promotion and moved to Florida."

Savannah swallowed hard. A female detective. Perfect.

"Guess what her rank was?"

So. Utterly. Screwed. "Sergeant."

"Bingo."

Anna wailed. Keeping an eye on Muñoz, Gina gathered her closer, anxiously trying to shush her before he turned his wrath on the child. Gina Sutton climbed plenty of rungs on Savannah's personal scale of decent people. No matter her past, she fought tooth and nail to save the squirming child in her lap from Muñoz. Between her and Georgia, they worked overtime not only comforting the weeping girls but also hiding Muñoz's interactions with their mother.

"I'll shut that kid up," Muñoz vowed. He jerked the gun toward

Anna.

Cold fear stopped Savannah's heart. "No! Not my children!"

The .45 swung back to her and fired. No time to think. No time to react. No time to pray. Just a bright orange flash and deafening explosion.

Children screamed. Voices yelled in a cacophony of noise that rivaled the ringing in her ears. Her heart shifted to Warp Nine and stripped a gear getting there. Her mind blanked. She froze, too frightened to move but her vision never strayed from the gun's black, cavernous muzzle staring back at her.

Something warm and wet trickled into her hairline above her left ear. She'd been shot – she felt the bee sting in her hand – but the wound took a backseat to the fact Muñoz looked extremely willing to pull the trigger again, this time with fatal results.

Lily and Anna kept screaming for her. Others joined in but Muñoz and Brozek blocked their view. Every moment without her answer to "are you okay" escalated the family's panic but base terror robbed her breath and voice. To be honest, she wasn't okay and she was terrified he was about to finish the job.

Blood dripped onto her cheek. A burning ache at the base of her pinkie finger forced her to glance at it. The bullet missed her head by scant inches and clipped her outstretched hand instead. The close call reduced her from a police officer trained to deal with dangerous situations to a mother and wife just wanting – trying – to survive.

Finally she dared to breathe. Her heart still pummeled her ribs like a wild animal bashing against its cage.

"*Are you okay?*" Ennis and Georgia shouted over the rest.

She wanted to say yes. Hell, she just wanted to *speak*. Muñoz's finger stayed taut on the trigger. *Save Daniel. Beg, promise, lie, whatever it takes to save your baby.* But that required the capacity for speech which currently abandoned her.

Behind Muñoz, she saw glimpses of people on their feet. Sanchez and Brozek must have corralled the rebellious family members who'd left their seats again to help her. For whatever reason Brozek allowed her sister to venture closer. "*Answer us,*" Georgia wept, "*please.*"

Ennis peeked around Muñoz's shoulder. By a nose, he placed second to Georgia in the race to see if the cop killer's shot hit its mark. Blood trickled from the corner of his mouth down his chin. Sanchez stood ready to deliver another debilitating blow with the rifle butt but decided to scream at the kids to shut them up instead.

"*Savannah, say something,*" a distraught Ennis demanded over the chaos. He sounded half-crazy and if she waited to answer she felt pretty sure he'd get killed trying to find out her condition.

Two hushed, trembling words fell from her lips. "I'm okay." She hated herself for lying but if she'd admitted the truth, someone – either Ennis or Georgia – *would* get mowed down for attacking Muñoz. No, she wasn't okay at all. The notch on her hand meant nothing. The now familiar, low-level ache marching across her back did and it intensified the longer she stared into the barrel's black abyss.

"Muñoz," Hadley griped, "you nearly shot me."

"Keep talking," he maintained solid eye contact with Savannah, "and it won't be 'nearly' next time."

The ache in her throat and jaw returned.  Savannah resigned herself to either Muñoz or her heart expediting her departure because those pills in her pocket might as well have been on the moon.

Muñoz moved just enough to allow his audience to watch him hold the muzzle mere inches from her right eye.  The family's aggressive attempts to reach her resulted in Sanchez getting a workout swinging the rifle and taking down the "heroes" as he called them.

For Savannah, the room shrank to two people, just her and the enraged killer.  Her lungs pulled for air but Muñoz loomed overhead robbing her of space while her body rebelled.  Her runaway heart pumped ice water through her body.  The meager breath she struggled for fought its way past her constricting throat and seemed to vanish.  "P-please," she stammered.  "Wait."  Her eyes tightened to prepare for a very loud, messy *no*.  The wait lasted forever and in the meantime the ache plaguing her spread and deepened.

His narrowed blue eyes gave him a feral, almost wolfish look, "You want another chance, don't you?"

She nodded.  The girls' crying ebbed to quiet weeping.  She heard Georgia and Gina attempting to settle them down.  No promises of "it'll be okay" though.  Savannah soon discovered how *not* okay it was...

Muñoz handed down the verdict, "Sorry.  No more chances."

"Hold on, Luis," Brozek called.  "She's learned her lesson, haven't you, Sergeant?"

Brozek's intervention dumbfounded her.  What child molester sacrificed an opportunity to get rid of the parents?  Only Alan Brozek.

Savannah nodded while fighting the instinct to close her eyes in case Muñoz carried out her death sentence.

The gun pressed against her forehead. "Say it. Say you've learned your lesson because I promise, next time I don't care if God tells me to stop, I'm killing you."

"I-I-unders," she swallowed hard and concentrated on speaking clearly. This wasn't the time for misunderstandings. "I know you will." To illustrate her point, she once more extended her shaking hands, wrists crossed, as a sign of surrender.

"Well, well, well," there was a smile in Sanchez's voice, "look at the big shot cop now."

Muñoz ignored his colleague but never moved an inch, "Brozek, tie this bitch up."

Brozek did as he was told. Once satisfied, Muñoz backed off. Savannah closed her eyes. Tears of relief slid from them. She concentrated on deep breathing but the angina (she prayed that's all it was) prevented it. It figured, she lamented. Saved from execution only to die of a heart attack.

Everyone was staring at her when her eyes opened. Georgia noticed her wincing with each breath. Savannah strove for that brave face people spoke of. Somehow she just couldn't muster it. Receding adrenaline exhausted her, leaving pain and worry in its wake. Daniel hadn't moved in the last several minutes. How much could a tiny human bear without repercussions? The intense confrontation weakened the dam of emotion and allowed the first tears to flow. She quietly cried, praying her stupidity hadn't harmed her baby boy.

Mama reached for her. If Savannah stretched, her mother-in-law sat within touching distance. The instant Mama's gentle grasp curled around her shaking hands, the dam of tears completely crumbled.

Jenny Lee centered on her. She seemed shocked to see Savannah openly weep.

Yes, was Savannah's fleeting thought, the "big shot cop" can cry rivers too.

Georgia caught her sister's eye. Her expression conveyed a mixture of sympathy and concern. "Are you okay?" she whispered.

Savannah nodded but if Daniel didn't pull through, she wouldn't be okay at all. *Forgive me, little one, I never should have put you at risk. Please forgive me.*

"Toss me the sergeant's phone," Muñoz told Hadley.

Savannah watched the smart phone sail over her as Hadley underhanded it to his cohort.

Muñoz powered up the phone which surprisingly chimed with voicemail messages. So it wasn't the storm preventing Joe Bob from reaching his sister. She'd simply turned her phone off or the battery ran down. Savannah bet on the former. Jenny Lee had an objective yesterday and it wasn't shooting the breeze with her brother or friends. No, she busied herself playing nursemaid and bartender to Ennis. Savannah also powered her phone down early to dedicate her full attention to him and in the process she missed a few messages.

Muñoz seemed impressed, "You're very popular. What's your voicemail passcode? I want to hear what your friends have to say."

Savannah gave him the code. He accessed voicemail then punched the speakerphone. A cheery greeting lilted into the room.

Sonya Porter, a friend from church, wanted Savannah's opinion on her new fundraiser idea and would she be interested in teaming up together for it. Yes, Savannah thought, if I'm still alive.

Next, a concerned Josh Hunter (hers and Ennis's captain) wanted an update on the storm and to know if they needed extra vacation time. Try forever, if these guys get their way, she mumbled under her breath.

Seth left a brief message saying all was well back home and to please let Georgia and Dane know.

Another was her OB/GYN's office rescheduling her appointment later the following week. Savannah prayed she and Daniel arrived for that new appointment.

John Mathis wrapped up the voicemails with a late-night ten thirty call. While Savannah fretted over her drunk hubby, their colleague tried warning them of impending danger. "Hey, Sarge. I know you and Rutherford are having a blast in Green Acres–"

Heat scalded her cheeks. She looked away from the family. They did not know Mathis the way she and Ennis did and probably took umbrage (even a little) at his phrasing. His idea of humor often offended others while Savannah and Ennis took it at face value and overlooked his rough attempt at wit. Still, she felt the sting of John's sharp words as sure as the family did.

"...another driver reported a car matching the stolen 4Runner passing through Amarillo. You two stay safe. Don't come back dead..."

A chuckle rumbled from Muñoz's throat, "Glad you didn't check your messages. Let's see what else you got on this phone."

Ennis mumbled to Sanchez. The latter pointed to Savannah, "He wants to know if she can sit on the couch with the others."

Muñoz frowned, "She stays. Consider it a very long time-out for bad behavior."

Minutes passed. Cold perspiration squeezed from her pores, dampened her hair, and began lining her forehead and back. The molten band burned across her back and adding to the misery, nausea arrived to the party.

The nitroglycerin's siren song grew louder. *Take a chance, Savannah. You'll feel better...* But sneaking one was the problem. If her family didn't see her, Hadley would since he practically sat behind her. Considering his earlier "have fun, sweetheart" comment about shoveling, she doubted he'd be as charitable as Brozek. *Just try. You're suffering and apparently it's only going to get worse.*

Georgia aimed her green eyes with such laser precision that Savannah squirmed. Her sister knew something was wrong. Of course anyone with two brain cells could tell that. Not many people enjoyed lying in the floor sweating and fighting for breath while curbing the urge to puke.

Georgia tapped her heart. Savannah was too miserable to hide it. She nodded. Her sister looked at Muñoz, about to speak. Savannah cleared her throat. Georgia turned back to see her sister pat her pocket. *I have the pills.* She cut her vision toward Hadley. *But he'll see me if I try for them.*

Georgia pursed her lips as she glanced at Brozek. Would he help, she seemed to ask. Savannah shrugged.

Unaware of the silent communication between the two, Muñoz

continued searching the phone, thumbing screen to screen after studying each application. "Nice phone. I like the pictures." Amused, he held it for everyone to see, "That's a hell of a sweater you're wearing there."

Savannah tried concealing her distress but the words strained past her constricting throat, "A present from the girls." She, Georgia and Leah wore colorful festive sweaters on Christmas Day. Lily and Anna spotted the garish attire on a shopping trip and put up a howl for them. The sweaters probably fell into the "ugly" category for some folks but Savannah opted for "cheerful" for her girls' sakes. Her daughters allocated one for their mama and the other two for their aunts. Snowmen adorned Savannah's powder blue sweater. For Georgia they designated the red sweater with white snowflakes and Leah a flashy red one showing a Christmas tree with so many vibrant colors, it looked like Santa's workshop exploded on her. Lily and Anna gussied up in their own holiday sweaters chosen by their considerably more conservative mother. The men of course wore their usual jeans and flannel shirts. That photo captured the essence of a perfect family Christmas. Everyone was relaxed and flashed their best smiles.

Muñoz cocked a brow, "Hope you enjoyed that Christmas. It was your last one."

"Excuse me," Georgia called Muñoz. Savannah nearly died on the spot. As if she and Monty hadn't stirred up enough trouble already, here came well-intentioned Georgia who would get an ass-kicking too.

"What?" he snapped. "I'm busy."

"I'd like to check on my sister."

"No."

"Luis," Brozek argued. "Let her do it. She hasn't been any problem."

"What are you?" Muñoz lashed out at his buddy. "Their patron saint? I said no."

"What about me?" Ennis asked. "Can I check on her?"

Muñoz glared, "Not a chance."

Fear drove her to reach out for Mama again. She gladly met her halfway, taking Savannah's cold, shaking hands in her warm, steady grasp. Many years ago Mama had witnessed her husband suffer a fatal heart attack in that very room. She recognized the signs and realized the urgency of getting help quick. Since that appeared rather unlikely, she provided words of comfort and reassurance and with each one, Savannah sensed Mama reliving her beloved's last moments.

Muñoz sneered at the two, rolled his eyes then began tapping the phone's screen, hunting and pecking his way around. "Let's see what the sergeant's been trolling on the internet."

What had it been? Ten minutes? Maybe twenty since she climbed out of trouble? Some sort of record for her that day because once Muñoz saw her "trolling", she'd be right back in that smelly creek without a paddle. She counted the seconds. *One... Two... Three... Four...*

"Uh-oh." Muñoz glanced from the screen to her, "This isn't good, is it? Hey, Brozek. Sarge had your number before you got here. She was checking you out."

Brozek leaned closer to the phone in his colleague's grasp, squinted at the article and his mugshot beside it. His expression clouded with a new emotion for Brozek. Indignation. He scowled at Savannah as if she'd cursed at him. Well, she assumed, that bridge is officially burned.

Muñoz delighted in heaving more gasoline on the inflammatory subject. "For a chickenshit, you're a really bad dude," his vision cut to Lily and Anna, "at least with young girls. Man, you are one sick bastard."

Brozek was too angry to speak. Muñoz merrily continued, this time reading the article aloud. In that time Brozek and Savannah squared off in a staring contest that she intended to win despite her misery. Yes, she checked him and the others out. Who wouldn't?

The story kindled Hadley's interest, "Get to the important parts, Muñoz. What does it say?"

"In a nutshell, Alan John Brozek was sent away for life after diddling a five-year-old in unimaginable ways. Ol' Sarge would blast him apart if he tried that shit on her kids. Am I right?"

There was no hesitation. Savannah nodded. Heart attack or not, she'd spend her dying breath protecting her children.

Muñoz nudged Brozek, "That look she's giving you is another incentive to keep her under control." He scrolled down, kept reading. "You strangled the kid, stuffed her in a bag full of bricks then tossed her in a lake?" He gave the child killer a look of utter disbelief, "Where the hell did you find bricks?"

On that, Savannah made damn sure Brozek understood her feelings. *Touch my kids and I'll rip your throat out.* Oh yes, his expression acknowledged. They understood each other perfectly now. "I worked construction," he answered, "I had easy access."

Muñoz's homicidal side resurfaced again, "You're genuinely sick, Brozek. If they'd put you in with me, my cell woulda been a single occupant by nightfall."

It was nice to see someone else taking the heat for once. What better person than a child molester?

Brozek's temper fired, "We'd still be in that shithole if I hadn't befriended those guards."

"And now that we're out," Muñoz spelled it out plain and simple, "your days are numbered, you deviant son of a bitch."

"There are children present. At least take the conversation out of the room," Mama's bearish side emerged again. Savannah winced, waiting for Muñoz to throw a shot at her.

Sanchez stalked toward her only for Muñoz to wave him off, "The old lady's right. I don't wanna hear Brozek whine any more than they do." He stabbed a finger at Brozek, "I can't stand you," then at Savannah, "and I can't stand her. Therefore, you are her keeper. Don't screw it up." He motioned to Hadley, "You. With me. Let's check out this map application and find another route to your brother's. Eventually we gotta get outta here."

The two sequestered themselves to the kitchen. They spoke in low, secretive tones that prevented eavesdropping. Brozek jerked Savannah's hands free from Mama's then stood guard beside her, silent and brooding.

Inches separated suffering from (she hoped) sweet relief. She planned to take advantage of the four fewer eyes in the room when Brozek wasn't watching.

For now she pulled at the air, willing it to fill her lungs and calm her heart. Desperation prodded, *begged* her to take reckless chances – except Brozek glanced down with annoying regularity. Moving her hands would draw his attention. If he caught her reaching in her pocket, well, the mere possibility of losing those precious pills was too excruciating to contemplate. But oh Lord, she was so everlastingly miserable. *Is it worth having Brozek maybe confiscate the bottle as payback? Which is worse – a heart attack or a bullet in the head? One might kill you, the other means Bye-Bye Butterfly.* She tried to shake clarity back, to rid herself of the pessimism. *You didn't kiss Muñoz's ass for the hell of it. You did it to survive. Take a chance, try for the pills. If the perv catches you, at least you tried…*

"Why do you let him bully you?" Georgia asked Brozek.

Who cares, Savannah asked herself. Does it matter? Georgia tipped her head in a small nod to her sister just before Brozek looked up to answer. Her big sis provided the diversion needed to maybe sneak some relief. Savannah nearly cried while whispering *thank you.*

"You've seen him," Brozek replied. "He's not above shooting anyone, including me."

Careful, she repeated to herself. Be careful and he won't notice the movement. She eased her hands toward the pocket. No sudden moves. Her fingers slipped in. The prospect of relief urged her to hurry but her hands began trembling. So close. So damn close. *Keep him talking, sis.*

"Why not stand up to him? After all, you're the reason the escape worked."

The index and middle fingers coaxed and pulled the bottle toward her palm. Her thumb closed safely around it, cocooning it in her fist.

Resentment crept into his voice, "I came up with the whole plan. He was eager enough to listen and participate but won't give me credit for it."

*Slowly withdraw your hand. That's it. Nearly there...*

Fingertips dug into her wrist. Brozek wrenched her hand from the pocket and pried at her closed fist. He used surprising strength in the battle for her lifeline but despite her distress, she held on. The struggle ended with his brutal backhand. "Not feeling well?" he taunted while pocketing the bottle. "Too bad. Lie there and suffer." He glared at Georgia, "And you, Auntie. Don't try anything else."

"There's nothing to gain by denying her the medication," Georgia's anger mounted. "Show some empathy. Your friends certainly don't have any."

"Please help Mama." Tears streaked Lily's cheeks. Her sniffling plea sounded as scared as Savannah felt.

If anyone stood a chance of changing Brozek's mind it was Lily however a tiny pill wasn't worth her daughter's innocence. The thought of her or Anna being alone with him caused the pain to worsen. A moan slipped out before she could contain it.

"*Please help her,*" Lily begged him.

And just like that Alan Brozek changed. He smiled warmth and sweetness to the little girl desperate to help her mother, "If I help your mom, I'll be doing you a favor. You understand that, right?"

"Lily, don't," Savannah struggled to sound normal. "I'll be fine. Don't ask him for anything."

Brozek's foot nudged her hip, "Shut up, Mom. This is between me and Lily." The hook was in but he needed to set it. A dash of charm, a cup full of sugar and the promise of Mom feeling better and he could reel Lily in. "Sweetheart, if I do you a favor, you have to do one for me."

The family campaigned to Brozek to give Savannah the medicine and leave Lily alone. The din of demands melded into a nonsensical, noisy stew.

"Lily," Savannah called. The family immediately quieted down, waiting.

She swallowed, willing strength back to her voice. She wanted to sound authoritative. Instead, she sounded pathetically frail, "Lily, please say no. You don't know..." she struggled for breath, "what he'll ask for. I do." Somehow Dumbo found his way on her chest. He pressed down, squeezing her lungs and forcing her to speak in short, strained hitches. "He's dangerous." How can I make her understand? How can I get this child to associate Brozek with evil? "He's worse than That Man last summer." Lily christened Jeffrey Holland with a new name last July. That Man. If anything stood a chance of helping the child comprehend the danger Brozek posed, that might. "He's *worse* than That Man... I want you safe... more than I want... the medicine."

Georgia, Gina and Ennis (as best he could) bounded from their seats first, followed by Dane and Mama. Cal, Jake and Monty weren't far behind. They meant to help Savannah one way or another.

A shot fired into the ceiling. It surprised Sanchez when no one obeyed his warning. They split forces, Ennis, Georgia, Mama and Gina headed toward Brozek. The others charged Sanchez.

Muñoz stormed into the room, "Whoever isn't sitting down in three seconds will be dead in four."

"All of you sit down," Savannah pleaded. Her mind played horrific images of her whole family dying just to save her and that drove the pain deeper. She pressed her fists to her heart, praying for the pain to recede, "Thanks, but please... sit down."

Gun in hand, Brozek shooed the four back. They begrudgingly returned to their seats while appealing to him to at least surrender the medicine.

Sanchez gifted each of his aggressors with a shove toward the couch.

Muñoz shook his head at Brozek, "Can't you do anything right? I leave for a minute and there's a riot." He informed the group, "I'm keeping your asses alive for a reason but these little girls? They can't shovel snow or chop firewood. Think about that, heroes." He turned and left the room.

Between the gunfire, skirmish and yelling, Lily cowered beside Bobbi who'd taken custody of the girls in that time. The girl's urgency brought the moment back into focus, "Mama needs her pills." She ordered Brozek, "Give her the pills."

From lion to lamb, Brozek reminded, "If I do I'll want that favor from you."

"Okay," she agreed before Savannah could say a word. Lily wanted to help and she knew only one way to do it. "Now help Mama," the girl finished with the diplomacy of a drill sergeant.

A sick, triumphant smile crawled across his features, "Yes, let's get Mama some help." He opened the bottle, shook out a pill out and leaned down. "Open up, Mama. Your little girl worked hard for this. Or will."

Anger and Dumbo worked in concert to steal even more breath. If it wasn't a heart attack before, it probably would be now. "Touch her and... I'll kill you... Somehow I will."

"Not in this shape you won't. Do you want the pill or not? Seems a shame to waste Lily's efforts." He taunted, "And you do look awful."

"Take it, Savannah," Ennis called from across the room.

"Yeah," said Jake. "We'll take care of the girls. Don't worry." That was easier said than done. He certainly sounded convincing but considering how the day progressed, she wondered how they'd successfully prevent Brozek from collecting on that favor.

Georgia brought Lily into her lap, "Take it, sweetie. We've got your babies."

Savannah felt tears slide from her eyes as she met Lily's gaze. Her innocent little face conveyed wide-eyed hope and a hint of a smile that she'd helped her mother.

Savannah's lips parted. She lifted her tongue. Brozek dropped the pill in then closed her mouth with a finger beneath her trembling chin. "There you go," he smiled back at Lily. "Everything's all better now."

## 15

If Brozek wanted her to suffer, she had, just not the way he'd initially intended. He capitalized on the nitroglycerin pills, holding them hostage for his favors. A "little" favor in return for one of "Mama's little pills". The bastard wanted to hand them out like candy now, repeatedly asking Savannah if she needed another one. Was she sure? Lily hated to see her mama in pain, he said, so anytime she needed one he'd "be happy to do Lily another favor".

The ache retreated to a nagging one like glowing embers of a dying fire but she would tear her own heart out before asking for or accepting another pill. No matter the level of pain or how weak the attacks left her, it paled in comparison to what lay ahead for Lily if Savannah requested more medication.

Her heart ached for a different reason now. Her beautiful daughter. To save her mama, the innocent girl agreed to Brozek's favor that he yearned to collect. Savannah concentrated on recouping her strength for that moment. If she died trying to protect her little girl, she'd use the meeting with God to ask her own favor regarding the four murdering assholes.

At one o'clock, Muñoz assigned Tyler then Zach to shovel the back walk like she had. Only their stay lasted twenty minutes, not forty, and they had the benefit of coats, gloves and hats to protect them. Savannah thanked God they did.

By two o'clock Muñoz granted her supervised parole and assigned Brozek as her warden. Don't get cocky, Muñoz warned, because her job was to "shut those damn kids up". Since the gunfire earlier, they recoiled and cried when he neared, raised his voice or waved the gun "willy-nilly" as Mama said earlier.

Savannah returned to her seat between Georgia and Gina. Lily and Anna migrated from Bobbi and Georgia to their places beside their mother. Muñoz seemed to relax.

The two angina attacks sapped her strength but this time recovery came slower. Nothing felt normal yet. Not her breathing, aching back or tight throat. A profound fatigue threatened to deplete the last of her energy. She vowed to use her meager reserves only in a dire emergency because it might be her last stand.

There was a special kind of hell apart from being held captive by killers. It was CNN. When the satellite reception worked, the channel aired repetitive commercials and recapped the "top stories" with such frequency Savannah caught herself memorizing them. She and Ennis avoided news channels at home. They dealt with plenty of bad news at work so why add to it? Plus they refused to expose their children to the world's evil, yet here it stood in the same room.

The dreary sky showed no reprieve from the snow. The wind

died down from the howling "Big Bad Wolf" (as Anna called it) to an occasional sorrowful moan.    Sanchez frequented the picture window, bemoaning aloud his wishes that Mother Nature switched off the snow soon. *Mother Nature's a bitch, and not an obedient one either* was John Mathis's mantra, usually after being drenched in a torrential rainstorm. Savannah could only imagine his thoughts on this winter calamity.

Anna and Lily snuggled tight beside Savannah who held their hands hoping to discourage Brozek.  He'd propped against the stairway railing watching Lily with a lustful, almost predatory gaze.  Savannah had seen the look before.  Years ago a deviant named Lonnie Pryor sat in the interview room staring at his victim's photo the same way.  It was her first child molestation/homicide case as a detective and she and Mathis showed Lonnie how they felt about that smile of his.  Once they taught him a lesson they turned his cellmates loose on him.  She recalled that day with Mathis, how sore her hand felt when they finished with Lonnie. The anger building in her while the simpering child rapist slumped on the table, begging for mercy.  She never claimed to be a perfect police officer but what decent human being didn't want to bust their knuckles on a degenerate who hurt and killed kids?  If Alan Brozek so much as touched her girls she'd do more than give him a beat down.  She'd bury him.  If she dropped from a heart attack or a bullet, the family would pick up where she left off.

Brozek ambled over to Muñoz and mumbled in his ear.  She tensed in her seat, preparing to confront him if he mentioned that "favor" again.

Muñoz's annoyance flared, "What's your problem, Brozek?

They're finally quiet."

Another mumble. Muñoz rolled his eyes, "If they get loud again, you pay for it."

Brozek started toward Lily. Round one had begun. The girl drew back, grasped Savannah's sweater and buried her face in it.

Shortly after she sat down with the girls, Savannah reinforced again how Brozek was worse than "That Man" last summer. This time using Lily's code name for Holland worked. Judging by their wide-eyed expressions using the nickname finally sparked the fear associated with Jeffrey.

Leaning on his knees, Brozek sounded more like "Uncle Alan", not the man who dropped his victim's body in a lake weighted down with bricks, "Don't be scared, Lily. I'm not going to hurt you. I want to be your friend."

If Lily curled any tighter she'd disappear, Savannah thought. "She's got enough friends." And they don't molest her.

He barely concealed an emerging scowl and focused on the little girl cowering from him. In a blink Mr. Molester vanished and "Uncle Alan" returned, "You wanna play Crazy 8s?" He removed a colorful deck of cards from his hip pocket. Cards illustrated with cartoon bears, lions and elephants.

Great. While the others gathered provisions and guns during their murderous spree across Texas, Brozek browsed the aisles for children's games.

"If you don't like that game, I've got Go Fish."

The small fists twisted harder in Savannah's sweater, anchoring herself to her mother.

"She doesn't want to play," Savannah answered for her.

"Lighten up, Mom," he countered, "I want to play cards with her."

*I'm a cop and a mother. You can't fool me, asshole.* "Let's ask Lily what she wants. Lily, do you want to play cards with That Man?"

"No."

"Now, Lily," a hint of authority laced his soft voice. "You owe me that favor."

That one comment did wonders for Savannah's adrenaline. If he kept pushing Lily, Mama Bear lurked close to the surface, reenergized with rage and ready to attack. She spaced the words evenly, "She owes you nothing."

Brozek's features hardened. He took a moment to remind her, "I have your pills. If you don't shut up, I'll pour them down the sink."

She stared, unblinking. *Here's a better idea. Let's you and I go outside, just the two of us, and I'll make Lonnie Pryor's beating look like a day at the beach.*

His persona switched back to the Good Ol' Uncle Alan persona as he tweaked Lily's sneaker toe, "C'mon on, let's have fun together."

She shook her head.

He stroked Lily's hair. She slapped his hand away. "Brozek," Savannah warned out of Muñoz's earshot. She came close to grabbing him by the throat and squeezing until his eyeballs shot across the room.

He curled a strand of hair behind Lily's ear, trying to coax her out of hiding.

"Brozek, I mean it," Savannah teetered on going ballistic. "Leave her alone." Every part of her daughter he touched was foreplay to molestation. He probably figured after two bouts of angina Savannah lacked the strength to fight him now. If she fought him, she'd make it count. *It doesn't take a lot of power to throat punch someone so don't push it.*

The Uncle Alan mask came off. *Try it, bitch,* those eyes dared. *Try and stop me.* His voice belied his expression, "It's alright, Lily. Mom doesn't mind if we sit right in front of her and play. Do you, Mom?"

*Oh, let's see. I mind it as much as being awake for an appendectomy.*

"Can't you leave Lily alone?" Georgia asked. "She doesn't like strangers."

The offending hand dropped to Lily's thigh.

Savannah struck fast. Her fingers dug deep into his wrist, "Do not touch her."

Muñoz stepped in with the .45, "There you go exercising your big mouth again." He yanked her to her feet so violently it knocked Lily to the floor beside Brozek.

No one liked Brozek. Not her, not the family and none of his cohorts so surely Muñoz could understand, "I don't want that pervert near my girls."

Brozek reached for Lily but she slapped and flailed like a swarm of bees attacked her. She clambered into Georgia's lap. Georgia held her close, warning Brozek, "Don't even think about it."

Savannah shoved Brozek back. His eyes flew wide either from surprise at her strength or shock she'd actually pushed him. He stumbled back then tripped over Gina's legs that she'd conveniently stretched into his path. He landed on his back (and his .45) with a pained grunt.

He cringed up at Savannah, pulled the gun from the back of his jeans just as something collided against the side of her head and sent her to her knees. The others tried forewarning her about Muñoz but rage consumed her until the sucker-punch took her down.

The Rutherford brothers – Ennis in particular – stormed Sanchez but the cocky Hispanic wielded the assault rifle with a brutal vengeance and swung it dead center into Ennis's diaphragm then followed up on Jake. Both ended up on their knees heaving for breath. In their own effort to help their sister-in-law, Cal and Dane got two steps further before meeting the same fate.

When she looked up, Savannah stared back at two guns. Muñoz towered over her, his .45 aimed straight at her nose. Beside him, Brozek – on his feet again – braced his hip with one hand while the other jammed the gun against her temple.

Muñoz seethed, "Step away, Brozek. She's mine."

Brozek cursed his compadre (and her) but followed orders. It must have dawned on him that he had carte blanche with the girls because he eyed Lily with such deep, lustful desire that Savannah doubled her fist.

"You got bigger worries than those brats." Using the gun barrel, Muñoz redirected her attention to him, "Because your license to live just expired, Sergeant."

"She was protecting her girls. Any parent would." Georgia spoke so fast Savannah barely recognized her, "You shouldn't hold that against her."

The .45 aimed at her. Georgia flinched and tucked Lily's head down in case he fired. He didn't. "You wanna die too?" he asked. "Keep talking."

"Georgia," Dane shushed her.

Savannah agreed with him. One of the sisters should have a chance at surviving this hell. Muñoz decided Savannah's fate the moment he discovered her occupation. Someone should be around to help Ennis raise the girls (should he survive), to teach them the ways of womanhood and things a daddy couldn't.

Her vision dropped to the .45. The haunting tattoo spanning the width of his chest came to mind. The large, gothic-style letters reading "F*CK THE POLICE" – with the expletive spelled in all its profane glory – along with the graphic image of a 9mm blowing a cop's brains out the back of his skull. Her imminent demise unless God granted her another stay of execution.

"But she–"

"Georgia, don't." Savannah fought to steady her voice, "Thanks but don't." No one could reason, bargain or beg him enough to save her, he'd made that crystal clear.

The .45 whipped back to Savannah, "Get up."

Brozek assisted in his own callous way. His fingertips burrowed between tendon and bone when he yanked her upright by the arm. It set off a rush of numbness from her shoulder to her hand that she'd not felt since the surgery last summer.

He jerked her closer then leaned to her ear, "I'm gonna have a party with your kids. And once I'm finished, I'm gonna cut their throats and burn 'em up, just like those kids in Decatur."

Brozek was an enigma. Other men emasculated him with one look but let one woman stand up to him and magically he grew a pair of danglies. He was about to learn this woman had her own pair, only these were made of brass. And if she died, she'd leave plenty of damage in her wake.

She launched her elbow into his nose. Brozek unleashed an almost girlish shriek when he staggered back. Blood seeped between the fingers cupping his nose. Tears trailed down his unshaven cheeks.

"You touch my kids," she put him on notice, "and you can kill me a hundred times and I'll come back just to send you to hell–"

Muñoz's fingers bore down around her throat like a dog going in for the kill. The pressure fell short of closing her airway or cutting off the blood but it did get her attention.

Muñoz smiled into her rounded eyes as his grasp raised her to tiptoe, "I'll shut you up. Open your mouth, bitch."

An ice cold swell of terror crashed against her heart and drained into her stomach.

Muñoz's smile broadened. He craved to see her fear and feel her tremble in his grasp and she fed that appetite very well.

She barely heard Ennis and the family begging Muñoz for clemency. Her heartbeat bounded in her chest, neck and ears. The plaguing backache made an impressive comeback. It progressed like a bomb's lit fuse, traveling across her back and into her jaw. The burning sensation felt akin to a severe sunburn. Fragmented thoughts flew through her mind. *Heart attack or bullet? Bullet's messy. Blood. Hard to clean blood. The girls will see. Can't help but see. And Daniel. Daniel.* Savannah's eyes swam with tears. *Our precious son will die.*

Ennis struggled to his feet after Sanchez's beatdown. He proposed a deal – *my life to spare hers.*

"Ennis," Jenny Lee cried, "no."

Muñoz rounded on her, thrust the .45 at her and laughed when she recoiled, blubbering *please don't shoot me.*

"Gimme a reason not to."

"B-b-because I didn't do anything." Jenny pointed straight at Savannah, "She did. She's the one c-causing trouble. D-don't shoot *me,* shoot–" her mouth snapped shut in midsentence, as if realizing how it sounded – or would sound had she finished it.

Savannah's breath and strength abandoned her. Her knees felt loose. *Don't shoot me, shoot her,* Jenny nearly said.

In the history of betrayals, Jenny's fell far down the list from Judas but somewhere in the neighborhood between Brutus and Benedict Arnold – at least to the woman sentenced to die. Savannah felt betrayed and screwed to the center of the earth. Jenny never minced words about her feelings toward her but to endorse her execution?

Amid the outrage spreading throughout the room, Jake sat pale and shell-shocked as if his fiancée knifed him in the chest.

Unbridled fury spurred Ennis into a wild fight. He thrashed against Cal and Dane's best efforts to hold him back.

Savannah barely recognized her husband when he vowed, "Jenny, I'm gonna kill you. I'll take you apart with my bare hands for this."

"And if there's anything left, I'll finish you off," Georgia vowed to Jenny. The only thing keeping her from bolting at the traitor was Lily who'd retreated to the safety of her lap.

The clamor continued until Muñoz turned to Savannah, "I said open your mouth." He aimed past her shoulder at Georgia and Lily, "Or that kid gets your bullet. You choose. Let's see whose ass you *protect and serve* today. Hers or yours."

"What did you expect a mother to do?" Another Mama Bear heard from. Caroline proceeded, "Why punish her for protecting her babies against a man even *you* detest?"

Muñoz's blue eyes shifted from Savannah to Mama. To normal people she posed a valid question. To the crazy about to blow a person's brains out, not so much. "Because I hate cops worse." He prodded the gun toward Lily, "Hers or yours, Sergeant."

Her lips parted slowly. The .45's cold barrel rammed in her mouth. It nudged the back of her throat, gagging her. Through watery vision she forced herself to maintain eye contact, wordlessly pleading for him not to pull the trigger, especially in front of her kids and family.

The men acted en masse once more against Sanchez and Muñoz. Cal managed to swat the assault rifle's aim askew then level Sanchez with a blow across the chin. Sanchez collapsed but somehow kept hold of the gun even as Dane wrestled him for it.

Muñoz fisted Savannah's sweater and pulled her closer as a shield. "Brozek, shoot her husband. Maybe they'll finally get the message."

The gun muffled Savannah's cry. Muñoz found her effort humorous, "Wait, Brozek. Let's see what Sarge wants these heroes to do."

Sanchez was on his feet. Muñoz turned Savannah partway. By cutting her vision to the side she could see the men within three painfully close steps of her. They'd nearly made it. Nearly.

She relied on hand gestures. Palms down, her shaking hands motioned them to sit. They refused. Scared and frustrated, she tried again, this time with more vehemence. The group stood their ground.

Sanchez sounded all too eager, "Okay, hubby. Looks like you go first." He raised the assault rifle.

Furious, Savannah screamed another emphatic warning. The barrel trapped her tongue, making it impossible to articulate. She struggled to form words without gagging – *Sit down!* She blinked tears from her eyes that locked on Ennis. *Please,* she motioned again, *sit down.* She couldn't say *at least try to leave our kids one parent* but according to his expression he understood.

Muñoz didn't wait for compliance. He pushed on the gun, "Walk, Sergeant. We're going outside."

Savannah stumbled backwards to keep up his pace. A frantic glance at her family revealed anger, frustration but mostly heartbreak. They continued fighting Sanchez, Brozek and now Hadley who stood between them and Savannah.

She couldn't bear to watch her sister's composure crumble as Georgia handed Lily off to Gina to join the fray. Bobbi cradled Anna, keeping the girl's face turned away. Savannah would die without one last look at her babies.

For a brief instant she and Muñoz established a harmonious stride, him walking forward and her backward from the living room toward the mudroom.

Bedlam broke out as they left, some calling her name and others pleading with Muñoz to spare her. Savannah heard scuffles and threats. Ennis repeatedly called for her until something (Sanchez more than likely) abruptly cut him off midway through her name. The girls screamed for both her and now their daddy.

Muñoz smiled when Savannah lost her footing and struggled to stay up. He added another incentive to their jaunt, "The gun comes out and I shoot you where you stand. Stay up with me... That's it. Very good."

She moved by memory to clear obstacles, sometimes misjudging distance and objects, all while wishing her hands were free to aid her already clumsy journey. In her haste to match his speed and stride, her elbow had struck the banister, her shoulders bumped walls and her heels clipped a threshold that came terrifyingly close to tripping her.

He smiled, "Watch your step, Sergeant. Falls can kill."

Along the way she battled the instinctive urge to wretch as the cumbersome .45 tapped and scraped the back of her throat. Then her back slammed into the mudroom's door jamb. She heaved.

The commotion in the living room grew louder. A frantic Brozek rushed in, temporarily halting the pair's trek outside. "This won't work, Luis. It's already a mutiny in there. What'll happen when they hear a gunshot?"

Muñoz couldn't care less about mutinies, "They'll think twice about screwing with us."

Judging by the uproar behind Brozek, the big ol' Rutherford brothers made little Alan pee his pants. Them and the roomful of Steel Magnolias ready to string him up by his doodahs with Mama's yarn. Brozek interacted with kids, not people who could kick his sorry ass to the moon.

Brozek cast a nervous glance behind him, "Don't shoot her. Leave her outside. We're in the boonies. She'll die before she finds help or it finds her."

The execution's delay aggravated Muñoz, "Get in there and take control before Sanchez kills them. If he does, you two become the workhorses around here. Ask this one how much fun shoveling snow is, right, Sarge?" He nudged the gun to get her moving again.

Savannah stumbled through the mudroom entry until her rear bumped the back door. She'd spent the trek terrified she'd trip or he'd pull the trigger. To her surprise Muñoz slid the .45 from her mouth, motioned her to turn, "Open the door."

It took two tries to slide the deadbolt back with her trembling hands. The gun pressed to the back of her head as a prompt to hurry.

The inner door creaked open to reveal a blinding white landscape as far as the eye could see. Only the steps and a deep depression on the porch marked Tyler and Zach's shoveling efforts.

An involuntary shiver shuddered through her. Standing there watch the snow and wind, she had one thought. *No one should die like this.* Then she recalled slipping on the icy porch steps that morning. It was a sign of hope.

Muñoz reached past, threw the door open. The .45 jabbed her in the back. She gingerly stepped onto the porch, keeping a tight grasp on the bitter cold railing. As expected her foot slid an inch or two forward. Savannah regained her balance quickly before baby-stepping down one step then another but kept a keen ear tuned behind her.

Muñoz's first step proved as treacherous as hers earlier. His boots skated on the ice. Savannah seized the opportunity and while he flailed for balance, she reached back, grabbed the scruff of his neck then clanged his forehead off the railing and shoved him down the steps.

The gun flew from his hand and sailed into a drift. Muñoz scrambled to no avail. As he went down, the side of his noggin slammed the railing's corner before he landed facedown on the porch.

Savannah hurried down the steps. The black .45 shined from the sea of white near the motionless killer. She wanted that weapon in *her* hand for once.

Muñoz expelled a groan as he pushed to his knees. Blood stained the icy, snow-covered concrete. Snow clung to his hair and dazed features. He glanced over his shoulder. A gash on his forehead dripped blood. He wiped his eyes to clear his vision then saw her scrambling toward the nearby drift.

The two plunged their hands into the snow at the same time. Four hands scrabbled for the .45. She claimed second prize by grabbing the barrel and Muñoz won the jackpot when his finger curled around the trigger. The tussle for the weapon quickly tipped in his favor when his other hand joined the contest. The man was a mutant. After taking a hit to the forehead and another to the temple, he still rallied enough muscle to almost overpower her. "Almost" gradually disappeared from the equation. His grip solidified and the gun slowly, steadily turn toward her. Instead of gaining an edge over Muñoz, she now channeled her energy into avoiding being shot while battling the spreading ache in her back and throat.

Slick and cold with snow, the barrel started slipping from her grasp. Muñoz's strength surpassed hers, pulling at the gun while angling it in her direction. Desperate for an advantage, she rammed a knee in his groin. The glancing blow – which was all her position allowed – stoked his fury instead of loosening his hold. Muñoz drew back and swung. The surprisingly solid punch nailed her jaw. A mutant, she thought just before stars exploded behind her eyes.

Muñoz struggled to his feet. Blood trailed down his forehead and cheeks. He wiped the blood from his eyes then repeatedly blinked as if focus eluded him. Now that he claimed the gun, clarity seemed to falter. He staggered back a step. The .45 wavered in his hand. "I shoulda killed you sooner. You and those noisy brats." The wobbly gun lifted.

Savannah stepped forward to charge him the way Monty had but her foot slipped, tipping her off balance. By the time she regained it, he'd regrouped. She backpedaled in the snow with hopes of putting distance between them before he pulled the trigger. She planned to run like hell – claw, dig, tunnel, whatever it took to live.

Muñoz stumbled forward and fired. The shot went wide. She turned, willing her legs to plow and push through the deepening snow to give her and Daniel a chance to survive. The drifts grew denser and taller

– calf, knee, thigh then waist. Had she not been so desperate to escape, she'd have fallen to her knees and cried. Legs churned, hands plunged in the snow, scooping frantically to dig a clear navigable trail – all at an excruciatingly slow pace. In a place where on a normal day "a person could watch their dog run away for two weeks", she couldn't move five lousy feet. Mother Nature blocked her in. *You're wrong, Mathis. Mother Nature isn't just a bitch, she's a–*

A second shot fired. Her right leg folded, sending her down in the deep drift, walled in by snow. She tried pushing to her feet but went down with a cry. The leg failed to support her. Savannah scrambled back, trying again to stand and failing.

Muñoz closed the gap between them. She cringed at the .45 bearing down on her. *A bullet point blank. Lord, if I knock on your door, please let me in – and take it easy on me. Someone needs to.*

Considering Muñoz's loopy condition, she figured a decent low tackle might knock him off his feet. It was her last hope.

He advanced too quickly. As though sensing her plan his foot reared back and struck with the power of a battering ram. The toe caught her temple. Her head snapped sideways and a vague sensation of falling registered as the world faded around her. In the receding consciousness she heard a gun fire.

16

"Did I say ya could lay there and die?" The put-out voice belonged to her father who stood in a blinding halo of light. He put his hands on his hips. His already formidable physique grew larger as he stepped closer. "Yer mama left me too soon but she didn't have no choice. You do. And don't give me any sob story about being shot or having heart attacks or freezing out here. Is that what we tell them girls when ya go in the ground? That their mama survived that sonuvabitch Holland just to go die in Texas?" R.J. shook his head and rolled his eyes, "In *Texas*, for God's sake." His tone suggested if her brains were ink, she couldn't dot an i. "And that baby in yer belly. My grandson. I s'ppose yer willing to sacrifice him too."

His drill sergeant shouting hammered the beastly headache to her soul. *Daddy, hush. My head hurts... No. It <u>throbs</u>. Back and leg hurt... Where... am... I? So cold... Numb... Frozen...*

R.J. bent nearer, "Hey, girl! Pay attention!" She did. In her youth disobeying her father caused hellfire and brimstone to rain down in a hail of lashings with a belt or willow branch. "If ya wanna live," he continued, "get yer ass up. Crawl if ya hafta but don't ya dare give up."

"Notgivin'up," was the slurred moan. Her tongue felt thick and, like her brain, as functional as a rock. "M'headhurts. Tootired."

"Oh," R.J. straightened. "Excuse me fer tryin' to help out. I thought ya gave a shit about yer family."

"Ido."

"Nah. Ya wanna wallow in self-pity. That ain't *my* kid. My kid don't quit. Even when I beat the shit outta her she still fought me. She paid fer doin' it, but she wasn't no quitter. Clear out the snow around ya. Show the world yer alive."

She cobbled together enough strength to move her arms. They wagged to and fro, collapsing the accumulation beside her, at least she thought they did.

The effort pleased her father, "That's my girl. Keep moving cause if ya stop, the next face you'll see might be St. Peter's."

She pushed her arms back and forth once, twice, then three times. Each swipe drained more energy but she pushed herself to continue like her father instructed.

R.J. walked toward the bright light. No, she called, don't go. She reached for him begging *Daddy, don't leave me* when the black curtain of unconsciousness dropped.

O O O

*Are ya deaf, Savannah Charlene, or just that anxious to meet yer Maker? If you die yer takin' my grandson who hasn't even had a chance at life.*

*Why send him back? It's not like you'll get a refund. <u>Move</u>.*

Whether her daddy's presence was just a dream or the bizarre result of a concussion, he prodded her to focus past the pain and numbness setting in. Her right leg throbbed and her brain threatened to thrash itself to pieces.

Sleep's siren song tempted her to slip away, to leave it all behind in place of peace.

*I said <u>move</u>!*

Savannah jerked awake when her father yelled. Her startled gasp flooded her lungs with frigid air – but it also sharpened her focus temporarily. Earlier the wind howled through tree branches making them sway and creak beneath the snow's weight. Now the wind and raging snowfall diminished. But the bright white glare squeezed her brain in an invisible vise causing her eyes to slam shut. How could she think or plan if merely *seeing* caused such agony?

*Clear out the snow around you,* her father had said. *Show the world you're alive.* Well, that task didn't require eyeballs so she swept her arms back and forth into the same drift a few more times then stopped. No need to waste reserves on an already accomplished job.

Without offending her head too egregiously she lifted it to view blurry surroundings. It took a moment or two to realize she lay in a collapsed drift. Something in the near distance slowly came into focus. The back porch railing and steps. Now she remembered everything. Forget shooting her dead, she bemoaned, that kick practically served the same purpose. Leaving her outside to freeze. Brozek's suggestion appealed more to Muñoz than she expected. Or perhaps the up close and personal meeting with the porch railing rang his bell the way his boot rang hers. Before he punted her noggin between the goalposts, Muñoz's bloody face rivaled Carrie's at the prom so unless that was a rock on his neck, he suffered a hell of a headache like she did. His lousy aim supported that notion. He had to know he missed with the last shot. *Maybe that's why Daddy keeps at me to move. Muñoz may be coming back to finish the job.*

A bolt of pain jarred her the second she moved. It shot from ankle to hip in white hot flames, lighting every nerve along the way. A sick whimper surfaced, a small concession to the shriek trapped behind clamped lips. She eased her numbing fingers down the thigh to her knee to try pinpointing the exact location of the wound. They skimmed over a sore spot below the knee but were too numb to assess the damage through the jeans. Blood stained her fingertips when she lifted them to her semi-blurry vision. Muñoz shot her in the leg to force compliance (or flat-out missed his target) but he reaped an added bonus. The ranch was too far from anywhere – neighbors or town (as Brozek said), to go traipsing for help and survive the trip. Unless she literally dug a path down to the barn to snuggle with Bertha, Sunny, Cocoa and the rest of the dairy cows, she had no access to warmth or water. She sighed. Less than a quarter mile separated her from shelter. Getting there – practically impossible in that snow and those drifts. Just the thought wore her out and she was so damn tired from the day already.

There had to be another place of safety. A closer one but where? She rubbed her head, willing the headache to subside so she could concentrate. The surroundings spun, setting off a sudden rolling nausea that forced her to ease back down.  Throbbing head, wounded leg, the encroaching numbness and damp, snow-covered clothes.  She considered those minor compared to the fact Daniel hadn't moved since she woke up.  Not one little kick or flutter.

Pain and nausea aside, she had to seek shelter fast to save him. Unfortunately the truth dawned as brutal as the storm.  She'd probably never make it to the barn, Jake's place or the ranch house but she had to try.  Soon, she promised Daniel.  After I get some rest, I'll start for the barn… I'm just so tired, sick and sleepy…

## 17

Something warm draped over her. It *was* warm, wasn't it? She felt so cold it was hard to tell. *Believe it's a blanket and it'll be true.*

She opened her eyes. Images narrowed to tunnel vision. Thoughts were fuzzy. So tired. Tired and confused. She was home again, not in Atlanta but Augusta. She lounged on the comfy couch across from a crackling fire in the fireplace. Her mama, busy in the kitchen, hummed "In the Sweet By and By". *Home. I'm really home with Mama.*

A sudden deep, racking cough shook her from head to toe. Pain registered in her throat and back. *Am I sick? Something's wrong but what?*

"Savannah, I made hot cocoa for you," Charlene called from the kitchen. "It's on the table beside you."

She thanked her mother. Charlene replied, "You have me worried, sweetie. You're not listening to Daddy. You know how he gets when you don't listen."

"When I get warm I'll try to find a place to go. Right now I'm too cold and I ache everywhere." Just the words made her shiver again. Savannah snuggled deeper into Charlene's handmade patchwork quilt, delighting in the sweet, flowery scent of her mama's perfume wafting from it.

The fire's orange and yellow flames lapped around the logs and stretched tall in a hypnotic dance. The rich fragrance of burning oak and the radiant heat wrapped her in a comforting embrace and enticed her to close her eyes. First, though, she'd indulge in a sip of her mother's cocoa.

An open book beside the cup gave her pause. The colorful cartoon drawings depicted Sam-I-Am and his Green Eggs & Ham. The book's text read correctly until veering into darker, inappropriate prose:

> I do not like them in a house,
> I do not like them with a mouse,
> I do not like them on the grass
> So everyone can kiss my ass...

A hand slammed the book shut, rattling the brimming cup beside it. "Shame on you, girl." Her daddy shook his finger at her, "You shouldn't read that crap to kids. It'll warp 'em forever." He shouted toward the kitchen, "Charlene, have you seen what this girl's readin' to our grandkids?"

Savannah glanced at the author. Manuel Sanchez.

R.J. stripped the quilt away, plunging her back in the deep freeze. "What're ya doin? Just passin' time till ya die? You were too hard to raise for us to lose ya now." Hands on hips, he bent eye level with her,

"Speak up. Ain't there somethin' you wanna say?"

No. She *wanted* to cry, not be harassed by her daddy. She'd been so cozy beneath the quilt, savoring her mother's sweet alto voice humming her favorite hymn. Enjoyed hearing her voice at all, really.

"Say somethin', Savannah. Say anything," R.J. prompted. When she failed to answer he leaned closer, "*Savannah.*"

She pushed two words past her lips. She scarcely heard them, "Help. Me."

R.J. broke into a rare smile, "There's my baby. Ya done good. Hang in there, girl, you'll make it." He retreated into a dense fog that disappeared altogether when something pressed against the side of her neck, startling her.

*Savannah...* A familiar voice called. A man's voice but not R.J.'s. Maybe Ennis?

The man's gentle touch reminded her of his. It had to be Ennis, didn't it? He brushed her hair back, touched her throbbing temple then stroked her cheek. *Come on, honey, wake up...*

Every ounce of energy went into being heard. "Ennis... Don't leave me..." Had she made sense? What she meant to say ended up garbled, incoherent. Nothing about her body worked right anymore.

*It's okay. I've got you. I'm not leaving you.* His voice faded in and out. Calm. Deep. Smooth as silk.

The same inquisitive touch probed the leg wound. It rekindled the ache enough she uttered a weak moaned protest. *What happened?* he asked. *Who did this to you?*

The faint scent of men's cologne drifted to her. Ennis never wore cologne.  He smelled of pure male and Irish Spring.  Maybe the cold affected her nose and she mistook the soap for cologne.  Who cares, she finally decided.  *This man – whom I will assume is my husband – is gentle and sounds kind.*

Strong arms scooped beneath her shoulders and knees.  Another spontaneous groan spilled from her lips.  To be warm again.  Warm and pain free.  She yearned for the home in Augusta, her mama and daddy, the fireplace and thick quilt, just to bask in the warm, idyllic moment a while longer.  She reached for the vision in hopes of retrieving it.  Her hands bumped something hard and raspy like sandpaper instead.

*Watch that right cross, honey*, came a gentle caution, *'cause I kinda need the chin and nose.*  This was not Augusta or even the afterlife.  God promised Paradise, not bone-chilling cold or physical pain – and every step he took ricocheted bolts of misery through her leg and head.

"Ennis, stop," she mumbled.  "It hurts."  Had he even heard her?

Apparently not.  He continued step after jarring step on his journey.  He stopped walking about the time she decided to exercise her "right cross" again, this time for real, not that it would amount to much.

The long trip exhausted him though, leaving his chest heaving against her side to draw in deep, heavy breaths.  *I'm setting you down but I'm right here if you need me…  Gotta dig the door free…*

During their travels she'd burrowed against him to greedily absorb body heat.  Now his warm, safe embrace and comforting voice disappeared, letting cold, isolation and loneliness creep in again.  She groaned for Ennis to come back.

*Give me a second, hon.  I'm trying to find a key…*

Something creaked – a door maybe?  Arms lifted her into their embrace – Ennis always handled her like porcelain.  He carried her from a bitter wind into temperate calm.  There was no breeze, no biting cold anymore.  She began drifting off.  Safety.  Finally.

Her head sank into softness.  A pillow?  When his arms withdrew she swore she lay on a bed.  *But you swore the fireplace, quilt and cocoa were real too and they weren't.*

"Hold real still," he said, "and I'll cut this rope."

Her brain accessed its Rolodex of voices.  Familiar yes.  Ennis?  Maybe, maybe not.

Cold metal slid between her wrists.  A gentle tug and the steady pressure released.  Her arms fell limp to her sides.

"Now the clothes come off," he said.

She'd blamed the wind and cold on affecting her senses.  She'd been wrong.  So dreadfully wrong.  "*You're not Ennis.*"  The thick, elongated accusation dripped out like cold molasses.  It was difficult to form words, much less verbalize them in a coherent sentence.  *I'm hurt.  I was tied up and carried to a bed.  Now he's stripping me.*  A sudden flood of panic crashed through her, destroying any previous notions of his identity – and that flood carried one name.  "*No, Jeffrey, no…*" she tried fending off the killer's hands grasping at the buttons on her jeans.

Those hands gently encircled her wrists, "Settle down, honey.  I'm not Ennis or Jeffrey but this still has to be done or you'll get sick."

Her feeble attempt sapped her reserves and stoked the brain-busting headache back to full power.  *He's trying to help*, she finally managed to reason then gave up.

His voice softened, "Good girl."

He went to work while the sliver of consciousness threatened to abandon her entirely. He removed her shoes and socks. Once sliding the soggy Levi's off he started removing her panties.

Her trembling hand reached to stop him. Like hell he'd strip her bare down there.

He pushed her hand aside, sounding downright amused, "Don't get feisty with me. I'm not looking."

Starting from her waist and working down, he patted the exposed skin dry with a soft towel. Next he draped a heavy blanket over her lower half.

"Sit up for me, honey. That sweater and bra are next."

She'd drifted again. His voice so close to her ear buoyed her closer to consciousness but she was wiped out and just wanted to sleep in the soft, toasty bed until her strength returned and her body quit aching.

Her hardheaded hero had his own agenda however and without a second thought or ounce of strain, propped her upright to strip the thick sweater over her head and arms. Before giving her a chance to fight or argue, he reached around her back. Her breasts fell free and the bra slipped away.

He dried her back and arms the eased her to the bed, "Lie down now. There you go. I'll dry you off then you can rest."

He took extra care around her breasts and baby bump, so much that the gentle motion relaxed her to the brink of drifting off. "That's right. Get some shut-eye and recuperate." The soothing Texas accent vowed, "I'll keep you safe."

The blanket tucked under her chin. *I'll keep you safe.* She couldn't explain why she trusted this man or his promise – if he was actually there. Her throbbing brain may have conjured him up like it had her mama, daddy and the house in Augusta. No matter how real he sounded or felt, she assumed it was a dream. A very annoying dream on occasion when the squeak of cabinets opening and closing tweaked her from slumber. Water ran in a sink then finally silence. The blanket lifted, startling a flimsy objection from her. First the quilt disappeared, now the blanket did too, except soon a different cozy, warm sensation, this one somewhat weightier, settled at the rise in her belly.

"This should help you and the baby warm up."

The blanket returned. He tucked it beneath her chin, "Found a couple more blankets for you too."

More pressure settled on top of her. Her hero (real or not) tucked the extra covers snug around her. She couldn't move if she had to. Delusion or not, the safety, warmth and quiet lulled her to sleep.

## 18

A white-hot fire in her right leg jerked her wide awake with a mild curse. She recoiled but something – no, someone – held her leg immobile by the ankle. No, *this* wasn't a hallucination. Pain this intense only occurred in real life. Adding to her misery, a swarm of invisible bees and colonies of fire ants attacked every nerve in her extremities. An inferno of blood circulated as if someone boiled it then transfused it back into her veins. Her hands, feet and face felt swollen and her head like a giant popcorn kernel on the verge of exploding.

No wonder she was miserable, she bemoaned. Except for her right leg, a mountain of blankets weighted her down.

Savannah focused to her right. Standing several feet away a space heater added several degrees to her increasingly unwelcome tropical vacation. The sight on the nightstand beside her, however, brought tears to her eyes. A five by seven of Lily and Anna. The man who saved her (and now tried broiling her alive) brought her to the ranch house – but who *was* he?

She struggled to her elbows. Her unlikely hero rendered her

speechless. Joe Bob Crawford sat near the foot of the bed, hunkered over her leg that he'd elevated on a pillow. He held a bottle of rubbing alcohol in one hand and a towel in the other.

"Mornin', Sunshine," he greeted with a chagrined half-smile. "Sorry for the rude awakening but I have to disinfect the wound."

Savannah debated over punching him or thanking him. Grandmama Prince did shit like that. Inflicting sometimes off-the-wall, archaic "cures" on innocent souls. She used "tried-and-true" old time remedies handed down from her mama and grandmother. Grandmama prescribed a spoonful of vinegar and honey for a sore throat, eating an onion to cure a cold, and turpentine wraps to bandage cuts. No one wanted to catch the flu at Grandmama's house because her cures scared the hell out of her grandkids. Even Georgia ran for her life when Grandmama opened her "medicine cabinet". After remembering the turpentine wrap, Savannah figured alcohol really wasn't any different. Either one was cruel as shit but they both worked.

Savannah lifted a hand to her head. Lord, she felt like she'd been pulled through a knothole. She cringed when she touched her temple then again when she assessed her chin. She ran her tongue over her teeth. All choppers were present and accounted for, thank goodness.

Joe Bob winced in sympathy, "You took a whupping, didn't you?"

A whupping and a half, she added. *Wait.* A frightening realization knifed past the scathing headache. *He'd said "morning".* Had that much time passed? She'd slept away valuable time while her family suffered and maybe died.

Outside the kitchen window a dull sun hidden by drab gray dreariness sat lower on the horizon. The sight relieved her a little. Evening. Not morning. The time of day when semi-melted snow froze to ice and wind chills plummeted.

There was a strange pressure on her stomach above her baby bump. Savannah reached down to move the tepid hot water bottle aside then shoved the blankets away and claimed the sheet to cover her breasts. She needed cooler air to moderate the massive hot flash steamrolling her. She hadn't perspired that much since her labor with Anna. Once her temperature regulated she'd go after the rifles and clothes in preparation for the trek back to Mama's house. Before night fell she wanted back in that house to save her family.

The rifles sat in locked cases atop the armoire, she saw those, but saw no sign of her clothes. Where were they, she asked Joe Bob.

He threw the covers back over her, "Your clothes were sopping so I laid 'em out to dry. Normally I don't go around stripping the clothes off unconscious women but I had no choice in your case."

She wondered why he felt the need to explain. Developing pneumonia sounded as delightful as catching the plague so why would she mind if he... Oh. *That's* why he seemed skittish about the subject. Somewhere in the recesses of her mind she remembered calling him *Jeffrey*.

She apologized to Joe Bob who replied, "No need to apologize. You went through hell so it sticks with you. I just wanted you dry and warm. I didn't look, I swear."

He could "swear" himself into next week because his eyes told a different story. He had no choice but see the residual number "10" Jeffrey Holland carved below her right collarbone and the resulting surgical scars to repair the damage. It didn't matter that while peeling off her wet sweater he viewed the scars crisscrossing her back from the killer's brutal caning. He'd seen the roadmap of misery Jeffrey inflicted simply because they were impossible to miss – and she couldn't care less that he had. That day, Joe Bob Crawford was her guardian angel, she told the sheepish fella standing beside the bed. She thanked him for bringing her to safety, tending her wounds and saving hers and her son's lives.

"Well, you did exonerate me with Guthrie and save me from breaking a tooth on his bologna sandwich. Stop fiddling with those blankets, missy. You're in no shape to get up. It hasn't been that long since we got here."

She flapped a hand at her face, "But it's hot enough to melt glass under here."

"You *think* you're hot but your body's still adjusting. Give it time."

Yeah, right. The one thing she didn't have. Time.

He reclaimed his perch beside her injured leg, "Judging by your restlessness you seem to be recovering from the cold and the other good news is there's no hole in your leg. Whoever shot you, though, put one impressive notch in it. Came thatclose to your knee." His thumb and forefinger indicated a frighteningly small distance that made her feel dizzy and a little sick. He continued, "It bled like a stuck hog too. At least the snow helped stanch the bleeding."

More like divine intervention if you asked her. God diverted plenty of bullets that day. Now she needed Him to lift the headache and other ailments so she could focus on getting back to the house. She wiped her brow, explaining, "I take a blood thinner. That's why it bled so much."

Speaking of divine intervention, what prompted Joe Bob to brave the worst blizzard (the duplicitous weather-challenged Windbag Willy called it) in over fifty years?

"Eldon said y'all seemed pretty tense and you gave him a lame excuse for that knot on your jaw. Tripping over luggage? Really?"

"Well," she shrugged, embarrassed, "it was short notice." She placed a hand to her belly. As far as she knew Daniel hadn't moved for hours. They'd literally suffered every step of this hell together. She'd made stupid decisions, some so reckless she doubted her ability as a mother. What good and decent mother endangered their unborn child?

Oblivious to her concerns, Joe Bob proceeded, "Plus, Eldon said the phone was dead at the main house and Mrs. Rutherford declined his offer to call Ma Bell. I already knew something was off when Jenny Lee never answered her cell phone. That's one thing my sister lives for is that ridiculous contraption."

He talked while he worked, she suspected, to distract her from the cold burn of alcohol pouring into the raw wound. "How'd you get here?" she asked.

He sat back, boasting, "Eldon let me borrow his tractor with the brand new fancy plowing blade. Did alright considering the amount of snow. Took a while to dig through a few drifts though. Had to come the back way since the main road was blocked with cars stuck in the snow."

"The one behind Cal's property?" Close to where I found Monty way back when, she guessed.

He nodded. "I parked the tractor down at Jake's and hoofed it the rest of the way. That's quite a cardio workout."

Yes. One that after today would have spelled utter doom for her and her son had she tried it. *But you laid there in the cold and snow so how was that any smarter?*

Joe Bob's vision settled on her hand stroking her stomach. He temporarily abandoned his work, "Problems?"

She swallowed the urge to cry while she could. *If Daniel dies, it's your fault.* She'd pushed Muñoz too far that afternoon but she'd be damned if she let her girls suffer at Brozek's hands. She would never regret protecting her daughters but she regretted her unborn son may have paid the ultimate price for her actions.

She pursed her lips to conceal the trembling and answered with a tiny shrug. A tear slipped down her cheek. She wiped it away.

"Any cramping or unusual pain?"

She shook her head then confessed in a scarcely restrained voice, "He's not moving."

He put a hand to hers, "He needs to recover too. Give him time and try not to worry."

His calm confidence probably should have assured her but this was her son they were talking about and she justifiably blamed herself for endangering him. What if she and Ennis had no baby to hold, no toddler to teach ABC's and 123's to, no grown man who shared his father's inner strength, handsome features and sweet nature? A man whose eyes twinkled when he spoke of a certain lady the way Ennis's did when he spoke of Savannah. And the day Daniel brought that certain lady home to proudly announce their engagement. Savannah dreamed of these things, held tight to them since the day she discovered little Daniel No Name Rutherford existed. She'd never be able to cope with losing this child, especially after goading Muñoz as she had.

Before she lost the battle of tears – or her mind, she tried sitting up, "I need to call Sheriff Guthrie then I need clothes. I have to get back in that house before I lose everyone I love."

Joe Bob's hand went to her shoulder, "I've already called. I told him how I found you and that I heard a bunch of guys shouting threats in the house. He's alerted the Amarillo police. If I know him, he's notified the FBI and every agency this side of Starfleet Command too."

"We need to tell him those are the four from Gatesville."

He tucked the blankets around her, "Somehow he knew it might be them."

Much to his exasperation, she propped on her elbows, "They know Ennis and I are cops. That's why I'm in this shape and I'm scared he's next."

He pointed to the bed, "Down, missy. Your job is to recover. You may not remember begging your daddy to come back or calling me Ennis but I do. That behavior says you got knocked cuckoo."

"Joe Bob, *I need back in that house.*"

"Guthrie and the cavalry will be here soon. Let me finish up here and I'll get you something for pain if I can find it." He reached beside him. Savannah braced hard in case he chose that spiteful rubbing alcohol again.

Joe Bob kinda chuckled, "It's not a rollercoaster ride. I'm just checking for debris."

She considered telling him to forget debris and check for a fire extinguisher because one more second of heat and she'd spontaneously combust. Between the space heater and blankets she perspired in places ladies shouldn't and the armies of ants beneath her skin tripled in number. She kept the sheet and threw the blankets back. He tossed them back over her. She frowned at him. He frowned back. Then something happened. A miracle – and that miracle happened twice. Daniel moved. Tears pooled in her eyes, "The baby kicked. Finally." She thanked God for that tenacious pressure against her ribs. *Keep kicking, little one. Kick all you want.*

Joe Bob's mouth slanted in a boyish grin, "That's the best news since I found a pulse in your neck. You're giving him Ennis's middle name Daniel, right?"

He applied the antibiotic cream with such a light touch it sent a shiver through her, "Yes. All we need is a middle name."

"How about your pa's middle name?"

No thanks. "Probably not a good idea for a few reasons." One being she'd suffered the brunt of R.J.'s beatings in her youth and he still wielded a short temper and mighty swing when angered. That and, "Daniel Jefferson Rutherford is so long it practically needs a caboose. Ennis and I thought about Ennis's daddy but Cal and Bobbi beat us to it twice. John is Tyler's middle name and they claimed Zach with their youngest."

"Feel free to use one of the Crawford gems.  Through the generations we've had Maverick, Flem, Enoch and even Vega to name a few."

"Flem?"

Joe Bob considered that.  "On second thought don't use Flem.  It sounds like a flu symptom and I don't want your boy getting whupped on the playground.  Vega seems more fitting."  He wrapped a bandage around the wound and readjusted the blanket over her, admitting, "That leg looks mighty painful and Doc's car can't motivate in this weather so until someone can give him a lift, we'll have to make do with whatever's here."  He went to the small kitchen to rummage the cabinets.  "Mrs. Rutherford keeps the cupboards pretty well stocked but I didn't see any Tylenol.  Even checked the bathroom."

"It's in the upper left cabinet, middle shelf," she directed.  "She keeps it up high, away from the kids."

"Found it."  He brought a glass of water then shook two pills in her hand.  "Maybe that'll dull the ache some."

On shaky arms, she pushed to a sitting position to swallow the meds.  To her surprise the earlier angina subsided.  Maybe between Muñoz's winging her and Joe Bob's trial by alcohol it decided adding additional misery just wasn't worth it.  Whatever the reason she was grateful.

"Your jeans were pretty damp so I hope you don't mind me emptying your pockets. Jenny Lee told me about your heart condition and I found the blood pressure pills, blood thinner and aspirin.

Normally they prescribe nitroglycerin but I didn't find any."

"Brozek took it."

He went quiet. His expression reminded her of Ennis and Georgia's the last several months. He considered her a time bomb.

"Joe Bob, my ticker's lasted this long so to quote you, try not to worry."

He conceded with a nod then ambled to the window facing the main house. He fingered the curtain aside an inch, "Where do those guys hang out in there?"

"Living room mostly. That's where they gathered the family. Scott Hadley stays by the liquor cabinet and keeps his .45 on the bar. Sanchez and Muñoz ride roughshod over everyone, Muñoz with his .45, Sanchez with an assault rifle. They searched the house and found the rifles and shotguns so they're armed to the hilt. All while that degenerate Alan Brozek salivates over my girls." She obsessed over his loving caresses on Lily's cheek and his fingers brushing her thigh. *I'm gonna have a party with your kids,* he'd promised. *And once I'm finished, I'm gonna cut their throats and burn 'em up, just like those kids in Decatur...*

"See," Joe Bob pointed at her murderous scowl, "*that* mood ain't helpin' you recover. Settle down before you need those pills you don't have. Give Guthrie a chance to round up reinforcements."

He moved to the kitchen, opened a couple of upper cabinets until finding coffee mugs. "You seem lucid enough to drink coffee if you want it." He poured a cup apiece, "Cream, sugar?"

Normally Savannah took cream with a little sugar but that day she craved plain old, strong hot java, "Just coffee please."

The aroma teased her since she woke up. When he approached holding the precious steaming beverage, she actually drooled.

He hitched a thumb at the empty gun rack hanging beside the door, "A gun rack with no guns?"

She eased the cup to her lips for a tentative sip. A small swallow of sheer bliss flowed past her tongue and down her throat. Judging by Joe Bob's expression, the moan she released sounded on the verge of lustful. She nodded to the top of the armoire where Mama Rutherford kept the long gun cases, "Two rifles in the cases on top. The keys are in–"

"Lemme guess," a flash of humor crossed his face. "In the cabinet with the Tylenol."

"Close. At the back of the drawer beneath the Tylenol cabinet." A sigh slipped out after another sip. Her eyes nearly rolled back in her head, "Best. Coffee. Ever. Thank you."

"There's plenty so drink up."

The caffeine rejuvenated her enough to try standing. She wrapped the sheet around her and prepared to swallow something far less enjoyable than coffee – a bitter blue streak a mile long. The wound already throbbed with a bone-deep ache. Her head wasn't any better but every passing minute brought her family closer to the brink of disaster. She refused to sit on her ass while they died.

Joe Bob put hands to hips, "I know it's killing you to take orders but I'm in charge right now so stay put."

The last two words and inflection harkened memories of Ennis when he lost patience with her. She obeyed. For now.

Joe Bob rounded up ammunition stored beside the locked rifle cases then freed up the weapons. After loading them he handed her the Winchester and kept the Remington bolt-action for himself, "There ya go. One for you, one for me."

Savannah sat the coffee aside to hold the newer version Model 73 and get the feel of the lever-action rifle. The blue steel beauty with a walnut stock and twenty inch barrel felt at home in her grasp. Perfect for taking out murderers and child molesters alike.

The phone rang. Joe Bob picked up on the second ring. It was Guthrie. Joe Bob relayed her information of the foursome's last known locations in the house then told him he and Savannah had enough ammo for a skirmish, not a war, so hurry it up. The topic switched to her. "She feels good enough to argue if that helps you assess her condition. Yep, and the baby seems fine too... What?" He did an eye roll, "Of course I disinfected and dressed her wound. I'm not dense. She should be okay until Doc can see her." He turned to Savannah, "Besides those four, who's in the house? Guthrie wants a list. The whole family and Jenny Lee, right?"

"Yes, and Gina Sutton."

Joe Bob's mouth fell open, "Gina Sutton's in there? Geez, it's a miracle no one's killed her yet."

"There was no shortage of volunteers last night," she agreed, "but she is trying to protect the girls. Personally I'm glad she's there."

His and Guthrie's exchange lasted another minute. When Joe Bob hung up, he instructed as parentally as possible, "Guthrie told us to stay away from the house. He's coordinating with the other agencies and needs us for periodic updates."

*Hmm... What part of me says "sit back, relax and let the 'other agencies fix this'"?* By the time the FBI "coordinated" themselves, her family would be dead. *Sorry, Guthrie. I won't take that chance...*

Joe Bob heaved a resigned sigh, "Yeah. How'd I know you'd balk at that? Listen, he doesn't want us charging into the place guns blazing. You for obvious reasons and me, well, because I'm me."

"Can't shoot straight?" she teased.

"For your information, Mrs. Rutherford," he bantered back, "I won my share of competitions in my youth and I still go hunting. But I'm more familiar with deer and pheasant, not cold-blooded killers and another plus – deer and pheasant don't shoot back."

Thirty minutes later Guthrie called back. Apparently the FBI and Amarillo PD were delayed due to road conditions and the choppers couldn't fly in the wind gusts. The stiff gales made an encore appearance, nothing steady but the strength and unpredictability had Savannah questioning if everyone was against them, including her old pal Mother Nature.

They're coming, Guthrie promised before hanging up, and in the meantime he and his deputies would start out toward the ranch and come in "the back way" as Joe Bob had.

Joe Bob nursed his coffee while taking a peek out the kitchen window then stiffened, "Any of those guys wear a dark jacket? Hard to tell but he looks sorta skinny."

"Probably Brozek."

"He's moving around the back of the house. I figure he's looking for you." Joe Bob sat the coffee down to angle for a better view, "Now he's checking the side of the house but the snow's too deep."

Savannah straightened in the bed.  Her hand rested on the Winchester in case Brozek (or whoever it was) grew inquisitive.  "He can see your footprints leading here."

"Unless he's blind.  The wind could've covered them but not that well.  Those were pretty deep drifts I went through."

"Let me know if he starts this way."  Yes, because she intended to send Mr. Brozek special delivery to The Man upstairs.

Joe Bob sighed.  "He's back inside."

This was ridiculous.  One person running between two different windows – sometimes three – seemed rather silly when even a gimpy individual could tend one of them full time.  "Hand me my clothes.  If Brozek's looking around, it's a matter of time before more of them join in."

"No can do, honey.  Those duds are soggy.  You'd catch your death in them."

Well, she wasn't about to fight a gang of murderers in the buff. Securing the sheet around her, she bore her injury's grievances behind gnashed teeth as she swung her legs down and pushed to her feet.  Tears blurred Joe Bob's image when her weight settled on the wounded leg.

Muscle and bone softened beneath her.  The room spun.  The marching band parading through her brain cranked up the volume and forced her to grope for the nightstand or fall flat on her face.  Shee-yet, she groused under her breath.  Reality sure knew how to humble a soul.

A strong arm encircled her waist and eased her to the bed.  Joe Bob bent until they met eye to eye, "Keep yourself parked before you keel over, ya dern mule."

"Joe Bob, if we're both armed and ready to fight, we stand a better chance when they venture down here – and they will. Brozek may be dumb as a post but the others aren't. As for clothes there's a change in the armoire in case of emergencies. I'll wear those."

He stared back in utter disbelief. Throughout her life she'd experienced the same frustration with her parents, siblings, husband and boss. The hopeless realization that this person, despite age or IQ, really might *not* come in out of the rain.

"Listen, honey, I can't keep track of them *and* you if you're gonna squirm around like an anxious kid. If I consider letting you help, you'll do as I say, no hemming and hawing, no questions, and no pulling rank. Got it?"

Got it, she said then pointed to the armoire.

"Not so fast. Look up."

The room's light speared her brain but she withstood it while he checked her pupils. Next, keeping her head perfectly still (she thanked God for it too), her vision followed his finger that moved left, right, down then up. Finally he announced *at least your eyes don't cross.*

She tried not to sound impatient, "Am I cleared for duty yet?"

He held his hand up in a peace sign, "How many fingers?"

"Two."

He moved his hand further away, lifted only his pinkie, "Now?"

"One."

He closed his fist, "And?"

"None, you cheater," Savannah half-joked. "So did I pass, Dr.

Crawford?"

"Yes, Sergeant Stubborn. Lemme check for the clothes first." Joe Bob's broad shoulders drooped on his way to the armoire. "I'll tell ya, my sister may be cockeyed but she's right about one thing. You are one obstinate female. I'm surprised Ennis hasn't snatched himself baldheaded."

He rummaged the top drawer, flung a pair of folded jeans onto the bed. Once he shook them out, his eyes bugged at the waist and butt, "Wow. Who do these big boys belong to?"

Jenny Lee wasn't the only cockeyed one, she thought. Her brow sank, "Are you sure a bull broke your shoulder or was it an irate woman? Those are maternity jeans from my last pregnancy, Joe Bob. Anna should have been twins as big as she was."

He handed them over, "I guess all Crawfords suffer hoof and mouth. Sorry."

"No problem," she smiled. "I can't stay upset with a hero. Can you check for a belt? I'm pleased to say these pants are too big."

He opened the second drawer, scrounged a bit then removed a red and black plaid shirt, "No belt but here's a nice flannel shirt for you. Put that on and you'll look like Mrs. Paul Bunyan."

"My life's dream."

Joe Bob shoved things aside in the drawer for another fishing expedition. "I don't see a... um..." he pointed to his chest.

"Bra?"

"Yeah," he blushed, "that." He rummaged again until tweezing his next find between his thumb and forefinger. A pair of cotton briefs.

"Uh, here," he thrust them at her without actually looking at them.

Funny how men played with old greasy cars, wore smoke from a BBQ as a badge of honor and stuck worms on the ends of fishing hooks without flinching but the simplest female possession could be their undoing.  For a man who rode animals weighing more than a U-Haul trailer and delved into the messy task of calving, she never expected Joe Bob to get squeamish over one pair of women's dainties.  Savannah plucked them from his hand.

"If that leg prevents you from slipping those on," he averted his gaze, "I can help you."

His shyness amused her, "I can manage but thanks."

"It was different earlier," he explained. "Takin' 'em off was a matter of life and death."

"It's okay, Joe Bob.  I understand."

He relaxed.  "Then I'll look for a belt," he pointed to the other bedroom, "in there."

She waited until he left for the kid's bedroom before tackling the panties.  It took a combination of adequate groaning, agility and luck to clothe that end of her body but she finally succeeded.

"You decent?" he called out.

"Depends on who you ask.  Yes, Joe Bob, I'm covered."

He emerged holding a western belt with a longhorn steer emblazoned on the silver buckle.  Not exactly her style but better than walking around with pants around her ankles.

He checked the window for activity at the house.  Savannah swung her legs out, grimacing against the leg's radiating ache.  While his back was turned she slipped on Ennis's soft flannel shirt, buttoned it then rolled the sleeves back to her wrists. At five nine few things in life made her feel small. Between the broad shoulders and longer arms, her hubby's shirts rated near the top of the list.

Joe Bob steadied her when she stood to pull up the jeans. She tested the leg by settling a tiny bit of weight on it. Instant regret paired with a muted whimper. An arrow straight from hell impaled her from heel to waist. He told her to sit down. She didn't argue.

"Hold on. One more thing," he said. Back to the armoire drawer. Out came a pair of wool socks.

Had he lost his mind? Her feet felt like overcooked sausages and he wanted her to stuff them in those? *You and what army are putting those on me?* her expression dared. His determined frown vowed *an army of one. Me.* "The socks go on or you're back in bed. Your choice."

Men. No, *Texas* men. Impossible. Infuriating. Bossy. She refused to entertain the fact Ennis used the same descriptors for her. But socks? *Wool* socks? Joe Bob's army of one better retreat because the giant Oscar Meyer wieners on the ends of her ankles were not being shoved in thick, *hot*, wool socks.

They visually squared off until that ridiculous promise of capitulation reared up. No hemming and hawing, no questions, and no pulling rank, he'd said. And stupid-like she'd agreed. Savannah's shoulders slumped, "Are they really necessary right now?"

"Does the Pope work on Sundays? You'll thank me later."

Later? Maybe. Now? No. "You and Ennis," Savannah

harrumphed. "Cut from the same cloth."

Smiling, he kneeled to slip the socks on her feet, "And that's a bad thing?"

"No, just frustrating sometimes."

Once her apparel met his approval, he helped her to the kitchen window then placed the Winchester on the counter within easy reach. When he grabbed a teaspoon from a drawer, it confused her. The guns she understood but a spoon? It wasn't until he brought a bowl to the stove that she noticed chicken soup heating in a pan.

Joe Bob served it up then presented it to her, "Bon appétit."

She heaved a pained sigh, "Joe Bob."

"Savannah," he countered, "chicken soup can't hurt you, besides you and Daniel need nourishment."

Clever, Joe Bob. Using the baby as leverage and topping it off with a big, fat cherry called guilt. "You sure you've never met my sister?" she asked.

"No hemming and hawing, no questions—"

"I know, I know. I'll eat what I can but no more mothering. I got two in that house down there – three if you count Mama herself – and I'm worried sick about them."

His hand rested on her shoulder, "I know you're worried but you've got yourself and Daniel to look after too. Even if you're not hungry, he probably is."

"Stop being so right all the time," she shared a little smile. "It's really annoying."

The phone rang. The brief conversation took a dismal turn.

"The sheriff and his guys are having a tough time getting here," Joe Bob said. "Abandoned cars are blocking the roads. He's called out the tow truck and plow to help clear the way."

"That could take hours and our families don't have it. After I eat, I'm out of here." She blew the steam off another spoonful and downed it. The time for humoring Joe Bob came to an abrupt end. He had no clue how these guys thought. She did and Muñoz and Sanchez were already antsy to leave at any cost.

"Give me time to prepare. I want to be ready in case those four buzzards get inquisitive enough to come here. And I need a few things if we strike out for the house later." He began opening drawers, "I saw some tools in one of these earlier–"

"Second drawer," she pointed across the way.

In seconds he'd gutted through scissors, flashlights, pliers, screwdrivers, a tape measure and other items. He selected the flashlights, a large coil of braided baler twine and a roll of duct tape. "You only need two tools in life," he crowed. "WD-40 and duct tape. If it doesn't move and should, use WD-40. If it moves and shouldn't, time for duct tape."

She really liked Jenny's brother. Smart with a fine sense of humor, he personified the chivalrous (yet a shade bossy) Texas male – at least the ones she'd encountered. Joe Bob redeemed the Crawford DNA and proved not all of them were half-baked.

## 19

Thirty minutes after Guthrie called, he rang back with worse news. The snow plow backed into two stranded cars and required a quick fix before being operational again. Guthrie sent word to the mechanic who had to dig free from his house, gather what tools he needed and find a way to the crippled plow. In other words, Savannah thought, it will take forever.

She looked at the clock. Seven thirty-four. A weak, cloud-covered moon replaced the sun's fading light. The wind exhausted itself to a steady gentle breeze. The snow finally, mercifully stopped.

While Savannah kept vigil at the window, Joe Bob spruced up the bed in anticipation of visitors. He fluffed and shaped two more pillows then threw the blankets over them. The "figure" tucked in nice and cozy appeared convincing enough to Savannah. She expected the ruse might temporarily fool anyone hunting down a wounded police sergeant.

In the meantime, her bra dried and wearing it restored a shred of femininity to her new rustic attire. Now if the cacophony in her head subsided and the warring nerves in her leg called a truce, her overall existence would improve as well.

She stared at the house down the road. Was her family okay or had Muñoz lost it again? And what about her babies? Oh, how she wanted five minutes alone with Brozek, the Winchester and that box of ammo on the counter.

Savannah cupped her hands to the window, squinted into the distance. Mama's kitchen light burned bright since the sun set but there was no sign of activity since Brozek's earlier excursion outside.

She leaned back to rest her eyes and leg. The chicken soup sated her appetite. It also made her sleepy and a full stomach and quiet house enticed her eyes to drift shut.

Savannah startled awake. How long had she been asleep? A glance at the clock brought a sigh of relief. One minute felt close to an hour but that precious sixty seconds left them vulnerable. She rubbed her eyes to sharpen her focus then reached to the coffee pot for a refill.

The mudroom light winked on at the main house. She sat straighter. Laid a hand on the rifle beside her. *Come on, Brozek, pop out for another breath of fresh air and as the game show says "come on down". "Mom" is having her own party and you're the guest of honor.*

Unless the conk on her head caused double vision, two figures stood silhouetted against the light. "Two of them just stepped outside."

The pair explored around the house then began an awkward, high-stepping gait through the deep snow. She updated Joe Bob who completed the finishing touches on the bed, "They're headed toward the barn or here. They both have shotguns."

Joe Bob took his position at the living room window for a better view of the barn, "If they're coming in pairs I guess they mean business now."

The two men hoofed it toward the ranch house. They wandered close enough Savannah recognized them. "The one on the left is Brozek. The other is Sanchez."

Sanchez pointed to Joe Bob's trail. The passing hours left a windblown depression marking his journey but it was obvious enough for anyone with eyeballs and half a brain to follow it to the ranch house's front door.

"Here they come," Joe Bob warned. "You ready?"

"More than ready." Minutes elapsed. She urged them to pick up the pace. What was taking them so long? They stopped at the barn and stables, every rise in the snow, every drift. Were they really that stupid? *You broke out of a maximum security prison, for God's sake. Can't you morons follow a simple trail?*

Finally they meandered close enough Savannah ducked out of sight. Brozek flanked Sanchez, their breaths clouding in the frigid night air. Voices approached the kitchen window. She overheard Sanchez berate his companion, "See Brozek? These are called footprints. If you'd opened your eyes earlier you'd have seen these tracks and I wouldn't be out here freezing my ass off. Since they lead to the door, what does that tell you?" He didn't wait for Brozek's reply. "I see a light inside. Let's go."

Savannah heard voices mumbling back and forth. Soon after, heavy footfalls tramped on the porch.

Joe Bob padded behind the door. She joined him, both shouldering their rifles.

The doorknob slowly rotated. The door edged open an inch, waited, then dared another two. The cold breeze rattled the family pictures on the wall. The smiling faces in those picture frames steeled her against her body's riotous pain. She gripped the rifle harder, her finger snug on the trigger.

Sanchez entered with caution, his shotgun aimed at the figure in the bed. He eased in far enough for Brozek to step inside. His shotgun also pointed at the bed.

"Wake up, Mommy," Sanchez called in a sugary sweet voice. "Manuel's got a surprise for you."

Brozek laughed. She and Joe Bob stepped from behind the door, his rifle at Sanchez's back, hers at Brozek's. "We've got one for you too," she slammed the door. "Lose your weapons and drop to your knees."

Neither did. Joe Bob cocked the Remington, "Listen to the lady or you'll go to the floor the hard way."

Sanchez and Brozek exchanged a glance. She jacked the Winchester's lever, "Whatever you're thinking, don't."

Sanchez took his time placing the shotgun on the bed. Brozek followed suit. Savannah questioned Sanchez, "Is anyone hurt or dead in that house?"

He shrugged.

*My family. Tell me about my family because*, "If you shrug again, it'll be the last thing you ever do. Is anyone hurt or dead in that house?"

Brozek answered, "They got out of control when Muñoz took you outside. Your husband and sister especially. When Muñoz came back, your husband took a beating but I managed to spare your sister. Otherwise everyone's fine."

Joe Bob shoved Sanchez to his knees, "They better be because my sister's in there too."

"Brozek the Brave," Sanchez taunted, "you saved her sister but tell Mommy what you did to her little girls, hero."

The world shrank to pinpoint. In her periphery she saw Joe Bob reaching for the duct tape. He warned Sanchez to shut up. For hours she agonized over horrific images of Brozek touching her girls, muffling their cries with a hand over their mouths as he unzipped his jeans and...

Savannah rammed the rifle butt into Brozek's temple, sending him flat to the floor on his nose. His earlier smile and cocky laugh vanished. She would make damn sure he never laughed again.

When she pressed the rifle to the back of Brozek's head, Joe Bob – busy with Sanchez – panicked, "Savannah, don't do it." He'd stripped Sanchez's coat off and hustled to tie his wrists behind his back.

From the instant Sanchez blurted his statement, she ceased being a cop. Whether Alan Brozek knew it or not, he was a dead man. "Did you hurt my babies, Brozek?"

"You should have heard them," Sanchez mimicked a child's voice. "*Make him stop! He's hurting me! I want Mommy! Where's Mom–*"

Joe Bob's fist collided with Sanchez's jaw to temporarily silence him. Jenny's brother turned to Savannah, walleyed as she braced a foot in Brozek's back and aimed the rifle straight at Sanchez. "Savannah, stop. Yes, they deserve it but don't pull that trigger."

She sighted the gun between Sanchez's eyes, daring him to, "Say it again."

He laughed until a strip of duct tape slapped over his mouth. Joe Bob pressed hard on Sanchez's mouth and jaw, ensuring he sealed off the murderer's words – but she saw the malicious smile behind the tape. Her eyes narrowed, her finger tightened on the trigger.

Joe Bob worked faster than a calf roper at a rodeo competition. He hogtied Sanchez, did a quick pat down and found a hunting knife that he tossed on the bed. In seconds he stood beside her, hand on the rifle and attempting to lower the aim. "Take a breath," he told her in a calm but insistent voice. "Take long, deep breaths."

She shook with fury. Thanks to Sanchez, she imagined her two sweet babies calling for her, begging for her help – and she hadn't been there. Instead of protecting her girls, Muñoz banished her from the house, shot her and left her to die. If not for Joe Bob Crawford, Muñoz would have gotten his wish. Grateful as she was to Jenny's brother, he *would* back off because she and Brozek had unfinished business.

She swung the rifle to Brozek. The sudden movement backed Joe Bob up a step while she ordered him to, "Tie this pervert's hands."

He tried reasoning with her, "Not while you're holding that gun and shaking like that. You might shoot–"

"I said *tie his hands.*" Did he lose the ability to understand simple English? "Remove his coat, tie his hands, search him then stand back."

He patted the air, "Okay, okay. Don't go all Clint Eastwood on me. You might also consider calming down before your legs loosen again. Just sayin'." He kneeled down, stripped Brozek of the tan Sherpa lined coat then cinched his wrists together with the twine.

Brozek prattled the usual diatribe child molesters told cops until the cops provided real incentive to confess their sins. Joe Bob advised him, "Jabbering like that ain't helping your cause. Shut up before you get us both killed."

Joe Bob centered on her shaking grasp then her murderous scowl, "You need to sit down. You're pale and sweaty and that trigger finger's too trembly for my taste, especially with me being near the barrel's business end."

He placed the hunting knife from Brozek's pocket on the counter. Relief washed over her when Joe Bob fished into Brozek's other pocket and found the nitroglycerin bottle. He sat back on his heels to appraise the pills then put the bottle on the counter, "At this rate you'll be needing these soon."

She ignored the comment, "Stand back. Brozek and I aren't done and spare me the morals and ethics speech. I want to know if he molested my girls. He just needs a little nudge to tell the truth." She braced a hand on the cabinet, lodged a foot beneath Brozek's hip and rolled him to his back. The rifle barrel stabbed his groin, drawing a sick whimper as he doubled up.

She forewarned Brozek, "I'll neuter you right now if you don't tell me the truth."

His wide eyes shifted to Joe Bob, begging him to intervene.

She drove the rifle into his crotch until he writhed beneath it. "*Did you touch my kids?*"

Across the way Sanchez nodded.

Heartbeats fell like hammer blows inside her skull. Brozek's pathetic whining worsened the unbearable pulsing. She felt one stop away from stepping off the sanity train, "You've got five seconds to tell me the truth then I *will* pull the trigger. Five."

Brozek cringed, not so much from discomfort but probably anticipation of getting his gonads blown off, "Please don't. This is cold-blooded murder–"

"Answer. The. Question. Four."

"Please, I didn't–"

"You say *please* again and I'll shoot you anyway. Tell me the truth. Three." She steadied her stance as best she could. The bandage on her leg felt sticky and wet. *That can be replaced. My girls' innocence cannot.* The thought tightened her grasp on the rifle.

Joe Bob reached toward it. One look warned him off as she counted down Brozek's life, "Two."

"Y-you're a cop," the child killer wormed beneath the rifle's pressure. "Y-you can't do this."

"Watch me." She pushed hard enough even Joe Bob cringed then she dropped the last word like a boulder, "One."

"No! He lied!" Brozek screamed. "Sanchez lied to you, I swear! I didn't touch them!"

"Why should I believe you? I recall you saying 'I'll have a party with your kids.' Sanchez told me the truth, didn't he? You raped my girls and I'll make sure you never rape another child again."

"Savannah!" Joe Bob yelled.

Her brain threatened to detonate from the volume. She blinked then slowly met his gaze. She was vaguely aware of tears spilling down her cheeks, of the sweat lining her hairline and back but most of all she felt the debilitating agony of failure to protect her babies.

Joe Bob centered on the finger still trembling on the trigger, "Savannah, back away from him. Check with the girls when you see them. Talk to them, not Brozek or Sanchez. Right now we need to get in that house and save our families. We can't do that if you waste ammo on these bastards."

One or two shots wouldn't matter. Hell, they had two boxes of ammo. Once she dispatched Brozek – which would take a grand total of a second – then they could focus on leaving.

Except standing on her leg spawned a pain that took on a life of its own. Its partner nausea joined in and kicked that precious focus out the door – until Daniel moved. Her son managed what Joe Bob couldn't. Redirected her from exacting revenge to concentrating on the one child she *could* protect. Her baby boy. In the heat of the moment, she forgot her emotions affected him too and right now another innocent life suffered needlessly.

Taking that mental breather let logic overcome the murderous rage. It occurred to her that she could beat the shit out of Alan Brozek or blast his nuts to pieces and she'd only believe what she wanted to. Her shoulders slackened somewhat from pain but mostly exhaustion.

Joe Bob relaxed a degree – as did Brozek. The former fetched the chair she vacated earlier then abandoned it when he saw the rifle barrel return to Brozek's crotch.

"Tell me where Andrea Tate is," she said. The child lingered in her mind since yesterday. The depraved images of her suffering haunted Savannah and now she associated those images with her daughters.

Joe Bob's brow sank. "Who's Andrea Tate?"

She poked the molester's privates again, "Where is that little girl, you warped son of a bitch? Did you rape her and kill her or leave her by the roadside to fend for herself?"

No reply. Savannah jabbed him hard. He retaliated with a kick intended for Daniel. The boot came within a whisper of her baby bump.

Joe Bob armed himself with the Remington pressed at Brozek's throat, "Try that again and I'll put you down myself. Answer the lady's question."

Being pinned by two rifles held by two people willing to use them prompted rapid fire pleas to spill out, most of them stuttering and stumbling for traction they never quite found.

Joe Bob whopped Brozek's forehead with the gun barrel hard enough to get his attention, "Where's the girl? Be specific or we'll show you the meaning of the word by shooting you one body part at a time."

A line of tears streamed from his eyes. "She's in the car about a half mile down the road from the house. She's not dead, she's in the car."

Joe Bob's shoulders slumped on a groan. Savannah's heart sank to her stomach. Brozek and the others left the child to freeze to death. Shooting cops, burning families alive, molesting girls and now leaving poor little Andrea Tate alone to die in a blizzard. Their cruelty knew no bounds. Still it was hard for her to believe, "You left that child to die in this weather."

"I wrapped her in blankets. I tried to help her."

"Tried to help her." The absolute idiocy of his statement made her teeth ache from clenching them. "Well, it's past time I *helped* you."

Joe Bob pushed her aim away from Brozek's danglies. "No." He dropped the word with finality, as if she had no say in the matter.

Future brother-in-law or not, she wanted to keep Joe Bob as a friend but the incendiary words burning her tongue promised to cripple, if not sever, their fledgling relationship.

These bastards massacred Andrea's family, stole her innocence, and wrecked her life, Savannah wanted to say. Why let them rot in prison when someone – a mother – could serve up justice in one second? Andrea spent long, terrifying hours witnessing and enduring trauma most people never experienced. Losing her family in a gruesome way, being carted off by the men who killed them and being abused in unconscionable ways. Then left *trapped* in a storm so immense it boggled even an adult's mind. Savannah trembled to think how impossibly surreal it looked to a six-year-old child (so close to Lily's age, her mind taunted). A little girl struggling to free herself from her bonds. Her screams for help answered only by the bitter, whistling wind battering and rocking the car. The view outside gradually vanishing as the falling snow climbed inch by inch, burying her in cold tomb and eliminating any hope of rescue. Angelic Andrea Tate robbed of her innocence, childhood and future. No first date, no first kiss. She would never feel her husband's caress on her cheek or the warm, soft sweep of his lips on hers or share the connection with a man, the one that completed her just being in his arms. Andrea's mother wanted those things for her daughter. Wanted her to grow up happy and live life to its fullest. Savannah and Ennis wanted that for their girls and in a few short hours, Brozek destroyed that dream. So, at that point, if anyone had a vote whether to expedite Brozek to St. Peter, it was Lily and Anna's mother.

Joe Bob fought against her to move the barrel aside. It must be a recessive gene, she gnashed her teeth, because for a man who showed such promise, he picked a hell of a time to catch a case of the Crawfords.

*Time for a Come-to-Jesus-Meeting, Joe Bob.* "If you'd seen a dead child on an autopsy table and listened to the coroner explain detail by excruciating detail what that baby went through, you'd let me finish this animal." She glared through watery vision at Brozek, "You let that child die. You didn't *help* her, you sentenced her to a slow, inconceivable death." She muscled the rifle back, this time at his nose, "*After* you violated her."

"I didn't touch her!" Brozek shrieked at an octave that contracted her brain inside her skull. "I swear on my mother's life I didn't lay a hand on her or your kids!" He fixated on Joe Bob, "Do something, man. She's gonna kill me."

Joe Bob refused to release the barrel. If they continued wrestling with the gun, she'd end up shooting a hole in the floor or cabinet, not that pinhead molester's nuts. If her bleeding heart partner refused to let her kill Brozek, she'd do the next best thing. "Fine. I won't kill him." The barrel slid down Brozek's chest just beneath his navel. She smiled grimly, "I'll shoot him and leave him here. If help comes in time, fine. If not, he'll have an idea of what Andrea went through. Feeling his life slip away and hoping, crying, *screaming* for help – and no one can."

Sighing, Joe Bob drew an arm across his forehead, "Listen, honey, after what you've been through today, I understand you're not thinking straight. Let me tie him up like Big Mouth over there, we go save our families and Brozek and Friends can live long, miserable lives behind bars. God'll get to them in due time."

Apparently every Crawford was stupid in their own special way. "*He let her die.*"

"We don't know if she's dead. There's nothing we can do except call Guthrie and tell him about the girl and where to find her. We've got our own crisis to deal with. We need to get to the house."

She realized that but she wanted revenge for Andrea – for every child Brozek violated including Lily and Anna if they added to his sick, twisted tally – because only fools believed a child molester's claim of innocence.

A rush of dizziness threw her off balance. She stumbled back a step. Joe Bob hurried to steady her.

Savannah cursed herself for wasting valuable energy on a bastard like Brozek. Joe Bob was right. They couldn't save the world but they could try to save their families.

Joe Bob slipped an arm around her waist, "Sit down. You're not looking good."

A high-pitched ringing drowned his words like she listened through a pillow. A gray fog clouded her vision and the room tilted. One hand braced on his arm to try righting the ship but it appeared she might have waited too long.

Joe Bob guided her to the nearby chair, "Sit here and rest. I'll let Guthrie know about Andrea after I'm done with Brozek."

"Tie him up till he turns blue." She wiped the sweat from her brow. Her vision passed across the family portrait. Lily smiling proudly in her daddy's lap and Anna's impromptu grin while sitting with her mama. The Fab Four. Tears welled in Savannah's eyes. She'd inadvertently jeopardized her family by expending precious reserves on Brozek. She'd be lucky to make it to the house now. Stupid, she railed at herself. Stupid, stupid, stupid.

Brozek glanced at her. His mouth curled into a slightly arrogant smirk – a first cousin to the one after he'd coerced Lily into that "favor" he later denied collecting on. He echoed Savannah's thoughts, "You'll never get to the house in your condition."

Using the rifle, she whacked him on the noggin Joe Bob-style, "Shut up, baby raper. When I come back, if you've moved one inch, I'll cure you of moving again, no matter how bad I feel." She leaned closer to make her point loud and clear, "And if I find out you touched my children, you won't see tomorrow."

Joe Bob employed his calf roping experience, fettering Brozek to match Sanchez. He completed the job by slapping a strip of tape over the molester's mouth. "Does this pass inspection?" he asked Savannah.

No. Nothing short of heaving the men outside *after* being shot would satisfy her. The same rules applied. Live or die. Dabbing more sweat from her brow, she nodded anyway.

"Just one more thing before we leave," Savannah pocketed the nitroglycerin pills on the counter. The brief respite allowed the shakiness to subside and strength and clarity to trickle in again.

Joe Bob frowned, "It doesn't involve rifles, does it?"

"No, just a little time." Against his ardent objections she pushed to her feet, "When I'm done, we'll drag him to the kids' bedroom and shove him in the closet and brace the door with something." She bent over. The room spun. She sank into the chair again.

Joe Bob's bewildered expression described how foolish she'd been to bend over in the first place. "What exactly were you trying to prove? That you can split your head completely open?"

Savannah pointed to Brozek's feet. "I was taking off their boots and socks," she groaned. More dizziness. More sweat. More nausea. *Dear God, help me get to that house without passing out...*

When Joe Bob reached for Brozek's bootlaces he uttered a muffled, defiant protest. Savannah's legs may have failed her but her tongue remained strong and sharp, "We're taking your boots and socks. We can either remove them or remove your feet. Take your pick."

Brozek grumbled behind the duct tape while Jenny's brother pulled the footwear off.

He finished removing Sanchez's boots and socks then dragged a still protesting Mr. Brozek to the kid's bedroom closet. Savannah heard the door latch shut. Joe Bob emerged with an update, "He ain't getting out anytime soon." He hitched his thumb at Sanchez, "Where do you want him?"

"Anywhere that'll slow him down should he get loose. I'll grab a pillowcase and gather what we need for our trip." Once on her feet, she tested her balance. So far so good.

Joe Bob chose the bed's footboard.  Considering it and the headboard were crafted from concrete masquerading as wood (or seemed that way), it was a good choice.  While he worked with Sanchez she dropped the two knives and Brozek's boots and socks in a pillowcase taken from the bed.  "I'll carry the pillowcase, a couple of guns and a flashlight if you can tote the other shotgun," she said when Joe Bob finished.

He toted Sanchez's boots over, "We'll get going as soon as I get these on you – they're kinda big but they'll do.  Then I'll get you another Tylenol, call Guthrie and redress your wound.  All the activity made it bleed again."

Savannah glanced down.  A fist-sized patch of blood seeped through her jeans.  She sat down with a sigh, "Yes, boss."

## 20

Every step with her right foot pulled at the wound. Sanchez's big dogs required some seriously large boots. Technically those boots probably weighed around two and a half pounds apiece but they felt heavier than cinder blocks.

Besides the torture devices laced to her feet, the most ridiculous looking piece of outerwear sat on her head and belonged to Ennis. Not that she accused her hubby of having an inflated head but his black Stetson gave her the elegance of a reject from Calamity Jane's School of Style.

The four items she was most grateful for during the quarter mile hike were the Sherpa coat, the gloves she found in the pockets, the unloaded shotgun she utilized as a cane and the Winchester cradled across her forearm. Between those and her partner they provided comfort and peace of mind she'd not had in several hours.

They trudged side by side, Joe Bob carrying his rifle and extra shotgun plus the pillowcase slung over his shoulder. He assigned her their only flashlight while he kept the twine and duct tape in his coat pockets.

Guided by soft moonlight reflecting off snow and the kitchen light as their compass, they retraced his earlier tracks back to the main house.

The monster storm blew out of the area, leaving her beloved country silence with an edgy eeriness. The normal sounds of rural life – traffic along roads, cows lowing in pastures – ceased to exist. She and Joe Bob walked another world, one of complete, deafening silence broken only by a few ice-encased tree branches clacking together in the stiff breeze. Several trees stood gap-toothed, their broken limbs protruding like bony brown fingers from drifts. The sight disheartened Savannah. Mama's fruit trees took a beating between the ice, clinging heavy snow and incessant, flogging winds.

"Quiet, isn't it?" Joe Bob mumbled.

"I've never heard it this quiet. Ever." It occurred to her that the silence worked against them as they neared the main house. Even with a blaring TV Hadley or Muñoz might notice small unusual noises, especially when she and Joe Bob moused around the basement entrance. Their first hurdle though, "The snow at the back of the house is crazy deep in places. It might take us both to clear it out," she said. Yeah, good luck with that bright idea, her leg ached in response. She grimaced at the intensifying pain flowing like lava along her leg. On a positive note the rock concert bouncing through her brain leveled off to a smaller cacophony from the percussion section.

Her comment neither surprised nor flustered him, "I'll do the digging. You stand watch. Is the basement's inner door locked?"

"Yes, or it should be. The key is in the generator room beside the house. Ennis and I have tried convincing Mama not to leave it so accessible but she refuses to listen."

He cracked a teasing smile, "I see you've converted Ennis to city thinking."

The ailing leg argued when forced to high-step the deeper drifts. She'd slowed down considerably since their trek began. The remaining distance to the house – a jaunt at a normal jog – equaled miles now.

Joe Bob stepped in front to plow an easier trail for her. Despite the chivalrous act, the mere motion of walking wore on her. She was becoming a detriment. Correction. She *was* a detriment. Slowing down, taking shorter strides and breaths while bearing the escalating pain. She relied more on the impromptu cane, trudging forward and wondering if she'd ever make it to the house and if so would she be any help once she got there.

Joe Bob slowed to her pace. "Need a breather?"

Sweat lined her chest and back beneath the coat. Between her groans and heavy breathing she sounded like an obscene phone call. Hell yes she wanted – needed – a breather but lives were at stake. "I'll rest later," she winced.

He shrugged, "Suit yourself." A few steps later he chuckled, "Y'know, Dane wasn't kidding about you."

Savannah was grateful for the change in subject. Anything to divert her from obsessing over that tempting breather he mentioned. "What did he say?"

"That you're one of the toughest women he's ever met."

She tried masking a cringe with a subdued laugh, "He meant bossiest."

"No, he said mentally and physically tough. Everything you've been through today and now you're hiking a quarter mile on a gimpy leg while pregnant? That's tough any way you look at it. Reckon God made another lady with your fortitude?"

"Do you want to lose your mind? I drive Ennis crazy. If you find a woman like me, my advice is run for your life."

"Nah. You and I get along really well so if I come across a lady like you, I think I'll chance it."

That was one thing she learned about Texas men. They liked to spoil their women but they also preferred their ladies with backbone. Ennis just never expected a backbone of iron. That's what drove him loony about her sometimes.

They approached the back of the house. Joe Bob flung the pillowcase in a drift and broke a trail to the kitchen window for Savannah. She ducked below the snow crusted screen to listen. CNN's muffled ramblings floated from the living room. The reception still sounded spotty. Yet another hiccup in their plan. No steady noise to camouflage their activity.

A half dollar sized portion of window screen provided a peephole into the kitchen. The tiny portal's limited scope revealed an empty room from what she could see.

"All clear?" Joe Bob whispered from behind.

She nodded. They baby-stepped through the deep snow for fear of tripping over land mines of planters, bird feeders and the basement doors that angled out from the house. Joe Bob relied on Savannah to locate the doors by poking the empty shotgun into the snow every other step. It slowed their progress but the threat of Muñoz charging out the back door kept her impatience at bay.

Another two steps. Poke. Another two. Poke. Where the hell *were* the doors? She'd estimated the distance from the back porch to their approximate location (or thought she had) but somehow her memory turned into the Bermuda Triangle. Information went in never to be seen again. Savannah poked ahead another step then twice more. Bingo. Bermuda Triangle be damned. She hadn't been that far off after all.

Jenny's brother plunged his gloved hands into the drift to begin scooping it away. Three inches. Six. Nine. Twelve. Fifteen. Over twenty inches buried the doors, a piddling amount compared to the mountainous drifts circling portions of the house.

The wet snow clung to his work gloves. He scrubbed his hands together then paused to catch his breath. He pulled a glove off, removed his Stetson and dragged his coat sleeve across his brow, "That's some mighty heavy snow."

Guilt weighed as heavy as the pain during their quarter mile hike. Joe Bob had plowed through snow and knocked down drifts to ease her passage – and that was *after* a roundtrip from Jake's to the main house and back again. Now he tunneled to China with his bare hands. It was far past time she pitched in to help.

Savannah laid the shotgun down, "I'll work on it while you rest."

He blocked her way. "You keep us safe and I'll get us in there."

It took a while to uncover the two sloping shutter-like doors. Once open, stairs led down to the entry door into the basement. Inside, the stairway leading upstairs opened into the mudroom. They needed luck and stealth to climb them. The risers creaked in places and considering Savannah's condition, both luck and stealth sounded laughable. Noises frequently traveled from the basement to the mudroom and depending on the racket it sometimes resonated into the living room. She never thought she'd count on the one thing she hated to help them out. Good old chatterbox CNN. If they kept their political crusades a'comin', she and Joe Bob stood a chance.

"Okay," Joe Bob rubbed the snow off his gloves, "let's grab the door key before we open these up." His long legs churned, knees lifting high to plow through drifts taller than mid-thigh on the six foot four Texan. Being shorter, she followed his trail, stunned (and growing ever more claustrophobic) at the snow gradually increasing in height on both sides of her. She'd never have made it, not alone. Not cutting trails in such dense wet snow or tearing down unfathomable drifts to dig the basement doors free. Joe Bob Crawford was a godsend and a strong one at that.

They plowed past a sharp depression in a drift that made Savannah wince. The wind blew a fresh layer of snow over bloodstains and smoothed the edges where she clawed a path in her desperate attempt to escape Muñoz. *Daniel and I should have died right there. Would have too if not for Joe Bob.*

The two plodded around the corner, perilously close to the back bathroom window. Since one never knew when nature might call a killer to pee, she whispered her question.  "How do we disable the generator? It's not as if we just unplug it, right?"

He found the question humorous.  "Never fear, City Girl, Joe Bob's here.  It's a matter of swiping the key to keep it from starting."

They reached the small generator shed attached to her late father-in-law's study.  The room provided a cushion for noise between them and the living room.  The bathroom, though, sat right where Joe Bob toiled his way to the shed door.  At least, Savannah thought, Mama kept the generator room unlocked for convenience.  She also prayed the door opened without too much fuss or clatter.

Joe Bob plunged his hands deep then scooped a load of snow aside.  Minutes later he leaned on his knees, huffing clouds of breath.  A short break later, he straightened with a hand bracing his back.  His crimson face and neck shined with sweat.  He mopped his brow with his coat sleeve, replaced his hat, "You ready?"

She nodded, keeping watching to both front and back yards. Anyone poking his nose around those corners would get a big surprise for his trouble.

A mild, subdued curse fell from Joe Bob's lips.  Ice coated the latch.  He stepped aside.  "You wanted to help so blow on that thing and try to loosen her up while I take a break."

She cupped a hand around the latch and did her best.  It wasn't thawing real fast but they only needed a little progress to break it loose. Joe Bob tested the latch then gave it a good, solid yank.  It snapped open.

A tug on the door revealed it was as frozen as the latch had been. It refused to budge.  "I may be full of hot air sometimes," she told him, "but I don't have enough to thaw *that* out."

"I gotta pull it loose," he said. "I'll try to be quiet. Be ready in case I screw up."

Joe Bob bumped it with his shoulder then pulled on the handle. A loud crack caused Savannah to wince in places and pucker in others. Only the deaf and the dead missed that piercing shriek, she thought while bracing the rifle against her shoulder. For several moments she stopped breathing. Her heart galloped in her chest. When would Muñoz come around the corner? And which corner, back yard or front? Or would he bust a window for target practice on a cowboy and wounded police sergeant? They'd literally be sitting ducks if he chose the bathroom window behind them.

Joe Bob scrambled to ready his rifle. He covered the front yard while Savannah guarded the back and window. Looking. Waiting. Prepared for any inquisitive homicidal lifers investigating the strange sound. She drew in a shaky breath. Willed her heart to calm down. Seconds stretched to one minute then two. Joe Bob lowered his rifle. Savannah couldn't bring herself to follow his lead.

She took just enough time to hand Joe Bob the flashlight then returned to guard duty. He stepped inside the small room and quickly zeroed in on the generator and basement keys. He handed them to her and she pocketed them in the coat.

Joe Bob crouched to avoid bouncing his forehead off the door frame. "Ain't no way they can make it work now," he said. "Let's go back to the basement. Stay on guard 'cause those doors probably creak worse than this one."

So much for the element of surprise. She moved to the back door, rifle at the ready and halfway hoping Muñoz might charge out the door. What she wouldn't give to thrust the butt of that thing right into his nose, drop him and finish the job. He'd put her through hell that day and deserved a healthy dose of payback.

Joe Bob gave the doors a quick, firm yank, dragging her from musings of revenge.

She nearly fainted when the layer of ice busting loose mimicked a small gunshot and the subsequent high-pitched screech sounded like a cat caught under a rocking chair. While Joe Bob lifted the left door and propped it against the drift beside it, she braced for one final confrontation with Muñoz.

Savannah listened at the back door, her heart rioting in her chest. Long seconds ticked by. No change inside. CNN's incessant droning actually served a purpose on the planet that day and if the satellite reception stayed semi-reliable she and Joe Bob stood a chance.

She signaled her partner with a *so far so good* thumbs-up. His shoulders sagged as he sighed a relieved frosty breath.

She stumped back to the basement doors and stared down into the black cavern. A single door stood between them and welcome warmth (warmer than the wretched outdoors at least) – and an opportunity to recoup strength and review their plan. They needed all three.

Joe Bob lit the way for her. She abandoned the makeshift cane, choosing the railing to descend the steps. He followed behind.

She pulled off the gloves to fish for the key in her coat pocket. It trembled in her grasp when she tried unlocking the door. Joe Bob reached around to steady her hand. When the door swung open, a pleasant wave of heat embraced her. The cool basement felt close to heaven compared to the iceberg outside and it tempted her to pause and luxuriate in the comfort.

The overhead light bathed the room in a soft glow when she flipped the switch.

Joe Bob went slack-jawed, "Wow. Look at all this stuff."

The basement stored a variety of items. Mama dedicated one side to gardening equipment and everyday tools. Savannah's vision locked on the two snow shovels leaned against the wall. A small puddle pooled beneath one. She sneered at it. The damn thing nearly killed her that morning from the exertion.

A rainbow of colors in Mason jars lined shelves on the other side of the room. Preserved pickles (both sweet and dill), apple butter, relish, peppers, corn, green beans, and tomatoes occupied one shelf. The one below contained peaches, cherries and blackberries from her coveted trees and bushes. The lower shelves stored canning equipment, ice cream makers, an eighteen quart roaster, dry goods and bottled water.

Joe Bob shook his head in awe, "Their ma is ready for anything. We could lose the guns and bash 'em with shovels, hit 'em with hammers or throw hatchets at their heads." He pointed across the room, "Even that ice cream maker would bean 'em good."

Savannah couldn't help but chuckle at Joe Bob's response. She shrugged out of the coat, draped it over a box beneath the stairway then laid Ennis's Stetson on top. She took a moment to finger-comb her hair.

Meanwhile Joe Bob meandered to the breaker box not far from the basement stairs. He accessed the panel and waved her over. "Just hit every switch on here. I'll get on in the living room then I'll holler for ya."

*Sorry, Joe Bob. Now our rolls reverse and you get to take orders from me.* Oh, he'd fuss and fume the way her very own Texan did when she beefed up her backbone – but he usually capitulated. She blocked the stairs, "The breakers are your job. That and covering our backs."

An unhappy Joe Bob flung his coat beside hers. His look accused her of being tetched in the head, "And leave you up there fighting those jerks? No way, honey, not with a baby on board." His hands rested on her shoulders. He applied gentle pressure to move her aside. She stayed put. In a hushed tone he repeated, "A *baby*, Savannah. Daniel wants to survive this too."

Earlier she bought a ticket for a guilt trip when Joe Bob dug through the equivalent of the Arctic by himself. She changed planes since then. Unless Joe Bob owned a shiny badge and took an oath to protect and serve, barging into that living room was her job, not his. Atlanta PD's motto was *Resurgens.* She intended to show Luis Muñoz that along with the city she protected, she herself managed to rise again – with a lot of help from a compassionate and hopelessly stubborn cowboy. So no, Joe Bob, "I've got the badge, not you."

"You're a mother."

She smiled, "You've got an answer for everything, don't you?"

"Yes, ma'am, and I'm having my way about this," he tried squeezing past again.

This time *she* stopped him with hands on *his* shoulders. She understood Jenny Lee's love and devotion for her brother. Joe Bob was a kind, protective soul and a fine man.    He did what he considered necessary to help a person, even if that meant using his lofty seven inch height advantage *and* an admirable frown to encourage that person to acquiesce.  Savannah lacked five good inches on her husband too and he rarely succeeded with that tactic.  "Not this time, Joe Bob.  If things go wrong, I'll need good backup."

"And if something happens to you or the baby?  Do you know how I'll feel knowing I stood back and let you do this?  Ennis would kill me and rightly so."

"Ennis fully expects me to take the lead in these situations."  *He hates it but expects it.*  "C'mon, Big Joe.  Let's go save our families."  As she climbed she sensed Joe Bob's nearness until his hand settled on her hip, "I'm at least seeing you to the landing *then* I'll go back down."  Mule-headed female, he grumbled.

"Still want a woman like me?" she teased.  She led each stair with the left foot then bit back a groan the second any weight settled on the injured right leg.  Pain-induced sweat returned with a vengeance.  The higher they climbed, the slower she moved.

"You're favoring that leg pretty hard." Joe Bob whispered.  "You won't make it ten feet on that thing.  Let me help you back down."

"No.  I can do this."  She dabbed perspiration.  Stared at the top step that might as well represent the peak of Mount Everest.

The headache and leg threatened to steal her focus and composure.  She pressed her lips tight.  They'd come too far to let one groan or whimper betray them.

"Savannah, let me by."

*Your family is in danger. You can do this. You will do this.* Those words became her motivation. *You can. You will.* "I got it. Just needed a break." And a new leg, please. "Last stair. You can go now. Thanks."

Ear to the door, she listened for movement and voices. Someone (she guessed Muñoz) shushed everyone as a CNN breaking news alert sounded. Savannah caught pieces of the report, "…four escaped inmates from Gatesville…" She pressed closer, "…been located west of Amarillo along I-40. No other details are available at this time…"

"Shit." She let the curse slip.

"What?"

"The media know enough to panic Muñoz. We've got to hurry."

The word "hurry" scarcely left her lips when Luis Muñoz's temper detonated.

"*Who called the cops!?*"

Savannah eased away from the door. No need eavesdropping now. The yelling thundered through the wall.

The TV volume cut off. He lashed out at the family, hurling accusations and leveling threats. "We took your phones. We disabled the phone line. You and you. You were the last ones in the john. Somehow one of you called 'em."

Savannah shook her head. Muñoz never bothered with logic. He stayed too busy reacting.

"There's no phone in the bathroom and you took my cell phone." Georgia.

"*You* then. You gotta have a phone on you."

"Brozek searched me this morning and found it. Remember?" Gina.

If this escalated, Savannah couldn't wait for Joe Bob to throw the breakers. She'd take them by surprise any way possible, lights or no lights.

Muñoz zeroed in on another victim, "How about it, Grandma? You got a cell phone stashed in the john? You went in there after I killed that bitch and you were gone a long time. Did you make a call while you were in there?"

"For your information, Savannah is…" Mama's voice caught in her throat. She was crying. "Savannah *was* a very sweet girl and I begged you for a bathroom break because I was sick to my stomach–"

"I asked you a question, old lady."

"No one in this house called a soul because we couldn't."

"I think you're lying to me. Get up."

"No."

Mama shrieked.

"Get. Up."

The bottom dropped out of Savannah's stomach. Mama was next on Muñoz's hit list if someone didn't intervene quick. She frantically shooed Joe Bob back, "Go get ready. I'll give the signal."

"Muñoz, look." A second later the TV blared to life again. The CNN reporter announced a slightly more precise location as "a small town" along I-40. She included a postscript saying FBI agents were assembling to move in as soon as possible.

Savannah wanted to groan. Just enough information. The woman released just enough vital information to compromise the family. God, Savannah hated CNN. The world may not figure out which small town but Muñoz and Hadley knew.

Muñoz transformed from armed bully to panicked fugitive, "Go find Brozek and Sanchez. We're leaving."

Hadley laughed. A laugh cut short by a loud thud reverberating through the wall. "Laugh again," Muñoz warned, "and you'll join that bitch cop outside. We are leaving and for insurance we're taking the older girl. Lily."

If Hadley kept pushing, he would discover no one ridiculed Muñoz and got away with it. And push he did, "Luis, explain how we're supposed to get out of here."

Muñoz's tone verged on incredulous, "It's a ranch, isn't it? Hey Grandma, you got a tractor like Elron's, right?"

Mama elected not to correct his faux pas, "Yes, we have a tractor."

"Seriously?" Hadley asked. Savannah sensed him barely restraining another chuckle, "A tractor? We're gonna look like O.J., only dumber. We can't cram five people in a tractor cab. The kid'll have to be a hood ornament."

Another collision against the wall. Hadley uttered pained acquiescence. Savannah guessed Hadley might soon sport bruises like her own. He broke the first two rules of "How to Get Along With Luis Muñoz". One, *Thou shalt not argue with Luis* and two, *Thou shalt not mock Luis.*

CNN's report brought out a new facet to the angry lunatic threatening to kill everyone. Muñoz transformed to a scared, cornered animal making irrational decisions just to survive and those irrational decisions included Savannah's child.

"We gotta get outta here now," Muñoz demanded.

"Get ready," Savannah whispered to Joe Bob. He acknowledged with a thumbs-up.

Muñoz asked, "Where's the tractor?"

No one answered.

"You want to end up like your *sweet* daughter-in-law? Where is the tractor?"

Mama refused to speak.

"In a building down thataway," Cal uttered in a rare clipped fashion. Savannah pictured him nodding in the direction she and Joe Bob came from.

Muñoz directed Hadley, "Go find the tractor. If you run across that thing I lost, take care of it."

Savannah's loose interpretation: Put a bullet between "that thing's" eyes and make sure she's dead.

Hadley's aggravation flared, "I've never driven one but isn't a key required to start a tractor?"

"Hangin' on the caddy at the back door," Cal's tone insinuated they were too stupid to find their asses with two hands and a map.

Hadley and Muñoz moved toward the back door as they spoke. She eased down a few steps in case they headed her way.

"Can tractors navigate snow this deep?" Hadley wanted to know.

"It's deeper than when that hillbilly brought the eggs and milk."

"We'll find out, won't we?"

"I can tell you one thing. Taking that kid along is a mistake. She'll be more trouble than she's worth and we need that cab space for us."

"If you want room in the cab, kill Brozek and Sanchez if you see them. That solves half your problem." Muñoz's voice neared the basement door. Savannah backed down the stairs as he told Hadley, "That kid keeps us alive. Cops won't risk shooting a kid."

She signaled Joe Bob. A second later the basement – and whole house – plunged into darkness.

## 21

Muñoz ordered Hadley downstairs, "The Feds are here. You know what to do."

Joe Bob shined the flashlight at the cubbyhole beneath the stairway, leaving it on just long enough for them to wedge into the cramped space beside Mama's boxed up Christmas decorations.

Footsteps approached the basement door. It swung open until slamming against the stop. Muñoz's ominous ranting at the family grew progressively out of control. Savannah urged Hadley to hurry. She wanted him out of the way so she could deal with Muñoz herself.

Methodical Hadley, however, moved at a pace that put tortoises to shame. His flashlight beam shifted across the room searching for intruders. A second, more thorough sweep, perused the area in detail beginning at the breaker box, then scanning across shelves of canned vegetables and preserves then to the door leading outside. From there it highlighted the tools then traveled to Mama's and plastic boxes filled with Christmas wrapping paper, ribbons and bows.

Muñoz yelled from the living room, "What's going on down

there?"

"Looks like a power outage. I'll check the breaker box."

"Once you get the lights on, get the tractor."

"Yes, Luis," Hadley answered then grumbled a sarcastic, "I'll get the tractor, kill Brozek and Sanchez then if I find her, I'll put *another* bullet in that bitch. You're lucky I don't put a bullet in you, you crazy bastar–"

The beam jerked back to the entry door across the room. Hadley muttered, "Maybe you're not so crazy after all."

Savannah tensed at the sight. They'd forgotten to mop up the melted snow from their boots. That one mistake cost them the element of surprise. When he rounded the bottom of the stairway, he'd be on guard and probably trigger happy.

Hadley moved the light around the room, "Let's see. Who dug through all that snow to get inside? Obviously not the Feds, no matter what that idiot upstairs thinks. Feds come in swarms." The stairs above her creaked. Guided by the beam, Hadley descended slow and cautious and with a swagger in his voice, eliminating possibilities along the way, "Can't be a police sergeant. Muñoz knocked himself screwy but he still shot her so there's no way she could dig those basement doors free."

Sweat chilled her. She tried to control the rapid, panic induced breaths. He was coming and they had to act quickly.

His footsteps dropped harder on the stairs, "Okay, game's over. Come on out."

He hit the bottom stair. Boots scraped the concrete floor in a lazy gait. No hurry, no worry. The light swung back and forth. The effect made Savannah dizzy and a little sick but closing her eyes made her vulnerable and would let her partner down.

Hadley rounded the base of the stairs. Joe Bob placed his hand on her arm to hold her back. She decided not to argue considering her overall substandard condition. She'd save her strength for climbing those miserable stairs – and beating the shit out of Muñoz.

Hadley gradually came into sight. The flashlight's beam arced across then jerked from the door right to their hiding place. The brilliant light speared straight to her brain.

Joe Bob struck with a cheetah's speed and agility. He kicked at Hadley's knee, dropping him to the floor. The flashlight and gun clattered to the concrete. The light spun and when it stopped, the beam shined directly in Hadley's face.

Savannah scrambled from the cubby, rifle at the ready. She poked Hadley in the back with the barrel, "Make a sound and that knee's the least of your worries."

"I see you're not as dead as he hoped," Hadley cringed.

"Not even close." She placed his .45 on a box containing wrapping paper.

Joe Bob shoved a hand in his coat for the twine and tape. He added a caution to Hadley, "You move and I'll turn her loose on you. And believe me, mister, she'll do serious damage." He stretched a length of twine to begin tying Hadley up.

Muñoz shouted. A shot rang out. Women screamed. Georgia's voice plunged like an icy hand into Savannah's chest. It seized her heart in agony so intense it nearly took her to her knees.

"Lily!" Georgia sounded so distraught it could only mean one thing.

*No, no, no. Not my little girl. Not my babies...*

Panic overrode pain. Much to Joe Bob's frustration and objections, she broke into a loping sprint toward the stairway.

Horrific images filled her mind and adding to them, Hadley's perverse glee as he laughed, "What's the rush? Your husband's dead and now your kid is too."

Joe Bob abandoned the twine for duct tape. He clenched a fistful of Hadley's hair, yanked his head back and slapped a long strip across his mouth. She'd rounded the stairway when Joe Bob uttered the same demand for her to wait then fought against Hadley who thrashed to free himself. He knocked Joe Bob back. Savannah saw her friend wrestle him flat again. "You got him?" she asked.

"Yeah, but you better wait for me. You're not doing this alone."

That's what he thought. She began the climb up. This time she intended to blast someone to kingdom come no matter what Joe Bob said. Dispatching Muñoz wouldn't bring Ennis or Lily back and blowing a hole in his head wouldn't relieve an ounce of heartbreak but it would let God sort the bastard out sooner than later. Her world crumbled, sending her into emotional free fall. Half of their "Fab Four" (soon to be five) vanished in the blink of an eye. *Too late. I'm too late.* She'd waited too long to journey back to the house. If she'd passed on the chicken soup or pushed Joe Bob to leave sooner – or not wasted precious time with Brozek – Ennis and Lily would be alive. Now they both lay dead upstairs. In one brief afternoon full of bad decisions Savannah lost her soul mate and her cherished firstborn. She, Anna and Daniel were left behind to bear unfathomable, overwhelming loss and try to piece their lives back together. Savannah couldn't promise herself or her remaining family much except one thing: Luis Muñoz would pay for killing Ennis and Lily. He would not leave that house alive.

Joe Bob planted a foot in Hadley's back. He still struggled with subduing him. Savannah knew he could handle the killer – he already had his hands tied – or he'd call her for help, not try to stop her from dispensing justice.

"Once I'm done with him," Joe Bob vowed to her, "I'm trussing you up next. Wait for me."

She heard his impatience and frustration but she'd wasted enough time that day and because of it the Rutherford house gradually became a killing field. She gripped the rifle in one hand and with the other pulled herself up each stair via the railing.

Another bout of yelling – Muñoz vs. Georgia – spurred her to climb faster despite the pain. Savannah already lost too many loved ones. She'd be damned if she lost her sister too. Georgia possessed a heart of gold but also a bold tongue and Savannah learned firsthand that bold tongues bought a heap of trouble called a bullet.

"*Savannah, stop.*"

"Not unless you need me," she answered Joe Bob's exasperated plea. She pursed her lips. If she uttered one more syllable, words weren't coming out. A scream was. Rage and revenge dulled only so much pain.

Muñoz stormed around the living room. The sudden blackout tipped his already unstable demeanor into the red zone. He shouted at

Hadley to "turn on the lights and get your ass upstairs to help me". The daunting task of keeping nearly a dozen captives under control – basically in the dark – fractured the last of his dwindling patience.

She took delicate, cautious steps through the mudroom to the hallway. Moving from tile to carpet, she eased along the hallway then paused when a shaft of light arced back and forth across the living room walls. The flashlight beam cast long, distorted, almost dizzying silhouettes onto the floor, ceiling and walls as he erratically waved the .45 between family members.

While his back was turned Savannah did a quick head count. Aside from two changes the assigned seating remained the same. She noticed everyone over ten years old had their hands *and* feet tied now, effectively eliminating the possibility of the family's help. And the most prominent change – and most heartbreaking: One seat sat empty. Ennis's.

Hadley's cruel declaration fed her worst fears. At some point while she recovered from her own close call, Muñoz murdered her husband.

She trapped an impulsive sob behind her lips. She couldn't explain why she believed Hadley except the whole trip went to hell the moment they stepped onto Rutherford soil. Now she'd lost her husband and Lily and... Where was Anna? Where was her baby girl? She couldn't have lost everyone in her little family, could she?

Peering around the corner, she finally let herself breathe. Anna found refuge in the unlikeliest of places. Jenny Lee's lap. To her credit, Joe Bob's sister wrapped the toddler in a shielding embrace and used a tender voice to settle Anna's sniffles and fussing. Savannah was grateful.

Muñoz blocked Savannah's view of Georgia but Savannah caught a glimpse of Lily's legs draped across her sister's lap. Georgia held her niece, shushing her as she cried and whimpered.

Savannah turned, her back against the wall. She fought the rush of tears and relief crashing over her. Lily *wasn't* dead. *Both* her girls were alive.

She looked to heaven to thank God for sparing her children. She also prayed fear drove Lily's crying, not pain from a gunshot wound. Muñoz hadn't taken Lily from her (*yet*, her mind taunted) but the cold, cruel truth was he'd ripped Ennis from her arms forever.

The crippling sorrow twisted inside until it wrung the life from her. The love of her life – gone forever. Now she and her kids would return to Atlanta with their husband and daddy in a casket.

A brief exchange between Muñoz and Gina quickly escalated to violence when he delivered a debilitating blow across Gina's cheek with the flashlight. It winked out. The darkness sent him into another rage, cursing her, cursing them all.

Savannah shouldered the rifle and padded across the carpet, using his voice as a guide. She could barely discern his burly outline in the room and crept within arm's length of her biggest nemesis since Jeffrey Holland. It gave her immense pleasure to jab the rifle into Muñoz's back, cutting off his tirade in mid-rant.

"Remember me?" she asked.

Georgia, Mama and Bobbi gasped. The room fell silent.

"Savannah?" A man's voice came from her right, around the spot

Muñoz nearly plugged her between the eyes that afternoon.

"Savannah, is that you?"  The soft, halting voice repeated, this time on the verge of tears.  Hope buoyed the words but not too much, as if he needed confirmation before daring to believe it was her.

A flutter in her belly – Daniel, maybe – seemed to recognize the voice.  She did too but… *It can't be.  He's dead, remember?  Ennis is dead.*

Her brain tried to make sense of it.  But Hadley said…  And Ennis's seat is vacant…  Could it be true, that he's alive?

Her heart forged ahead.  I know that voice, it said, and so do you.  You've heard it for nine going on ten wonderful years.

The crushing weight of loss began lifting – but like the hesitant voice nearby, Savannah required proof before letting herself believe the voice belonged to, "Ennis?"

Light flooded the room.  Jaws slackened.  Eyes bulged.  Yes, it's me, just worse for wear, she wanted to say but busied herself looking between Mama's rocker and the bar.

"It is Savannah!" Georgia rejoiced.

"Mama's back!" Lily cheered.  "She's really back!"

Savannah had her own reason to cheer.  Not only were her daughters among the living (apparently without a scratch on them) but slumped against the bookshelves sat her soul mate sobbing, "You're alive.  Thank God you're alive."

During their hours apart Ennis suffered his share of beatings.  His left eye swelled and a sizeable knot jutted from his jaw.  Through his tears he stared at Savannah as if she'd risen from the grave – and she figured she looked like it too between her own bruises, the loose, tangled curls, her hunched shoulders and the blood-stained pant leg. "Mrs. Paul Bunyan", as Joe Bob labeled her, lived to fight another battle – this one against a blue-eyed bastard who terrorized her family and now grabbed for Lily...

"Don't do it, Muñoz. Drop the gun and get the hell away from my family." Savannah's command silenced the family.

Muñoz ignored her. He realized her predicament. Lily and Georgia sat too close to her line of fire. Shifting to either side put other family members in jeopardy. Murphy's Law, she lamented, still present and accounted for in the Rutherford house.

Lily's shriek pierced the air as he yanked her from Georgia's lap. There was an instant when he leaned down that the .45 strayed from Lily's head – a near perfect opportunity for Savannah to act – except (Murphy laughed again) the shot's trajectory might have taken out Georgia as well.

When he turned to face Savannah, he'd braced Lily to his chest. "You want me to drop the gun, Sergeant? Then take it from me."

The girl centered on the rifle pointed at her. Savannah's aim rose to Muñoz's face as he pushed the .45's muzzle beneath Lily's chin. "You willing to risk your daughter for this gun?" he asked. "It means that much to you?"

Lily's wide eyes locked on the weapon in her mother's hands. Savannah never felt more traitorous than aiming a gun anywhere near her daughter. *Are you steady enough to take out Muñoz and not Lily? Are you willing to risk your child's life because her head is meager <u>inches</u>*

*from his – and he's anxious, fidgety. See how he keeps moving? How he shifts back and forth ever so slightly? You might miss him and shoot her by accident or if you pull the trigger, he might too.*

Muñoz's mouth curved into the smug, telltale smile Savannah remembered when he marched her outside and shot her. He taunted her, verbalizing her inner struggle, "You shoot me, I shoot her. If your aim is off, you shoot her. Decisions, decisions."

Savannah made the mistake of meeting Lily's watery gaze. Tears trembled in her eyes as if her mother targeted her, not Muñoz – or maybe the youngster noticed the tremor beginning in her hand.

Savannah's job depended on a steady aim but after Jeffrey's slicing and dicing and the subsequent surgery, occasionally it faltered under duress. The rifle's firm pressure against her shoulder hastened the tremor to return. The muscles tensed and trembled, skewing her accuracy a shade and shaking her confidence as a cop and as a mother attempting to save her child. "You still want to kill me? I'm right here. I'll trade places with her."

The family objected with a level of vehemence and volume that compressed her brain inside her skull. The racket also derailed her train of thought. No matter their accusations or assumptions, she hadn't blindly volunteered to die. She had a plan to save both Lily and herself – or did until all hell broke loose among the natives.

Savannah saw movement behind Muñoz. Georgia hurriedly mined for the .38 between the couch cushions. "Not now, Georgia," she warned.

Heaving a furious sigh, Georgia slowed her search but fell short of actually obeying.  Although she did, once more, accuse Savannah of being suicidal and stark raving mad.

"Get rid of the gun first," Muñoz said.  "Any tricks and I kill the kid then you."

"Savannah, what about Daniel?  You're not just sacrificing yourself, you know," Georgia reminded.  The verbal chaos ebbed several decibels when she mentioned the baby.

Savannah squeezed tears from her eyes, "Shut up, Georgia." *I've got enough to deal with.  I don't need guilt too.*

She laid the Winchester down.  "Let Lily go."

Lily's feet hit the floor.  Muñoz shoved her aside.  Savannah winced in sympathy.  The push nearly sent the child sprawling in the floor.

The child scrambled to her feet then rounded on Muñoz.  Most kids would have run for cover, Savannah reflected.  Not her kid.  Standing up to bratty Jenny Lee was one thing but confronting a murderer was another.

"Lily, go to Aunt Bobbi," Savannah ordered.  *Now's not the time for the Prince genes to kick in.*  Those little microscopic bastards caused trouble for generations in the family.  Firefighters ran toward fire.  Cops rushed into danger.  Princes bulled headfirst into brawls and if there wasn't a brawl, they'd create one.  "*Go to Aunt Bobbi,*" Savannah repeated, hoping to stave off disaster.

Lily stood her ground then tried for some inexplicable reason to induce that heart attack Savannah worked all day to avoid.  She charged toward Muñoz like a bully's victim who'd taken a bellyful from her aggressor and decided to turn the tables. The girl swung her fists back like a batter eyeing a home run pitch.

Savannah and Ennis started early teaching their girls self-defense. Bite, claw, scream and kick. Anything to draw attention, anything to save themselves. Seeing those lessons in action, Savannah briefly tried to recall if they covered the subject of "What to do if a crazy man holds a gun to someone's head". Lily wanted to save her mother but while Savannah watched her fists launch toward Muñoz's crotch, all she saw was certain death for herself then her brave firstborn – or vice versa.

Muñoz took aim on Lily. The girl's punch smashed into its target at the same time Savannah knocked the gun's trajectory upward. Muñoz fired. The shot went over Lily's head but she stood frozen with fear.

"*Lily, run!*" Savannah yelled at her daughter.

Lily ran straight for Bobbi.

In that split second before Muñoz targeted her child again, Savannah grabbed the gun barrel, forced it downward and drove the heel of her hand against the inside of his wrist. For the first time that day, she gained the upper hand. No one on the planet stood a chance of prying that .45 from her grasp. She took dead aim on his chest while evading his attempts to snatch the weapon from her.

Georgia got to her feet. She secured the .38 in both hands and shoved the muzzle against his temple with a command to drop to his knees. There was only one problem. Muñoz didn't give a shit if a cannon pressed against his head. He wasn't giving up.

He advanced toward Savannah, determined to reclaim the gun

and finish the job.

She employed her cop voice, "Listen, you sorry son of a –" she stopped herself before cutting loose with coarse language. "When you're told to drop to your knees, you drop." She balled her fist, summoned every ounce of power and momentum and slammed her knuckles into his chin. And he dropped.

Venomous slurs spewed out. The attack may have temporarily disabled him but it also stoked his rage. "I don't need a gun to kill you."

She saw his muscles tense and stepped back.

"Don't move, Muñoz," Joe Bob made a beeline beside Savannah. He braced the Remington against his shoulder and sighted straight at the killer. "She's in a very bad mood today. Just ask Brozek."

Georgia added a little extra incentive, "I've got five shots just waiting for you."

Savannah hated to tell Georgia but any shooting was her responsibility. It was her child that scarcely escaped death. The day Savannah joined the academy she signed up to meet danger head-on. Her daughter hadn't and the bastard tried to kill her. For that he would pay.

She leveled the gun between his eyes. Now she'd see how he enjoyed being on the business end of a loaded weapon, "You tried to shoot my little girl. *You tried to kill her.*" It still sounded so surreal, that someone not only took aim on her daughter but also pulled the trigger. By the grace of God his shot missed. Savannah's wouldn't.

"Lily," Ennis frantically summoned, "come here quick."

The ringing subsided in Savannah's ears enough that voices and noises sharpened. Those voices begged her not to shoot Muñoz. They couldn't see what she saw. The determination in his eyes. His clenched teeth. He wanted that gun and intended to get any way possible. Giving up never entered his mind despite her busting him in the jaw and having his nuts jangled by a child's impressive punch. Now for some reason he started mocking the woman about to shoot him.

"Savannah, ignore him and step away," Georgia told her. "We've got this."

And here came her moral compass. Joe Bob offered his two cents in a kind but firm, "We discussed this earlier, remember? Killing these animals won't do any good. Let the law have him. He'll die of old age in prison."

"No, he won't," she argued. "He'll get out and come after me and the girls. It happened with Jeffrey Holland."

"Damn right, I will," Muñoz vowed. "You'd better shoot me unless you want me on your doorstep someday, Sergeant. You won't though. You're a coward. Anyone else would have shot me already. Guess I'll be seeing you again soon."

Georgia focused on her sister's trigger finger. "Listen to me, Savannah. Ignore him. Put the gun down."

Lily's close call replayed in Savannah's mind. One small hesitation meant death for her little girl. She wanted revenge for her daughter, the family and herself. They'd gone through hell and barely survived. If she let him live, he'd show up again like Jeffrey had. He'd escaped prison once, why not twice? No, this time she'd make sure there was no killer on their doorstep sooner, later or ever again.

A vigorous tugging on her shirttail diverted her attention. Lily. She yanked feverishly until Savannah glanced down at her. Her daughter expressed three of the most beautiful words Savannah ever heard, "I'm okay, Mama." Then she made a simple request, "I want a hug now."

Seeing her baby's sweet face snapped her from the murderous rage. She experienced that depth of anger only once before. The day she tried to kill Jeffrey Holland. Golf driver gripped tight in her hands, she took the granddaddy of all swings at him to finish off the killer – until Ennis stopped her.

In those moments before Lily tugged at her, Jeffrey's face and voice replaced Muñoz's, sending Savannah back years when she came within a second of the driver colliding with Holland's head. She'd been so immersed in that vision – in eliminating the threat – that she lost total awareness of her surroundings and the fact her children were watching.

Savannah suspected Ennis sent Lily to intervene before his wife turned into the Terminator. They exchanged a glance. His nod confirmed that yes, he was the culprit. Years ago he wrestled that golf club from her hands to prevent a killing. Today he sent their daughter to talk her down. Ennis knew her too well, she thought. Who wanted to hold a gun when they could hold their child?

She held the gun but only to keep Muñoz from reaching it and allowed Georgia and Joe Bob to take over while she drew Lily into her arms.

"Sorry I was late getting in here," Joe Bob apologized. He laid the Remington across his arm to access the roll of twine in his coat. "That fella downstairs is stronger than he looks. By the way, is there an

'I' in 'team' that I missed? What happened to us doing this together? You coulda been killed."

She held Lily tighter, "I was afraid," she swallowed hard to contain her emotions, "I was afraid Lily was gone."

What sounded like an army pounded their way down the hall. "Drop your weapons!" a voice shouted behind her. Ah yes. It had to be the Friggin' Bunch of Idiots coming to the rescue. Some cavalry, she thought. They're more like the clean-up crew.

A swarm of men dressed in full combat gear invaded the room. She caught sight of the white lettering on their chests. Sure enough. The FBI.

With his assault rifle trained on Savannah, the walking bullhorn stepped to her right and again practically yelled *drop the gun* at her.

Georgia and Joe Bob already followed orders, slowly setting the .38 and Remington aside.

Another agent jerked Lily away. She screamed and flailed in his grasp. *Bite, claw, scream and kick.* Apparently the child utilized them to free herself. Before the Fed went down with cracked walnuts like Muñoz, Savannah reminded Lily that although incompetent, they were in fact police.

Savannah placed the gun on the floor, painfully straightened with hands lifted in surrender. She hadn't come that far to be blown away by a dipshit who likened himself to John Wayne.

"No, *you're* the police!" Lily shouted to her mama. "You saved us!"

A hand clamped around Savannah's wrist and twisted her arm

behind her.  Handcuffs rattled.  Her shoulders sagged as metal cinched down around one wrist then the other.  Seriously?  *Handcuffs?*  The day's indignities never ended.

The cuffs sent Lily into orbit, "I have her badge!  Look at her badge!"

From the corner of her eye, Savannah saw her open the wallet and shove it right in the agent's face.  He looked then nodded to his partner.  The cuffs came off.

Before they slapped a set on Georgia or Joe Bob, Savannah explained who they were and that they were harmless.  Harmless to the good guys, she added, hoping they might take a hint.

The agent cut Lily's hands free and she raced back to her mother.  Lily's strength surprised Savannah when her arms cinched around her in an embrace so strong it seemed to dare anyone to try separating them again.

In that instant a deep calm settled over Savannah for the first time that day.  The bear hug amounted to heaven on earth.  The Fab Four (soon to be five) remained intact.  A whole lot wearier, bruised and injured but alive nonetheless.

More Feds made the rounds cutting the ropes binding the family's hands and feet while the biggest, burliest agents Savannah ever laid eyes on swarmed Muñoz with cuffs and orders not to move.  A young, fresh-from-the-academy rookie searched his pockets.  He seemed shocked to mine out a handful of gold bands and diamond rings.  The young man waited patiently for the ladies and gents to claim their rings.  Savannah yearned to wear hers again.  To some people it might have sounded strange but she felt incomplete without it.

When his palm emptied, though, Savannah was the only one left without a ring. "Where's mine?" A thread of panic laced her voice. "He put it in his right front pocket. Is it gone?"

Lily held her hand whether to console her or prevent bloodshed because Savannah intended to beat Muñoz to a pulp if he lost her wedding ring.

The agent holding Muñoz by the arm jammed his hand in the killer's pocket a second time. Tweezed between his thumb and forefinger was the symbol of Ennis's love for his wife. The facets glinted in the room's light for all to see. "Is this it?" he asked.

Oh yes. That was the ring alright. She blinked back tears while slipping on her cherished wedding ring and held it to her heart. She felt complete again. To some people a wedding ring signified a union of two people. That sparkling ring told the world of their immeasurable love, their past, present and their future. Savannah closed her fingers around the precious ring then kissed it.

Jenny Lee helped a squirming Anna to the floor. The child's feet bicycled before hitting the ground and stretched her arms out to hug her mama. When the three bunched together in a long, tight embrace, Savannah *thought* she saw a smile on Jenny's face.

## 22

After the Feds lugged Muñoz out, reunions began in earnest. For the first time that day hugs, kisses and laughter filled the room and tired smiles supplanted stark fear.

Agents mingled around the house while most of the family lined up to welcome Savannah back. She hadn't moved an inch since the arrival of the Federal Bureau of Incompetency. She was grateful the crisis ended but she still hurt like hell and hated riling the pain by moving.

Mama, the boys and their parents greeted her first. Dane, Jake and Gina followed behind. Savannah noticed after Jake hugged her, he sequestered himself to the opposite side of the room as far away from Jenny as possible.

Georgia brought Savannah into a hug that expressed how much she missed her – and also realigned a few vertebrae in the process. Tears flowed freely between the sisters as they spoke to each other. Georgia then smiled at Ennis who'd stood by, allowing everyone their turn to speak with Savannah first.

"I think someone's been very patient with us all," Georgia said.

"Thanks, Ennis." Sweeping tears from her cheeks, she headed off to join the ladies in the kitchen.

The moment the sisters parted, Lily wrapped her arms around her mother while Anna clasped Savannah's right hand in a double handhold – so her mama "stayed put".

She had every intention of "staying put" she told her baby girl. And while "staying put" she had intentions of getting a kiss from her beloved. Two, maybe three, in fact.

Pain and weariness set in since the adrenaline ebbed. Only one thing pushed it back. The thought of finally being in her husband's arms.

Cal herded Lily and a protesting Anna to the kitchen to give Savannah and Ennis alone time. Granna had snacks hidden in the kitchen, he said, and it was up to the girls to find them.

Anna glanced back to remind both parents, "Stay put."

Dane and Joe Bob lounged on the couch conversing, Jake went on shunning Jenny and Jenny continued sulking. Tired yet upbeat conversation drifted from the kitchen as the ladies murmured sweetly to the girls and chatted with Cal's boys.

The people and noises faded away when Savannah and Ennis locked gazes. For long, agonizing hours she yearned to go home. Ennis was her home. Her refuge. He was her heart and soul, her everything and when the end drew near, in the final hour of her life she wanted to lie in his arms as she drew her last breath. That evening they would spend in each other's arms for another reason. They still had each other.

In their gaze, husband and wife conveyed their eternal love for one another and acknowledged their innermost fears of losing each other. Of losing their family. She and Daniel should have died that day whether by Muñoz's hand, hypothermia, a heart attack or plain old chaste terror. The Lord sent an angel in the form of a cowboy whose concern for his sister led him to Savannah before it was too late. Everyone in the house was a walking miracle thanks to the Man above.

Ennis stepped closer. His misty coffee brown eyes seemed to express a need not unlike her own. The need to hold her best friend, lover and soul mate. The need to savor his embrace and stay in his arms knowing the danger had passed and they were truly safe. And the need to feel the velvet caress of his lips, to have his kiss sing through her veins.

Trembling hands buried in her hair. Warm, soft lips brushed hers so lightly it sent a tiny shiver through her. *I love you* he whispered before reclaiming her lips, crushing and parting them to devour with a hunger that had her clinging to him, barely able to breathe. One arm eased down to clasp her tightly to him, the other he left threaded in her hair, holding her to the kiss. Savannah relaxed, sinking into his embrace. Home. She was finally home.

Dane blew out a breath, "Is it getting hot in here?"

Jake mumbled *uh-huh*. As the two made their way to the kitchen he muttered, "Get a room, guys."

Savannah reluctantly parted from the kiss to catch her breath, "Well, that kiss answered my question."

He caressed her cheek, "What question?"

"If you missed me," she teased.

He dove in for another kiss, this one slower and softer.

"My goodness," Sheriff Guthrie drawled. "That's what I call a reunion."

Ennis and Savannah both smiled. He eased away from the kiss, rested his forehead against hers but shored up his embrace. She figured they probably looked like lust-driven teenagers necking on her parent's front porch. Neither of them cared. Ennis replied to Guthrie, "Just expressing our love for each other."

Savannah surveyed the room. Their display cleared the room except for Guthrie, Joe Bob and a shocked Jenny Lee. Joe Bob's sister gawked in stunned silence at the openly affectionate couple.

Ennis nodded toward the dining room and kitchen. He murmured in her ear, "We've got an audience."

She turned and immediately blushed. Numerous faces filled the kitchen and dining room doorways. Cal's boys spied on their amorous aunt and uncle. So had Georgia, Dane, and Bobbi. Lily and Anna snuck a peek around the door and actually giggled.

A flash of humor crossed Ennis's face, "Busybodies." The two limped hand in hand toward the couch. Savannah really dreaded sitting. The leg despised bending plus, during the reunions and Ennis kissing her silly, the muscles stiffened to boards. Instead of exercising her extensive four-letter word vocabulary, she groaned when her rear hit the seat.

Guthrie fetched a small footstool to elevate her leg. Much better, she sighed with thanks.

Ennis settled beside her and pulled her close. She snuggled in, yawning. Oh yes, she thought. Much, *much* better...

Guthrie made himself at home in Mama's rocker, "You and ol'

Joe Bob left us a few Easter eggs.  Found Alan Brozek and Manuel Sanchez hogtied down at the guest house and Hadley tied up downstairs. I give Joe Bob credit.  He knows his knots." He cut his vision to Joe Bob who had moved to Hadley's spot at the bar, "I complain about him but overall he's a pretty good fella."

Joe Bob sounded surprised at Guthrie's praise, "So, you're not arresting me for anything?  Because Eldon let me borrow the tractor.  I didn't steal it.  And I'm hoping the Rutherfords might argue if you hauled me in for trespassing on private property."

Guthrie snorted at the overblown dramatics, "Crawford, I'm hoping to retain my job.  If I toss you behind bars the whole county'll run me off in shame.  I *was* going to commend you for your efforts. You saved Mrs. Rutherford and you both worked well together."

Joe Bob's jaw slung open.  He turned to Savannah, "A genuine compliment from the sheriff.  Must be a blue moon tonight."

Guthrie's mustache fattened over his pursed lips, "Don't get the big head."

In the kitchen, weary ripples of laughter ended on yawns.  FBI agents milled around, taking statements and generally being an annoyance in various ways (in Savannah's opinion, at least).

Ennis's gentle embrace and the sound of easy, flowing conversations should have promoted relaxation but the Feds were anything but quiet while performing their duties.  The constant talking, unnecessary noise and activity put her on edge.

The back door slammed.  The sudden sharp report startled her so bad her elbow snapped back into her husband's ribs.  She apologized when Ennis put a hand to his side with a flinch.

The sheriff chewed out the culprit trekking through the living room, "You fellas hold down the racket. These folks are trying to relax." Ya nitwits, Savannah heard him grumble behind the mustache.

Ennis clasped her hand. He placed a kiss to her temple, whispered *calm down.*

Savannah pitied her husband. Pitied her whole family, really. Aftershocks of Jeffrey's attack lingered on and off the last several months and her family helped her deal however they could. Even now Ennis stayed up with her on sleepless nights or woke her from nightmares. He checked and rechecked doors and windows, making sure they were locked.

The kids never understood why their mama hovered and never let them out of her sight unless a relative supervised them or they were at school. After so many months, tireless effort and endless support, she'd improved and climbed from the pit of paranoia and knee-jerk reactions. Well, for the most part anyway. Now they had it all to do over again.

Guthrie took advantage of the quieter atmosphere to offer Joe Bob a job running a snow plow. "I hired Becca's son to drive it but he hit two cars and was grinding the gears to dust. No one told me he couldn't handle a stick. Had to get Will Johnson to run it up here for us but his wife is sick and he had to get home to her."

"I'll take the job," Joe Bob yawned. "Any chance of a catnap first? I'm flat tuckered from Darcy calving last night and everything today."

"Make it quick. Plow's parked at the road beside Cal's place."

The men's discussion lulled her to drift and reflect on the day's events. It began innocently enough until darker memories crept in. The sight of Muñoz's .45 centering on her, firing and missing her head by a meager breath. Then the tussle outside with Muñoz took center stage. (You nearly won that battle, her mind taunted). The fight for the gun and the fear as she clawed through the drift to try and save herself and unborn son before Muñoz killed them.

Her mind switched to Andrea Tate. When would they find her? Tomorrow? In two days? A week? Would she be in the car or a nearby field, or (the thought made Savannah ill) mere yards from Mama's house? Andrea prompted worries about Lily and Anna. Had Brozek's sick appetite for children driven him to fulfill his promise to 'have a party' with her girls? Had the twisted bastard lured them—

"Babe," a gentle touch drew her from her mind's agonizing what-ifs. Ennis nodded to the sheriff, "Guthrie said Doc's coming to look at your leg. It'll be a while before he gets here."

"He's no spring chicken, you know," Guthrie added. "Takes him longer to get moving these days, especially when the weather's cold and damp."

Doc Lucas's lengthy, prestigious career spanned at least three generations of Rutherfords from Mama and her husband all the way to young Zach. Residents held him in such high regard they referred to him as the town's backbone. No way would Savannah allow the "town's backbone" to risk developing pneumonia or breaking a hip just to wrap a bandage on her leg. Shouldering that guilt would polish her off. "There's no need," she said. "Joe Bob cleaned and dressed it. Tell Doc to stay home–"

Guthrie raised a hand, shushing her. "He insisted. He attended your wedding and chats you up when he sees you. He wants to check that leg and nobody argues with that man."

The others trickled in, couples claiming seats together on the couches, the singles taking chairs. Georgia offered to make sandwiches for her and Ennis but both declined. She wanted to settle in first to give her appetite time to return.

The girls raced to their mama and daddy, beaming the whole way. Lily climbed in beside Savannah while Anna straddled the state line to sit between her parents. Reality began sinking in as Savannah welcomed her children. Her family – her whole family – was safe.

But what about Andrea Tate? The sweet face with the dimpled smile remained ever present in her thoughts. The horrors an innocent young soul should never see or suffer. Left to die scared and alone. "Sheriff, has anyone found Andrea Tate yet?"

Guthrie glanced down, "Oh." He uneasily cleared his throat, "When Chris – that's Becca's boy – drove the plow, he literally ran into the 4Runner from Decatur. Said the back door was open and he ended up tearing it off. My deputy was with him and they checked inside and in the trunk. They scooped out the snow that accumulated in the car but no one was inside. All I can figure is the girl struck out on her own."

His comment cast a pall over the group. They silently acknowledged the unspoken truth. The odds of Andrea being found alive rated up there with winning a lottery.

Guthrie quickly added, "Besides her family, you'll be the first to know if I hear anything."

Savannah drew the girls closer, needing to feel their nearness. At least they were alive and safe. Posing the question about Andrea was difficult but broaching the subject of Brozek to her babies proved to be impossible. She struggled to find a sensitive, tasteful approach but hit a roadblock every time. The inability to find the words frustrated her. She'd done this before with other children. Knew the basics of how to talk with them about it. Her training came through in the past, why not now? *Because they're my girls. Thanks to that bastard Alan Brozek, the most unconscionable crime has hit home with my own children.*

Lily looked up at her mother, "What happened?" The child blinked her gorgeous blue eyes that always expressed love, devotion and trust. Eyes that could break her mother's heart when they shed tears then mend it when they smiled again. They held the promise of hopes and dreams for the future. What they did not have: the power to persuade her mother to answer that question.

Savannah placed a tender kiss to her daughter's hair, "We'll tell you someday, angel, just not now." She stroked a hand down her daughter's long, soft tresses. An image of Brozek doing the same thing to her little girl turned Savannah's stomach. She remembered his lascivious leer as she read to her girls. What happened in her absence? Had Brozek allowed Georgia, Bobbi or Mama to take the girls to the bathroom? Or had he assumed the role of escort to trap Lily in the small room? Had he slid his zipper past the growing bulge in his crotch? Had he told Lily it would be okay, that it would be their little secret? Had he threatened that if she told anyone, he'd hurt her family? Then backed it up with,

"Your mom is already dead. Do you want your daddy to die too?"

"We need to talk with the girls before the FBI leaves with Brozek." She blurted the demand, inadvertently cutting off Guthrie and Ennis's conversation. She didn't know what the subject was and didn't care. She wanted answers. If Brozek violated Lily or Anna, being tied up in a closet was the least of his worries. She'd hike to Amarillo or the moon to kill that child molesting bastard – witnesses or no witnesses.

Joe Bob pulled an agent aside. He mumbled to him and the Fed pointed to her and scoffed, "In her condition? I doubt it."

The casual dismissal rankled Joe Bob, "You'd be surprised what that woman can do on a gimpy leg. You better lock Brozek up tight."

The twenty-something agent appraised Savannah again just to appease Joe Bob. He shrugged, still unconvinced.

Guthrie asked him, "Son, do you have kids?"

He nodded. The light seemed to switched on in the cavernous area between his ears, "*Oh.*" He hurried out. The back door slammed.

Savannah turned to Joe Bob. Her brow plummeted. She let the frown speak for itself.

He held his hands in surrender, "Just lookin' out for my future sister-in-law. I'd like to see you on this side of the bars, not Brozek's side."

"Calm down, hon." Georgia's motherly tone intervened from down the way. She leaned forward in her seat, "Brozek wasn't alone with them for a second. You can relax."

Tears trailed down Savannah's cheeks. Her babies were truly okay. We have your babies, Georgia had promised that afternoon. And they had. The family – and Gina and Jenny – kept them safe.

Lily's expression questioned her mother's unexpected show of emotion. Everyone's happy, it seemed to say, so why is Mama's chin trembling and her cheeks all wet?

An agent stepped from the dining room, "Sergeant? We need your statement."

Lily's bold streak reared up, "Mama's upset right now. Hold your horses."

"Yeah," Anna chimed in. "Hode ya hawses."

Chuckles rose throughout the family. Savannah wiped her tears, laughing, "They are their father's daughters." From the corner of her eye she saw proud satisfaction in Ennis's features.

She asked the agent, "Is there any way you can ask those questions right here? If the subject matter gets too uncomfortable, someone with two operational legs can take the girls to the kitchen."

"Sounds good. And Sergeant? Sorry about earlier. Just doing my job."

Surrounded by her husband, kids and the rest of her family – knowing the danger passed – erased a lot of hard feelings. But, "You can make amends by chaining those four to the back of your SUV and letting them run to Amarillo."

## 23

Andrea Tate hung heavy in Savannah's thoughts. Tried to imagine the terror filling the child's mind when she realized she was alone, left in an unfamiliar place with bitter winds and mountains of snow.

First she had to fight her way out of the car before the winds drifted and buried it – and probably fight her way out with her hands tied. If she managed that, the storm itself became the next obstacle. The raging blizzard obscured the only viable refuge down the road. Her only hope of finding it was the sight Lily and Anna eagle-eyed to locate Granna's house – the black steel "Rutherford" sign arching over the ranch entrance.

*That's a hell of a trek for a kid practically Lily's age and height – and Lily's tall for nearly five years anyway. She couldn't plow those towering drifts to get anywhere, much less this house.*

Savannah winced at the memory of trudging behind Joe Bob after he'd broken though knee and waist high drifts. The journey exhausted two adults so Savannah realized it was impossible for a child.

Maybe she was underestimating Andrea. Maybe by the grace of

God she *did* find help. The will to live overrode a lot of adversities. Maybe (hold on to that hope) she freed herself from the car and instead of a white horse maybe her knight drove a dashing green John Deere tractor. He motored by and saw the child hiking along the road. Can't you see this mystery man (Andrea's very own Joe Bob) gathering her in his arms, driving her home – a place with a fire blazing in the fireplace and maybe a June Cleaver wife armed to the teeth with bowls of hot chicken soup and cups of cocoa? A couple who wrapped her in blankets and love.

Ennis kissed her cheek. "You okay?"

The quaint little fairytale disappeared but she'd hold on to hope a bit longer. Not too hard though. Holding things too hard tended to crush them. She hugged the girls closer to combat the encroaching depression. She nodded, "Just thinking."

By his expression, he read between the lines. Her husband honed that expertise during their marriage. Hell, he did it before they got engaged. Now he was a pro and her pro always knew how to divert her attention. He handed her cell phone over, "Here's something different to concern yourself with. You have twenty voicemail messages."

Savannah nearly swallowed her tongue. "Twenty messages? Do I even know twenty people who want to leave messages?"

While the agent interviewed her, everyone else contacted family and friends. Georgia handled Seth, their daddy and Savannah and Ennis's captain Josh Hunter. Ennis spoke with his and Savannah's colleague John Mathis and a handful of cousins. He also contacted Savannah's church buddy Sonya Porter for her, he said, because she'd left a flustered, two minute rambling message on his phone. The highlights consisted of: *Savannah isn't answering her phone and now you aren't either. Is everything okay? I've heard snow totals upwards of thirty-five inches – is it true? When will you be able to come home? Will Savannah be available for the charity golf tournament we scheduled for next Saturday?* Ennis had corrected the thirty-five to twenty-nine inches. Yes, everyone was fine now (he hadn't mentioned the home invasion part since Sonya hadn't) and said he'd let Savannah explain everything later. He offered no answer as to when they'd be home. Like snow totals, no one in authority could predict when highways and airports might open. And she'd better schedule a substitute for their "star" golfer on tournament day, he said, because Savannah was out of commission. If she was home for the competition, he told her, she might feel up to serving as the team's coach instead.

Ennis said, "Most are from Seth but a few are from Josh and Mathis. And Sonya Porter. Save her for later unless you enjoy headaches. She's bouncing off the walls because of the blizzard and the fact you're not able to play in the golf tournament. I didn't tell her anything else though. She was already upset enough."

"Wait to call Seth too," Georgia forewarned. "I told him what happened but his mood is pretty raw right now."

Savannah rolled her eyes. Good old Seth. Great brother, lousy temper. She'd delay calling him since she'd endured enough anger and turmoil for one day.

Georgia's comment confused Cal's boys. "You mean he's mad at her?"

"He's mad at the situation, not me," Savannah answered. "He gets frothy when he can't fix a problem like this. He'll be alright in a while. Seth is an odd duck."

Who was she kidding? Most of her family were backwards in their own special ways. Their big brother, bless his heart, had difficulties separating anger and fear so when fear reared up, his ire did too. Getting scared meant Seth lashed out without meaning to. Once his better half got hold of him he'd dial down his anger. Until then, Savannah intended to make other calls.

Ennis cautioned her sister to treat Mathis with kid gloves as well.

"Mathis? What's *his* problem?" Savannah wanted the lowdown before she inadvertently contacted another hothead – and like Seth, Mathis wielded a devil of a temper – plus his moods equated to spinning the wheel of misfortune. Or as Forrest Gump so eloquently put it, *you never know what you're gonna get.* A lot like Texas Panhandle weather, she grimly reflected. Again, she'd dealt with enough volatility that day, thank you, so she'd tread lightly and hope Mathis behaved.

"You got shot," Ennis reminded as if she needed it. "*That's* his problem."

Had her husband lost his marbles? "Why'd you tell him?"

"I didn't. Hunter did. Jump on him, not me."

If she could dread a call any worse she wasn't sure how. Then she thought about her father's likely reaction to what happened and realized Mathis *and* Seth were a walk in the park compared.

Before leaving, the FBI agents informed them they would be without landline phone service for several days. Savannah told them phone service was overrated because the family needed rest, not an influx of calls. Once the foursome's capture hit the news they could kiss their peace and quiet goodbye if the house phone worked. She figured as long as the cell phones connected they'd be fine. Few people had those numbers and none were reporters.

Mathis picked up on the first ring. The whole conversation lasted five minutes (Mathis kept his lectures brief). When she hung up, she smiled.

"That's not the look of someone who got reamed out for not ducking," Ennis mentioned.

"He was surprisingly kind. Not one obnoxious remark."

"Well, you are his boss."

Really? Apparently a few of her hubby's marbles *had* gone MIA. "Since when has that stopped him from speaking his mind?"

"I'm hungwy," Anna rubbed her belly. "Can I have a sammich?"

"Another one?" Georgia teased.

Savannah put in her bid, "I'd like a sammich too, sis, if you don't mind." Ennis dittoed the idea.

Georgia got up, "I'll feed the littlest ladies again then whip together sandwiches for their mama and daddy."

Bobbi and Mama also headed to the kitchen. Cabinets and the fridge and opened and closed. Silverware clinked on china. Fragments of conversations combined with requests for spoons, saucers or peanut butter. Bobbi: *Did you see Muñoz's face when he saw her standing there? Pass the grape jelly, please.* Mama: *Here you go, darlin'. I'm sure he probably thought he saw a ghost.* Georgia: *I know I did. Is there any roast beef left?  Dane's crazy about it.*  Bobbi: *Found it.  Don't you reckon Muñoz probably thought she was Lazarus back from the dead?*  Georgia:  *Muñoz never struck me as religious so he likely didn't know who Lazarus was.*

Savannah glanced at brooding, withdrawn Jenny isolated at the end of the couch.  Whatever she mulled over, it appeared almost painful.  Savannah wondered if, by chance, she regretted the *don't shoot me, shoot her* crack to Muñoz.  The betrayal reached a part of Savannah's soul she never knew existed, at least where Jenny was concerned.  For some reason it truly bothered her that Ennis's ex, jealous as she was, hated her to that degree.

"Savannah, what kind of sandwich would you and Ennis like?"

Gina's demeanor appeared more at ease around the family, especially Ennis.  Oddly, Ennis exhibited no penchant to strangle her either.  The brothers' animosity toward her diminished as well.  Was Savannah the only one who noticed?  Whatever happened, the lack of hostility pleased her.  They'd gone through hell together and survived.  That should count for something.  She smiled at Ennis's ex-partner, "PB&J sounds perfect to me.  Thank you, Gina."

"Make that two.  Thanks," a friendly Ennis replied.

His geniality – not to mention the thanks – surprised her.  She waited for Gina to leave before asking what thawed his attitude toward his former colleague.

Ennis hesitated then swallowed back rising emotion.  "She protected our girls when no one else could.  Meant a lot to me."

Dane lumbered by, tapped Savannah's good knee and smiled,

"Glad to have you back, Peach. We missed ya." He moved to the kitchen doorway to summon Georgia, "Darlin', my tummy ain't so little according to Eldon but it's so hungry I'm about to turn inside out."

She salvaged his pride by saying, "Your tummy's just fine and your sandwich is next on my list." She pecked a kiss to his lips as she toted out a Coke in one hand and a saucer holding a sandwich in the other, "Would you fetch Ennis's and bring it too?"

"Here's a late supper for you," she told Savannah. "Gina offered to make your sandwiches but I was already working on them."

Lily and Anna stared longingly at the saucer. Georgia assured them, "Don't worry. Granna wanted to fix your sandwiches. She's nearly finished."

Savannah swore she stared back at her mother, not her sister when Georgia instructed, "I want to see an empty plate, hon, so eat hearty."

"I intend to. Thanks, sis."

"Absolutely. It's the least I can do for you. You and Joe Bob saved our lives."

Joe Bob shook his head in amazement, "That woman'd charge hell with a bucket of ice water to save her family."

"I didn't see you resting on your laurels either, cowboy," Savannah replied as he departed for the kitchen.

Georgia bent closer, "I like him. He's nothing like Jenny Lee."

And I thank God for that, Savannah thought.

Meanwhile Jenny Lee still looked like she tried to pass a mental kidney stone. Leaving her to whatever she toiled over, Savannah sank her teeth into the sandwich. She moaned at the first taste of creamy peanut butter and the sweetness of strawberry jelly caressing her taste buds. The sound drew the room's attention – and made Ennis blush.

Dane delivered Ennis's meal which included a Dr. Pepper. He nodded to the Coke in Savannah's hand, teasing, "I told Georgia you deserve a Dr. Pepper but she maintains you prefer that ol' Coca-Cola stuff. You're missing a real treat."

She thanked him for his generous offer but, "Why don't you enjoy a Dr. Pepper on my behalf?"

It wasn't long before Joe Bob swaggered in munching on a double-decker BLT sandwich and holding a coveted Dr. Pepper. Savannah told Dane, "I see Joe Bob rated a can of your treasured stash."

He shrugged a shoulder, "Aw, I guess. It ain't every day he saves our family. Props to you too, Peach. You came back from the dead and led the charge."

"You'd be amazed what I'm capable of," she joked.

Mama delivered meals for the girls then returned with her own. Sheriff Guthrie vacated the rocker and held it steady while she eased into it. He declined her offer of food and drink but excused himself to make a phone call.

The group settled in and fell silent while digging into their meals.

Guthrie peered in the living room, "Doc's here. I'll help him in."

"I don't need any help, thank ya," a voice projected from the back door. "Gimme a minute to get these boots an' coat off an' I'll be right there."

Dr. Lucas "Doc" Garrett, toddled in carrying an old-time, well-used black medical bag. Stooped over but still spry, Doc still practiced the long lost service of house calls when a person's situation dictated it. His heavily-lined grandfatherly features and slim frame gave him a frail appearance but his voice, like his handshake Savannah learned over the years, remained Texas strong. "You've had quite a day so I hear," he told her. "Let's have a look at that leg."

Georgia supplied a footstool that Doc requested. Before sitting down, his smiling eyes lingered on her an extra second or two. Savannah knew why. Years ago when Doc met Georgia, he confessed an enchantment with Rita Hayworth. Rita and their mother Charlene shared an almost uncanny resemblance and Georgia inherited the majority of their mama's looks. Savannah favored their mother but not like Georgia. So seeing Doc's wistful admiration wasn't a surprise. Georgia's self-conscious blush was.

"It always amazes me," he said, "how much you and your sister resemble Rita Hayworth."

Savannah curbed a chuckle when her sister darkened to a ripe shade of plum. Doc retreated into dreamy nostalgia to retell a story they'd heard at least twice before, "Back in the day I was quite infatuated with Rita." Before beginning his work, he slid on a pair of glasses that reminded Savannah of Mathis's Ben Franklin specs. "Drove my wife crazy. I went to Amarillo three times to watch 'Affair in Trinidad' at the Paramount. That was the city's finest theater at the time. Rita deserved only the best."

He rolled up Savannah's pant leg then peeled away the bandage. For the raw misery it caused, she expected her calf to resemble a giant stick of salami with a bite chomped out of the side. It felt worse than it looked – to her at least – until hovering onlookers retreated a step with groans and grimaces. She debated over either feeling vindicated about the salami comparison or feeling close to death's door.

Doc examined it, his expression inscrutable, "Who cleaned and bandaged this leg?"

Savannah nodded across the way, "Joe Bob."

Doc's brow shot up. He seemed equally surprised and pleased, "Joe Bob? I know he's got a gift for calving and foaling but doctoring people?" He peered over his glasses at Jenny's brother. "Exactly how did you learn to clean a gunshot wound? From experience?"

"Probably," Guthrie ribbed.

Joe Bob took mild offense, "This will come as a shock to you but I'm not a complete idiot."

Doc got down to brass tacks with his patient, "Wouldn't hurt for the hospital to check this out too. You can limp along – no pun intended – on what I give you but I'd like you to get another opinion."

She declined. "You and Joe Bob have me on the mend. I'll be fine."

The frowny wrinkles on Doc Garrett's face deepened, "Young lady, do you argue with your doctor back home?"

"Yes," Ennis freely (and gleefully) tattled.

Savannah shot him "the look" then told Doc, "On rare occasion."

Ennis scoffed while Georgia pointedly cleared her throat.

Yes, yes, so she was a difficult patient but that night she'd have her way. "I appreciate your advice," she told Doc, "and if the wound was worse I'd go.   But right now I'm enjoying being with my family and frankly, I'm pooped out from the whole day."

Ennis sighed.   Georgia crossed her arms, displeased with her sister's refusal.

"Well, it's her decision.  I can't make her go," Garrett said.  He did, however, choose to play dirty by asking the girls for help, "Can I count on you to make sure your mother takes care of herself?"

Each answered with a decisive nod.

Georgia winked at her nieces.  A wink that seasoned veterans in the family knew meant General Georgia called her two best spies to active duty.  If their mama so much as sneezed, Aunt Georgia would hear about it.

Savannah forgot the biggest spy in her sister's army.  Ennis and Georgia exchanged a glance shortly before he spilled the beans about his wife's chest pains that morning.

"Chest pains?"  Doc snapped around to his patient, "You're not fooling around with those, not on my watch.  At the very least you need an ECG and blood work to monitor troponin levels.  I don't know if you know this but that's a protein that reacts to heart muscle damage even hours after a heart attack.  You need a hospital."

Like hell she did because, "Ennis needs one worse than I do."

"How do you figure that?" Garrett shot back.  "Minus a few bruises he looks fine."

"Believe me, when I'm done with him, he'll need serious medical attention.  Doc, I'm fine.  I'm not going."

"She's got a granite skull," Ennis groused.

Doc rubbed the back of his neck, "Your physician should charge you double for being so everlastingly stubborn." He fetched the stethoscope from his bag, "Let's check your heart *then* see if you're staying here or going to Amarillo." He eyed her critically, a silent warning that he was the boss now – no more negotiating allowed.

He spent enough time listening that Savannah wondered if there *was* something wrong. Doc leaned back, sighing, "Nothing obvious but I still think you should go. Now what about that bruise on the side of your head?"

"Muñoz kicked me."

"It knocked her loopy, Doc," Joe Bob expounded.

If another person sold her out there'd be a maiming. She sighed with frustration, "Et tu, Joe Bob?"

He shook a finger at her, "Had I known about those chest pains, missy, I'd have left *you* tied up in the closet, not Brozek. I wouldn't have let you hike down here. So like I said before I'm just looking out for my–"

"Your future sister-in-law, I know." She turned to Doc, "You can add Joe Bob to my list. He and Ennis can share the ambulance ride."

He waved her off, mumbling, "Ya pigheaded little… Worse than any two-year-old I've ever treated… Ennis, how do you put up with this?"

"Like I would a runaway train. I step aside," her husband answered.

Doc made solid eye contact with Savannah, "Here are the ground rules, young lady. Fail one of these tests and you're headed to Amarillo, either by choice or by way of the sheriff. I realize it's not exactly legal to do it but judging from the faces around here, I have the majority vote, not you. I bet between all these men, every one of them would pitch in and tote you to the sheriff's truck no matter how much you fight or wiggle."

A quick survey around the room supported his threat. There would be plenty of muscle to carry out Doc's wishes. They only needed the go-ahead. "It's still my decision," she reminded Doc's minions. "Go on with your tests, Doc. Let's get this over with."

By the end of his exam he admitted, "Guess your noggin *is* made of granite. Now, how about the baby? Any problems or issues?"

No, she replied, folding Mama's knitted afghan down to reveal her baby bump. He pressed the stethoscope to her belly. He asked, "He's been active today?"

Yes, she said. He asked, "Any cramping, discomfort or signs of bleeding?"

Savannah shook her head. She may have been hardheaded but she hoped Doc understood she'd never endanger the baby by declining immediate or necessary medical attention. One sign of trouble and she'd have begged for that ride to the hospital.

"Good." He moved the stethoscope and listened again. "Heart sounds strong, steady..." Daniel kicked at the pressure, startling Doc. He laughed, "He's got quite a kick. Doesn't like ol' Doc Garrett eavesdropping on him. What's his name again?"

"Daniel," Ennis announced with a generous ring of pride.

"They ain't decided on a middle name yet," Zach said. "I want it to be Zach."

"*Haven't* decided," Bobbi corrected.

"Tyler sounds better," Tyler (of course) argued.

"Boys," their mother admonished. "Stop campaigning. Ennis and Savannah will decide in their own time."

Nothing proved more challenging than Daniel's middle name. Lily Christine and Anna Rose clicked into place like Swiss clockwork. To Ennis's great joy, Daniel topped Savannah's list from day one for their son's first name. But that pesky middle one tripped them up every time... until a few hours ago.

Call her delirious or coasting on an endorphin deficiency but one name stood out during the grueling journey through the blizzard's wake. She checked off the traits she and Ennis wanted their son's name to reflect. Strength? Check. Fortitude? Yes. Kindness? You betcha. An all-around solid individual? Present and accounted for. It, unlike hundreds of others, sparked that "Eureka" moment she experienced with Lily Christine and Anna Rose. Coupled with her hubby's name, this one was a surefire winner in her opinion – and prayed Ennis agreed. "I've made my list of middle names."

"What?" A shell-shocked Ennis wanted to know, "When? Twenty-four hours ago we were both at a loss."

Dane leaned onto his knees, not-so-subtly rooting for – what else – the name Dane. Months ago he put in his bid hoping "first come, first served" applied.

Georgia shushed him with a nudge while Cal assumed, "We know it's not Jake."

The assumption evoked a prickly *you don't know that* from the youngest brother.

Cal reminded, "After the way you treated Savannah on her first visit, I'd veto your name myself. That teasing verged on rude."

"I apologized for that years ago."

Ennis shooed off the extraneous conversation, "Be quiet. Let's hear the names."

Except Jenny Lee, the whole room awaited a list of probably four or five names. How would they react to a list of one – and an unexpected one at that? "Well, it's really only one name."

Confused expressions replaced anticipation. Bobbi, along with the others, couldn't believe it, "Just one?"

"One." She gathered the nerve to confess, "I like the name Joseph."

"Joseph?" Ennis asked. "We tried Joseph. We agreed it didn't fit right."

"It didn't fit right because it had no meaning to us." She turned to Joe Bob, "Now it does. It would be a namesake."

Joe Bob beamed. Jenny Lee drifted from her introspective fog. She appeared genuinely stunned.

"I like it," Doc gave his stamp of approval. "Good choice."

Mama's face lit up, "That's a lovely name. Strong, bold, Biblical and–"

"His," Dane thrust a finger at Joe Bob. He was not happy. "It's *his* name. Peach, you're not thinking straight." He received another subdued jab courtesy of his frowning wife.

Dane defended himself to Georgia, "He got a Dr. Pepper for his efforts, now he wants a namesake too? She got hit in the head harder than we thought."

A smiling Bobbi gave the name a test drive, "Daniel Joseph Rutherford. Has a ring to it, don't you think, Cal?"

He levered to his feet then winked at Savannah, "I do like the way you think."

"I call dibs on their next son," Dane halfway joked. Halfway.

A quizzical Georgia asked, "If they name their next son Dane and, God willing, we should have a boy some day? What do we call him?"

"Screwed," Jake volunteered.

Other than Dane's mild objections (Savannah could tell his protest was halfhearted since he and Joe Bob were lifelong pals), the general response to her suggestion went over well – until Ennis remained discouragingly quiet. The name came as a shock, she understood that, but it seemed apropos in light of the day's events. Plus, in her heart Joseph fell into place like the missing piece to a puzzle. She hoped Ennis approved but the stretch of silence lengthened to the point she grew uncomfortable. "I need a thumbs-up or a thumbs-down," she mumbled to him.

Instead of Ennis voicing his opinion, Jenny Lee broke her long silence, "You mean you wanna name your little boy after my brother?"

Savannah wondered if IQ tests registered in the negative range for certain people. Between Jenny's obvious lack of common sense and the fact she so willingly offered Savannah as a sacrifice that afternoon, she suspected the Crawford genes turned backward on the youngest sibling. But to play nice, she replied, "Yes, I do. He's the reason Daniel and I are still among the living."

Joe Bob flushed past his ears, "Honey, that's awful nice of you but my name isn't faring well with all the brothers or the nephews."

She shrugged, "They'd get used to it."

He pointed beside her, "Ennis has a green tinge too, and his opinion *does* matter."

"Daniel Joseph Rutherford," Ennis tried the name. How many days and nights had they repeated the process, using a variety of middle names only to come to the same conclusion – it wasn't The One? "Daniel *Joseph,*" he emphasized. "*Daniel Joseph Rutherford.*"

"Happy now, Peach?" Dane folded his arms across his chest. "He's babbling."

"*Be quiet*, you rascal," Georgia playfully slugged his shoulder. He sat back on the couch heaving a long, defeated sigh.

"I like it," Ennis finally said.

A thoughtful smile curled Joe Bob's mouth, "I'm mighty flattered y'all are considering it but you don't have to–"

"Let 'em do it, Joe Bob," Jenny Lee's voice caught in her throat. "You deserve it. You saved her and her baby. I'm the reason Muñoz shot her in the first place. I'm so sorry, Savannah. So, so sorry for what I did."

The words sounded sincere. The tears seemed to be inspired by pure regret yet no one believed her, not even Savannah.

Jenny slumped on the couch, face in hands as she sobbed *I'm so sorry* over and over.

Joe Bob eased beside her, handed her his hanky and held her while she cried since no one else volunteered to.

All eyes centered on her meltdown. Savannah attributed most of it to adrenaline letdown from stress. People dealt with danger's aftermath in their own way – tears, anger, silence. Savannah recalled the first time someone took a shot at her. She'd lost her lunch after the crisis was over.

Jenny's breakdown dragged on until Mama joined Joe Bob to console his sister. In a moment of folly, Savannah questioned whether Jenny crashed from stress, genuine remorse or both. The memory of Jenny jabbing a finger at her and telling Muñoz to shoot her still weighed pretty heavy with her.

Jenny's hands fell away from red, tear-streaked cheeks to meet Savannah's gaze, "I was terrified when Muñoz pointed that gun at me. I don't know why I said what I did but I never wanted you hurt or dead. I'd never wish you dead, I swear." Her apology melted into an intelligible gibberish.

Once the tsunami of tears ebbed, she blew her nose. "There's nothing worse than hearin' those children cryin' for you or seein' Ennis and Georgia so distraught. All I could think about was your kids growin' up without you. I thought about Ennis pinin' for you forever. After hearin' him grieve for you, I realize how much he truly loves you. I feel horrible for what I did. I couldn't even look at Ennis because he blamed me, everyone blamed me, and they were right.

"I don't deserve forgiveness but can you give me one more chance? I can't believe I acted that way or said those things. That's not who I am," she bawled. "It's really not who I am."

The ability to speak abandoned Savannah. Since when did Jenny consider another's feelings over her own or express genuine remorse for anything she said or did? Never, that's when. So why did Savannah kinda believe her? Maybe Dane was right. She got hit in the head too hard.

Not even Georgia seemed sold on Jenny's apology and that spoke volumes. The spotlight shifted to Savannah who looked to Mama Rutherford. The older woman possessed a hell of a poker face. The only one affected by Jenny's sobbing? Joe Bob. His sister's despondency seemed to literally break his heart. She curled in his embrace and began weeping again. He turned to the one who could, with a few words, stop the tears. Savannah.

Charlene lived and preached the Bible's *turn the other cheek.* She knew her youngest child clung to grudges the way a drowning person clutched a life preserver. That troubled her until her last breath too. Savannah turned her cheek so many times with Jenny that her face hurt just thinking about it. There were others to consider though. Besides Joe Bob there was Jake and judging by that fiancé's glacial glare, the earlier lovey-dovey affection toward Jenny left the building and hung an "Out of Business" sign on the door. As unconscionable as Jenny's actions were, Savannah refused to stand in the way of their relationship if it was salvageable.

Jenny waited. Each passing second drained her hope to crestfallen resignation.

Savannah extended her hand to Joe Bob's sister, "Everyone

deserves a second chance."

Except for Mama, jaws dropped. No one said a word for the longest, not even Doc or Guthrie who gaped in mute shock at the soap opera unfolding in their presence.

Savannah couldn't tell if Ennis approved or not. Dane, as usual, let it all hang out, "You're kidding. A second chance? This is her millionth chance. You're too soft-hearted, Peach. That or crazy."

Mama shushed him. "It's Savannah's decision, not yours or ours."

Jenny's eyes brightened, her fingers curled around Savannah's in a gentle squeeze, "Thank you. I promise things'll be better between us. I may slip up but I'll work hard not to."

"Sounds like a plan." That emerged way more confident than Savannah felt because she certainly wasn't stupid. Insulting and demeaning Ennis's wife came second nature to Jenny. Swearing off that behavior with only a few "slip ups" sounded like an alcoholic promising to never get sauced again.

A handful of family members (mostly Cal's boys) questioned Savannah's sanity but Georgia, Cal, Bobbi and Mama realized her goal. To live in peace or at least coexist with a truce.

Cal nodded to her, "You have a big heart, Mrs. Ennis. Not many people would be so forgiving."

"I'm one of 'em," Jake drilled Jenny with a piercing scowl. "Savannah may have forgiven you but I won't."

Jenny's expression evolved to one Savannah recognized very well. It reminded her of Georgia's when her first husband Matthew filed for divorce. He might as well have reached in and ripped Georgia's heart out. Jenny's face said Jake hadn't stopped with her heart but grabbed a few more vital organs along the way. If Savannah doubted Jenny's love for Jake (and she had), that cured her quick. Joe Bob's sister fumbled for words, "But Jake, I regret what I did."

"Doesn't change the fact you threw her under the bus." He stalked toward her. Rutherford men weren't violent but patience and tempers ran thin after that day and nothing set a person off like their family being betrayed.

Savannah seldom recoiled but a man Jake's size with his brawn and lightning fast temper made her shy away too.

He loomed over Jenny, seething, his hands balling to fists.

Savannah flinched when he thrust a finger not at Jenny but at her, "He shoved a gun in her mouth, took her outside and did exactly what you told him to do. How can I marry a woman who has no regard for a person's life?" He stepped uncomfortably close, leaving Jenny shrinking back from his scathing tirade. He leaned down face to face, "We spent most of the day believing she was dead *because of you*."

Guthrie edged closer, telling Jake to step away. Joe Bob reiterated the statement using an *or else* undertone. "She knows she did wrong," he said. "Savannah's willing to give her another chance. You should too."

Cal pushed to his feet then grimaced while stretching his back, "Jake, let's channel your mood into chopping ice and feeding cattle. I'll take all the help available."

Dane sighed, "Don't tell me. I've just been drafted."

"You said it, I didn't," the oldest Rutherford said on his way to the mudroom. He stopped then turned. Exhaustion etched his features. Small lines at his eyes deepened. His posture, once straight and strong, sagged somewhat as if gravity pulled hard on his broad shoulders. He crooked a finger at the boys, "Monty, Tyler, you too."

Jake rooted to the spot, seething. Dane waved him off, "Quit blustering, Jake. You ain't gonna touch Jenny and you know it cause it ain't in your nature." He pecked a quick kiss to Georgia's lips before leaving for the mudroom.

Ennis grumbled, "Jake, I understand and agree with you but it's Savannah's grievance to forgive and she's giving her another chance."

No one seemed to approve of Savannah's decision – including herself if truth be told. Georgia and a few others understood why but understanding it and approving of it were strangers that spoke different languages. Mama, Bobbi and Cal outwardly supported her but they probably thought she needed a CAT scan to ensure her brain hadn't fallen out.

The only things on Savannah's mind – if Jake found true love with Jenny Lee, she'd be damned if she broke them up by shunning Jenny and two, like Charlene, she wanted to be a good role model for her kids. Charlene exercised forgiveness even when her sisters spent a lifetime mistreating her. If Savannah's precious mama found forgiveness for those two wretched sisters, surely Savannah could forgive Jenny.

Turning the situation around, she tried seeing it through Jenny's eyes. A crazy man waving a gun at anyone who moved. No one, not even her fiancée could step in and stop the madness of these four murderers terrorizing her and her future family. And one of those murderers just centered on her. A woman who (as Ennis and Joe Bob said) had been pampered and protected her whole life. Until then problems were solved by her parents or brothers. But this one moment in her life, if she wants to live, the solution depends on her, not someone else intervening for her. And this lunatic with a gun wants a reason not to kill her. Not because of some shenanigan, say, arguing with him or refusing to do as she was told (as Savannah had) but because she reacted to something Ennis said. Two little words could buy a death sentence. So what words bought her a reprieve?

How *would* she – in Jenny Lee's shoes – try saving her skin? Begging? Bargaining? Shifting the focus as Jenny had done? Savannah doubted few people, if anyone, could predict their reactions under similar circumstances. Unarmed and staring down a loaded gun that might fire any second – that level of terror even crippled seasoned police officers and soldiers. She couldn't fathom what went through Jenny's mind.

Dane leaned around the corner, "Peach, I honestly believe your brain got knocked loose, what with forgiving Jenny and overlooking a prime, Grade-A name for your son. Ain't nothing wrong with Daniel Dane Rutherford. Nothing at all."

Ennis wearily shook his head, "For the hundredth time, there's nothing wrong except the stutter we'd both develop by saying it."

"You're afraid the boy would prefer Dane over Daniel. That's why you won't give him my name."

"No," Ennis shot back, "it's because he'd grow up to be nuisance like his namesake."

Yep, Savannah smiled inside, in some ways the Rutherford house slowly returned to normal.

## 24

"Ma! You oughta see it out there! You won't believe it!"

The hollering drew Savannah from slumber's abyss. Monty raced into the living room just as her eyes sluggishly parted. Fatigue plunged her so deep she awoke disoriented and thinking she was home in Atlanta.

Bobbi shushed her son with a glance to Savannah who yawned. A resigned sigh later Bobbi wanted to know, "Well, what's so all-fired important you have to wake ever'body up?"

Cal, Dane, Joe Bob, Jake and Tyler filed into the mudroom to shed their winter gear. Most expressed amazement and shock regarding the amount of snow. Joe Bob just laughed at their disbelief.

In the meantime Monty regaled the ladies with tales of the tractor pushing through snow three feet high – and higher. He used his hand to illustrate the depth. Savannah estimated the height at five feet. That must have been one hell of a tractor, she thought. Her nephew suffered "Fish Tale Syndrome". Neither she nor Joe Bob trekked through five feet of snow along the road itself. Three feet? Sure. But five? The family would still be dodging Muñoz's bullets and she'd be outside frozen harder than an ice cube. But Monty reveled in the attention so she refrained from correcting him. Plus, by then, the other men wandered in from the mudroom. They looked as wrung out as she felt – except Tyler and Monty, of course. The joys of youth, she mused wistfully.

Cal agreed the pasture roads took the longest to clear with the plow and shovels. He opted not to correct his son either.

Tyler recounted his version of amazing sights left behind by the blizzard. He too put sauce on the details to liven up the already staggering results. Savannah began to ache at the mere thought of snow, sauced up details or not.

Monty raved on about digging the barn door free. For some reason he chose not to exaggerate the depth of the drift blocking the door.

"It wasn't *quite* that high," Cal amended, "but a couple of shovels and strong backs cleared it out."

For some reason Cal downplayed the severity. Savannah saw that drift herself and Monty had not embellished the height.

Tyler stood on one foot then the other until being able to announce, "Ma, our house is buried!"

"*Tyler*," Cal lightly admonished.

Bobbi paled. Savannah now understood Cal's reluctance toward the unvarnished truth. His wife wilted at the news despite Tyler's overblown account. Of course who wouldn't? Barns were one thing. Home was another.

Tyler dialed down the drama a fraction, "Well, our front porch is buried for sure!"

Cal and Bobbi's place sat near the pasture's entrance so the men got a front row seat to the storm's power. The two story structure's protection totaled half a dozen trees. Great for wind and sun, not so great for snow drifts. After seeing the ranch house and Jake's house across the way from it, Savannah knew those "strong backs" Cal mentioned would stay busy.

She questioned the boys' intentions because Monty's next announcement nearly made his mother faint. "And your car's buried too! It's a big white lump in the driveway!"

Bobbi's shoulders slumped. Her mouth gaped.

"That part is true," Cal hesitated to agree, "but in the morning we'll go dig that and the front door clear."

Bobbi stood on wobbly legs, "You're... You're *kidding. My Yukon? Buried?*"

Her husband hugged her close, "Don't worry. Your Yukon will be visible long before the spring thaw."

Bobbi prized the SUV the way Savannah loved her Camaro years ago before some moron torched it. And the thought of such a precious, dependable chariot being victimized by the elements deflated Cal's wife. "It's really buried?"

Monty raised his hand above his head, "That deep."

Cal opted for the unvarnished truth this time by lifting the boy's hand six inches higher, "No, it's that deep due to drifting around those trees."

Bobbi sat down in an attempt to grasp the concept. Savannah sympathized. Until a person actually witnessed the depth or tried walking through it, those kinds of descriptions sounded on the verge of mythical.

All the talk of snow drifts wore her out. She yawned to Ennis, "I'm bushed. I'm grabbing a quick bath and going to bed."

Georgia stood up, held her hand out, "I'll help you."

"Let one of the boys help her upstairs, honey." Mama resumed knitting the last half hour. The progress in that short span promised a completed pair of baby booties before sundown the next day. Savannah watched with envy as the needles click-click-clicked back and forth with frenzied accuracy. She felt older than Moses while the eldest member of the family knitted booties like a human sewing machine.

Before fatigue pulled her deep into its undertow, she wanted a nice, warm bath then she'd collapse in bed. If she waited any longer, she risked falling asleep wearing the day's sweat and overall grunge.

The trick was getting up those miserable stairs, help or no help. She'd hiked a quarter mile in the freezing cold on a bum leg. She'd climbed the basement stairs twice on that miserable thing so why all of a sudden did one simple stairway appear insurmountable?

Ennis noticed her eyeing the stairway, "Dane, will you or Cal carry her? I'd do it except…" he pointed to his knee.

Dane came to his feet alongside his wife. "Except bouncing down a flight of stairs might actually finish her off because that'll happen if you try carrying her. Don't worry. I'll take care of Peach then Georgia can help with the bath."

Exhibiting a dash of adolescent swagger, Monty strutted beside Dane, "I can carry her."

The other men smirked and snickered. Savannah admired the teen's spirit but to be honest she felt more secure with experience, not ambition.

"Guys, stop laughing," he said, visually appraising Savannah. "I can easily pick up a calf so she can't be too much heavier than a young heifer."

The laughing stopped alright. Mama mumbled *oh dear.* Bobbi shook her head, "I see my son inherited the Rutherford hoof-and-mouth disease."

Savannah wanted to crawl in a hole. Monty compared her to a farm animal? She didn't know how much a calf weighed, much less a young heifer, and did not care. "Ennis, darling, if I ever approach the weight of a heifer of *any* age, put me out to pasture and let the Lord have me."

Monty blushed and apologized. Dane schooled the boy, "Got a lot of learnin' to do about the opposite sex, young man. If you were married, you'd be sleeping in the barn tonight – *with* the heifers."

Monty's shoulders drooped. Now she felt guilty for teasing him. His offer to help received jokes and giggles instead of a carefully crafted, easy-on-the-ego *no thank you.*

She waved him forward, "Dane can carry me but I'll get Monty to help me up. This ol' heifer can't manage by herself."

Ennis disapproved of the idea but held his tongue – sort of. He uttered a mild caution to his nephew about being extra gentle.

Monty's strength surprised her. She'd never have guessed he spent the last few hours battling snow drifts, feeding cattle and swinging an ax to chop ice in water tanks.

Monty held steady to his aunt struggling to balance on her good leg. The Rutherfords and Joe Bob winced in sympathy when she accidentally shifted onto her wounded one. A blinding arrow shot along her leg forcing her to bite back a complaint.

"I can't watch this anymore," Jake shouldered past Dane. "Savannah, I'll carry you upstairs. It'll be less painful for us all."

She opened her mouth to protest only for him to cut her short. "My ex got you into this mess, the least I can do is take you upstairs so you can rest. Hold on to me," he said just before sweeping her into the cradle of his arms. "Bedroom or bathroom?"

Bedroom she said. She needed a few things before taking her bath.

Other than Savannah thanking him for his help, they spent the trip upstairs in silence. She heard Jenny crying as they climbed and saw Jake's icy glare aimed at her.

Days ago the inseparable couple delved into groomsmen, bridesmaids, colors and menus, immersing themselves and the family in their impending nuptials. Now Jake might favor being hit by a bus rather than exchange vows with Joe Bob's sister. Savannah sensed his anger mixed with another powerful emotion – whether he admitted it or not. No amount of yelling at Jenny or throwing her the stink eye cured his condition. He truly loved the silly woman with a voice rivaling a chainsaw. Somehow her presence smoothed his rougher edges. Oh, he remained flinty enough and his sense of humor needed a shovel of sugar but he smiled and laughed more with Jenny than ever before. Savannah considered that a miracle and she couldn't, in good conscience, let the two part ways because of her.

Jake froze at the bedroom door, shocked at the room's chaos. That morning she and Brozek left the room organized. Only open suitcases and the medicine case lay on the bed when he escorted her to the bathroom. Now... Whew, she thought. Talk about a mess.

In their search for guns and valuables the felons upended the suitcases and medicine case, leaving clothes and supplement bottles strewn across the bed and floor. Mama's little trinkets and pictures on the nightstands and dresser littered the floor. Dresser drawers yawned open and the closet gaped wide from the pillaging. How they overlooked Ennis's gun she'd never know but was grateful they had.

She closed her eyes on a sigh. Once she bathed she'd begin straightening the room enough she and Ennis could safely navigate the room that night. She'd leave the remainder of the mess for tomorrow.

Jake eased her onto the bed between pieces of crumpled clothing, "While Georgia's helping you with a bath, I'll tidy the room a bit and pick up your clothes."

"Thanks, Jake. If you wouldn't mind refilling the medicine case and picking up glassware and pictures, I'd appreciate it. Georgia can help me with our clothes and the rest of it." She fished the prescriptions from her pocket, returned them to their respective spots in the medicine case.

"Sure thing. I'll put the meds right here," he pointed to the nightstand, "in case you need in there tonight."

This soft-spoken, compassionate side of Jake Rutherford caught her off-guard. Oh, he had a soft-spoken, compassionate side alright, but it rolled around as often as a leap year. She also detected something new in his voice and it bothered her. Resignation.

Savannah took his hand, thanked him then braced for a conversation that might resurrect the old Jake who often took exception a tad too quickly. "This isn't my business," she began, "so I'll hush if I'm overstepping."

He tensed. Yep. Old Jake returned, armor equipped and ready for verbal combat if required.

*No matter how I phrase it, it'll sound intrusive and rude.* So in the wise words of Ennis Rutherford, she *let 'er rip.* "Do you love Jenny?"

She fought the instinct to lean away. When he felt people muscling in on his life decisions, he too *let 'er rip*, and sometimes in an unkind way.

But Jake deflated on a sigh, shoulders slumping, "Yeah, I do but I can't get past what she did to you. I mean, how," he shoved a hand through his hair, "*how* could a person do that?"

Savannah scooted a rumpled sweater aside and patted the bed. He sat down. "Jake, fear does strange things to people. In her defense, it's never easy to cope with a gun in your face. After today, you know how stressful it can be. All you want to do is live."

He swiped a hand down his tired features, "Yes, but none of us would sacrifice our family to protect ourselves. None of us did. Only her. Besides, even if I wanted to marry her, I couldn't because the family won't approve or accept her. At best they've tolerated her. Now they just hate her."

"Using Mama's wisdom, it's your decision, not theirs. If you love

Jenny, I think they'd warm up to her again. You heard her apology. I think it was sincere. I accepted it as sincere, at least."

One brow lifted higher. "You really believe that? After the hell she's given you over the years?"

An easy smile curved her mouth, "I'm not naïve enough to think it'll be Utopia however I am hopeful she'll try to get along. Jake, if Jenny is the one for you, don't let anyone stop you from marrying her."

He debated the advice. A full minute lapsed before he heaved one more deep sigh, as if the energy to think sapped the last of his strength. "Cal's right. You do have a big heart. Thanks, Savannah."

## 25

Nightmares stole precious rest. More than once she awoke drenched in sweat, a scream poised at the back of her throat while Ennis snored beside her.

The Gatesville Four prowled the nighttime hours, turning the opportunity for peace and repose into another struggle to survive. Instead of sleeping she spent the hours watching her family die or feeling cold steel ram in her mouth. Just as the gun went off she jerked awake with a stabbing pain in her head. The headache resurfaced again and, she supposed, prompted the nightmare.

Mama's clock downstairs chimed three times. Three o'clock. She'd been in bed one lousy hour. It felt more like two days.

When she drifted off again, Brozek emerged from the bathroom holding Lily by the arm. The girl's hysterical sobbing and his expression meant only one thing. She fought to free herself, to run into her mother's waiting arms, but Brozek pulled her back. He leaned to Lily's ear whispering, "Remember. It's our little secret."

Savannah gasped awake, hands poised in mid-air trying to

strangle Brozek. The vivid nightmare was so real his pulse pounded against her fingers as they dug deep into his neck.

She spent several minutes talking herself out of checking the girls and reminding herself that Brozek and his cohorts sat behind bars thirty miles away.

She wiped the sweat from her face. A glance at the bedside clock revealed how excruciatingly slow time passed on a bad night. Maybe she should get up. One quick check on the girls wouldn't hurt. After that she'd head to the bathroom and splash cold water on her face.

The second she moved, she abandoned the idea. Besides the aching leg and head, every conceivable muscle either turned to stone or felt stretched to the point of breaking. Moving meant serious pain and serious pain meant groans so loud they woke others (probably her husband and owl-eared sister) who would feel obligated to help or stay up with her.

She propped on an elbow and settled for a drink of water. She reached for the glass on the bedside table, thankful for Georgia's forethought. Along with the water, her sister placed two Tylenol beside it, also a flashlight and, of all things, a tried and true cowbell with "Vega Longhorns" – the town's high school – stamped on it in black and gold. Ring if you need help, Georgia told her. The irony verged on laughable. The heifer had a cowbell.

The cool water quenched her thirst. It also caused a continuing shiver, forcing her to pull the covers to her chin and snuggle closer to Ennis.

At four o'clock she floated into a light sleep and into a raging blizzard. Muñoz and Brozek had abducted the girls and Savannah, alone, headed into the storm to find them. She shouted their names until reducing her voice to a hoarse rasp. She pushed through thigh-high snow drifts until her back throbbed as she broke a trail down a road obscured by blinding, wind-driven snow. Looking, calling, praying for her babies.

Exhaustion set in, muscles stiffened, breathing quickened. Sweat trickled down her back from grinding and inching her way down the impassable road. Landmarks disappeared. Visibility dropped from several yards to a few feet. She was lost. She walked right into a solid wall of snow eight feet high that blocked her path.

Cold, numb fingers clawed and dug into the snow until scraping something solid. It was the back door of an SUV. A sheen of ice coated the vehicle, obscuring the view inside. Savannah screamed the girls' names, hoping to hear their voices but the wind's howling gusts answered instead.

Ice slicked the door handle and froze it solid. Her fingers repeatedly slipped off when she tried opening it. Anger and frustration took over. She kicked the door again and again. Each jarring impact rocked the car. Nothing, not even a layer of ice would separate her from her children.

Finally the icy coating cracked. She yanked the door open, leaned into the car, waiting to kiss her babies and enfold them in a hug they'd not soon forget. Hot tears blurred her vision when she discovered the car stood empty.

"Mama! Help!" the girls shouted in unison. Their voices faded in and out like an old, far away radio station.

Savannah spun, listening, searching for a location – a general *direction* at least – of where Lily and Anna might be. "Where are you?" she shouted back. Black fright swept through her. She *had* she heard them, right? The voices were real, weren't they? It wasn't the wind playing tricks, was it?

She trudged through dense drifts that graduated in height the further she went. Finally she leaned on her knees to catch her breath. Her lungs burned. Her heart raced but she forged ahead until facing the most formidable obstacle along the trek. A wall of snow as tall as a tree.

"Mama, hurry!"

She found them – they were behind the massive tower of snow. Savannah dug and scooped, tunneling as fast as possible. They were there – she heard them on the other side crying for help. How could she have been so foolish to think she'd conjured their voices?

"He's touching me, Mama! He's hurting me!" Lily screamed. "Please hurry!"

Arms and hands plunged deeper, dug harder and faster. Muscles burned and trembled from the strain. Her body begged – no, *warned* – her to quit. She gasped for air, ignoring the acute pain blooming in her chest. Once she got ahold of that bastard, she'd–

"*Savannah.*"

She looked around. Who was that? Ennis? "The girls," she cried. "Find the girls."

"*Savannah, wake up.*"

A touch on her shoulder snapped her awake, her eyes wild and searching. Breaths heaved from lungs that felt two sizes too small. Her

heart hammered fast and furious against her ribs.  She closed her eyes.
Another nightmare. *I should be used to this after last summer.  No peace
day or night.  Again.  First Jeffrey, now Muñoz and Brozek.*

Ennis hugged her tighter then pressed a kiss to her shoulder,
"Calm down, babe.  You're safe.  Everybody's safe–"

"Mama!  Daddy!"

Nothing launched a parent into a panic quicker than their child
screaming for them.  Echoes of the nightmare still reverberated in the
back of her mind as Savannah threw back the covers and switched on the
bedside lamp.

"Stay put," Ennis reached for her but she'd tossed back the
blanket, burying him with it in her panic to check on the girls.
"Savannah, stop.  You're gonna hurt yourself–"

No sooner had the words left his lips and she groaned a drawn
out, agonized, "Shee-yet."  She'd halfway pulled her wounded leg from
beneath the nice toasty covers when pain paralyzed her.  A body never
fully appreciated good health or warmth until spending a small lifetime
wounded in a raging blizzard.  She'd never take either for granted again.

"I'll see to the girls," Ennis assured, expelling a deep, weary sigh.

They were all so dead tired, she thought, and no one's getting
much sleep.

He added, "Lily probably thinks there's a monster under the bed
again."

Well, she'd seen enough monsters that day, Savannah replied, so
it made sense.

The hallway light blazed beneath the bedroom door.  The whole house probably came to Lily's rescue while her parents struggled to simply sit up. Sure enough Lily's fussing soon quieted down.

A knock rapped softly on the door. Ennis limped over and opened it. Eyelids drooping and shoulders slumped, Georgia and Dane stood wrapped in their own robes, each with a child propped on a hip. Lily and Anna, red-faced and sniffling, clung to them as if their aunt and uncle rescued them from the devil himself.

"Two little sheep are missing Mama and Daddy," Georgia yawned. "We heard them calling for you so we checked on them."

Savannah thanked them. Dane eased Lily to the floor, "No problem, Peach. However I do believe your bed is about to get mighty crowded."

Dressed in purple pajamas with pink butterflies, Lily clutched her princess doll to her chest. She ran to her mother, "Can we sleep with you and Daddy? *Please?*" She cupped her hand around Savannah's ear, whispering, "We're scared those men will come back."

She caressed Lily's cheek, "Honey, I promise they're not coming back but if it helps you two sleep, climb in."

Anna clutched her teddy bear to her chest, "Can Dallas come too?"

"Yes," Ennis lifted her from Georgia's arms, "Dallas can come too." Minnie Mouse's peppy grin shined out from Anna's red pajamas. The goofy smile seemed out of place at that insane hour of the morning, especially when Anna sniffed back tears and looked as cheerful as a kid forgotten on Christmas.

Ennis thanked Georgia and Dane and apologized for the kids

waking them.

Georgia smiled sleepily, covered her mouth to yawn again, "We don't mind. We can navigate faster than either of you right now."

Lily eagerly climbed into bed.

"Careful around Mama's leg, sweetheart," Ennis gently cautioned the rambunctious youngster. She scrambled under the covers and snuggled tight beside Savannah.

Ennis placed Anna next to her sister before crawling in beside his trio of females, "Thanks again, guys."

Dane tipped an invisible cap to them, "Sure. See y'all later."

Georgia bid them goodnight then quietly closed the door. They look like four little bugs in a rug, she told her husband. Yes, they were, Savannah thought. Four bugs in a cramped, queen size rug and it was absolute, sheer delight.

## 26

Children's voices pulled Savannah up the dark tunnel of slumber. The gray matter coughed and sputtered to life – or tried to anyway. Dear God, she thought, it couldn't be morning yet, could it? Already? She spent the night fighting nightmares in her sleep and when semi-conscious, played tug-of-war with her oldest daughter for her share of the pillow. The latter battle finally ended in a truce.

Ennis quietly shushed the girls. Anna whined about being hungry. Lily whispered *when will Mama get up 'cause then we can eat.* The girls woke up bright-eyed and bushy-tailed as opposed to their middle-aged, decrepit mother. She was neither bright-eyed nor bushy-tailed and she'd punch the first Pollyanna who accused her of it.

"Mama's tired," she heard Ennis say. "Gimme a minute and I'll get up." The covers eased back. He uttered a well-curbed grunt of discomfort. The girls bounced and jounced out of bed much to Ennis's dismay.

They rounded the bedside and didn't seem one bit surprised to see their mother's eyes open. "She's awake!" Anna shouted at her mother who cringed.

"That's debatable," Savannah's rusty voice argued.

"Give her room, girls." Ennis shooed them while hobbling around to his wife. He apologized for her rude awakening.

No big deal, she lied then tossed the covers back. The kids converged, crowding their daddy out to greet her with a cheerful "Good Morning". Morning? Yes. Good? Yet to be determined, at least physically. She returned their greeting with a kiss to each girl's cheek.

"Okay," their daddy said, "you've said hi to Mama, now go get dressed. Lily, help Anna with her clothes. I'll be in shortly."

Savannah waited until he closed the door to try moving. She'd eat nails before allowing their kids to witness her vast repertoire of cuss words – and there *would* be cussing once she moved that leg.

Bracing herself, she pulled, willing her leg to slide over the bed's edge. Muscle and bone protested. That vast repertoire of profanity grew by leaps and bounds. Somehow only a strained groan emerged. She never considered herself a sissy. Between her daddy's drunken beatings, Jeffrey Holland's brutal caning, giving birth to two kids – one of which nearly bought her a C-section due to her stubbornness (Anna), Jeffrey's last stand and a host of other maladies, she'd seen her share of misery and pain. The notched leg looked deceivingly minor but it hurt like hell.

"Hold on to me," Ennis said.

She waited for the pain to subside before reminding (as if he needed it) that he too had a game leg, "What, and take you down if I get overbalanced? Just slap a hand over my mouth if I get loud."

Savannah sucked in a breath then shoved the leg over the bedside.

The damn thing turned wooden overnight, strutting itself into a scarcely bendable limb.

Ennis couldn't bear to watch, "Let me get you on your feet. Here." He handed her the cane Mama loaned her the night before.

Hands beneath her arms, he brought her upright with little or no effort. She was both impressed and jealous.

They hobbled across the hall for Ennis to check on the girls but they were already downstairs chatting with the men so she and Ennis proceeded to the bathroom.

After freshening up, they stood at the stairway landing. Descending those stairs was either going to be a test of character or a total disaster.

Flashbacks of the previous morning crept past the dread of tackling the stairs. The deafening silence, the fear that engulfed her when she saw Mama in the rocker with her wrists tied and the sight that sent her stomach into free fall – the imposing Luis Muñoz smiling down at her from the landing when she turned to retreat.

"You ready?" Ennis asked.

She swallowed the sudden lump in her throat then nodded, grateful the question dragged her from the memory. With more confidence than she felt, she white-knuckled both the cane and railing while following behind her husband.

They baby-stepped down four stairs when a swarm of Rutherford men converged, demanding to help.

Jake and Cal chose Savannah. Dane and Monty went to Ennis who waved them off. Savannah welcomed the assistance though. It was nice having a strong grasp steady her on the potentially hazardous journey. Sometimes, she conceded, pride was overrated.

Long after midnight, the house's head count returned to normal except for Jenny Lee who surprisingly stayed the night again. Joe Bob and Doc left and Gina hitched a ride home via Sheriff Guthrie – but not before she and Ennis held a powwow together. By their demeanor, they'd parted ways on a friendly note. Savannah wanted to believe that despite the wounds from their past, this ordeal began to heal them at least in some way. When Gina put herself in harm's way to protect Lily and Anna, she climbed several spots in Savannah's book. When Ennis and Gina parted ways with smiles and a sincere handshake, apparently he felt the same way.

With the exception of Jenny Lee, the rest of the family followed Ennis's lead to treat Gina far kinder than when she arrived at the house. Ennis discovered that reasoning with Jenny was like administering medicine to the dead. Jenny shunned Gina until the woman walked out the door.

The succulent aroma of fried bacon and the melodic sound of women's laughter drifted from the kitchen. Both drew Savannah in hopes of joining the revelry and work. She yearned to prepare biscuits by the boatload and chat on familiar and pleasant topics. She actually looked forward to Jenny Lee setting the forks and knives ass-backwards and hearing Dane complain about it.

A glance in the kitchen revealed bustling activity. Georgia and Bobbi stood at the stove working on the bacon and gravy. Mama busied herself at the dough board cutting biscuits. And passing by the dining room she witnessed a miracle. Jenny Lee Crawford paused at each chair to set a textbook dining table, from plates and glassware to silverware and napkins. Savannah smiled, thinking how impressed Charlene would be.

The group's work commenced with flawless precision, similar to times when Savannah pitched in to help. Their efficiency – especially with Jenny – dashed her hopes of being included. Hopefully there would still be a job for a lame yet willing worker. "Good morning," she greeted.

Three beaming smiles and a respectable attempt at one (Jenny's) welcomed her. "Good morning, sleepyhead," Georgia replied. Bobbi and Mama joined her while Jenny Lee added her own (Savannah dared say) genuine acknowledgement.

"Can I help?" Savannah wanted a job, however small. Any available task to feel useful again. "Anything'll do."

Bobbi offered a way too chipper, "I'm doing fine here. Georgia?"

"Me too. Mama?"

"Biscuits are coming along. Jenny?"

"Table's done except the orange juice and milk glasses. I'll pour those when it's time."

Ugh. Such annoying efficiency. Unable to mask the disappointment, her shoulders slumped, "Oh. Okay."

Bobbi suggested, "You should sit down and relax. Get off your leg a while."

But she spent the whole night "off her leg". Truth was, they didn't really need her though, not with so many busy, capable hands. So she resolved herself to Ennis's role the past two days. Couch potato. No wonder his patience wore thin, she grumped. Sitting was foreign to them both and sitting while others worked? An utter disgrace. "I guess I'll sit down with Ennis then." She stumped to the door.

"Savannah," Mama called.

She swiveled back, figuring she'd be assigned referee duty for the kids if they argued over TV programs. Nothing as prestigious as washing dishes (yes, she was *that* desperate to help).

Mama waved her toward the stove, "If you feel up to it, you can stir the gravy. That'll free up Bobbi to start cracking eggs. Lord, those men are starving. I think we all are."

Couch potato no more. Savannah headed to the stove, anxious to get busy, "I'd love to. Thank you."

Bobbi relinquished the spoon, amazed at her enthusiasm, "If only my children were as eager as you."

O   O   O

A more serene atmosphere filled the Rutherford house at breakfast. No taunts or criticism. No snide scowls or frowns surrounded the table. Just famished appetites breathing in intoxicating, delicious smells and waiting to consume the bounty before them.

Between the milk and eggs, a good portion of Eldon Killibrew's delivery graced the table. A heaping bowl of scrambled eggs and a platter stacked with fried bacon waited to be passed around. On each end of the table Mama placed a pan of white cream gravy and beside them a decorative bowl covered with a red and white checked towel to keep the biscuits warm and ready for butter, jam or a ladle of gravy.

Everyone joined hands then sat reverently while Mama offered the prayer. By the time *Amen* rolled around, many used their napkins to dab tears.

The procession of dishes began. Serving spoons plunged deep into bowls. Bacon left the platter in threes and fours and biscuits by pairs. Contrary to days before, not a soul complained of temporary traffic jams, delays or the amount of food on someone's plate.

The room fell silent aside from groans of contentment. Silverware clinked and scraped plates. Calls for seconds and thirds were frequent. The minimal conversation revolved around the snow and planning the day's logistics on livestock care. No one dared mention Muñoz or the day before.

Cal leaned back with a long sigh, "Ladies, that was one fine meal. Hats off to each of you." He looked at Savannah, "even the expert gravy stirrer."

Dane heaved his own contended sigh, "No kidding. I can't hold another morsel." A burp slipped out. Kids giggled. The rest smirked. He muttered a sheepish apology.

"I'm full as a tick too," Ennis patted his stomach. "If I eat one more bite, I'll explode."

Sitting a few chairs down from Ennis and Savannah, Jake and Jenny Lee sat together. Savannah slanted a covert glance their way. Jake slipped Jenny a sly grin then murmured in her ear. She tittered loud enough to draw attention.

Dane made a face. His subdued *yuck* earned a quiet *shush* from

Georgia.

Since Jake hadn't shunned or shouted at Jenny that morning (or heaved her headfirst in the snow as Dane suggested), Savannah assumed the engagement was back on. "Wedding on track again?"

Jenny – in her own world with Jake – replied dreamily, "Full steam ahead."

Ennis's lip curled, "Maybe so but this isn't your honeymoon and our kids are watching this display. Knock it off."

Elvis Presley's "A Little Less Conversation" cranked up on Savannah's cell phone in the kitchen. Mama Rutherford enforced one house rule with an iron fist. No cell phones during a meal. No problem for Savannah. She'd chucked it on the counter and answered another call. The call of breakfast. Now that the phone was singing its head off, she wished she'd left it powered down because it interrupted "one fine meal" as Cal so aptly praised.

Early morning phone calls meant relatives. In her case either upset relatives or *drunk* and upset relatives. That meant her brother or her daddy, respectively. While Elvis sang about "a little more bite and a little less bark" she debated over suffering a whole lot more bite *and* bark if she answered that phone. Retaining her sanity sounded way more appealing so she decided to ignore it.

Surprisingly Mama fetched the phone for her even after Savannah asked her not to. Her reason? "I'd rather not break the rule of cell phones at mealtime." Okay, she admitted it. She'd use any reason to avoid this trial by relative.

"Today is an exception," Mama said.

Great. Permission. Just what she didn't want.

"You'd better answer it," Georgia pressed. "It's probably Seth or Daddy."

Thank you, Captain Obvious, she frowned in response. That was the reason she tried chickening out in the first place. Speaking to either one left a person feeling less than warm and fuzzy or left them emotionally laid out from their self-esteem being KO'd. Their big brother inherited their daddy's moodiness, temper and general unpleasantness when things went wrong. She'd hoped for a longer break before suffering his wrath. And her daddy? Whew. She needed privacy for that skinning.

Savannah chanced a look at Caller ID. Seth.

Ennis's mother put a hand to her shoulder and offered a sympathetic *good luck, darlin'*.

Yes, that and a suit of armor might prevent him from carving her up.

As expected he wasn't mad, he was furious. Why hadn't she called yet? Didn't she realize they were worried? Didn't she care that her niece and nephew couldn't sleep until hearing from her?

Savannah rolled her eyes at her sister. Georgia warned her to wait before calling Seth but neglected to add *until Lily and Anna enroll in college.* Savannah waited out his list of indictments and guilt trips then he progressed to haranguing about her "dangerous" job. She was a mother, he lectured, a *pregnant* mother…

Had the week not turned upside down, she'd have refuted him point by point. One, she wasn't tardy with her call, she was merely waiting until after breakfast to contact family and friends. Two, yes she cared about them all, especially Lindsey and Dylan *and* their feelings so let's not go down *that* road, Big Brother. Three, Muñoz would have shot anyone, cop or not because that's what psychos did. The last thing she wanted was another fight so she softened her replies to each charge. Her efforts paid off.

He dialed down his inquisition to a gentle accusatory, "So did my unborn nephew spring a leak from a stray bullet?"

"Daniel's fine. Everyone's fine."

Only then did he truly calm down, "You gotta be more careful, Van, and consider retiring. It's time to just be a mom."

Listening to his mind-numbing spiel wore her patience to the bare bones of common civility – and made stabbing an ice pick in her ear seem almost merciful. Before she resorted to that, she needed to finish the conversation then return her daddy's four messages, two last night, one bright and early at six-twenty that morning and the last he left while she served as gravy stirrer.

According to R.J.'s first voicemail (he was so plastered she barely understood him), he'd seen the news at the bar after fielding a call from Seth's wife Leah. *Oh, that's how Daddy found out. Note to self. Call and "thank" Leah for her help...*

By the third message, he demanded action. "Call me when ya get this," his surprisingly sober voice said. "Don't make yer old man wait all day *again*." So she didn't. Once she collected the meager shreds of her dignity from Seth's reaming out, she dialed her daddy. Things went one of two ways with him. Okay or completely shitty. That day started off in the *okay* category. She sat tense as a bowstring during the call because one misstep meant disaster for his mood.

While the family pretended not to hear the loud voice projecting from the phone (he always shouted when a "damn" cell phone was involved), Savannah tip-toed around the conversational minefield, hoping to survive it. R.J. chewed her out for "ignoring" him the previous day.

"Daddy, I wasn't ignoring you," she assured. "This is the first chance I've had to call anyone."

"Yer sister *made* time to call last night." He said it loud enough the family, Jenny and the next county heard him.

Georgia winced then mouthed *sorry*.

Savannah just shrugged, "I'm glad she did, Daddy. I'll do better."

"You ever thought about ditchin' that damn job? What would we tell them girls if ya went in the ground? You barely survived that sonuvabitch Holland. How many more of these close calls ya got in ya, girl?"

A cold shiver shook her. Her daddy's choice of words echoed in a memory from the day before. Though not exact, they were familiar enough to genuinely unnerve her. "What?" she asked to make sure she heard him right.

"Somethin' wrong with yer hearing?" he huffed then repeated what he said.

Oh yeah. No question about it. She'd heard a choice few of those words yesterday, lying in the snow after Muñoz dropped kicked then shot her.  Everything went black until her daddy's voice – *Did I say ya could lay there and die?*  He'd proceeded, full of hellfire and brimstone, only instead of preaching the Gospel, R.J. preached Shit or Get Off the Pot:  *Don't give me any sob story about being shot or having heart attacks or freezing out here.  Is that what we tell them girls when ya go in the ground?  That their mama survived that sonuvabitch Holland just to go die in Texas?*

"You still there or did that damn phone cut me off?  I hate those things and ever' one of ya has one."  R.J.'s voice blasted from the receiver.

She held it away from her ear, "I'm here, Daddy.  What were you saying?"

"I *said* yer sister needs help at the shop.  I want ya workin' with her."

She smelled a conspiracy.  First Seth now her daddy – and Georgia called them both the night before.  Probably chatted them up, told them how Muñoz targeted her for being a cop.  "But I do work with her every Saturday I can."  But baking pies for a living?  Um, well…

"Yer not stupid, Savannah.  I meant I want ya workin' full-time with her.  Ain't nobody killed a baker for bein' a baker.  Ya nearly died last summer and it scared the hell out of us.  Quit yer damn job an' help Georgia.  She needs ya."

Savannah arched a brow at Georgia who crossed her arms and stared back defiantly.  One thing about her sister.  If she inherited anything from R.J. it was his tenacity.

She detoured around the issue by saying *I'll think about it.*  Georgia shook her head.  R.J. grumbled.  They both knew she lied.

A few seats to Savannah's right, the romance died thanks to her daddy's turbulent fit. Jenny's mouth slung open during R.J.'s tirade and she whispered to Jake. Savannah overheard *he's as mean as a mama wasp.*

For all his arguing and demanding, she knew her daddy cared about her. He may have been hell to grow up with but God help the fool who messed with his kids. His desire for liquor never skewed his aim with his trusty twelve-gauge scattergun he called "Old Faithful" and if given a chance, he'd have blown Muñoz and Friends straight to Jesus for a one-on-one chat – in itty bitty pieces.

When the call ended, Savannah realized how bugs felt when they were flying along and suddenly saw a windshield coming at them. She was also royally peeved that her family jumped on and rode her about her job. *Again.*

Lily tapped her arm with a hopeful, "You're really gonna work for Aunt Georgia?"

*Oh no, not the kids too.* By Lily's inflection it seemed the decision had been made in Savannah's absence. "That's dirty pool, sis," she told Georgia. "Recruiting my children?"

"They voluntarily enlisted long ago," Georgia defended.

She answered her inquisitive daughter, "I don't know yet, baby. We'll see."

Lily emulated her aunt by folding her arms, fuming, "That means no."

Georgia nodded to her little ally, "We'll work on her, sweetie, don't give up."

"You do make mighty fine fare, Peach," Dane added, "and you and Georgia are dynamite together."

She presumed the comment earned him a promotion in Georgia's ranks. The family agreed but in a Switzerland sort of way. No digs about quitting the job or references to last summer's close call with Jeffrey.

She loved working with Georgia but loved being a cop too. The bottom line: a sergeant's salary paid better and provided benefits her sister did not. Their medical bills piled up after last July and when Daniel came along, that salary bump would be invaluable. She and Ennis poured over figures every month to plan for their baby boy's arrival, their family's future and still keep food on the table and a roof over their heads. So "quitting her damn job" as her father put it, had to wait.

Johnny Cash's "Ring of Fire" mercifully interrupted the awkward moment. Mama quirked a brow but said nothing when Cal's phone sang. That's all it took for an apple red blush to darken her oldest son's cheeks. He'd broken the cardinal rule of no cell phones at the table, but as Mama pointed out, today was an exception.

Cal muttered a chagrined apology and took the call in the living room. Georgia excused herself to go check her messages. Cal's boys, Lily and Anna departed to the TV while Savannah powered down her phone. She was tired of hearing both it and her ears ring.

In the living room Cal m-hmmed through his conversation. Before breakfast, he'd fielded calls from neighbors and friends offering help caring for the livestock. This call sounded serious, almost somber.

After the call ended, Savannah heard Georgia and Cal talking in subdued tones. Not long passed when the two stood at the dining room doorway. It didn't take a genius to read those faces.

"What's wrong?" Savannah asked.

"That was Sheriff Guthrie," Georgia replied.

Ennis braved the subject, "Andrea Tate?"

Cal nodded. An iceberg slid into Savannah's stomach. Searchers probably found Andrea frozen ten feet from her four-wheeled prison. The girl spent her last days watching her family die horrific deaths, had probably been molested numerous times then was left to die alone in a blizzard. The child stood no chance.

*I should've pulled the trigger on Brozek,* Savannah seethed. *That regret will haunt me forever. I let Joe Bob talk me out of sending that pervert to hell.*

A warm grasp curled around hers. Ennis.

Cal cleared his throat, "Scott Warren found her. He couldn't tell Guthrie when or why he was out in the storm but he managed to get that tractor far enough to see the car. He said she was still inside, unconscious and covered with a blanket and her hands and feet still tied."

A mix of emotions rose from the family. Joy that Scott found Andrea and worry about both their conditions. The whole community realized elderly Scott Warren suffered memory lapses reminiscent of Alzheimer's. The fact he drove around in a blizzard at night was already cause for concern. Finding him walking along the road wasn't uncommon since he occasionally forgot to gas up the pickup. Everyone discouraged him from driving but their appeals fell on deaf, very stubborn, ears – *It's still a free country,* he once told Mama, *and I won't surrender my truck or my guns.* But he didn't mind losing two cell phones that his son Luke provided (he lived two hours away in Lubbock) or misplacing the third (it ended up in the freezer) so keeping in regular touch sometimes meant a long drive to Vega for his only son or calling a neighbor to check on him. Luke searched for alternatives for his father's care and in the meantime friends and neighbors tried looking after Scott.

Cal proceeded, "Scott misplaced his phone again but found it early this morning and called Guthrie about the girl. He'd taken her back to his place, wrapped her in blankets and laid her near the fireplace. Guthrie said he sounded coherent at least."

"Luke not here, I guess?" Jake.

"Tried the night of the storm but between Lubbock's slick roads and the snow here, he had to turn back. Anyway, Scott and Andrea are at the hospital and Guthrie just got an update. They're keeping him for observation and she's in serious condition and thankfully no sign Brozek touched her. Once the airport opens, her brother and aunt are flying in to be with her. At least so far there's a happier ending than we expected."

Savannah decided against asking questions. For once she would indulge the silly optimist in her. Today she decided to look through rose-colored glasses where the dragon is slayed, Prince Charming comes to the rescue, and everyone lives happily ever after. Soon Andrea Tate would be surrounded by the loving family she had left. Savannah recalled last summer when her own family's presence freed her from the prison of unconsciousness, worse for wear but she was able to recover enough to continue living her life. She prayed Andrea's brother and aunt did the same for her.

## 27

Certain faces caused it. The timbre of a voice, a certain laugh or a dream. The strangest things unleashed the fear, the images, the pounding heartbeat. To that day the smell of hospitals and antiseptic brought memories of Jeffrey's smile and his unnerving placid voice. The coppery odor of blood breathed life into the serial killer's cold, methodical touch and brought to mind the unbearable suffering those hands inflicted with a cane and scalpel.

Those were Jeffrey's triggers. Muñoz's were loud, sudden noises – voices, guns, doors slamming, anything unexpected. Logic (and people) told her to calm down, that the danger passed but logic was a stranger at those times. Anyone suffering PTSD knew relaxing meant letting their guard down. Danger lurked around corners, hid in dark rooms. Every shadow represented a threat. Be prepared to react, it warned, because you're never safe – *and here's why*, it sadistically taunted while plunging the person into a flashback. PTSD nagged and eroded a person's peace of mind and never let them relax or forget, not even during the sacred hours of sleep.

She realized her behavior and overreactions confused others but the fear was as real as the wound on her leg.  A shrink she visited years ago summed it up perfectly.  "Your body is here but your mind is still there.  There's a door and you walk through it to escape that traumatic event, except when you step through, it leads right back to that moment.  You do this repeatedly hoping to escape but you can't.  It won't let you.  You go right back to the traumatic event every time.  So you stop opening doors, knowing nothing will work."  The shrink ended on a glimmer of hope, "There *is* a door leading out, Savannah, and we will find it together."  And they had.

Four and a half years passed since she saw the shrink who found the door leading to peace and after yesterday Savannah really needed to see her again.  She toughed it out last summer, riding the wild emotional roller coaster without buckling in first.  What a fool she'd been when help sat one phone call away.  Her family deserved better so this time she'd contact the doc and pray for an appointment.

Until then she would try powering through – as her brother called it – while blaming her skittishness on fresh raw nerves.  It's not every day someone takes you outside to execute you, she reasoned with herself, so surely they will understand.

They tried, bless their hearts, but nothing prepared others to cope with someone suffering PTSD.  No one meant to test her good nature (and reflexes) slamming cabinets, busting out in sudden boisterous laughter or turning the TV volume too loud.  No one intended to drive her nuts but she felt sanity gradually slipping away.

By evening the family recovered enough to mention playing a

game.  But which one?  Cal and Bobbi mentioned playing Forty-Two.

"Savannah can't play Forty-Two," Ennis answered for his wife.

"She can too," Dane argued then winked at her.  "She just plays badly."

Forty-Two.  The mere mention of the domino game gave her hives.  For Ennis's sake she gave it the old college try but she couldn't keep the tricks, honors, trumps and twenty-three skidoos (or whatever they were called) straight.  She finally gave up.  Only then did she learn Ennis played because like ranching, a Rutherford was born into the game like some kind of birthright.  He was the only Rutherford to buck both.

"How 'bout poker?" Jake asked Savannah.  "You can play poker, can't you?"

M-hmm, she nodded.

"You playing with real money?" Ennis asked Jake.

"Of course.  Why else play?" Jake replied as if his brother turned stupid.

"She'll clean you out."

A smile touched her lips.  Why did Ennis sound proud of that, she wondered.

Bobbi suggested they use beans as an alternative.  By Jake's reaction she might as well have farted.  "Oh, forget it," he said.

Mama suggested a movie.  Savannah loved the idea.  A lighthearted comedy or engaging adventure, anything to keep her mind diverted to brighter thoughts.  Again the unanimous vote stopped with "movie".  The ladies chose a comedy, the men a drama, Lily and Anna put in a bid for The Little Mermaid and Cal's boys campaigned for

Rambo.

"No," Bobbi said. "It's too soon to hear more guns."

Ennis and Georgia seconded the veto while the latter pointedly glanced at Savannah.

She guessed her big sis and hubby probably enlightened the boys on PTSD. *Too many loud, sudden noises and it's Catch Ya on the Flip Side, Clyde for your Aunt Savannah* or something to that effect. Yes, loud noises scared the hell out of her but she refused to deny those boys their movie. They'd suffered alongside everyone else yesterday, hadn't they?

*I can do this. I can sit through this movie and prove to them I'm not going crazy.*

The boys halfheartedly opted to watch a nice, clean, gun-free comedy about dogs, but their eyes glazed over with the same zombie-like boredom Savannah got after playing the girls' favorite movie *Frozen* over and over.

Out of the blue, she agreed to watch Rambo. The boys cheered. The family balked. An extended discussion took place. In the end, they reluctantly agreed to the movie but with a stipulation the volume remain low.

Low volume or not, the noise put her on edge when sporadic gunfire erupted. She tried not to flinch. Everyone's watching, especially Ennis, Georgia and Mama, she told herself, so fake it. Make them think you're okay.

The shooting drew her attention to the half inch sized bullet hole in the bookcase between Mama's rocking chair and the liquor cabinet.

Muñoz had barely missed Savannah's head but he nailed Louis L'Amour's "Sacketts" right in the spine. The hole brought back a flood of memories. Muñoz wheeling and shooting. The flash, the pinching pressure on her hand then the blood and hot, throbbing ache. She flexed her sore hand, grateful his aim skewed that tiny bit. Two more inches to his left meant death for her and Daniel.

She tried tuning out the violence on TV. The trio of worrywarts quietly, regularly checked on her. That made it worse.

She glanced at the clock. In thirty minutes the hell would end. *Who am I kidding? In thirty minutes I'll be a basket case. What I need is something to dull the memories. Just enough to see me through...*

Her vision strayed to the liquor cabinet. Inside sat a balm to her misery, however temporary. Her tongue swept over her lips as the longing for a healthy slug of the Wild Turkey grew from a nagging to an urgency. She could almost taste the warm, sweet elixir sliding past her tongue and down her throat...

She forced her attention away from temptation. Her vision passed across Mama and stopped. Her mother-in-law had ceased knitting and caught her ogling the bar. Shame washed over Savannah. *What the hell is wrong with me? I've never taken a drink while pregnant and I won't start now.* But she would try a different route for relief. She got up to stretch her back. She needed to exercise her stiff muscles, she said then fetched her purse and cane and retreated to the bathroom. Once she locked the door, she expelled a long, shaky sigh. Safe from worried stares and questioning glances. Safe from making a damn fool of herself.

Savannah searched her wallet for the shrink's business card. *I bet she's not even practicing anymore.* A white card slid from behind her insurance cards. Beneath a drawing of a blue dove with outstretched wings read Dr. Lisa Coates, M.D. *If she is still practicing she won't remember me. It's been too long.* But calling couldn't hurt, right? It was the weekend. No shrink worked on a weekend, did they? *If the number works, at least I'll know there's hope.*

Her thumb trembled over each number then hesitated. A mental tennis match played out in her head. Do I or don't I? *Well, it's either this or Ennis will have to lock the liquor away from <u>you</u> this time.*

She dialed the number. It rang three times. "Hello, you've reached Dr. Lisa Coates. If you have an emergency please stay on the line to speak with the answering service. Otherwise please press three to leave a message and I'll return your call as soon as possible. Thank you."

Savannah panicked. Coates was literally a thousand miles away – what could she possibly do to help? Shrinks wanted you there in person, not begging for help on the phone and she needed help now, not later. Do I leave a message or don't I? Do I or don't I? She pressed the three. "Um," she stammered, "this is Savannah Rutherford. I, uh..." *Need your help.* "It's been years since I've seen you but..." *I was hoping you might be there to talk a moment.* "I'm sorry, just forget I called." *Idiot. You sounded so stupid, indecisive, incompetent. So... lost.* She decided to hold off until they got home to try again. By that time perhaps her professional self might make a surprise appearance instead of the bumbling dummy who bungled one simple message.

She carried the phone to the living room in case she decided to

call Sonya Porter.   This was one problem she *could* resolve herself.
Hyperactive Sonya, a genius at fundraising, wigged out when one detail
unraveled.   This time that one detail was her pal Savannah dropping out
of a golf tournament meant to fund a youth summer mission trip.  A call
for damage control seemed in order.   Since Sonya relied on her to
organize and play in the fundraiser (Mrs. Porter knew bupkus about
golf), Savannah planned to support Ennis's suggestion that she coach one
of the teams.

The instant she sat down she noticed a vase of artificial flowers
blocking the bullet hole that murdered the Sacketts.   She glanced at
Mama knitting up a storm to finish the little blue booties.   Ennis's
mother never looked up but Savannah knew who covered the reminder.

On TV, Rambo went on a rampage with his M60.   Fifteen
minutes left and the good guys won and Savannah could pry herself off
the ceiling.

Ennis put his arm across her shoulders, drew her close.   An
anchor in the storm.  She was grateful.

Machine guns fired at regular intervals toward the movie's finale.
The sound plunged her back into the same acidic, nauseating terror of a
cop killer aiming a .45 at her and pulling the trigger.

She closed her eyes hoping to clear her mind but each time a shot
fired on TV, her stress mounted.

Ennis's arm relaxed.   His breathing deepened.   He was drifting
off.   She thought about elbowing him awake.   How could he sleep
through that racket?   Didn't he realize she felt trapped in this room?
That because of these hideous flashbacks she dodged bullets all over

again? That she was going crazy? Her inner critic shook a finger at her – *No, no, no. Remember saying the boys deserve to watch their movie? That you'd be okay with the noise? Remember that? You knew the risks. Now you get to deal with the repercussions of that big, bold decision.*

Normal, she implored herself. Try to act normal. It's a movie, for God's sake, just a movie. But Muñoz stood above her, gun aimed straight at her face and fired.

The memories replayed in disjointed pieces, some real, others based on her worst fears.

*Your license to live just expired,* Muñoz's words whispered in her mind. *Open your mouth or that kid gets your bullet.*

Her wide, watery vision stared back at the soulless, ghostly eyes of a man who tormented for thrills and killed on a whim.

Her lips parted. Cold, bitter metal flattened her tongue, scraped her molars and bumped the back of her throat. She struggled to breathe. The drumbeat of her heart pounded in her chest and ears. The gun fired.

Savannah jerked like someone hit her with a cattle prod. Her eyes flew open on a long gasp. They darted wildly, searching for danger, for Muñoz.

It took a moment to reorient herself and realize people were calling her name. Muñoz didn't stand in front of her. Mama Rutherford did. Her hand clasped Savannah's and gently squeezed again, trying to calm her and settle the shaking.

"It's okay, honey," Mama assured. "You're safe."

Georgia was on her feet, ready to step in but Mama had beat her to it. Bleary-eyed, Ennis blinked focus back. He took one look at his wife and knew exactly what happened. He took her other hand, kissed her cheek, and whispered an *I'm sorry* for falling asleep.

He regretted getting rest. How awful was that? She needed that appointment with the shrink worse than she thought — not only for herself but her family. She couldn't forgive herself if they suffered again because of her inability to cope.

She swallowed the immediate fear and took those deep breaths everyone raved about in hopes of settling her runaway heart.

*I told you Rambo was a bad idea*, Bobbi told her boys. The TV switched to Disney.

With the room's attention solely on her, she turned away, unable to meet anyone's gaze — and the concern and pity in their eyes.

"Come on, darlin'," Mama tugged on her hand. "Let's go find more baby blue yarn. I'm making Daniel a blanket."

Mama led her to the master bedroom then opened a closet revealing what resembled six-foot wooden wine racks mounted side by side. In the cubbies she stored dozens of yarn skeins arranged by color. *Start worrying when Ma runs low on yarn*, Dane had said. *If she runs out of that, then the world ends.* If so, the world could rest easy for decades.

"What do you think about a two-tone blanket?" she asked Savannah. "I have some lovely blue chenille yarn I'll show you."

Savannah realized Mama tried small talk to divert her attention onto more pleasant subjects. What the hell, she shrugged, it couldn't hurt to try.

She laid her phone on the dresser, replying whether one or two-tone, anything she knitted came out beautiful.  She also added an apology for her odd behavior.   Thanks to her the whole family walked on eggshells now.

At five-two Mama stood considerably shorter than Savannah's five-nine.  She reached up to cradle Savannah's face in her warm, steady hands.  "Now let's get one thing straight, sweetheart.  You have nothing to apologize for.  You've suffered greatly this past year, far more than any of us realize.  Healing is a journey and you will not travel the road alone. We will help any way possible."  Mama hugged her, "And never hesitate to lean on us.  We'll be here."

"A Little Less Conversation" began playing on Savannah's phone. To save her a step Mama handed it to her, "I'll be back shortly.  Take your time."

The name on Caller ID explained Mama's speedy exit.   She remembered Dr. Lisa Coates from years ago after Jeffrey Holland's first attack.   She'd been one of the choir's loudest voices advocating professional help.

It surprised Savannah that Coates bothered calling back, especially after the silly message she left.  Most doctors wrote a person off after four and a half years, right?  The fact the doc returned her call lifted her spirits.   Can you spare a few minutes, she yearned to ask but wouldn't.

"Savannah, this is Dr. Coates. I just checked my messages."  The instant she spoke, the doctor's velvet voice washed over her like gently lapping waves.  The woman had an uncanny knack for settling her using that soothing voice, probably because the pitch reminded Savannah of her mother's. "What can I do for you?" the doctor asked.

*Talk me out of losing my mind.* "I need to see you but we're visiting family in Texas and we're snowed in. Twenty-nine inches."

"Goodness, you won't forget that trip anytime soon. Let me check my schedule."

Keys clicked on a keyboard. A pause. A longer pause. The doc muttered a disappointed *hmm*. Great, Savannah thought, she can't fit me in. What did I expect after so many years anyway?

"I'm booked this week and most of the next. Is next Thursday afternoon at three okay?"

The light brightened at the end of the tunnel. There was hope, after all. Even if she had to wait over a week. "Thursday's great. Thanks, Doc. I was afraid you wouldn't have an opening. It's been so long since I've seen you."

Coates chuckled, "I can always find an opening for you. You kept our friend from rotting in prison for something he didn't do. I was halfway expecting you to call last summer or fall. He mentioned you might."

Following Jeffrey's first attack, their mutual friend Duke Shelton recommended Dr. Coates. Savannah was grateful for that too. It surprised her Duke forewarned the doc to expect a call last year. But that was Duke. He was a little weird but he was kind and he cared.

She and Duke formed a friendship after she proved him innocent of killing several women. Jeffrey and his stepbrother tried to frame the millionaire for the murders and used his controversial lifestyle against him. Duke chose a dominant/submissive lifestyle where many of his submissives lived with him but others did not (it was the woman's choice where she resided).

Coates was one of Duke's "girls" but lived in her own home. Savannah recalled visiting with the doc in Duke's mansion during an undercover assignment as his submissive. The assignment to find a killer in the BDSM community tested her stomach, old-fashioned Southern upbringing *and* her marriage to their limits so Coates played a dual role, obedient submissive to Master Shelton and therapist to Savannah during her stay.

The doctor's reference to Duke brought to mind the vast difference in the woman's appearance at work and her off hours. At the office she wrapped her hair in a bun and wore conservative, darker toned business suits. As Duke's submissive she let her luxurious dark brown locks flow to the middle of her back and was elegance personified when she descended the sweeping staircase in her pink chiffon gown.

"How are you doing after last summer?" Dr. Coates asked, probably curious why her patient suddenly went mute.

"I should have called you," Savannah told her, "and wish I had." Three words stuck in her throat. She hesitated to say them because those words exposed weakness (or she thought they did) and cops were supposed to be rocks. Reliable. Strong in body and mind. The ones people called for help, not the ones doing the calling. But this cop reached the end of her rope. In reluctant, trembling syllables she confessed, "I need help. After yesterday..." Shit. She sounded as desperate as she felt.

Coates's voice softened to the silken therapist tone, the one that always managed to coax the bare truth from her, "What happened yesterday?"

"Have you seen the news about four prisoners escaping from a Texas prison?"

The realization dawned on the doc, "Oh no. *Vega.* That's what Duke meant when he mentioned your in-laws. I think the last we heard was they were located west of Amarillo near Vega. You mean they stopped at your in-laws' ranch?"

Savannah uneasily cleared her throat. *Hold it together.* "Yes. It was a wild ride for several hours." *And I pretty much crashed.*

"I'm so sorry, Savannah. Is everyone okay?"

Her throat tightened again, "Physically, yes. Bruises and lots of near misses." The knot in her throat refused to budge. *Don't cry. Do. Not. Cry.* "I could really use your help, Doc."

The doc's reply was music to her ears, "If you've got time now, let's see what we can do in the interim. Forget the Thursday appointment. I'll pencil you in on Monday evening after hours. Sound good?"

"Sounds great." No, it sounded like a godsend.

O  O  O

Most of her life she considered shrinks a bunch of snake oil salesmen, handing out placebos and charging for common sense advice. To each his own, she'd maintained. If a person needed to vent to a stranger, who was she to judge? Just don't ask *her* to visit The Couch. She dealt with life herself, thank you very much. Or she had until Jeffrey abducted her, stripped her naked, tied her up and beat her half to death with a cane. She'd not dealt very well after that. She slid downhill fast after spending weeks reliving the nightmare day and night – and she had plenty of time on her hands. Barely able to walk and having to rest in bed on her stomach while Ennis or Georgia medicated and bandaged the raw, open wounds to prevent infection. Weeks of constantly reliving the trauma convinced her The Couch wasn't such a bad idea.

She realized deep emotional wounds required treatment as much as physical ones or a different type infection festered, this one with poisonous paranoia and thoughts that grew darker each day.

When she met Dr. Lisa Coates, the curtain of depression began to lift. The doc's prescription – twelve weeks of cognitive processing therapy – slowly reduced the infection to a survivable level. Therapy didn't cure it but it sure helped. The doc delicately finessed Savannah into sharing deep-seated feelings – things she'd never reveal to Ennis or Georgia about the trauma of Jeffrey's brutality and innermost fears regarding the killer. Coates listened, baby-stepped her patient through the minefield of painful memories, implemented her treatment plan but never once promised to cure her. She promised to improve Savannah's abilities to cope and live a better life. For one hour each week Lisa Coates walked Savannah through hell again, coaxed the most difficult details, pushed her a little further and by the end of the session, Savannah felt wrung out but as promised, somehow better.

The over-the-phone therapy session limped Savannah through the evening. The wheels came off at night, though, no matter the doc's advice or refresher courses on cognitive processing therapy. No amount of controlled breathing or identifying adverse thought patterns (*distortions* Coates called them) blocked the cold barrel of Muñoz's .45 from sliding over her tongue and jamming against the back of her throat. How could she identify and redirect unhealthy thoughts while biting down on a gun? Avoiding "catastrophic outcome" scenarios? Right. Her brain embraced them like old friends. In those quiet hours of the night Muñoz repeatedly fired the .45 at her, splattering her children, husband and the walls with blood and brains.

At two, Savannah gasped awake for the third time that night, a scream poised in her throat, her body soaked in sweat. Her heart galloped in her chest. Hard, labored breaths strained to pull air in her lungs.

Ennis's hand went to her shoulder, "You okay?"

Nausea pushed up her throat. This bout of sickness meant business. "Yeah," she swallowed hard. "Just need the bathroom."

She rushed, tottering on the cane as fast as possible to the bathroom where she spent several minutes splashing cold water on her face and debating the need to painfully kneel at the porcelain throne. In between, she tried talking herself out of going nuts. *You had twenty minutes with the doc. It's too early for improvement at night. It took months of therapy before dreams outnumbered nightmares after Jeffrey's first attack. You know this. Twelve weeks of cognitive processing therapy and you still fought demons at night – just not as many.*

She pressed cold hands to her cheeks until she shivered. Dear Lord she looked forward to Monday evening's appointment. Coates mentioned adding a new therapy to her treatment this time. Eye Movement Desensitization and Reprocessing Therapy. Whatever the hell that is, Savannah thought but knew better than to pooh-pooh it. Something about revisiting the traumatic incident while the therapist wagged a finger in front of the patient like windshield wipers. Truthfully she couldn't remember heads or tails of the doc's explanation and didn't care what it entailed. She only wanted relief at the time, not a summary of her treatment plan. *I do recall her saying it's worked with soldiers and rape victims over the years. No matter how goofy it sounds, she hasn't steered you wrong yet. For now just try to get through tonight.*

She cupped more water in her hands for one last splash. *Now's not the time to fall apart. The family needs normalcy. You can do this. A couple of days and we'll be home. Home sweet home. Until then, pretend. Pretend you're fine.*

## 28

Morning dawned so bright she expected to see Jesus at the window. A laser of sunlight shot between the cream colored curtains, ricocheted off a picture frame and drilled her right eye. The sun came out for a second glorious day. That meant additional snowmelt and the promise of going home soon.

Savannah made her way to the window to behold the brightest white she'd ever seen. A thick snowy blanket spread as far as the eye could see. Flecks of sun sparkled like diamond dust along the tops of massive drifts. Long glassy icicles hung from the house eaves in jagged spears. For the first time in days she could see and appreciate the beautiful view instead of recalling memories of battling bitter winds and plowing thigh-high drifts.

Snow-laden tree branches drooped and swayed in the breeze. That morning clumps of the heavy white plague began tumbling onto lower branches. The overall sight sparked thoughts of seeing her home before Social Security kicked in.

She longed for the hustle and bustle of Atlanta traffic, the treadmill of the job, the sights and smells of home and the soft comfort of their bed. Most of all she missed the routines of their four person brood and the casual – and sometimes chaotic – life as they knew it. Dorothy was right. There's no place like home.

O   O   O

Mama Rutherford sighed, shook her head. These girls are incorrigible, she grumbled. "These girls" being her daughters-in-law. The three – plus her future daughter-in-law Jenny – commandeered the kitchen after breakfast, taking over clean-up duty and leaving Mama nothing to do but sit and utter halfhearted complaints of not being allowed to help. Anyone who knew Caroline Rutherford realized she took that "idle hands" business to heart and actually *having* idle hands left her two steps short of crazy. She stayed busy throughout the day whether cleaning, doing laundry, cooking, canning or other activities. That day she begrudgingly accepted the supervisory role but Savannah noticed she'd sneak a quick swipe at a counter when she thought no one was looking.

Georgia took over washing dishes while Savannah grabbed a dishtowel for drying duty. Bobbi put the dishes away and Jenny Lee rounded up the remaining plates and silverware from the dining room and placed them in the sink for Georgia.

"Girls, this is ridiculous. Let me wipe down the counters or sweep. Anything," Mama practically begged.

"I'll wipe the counters," Georgia volunteered.

"And I'll sweep the kitchen," Jenny Lee added.

Mama slumped, defeated. Another minute passed. She'd "lapped up" all the pampering she could stand. "Savannah, we'll trade places. You need to rest that leg."

*Nice try, Mama.* "I'm doing fine but thanks." No way would she surrender her dishtowel. As mundane as drying dishes was, it beat sitting on her can watching others work. She'd propped the cane in a nearby corner and leaned against the cabinet to rest her leg but she would *not* surrender her dishtowel, not unless God Himself ordered her to.

Savannah handed a plate to Bobbi who nodded beside her, "Looks like you've got a visitor."

A tugging on her sweater told Savannah her daughters' patience equaled their Granna's. Granna yearned to slog through dirty dishes and wield brooms and mops while Lily and Anna champed at the bit to build a snowman.

Anna stared up at her mother, her big brown eyes wide and hopeful. "Is it snowman time?"

Lily peeked around the kitchen doorway, coaching her sister *say please.* Bobbi and Georgia curbed a smirk.

Anna dutifully followed Big Sis's instructions, "Pweeease."

The scene played out with regularity at home, Lily banking on her sister's "baby of the family" status to wheedle Mama and Daddy. No one said no to the baby, their oldest believed. Savannah's personal experience said different. Growing up, "no" was her middle name. "No, honey, not right now," she replied, handing a glass to Bobbi.

Anna trudged away, sulking to Lily, "I twied."

"Anna's mama is a meanie," Georgia teased.

Bobbi chimed in, "How can she resist those puppy dog eyes? Little Anna looks *so* sad now."

Savannah resumed drying dishes, "Y'all keep talkin 'cause I ain't buying a ticket for this guilt trip." All kidding aside, she waited for the second round to begin. Their kids made a habit of tag-teaming Mama and Daddy when they wanted something.

The two young sisters conferred. Almost on cue, shoes shuffled slowly across the floor. Her oldest drama queen played off her aunts' comments by hanging her head. Savannah paused drying another glass to face the child.

Lily armed herself with such a downtrodden expression, a novice mother might actually fall for it. The girls forgot their mother was a veteran at the parenting gig so when Lily declared *Daddy said we could* Savannah returned it with a skeptical, "Did he then?"

So Ennis supposedly suffered a brain fart that erased his and Savannah's timeline for the girls. First, Monty and Tyler would shovel the porch and sidewalk *then* Lily and Anna could build their snowman.

If Lily wanted to finagle a parent, she chose the wrong one – but Savannah played along anyway, "And you're sure he said you could build a snowman right now? Absolutely, positively, cross-your-heart sure he said that?"

The women, including Jenny Lee, ceased their work to watch the scene unfold. Neither Georgia nor Bobbi uttered a word. They knew Lily lied and now her enthusiastic nod only compounded the fib.

…And like a loyal little sister, Anna nodded too.

Savannah laid the dishtowel aside for her cane. "I think I'll ask

Daddy myself just to be sure."

"No," they both said in unison. Lily added, "He's busy."

"Daddy's never too busy for me." She waited a beat for the two imps to retract their lie before she called Ennis.

"Mama, don't," Lily begged.

Savannah raised a brow, "Daddy didn't say it, did he?"

She toed the floor, pouting, "We just wanna build a snowman."

"Honey, I promise you'll get your snowman but shoveling snow is very hard work. Monty and Tyler are tired. They and your uncles spent yesterday digging out Aunt Bobbi's car and clearing snow from the front of their house. Give the boys another hour to finish then we'll talk about your snowman."

"Yes, ma'am," Lily plodded off.

Anna looked confused, "How long?"

"An hour." Savannah pointed to the wall clock, "When the big hand goes all the way around to the four again. Remember how long Pastor Andrew talks on Sundays? That's an hour."

The second she mentioned the Sunday service, Anna heaved a dejected sigh, "Oh. It'll be foe-eveh."

O  O  O

During that hour Mama and Savannah scrounged the necessary items for a proper Frosty. Savannah grabbed a carrot from the fridge while Mama disappeared into her bedroom for a short while. She returned with six large black buttons for eyes and a mouth – plus two bonuses. Her "old" shamrock green scarf and her late husband's well-worn green and yellow John Deere cap that boasted *Nothing Runs Like a Deere.* Savannah objected to the hat because it was a precious memento to keep, not something to donate to the children's whimsies. Mama opened the storage closet wider. Four more hats lined the top shelf along with John's collection of Stetsons. She patted Savannah's arm, "I've got plenty to spare, honey, and he'd want to be part of the girls' fun too. This way he can be."

Outside Monty and Tyler horsed around while shoveling snow at a rate that both amazed and exhausted Savannah. She wondered if she ever possessed that amount of energy, much less the ability to complete that task with such light-hearted revelry.

Lily and Anna stared longingly out the window. Both complained about the "melting snow". If only, Savannah lamented. Personally she'd yet to see much progress. Icicles drip, drip, dripped but it appeared even the sun struggled to overcome nature's winter wrath.

Monty and Tyler took regular breaks from shoveling and each time they stepped inside, Lily and Anna converged on them the way reporters crowded Savannah and Ennis at crime scenes. Lily unloaded a barrage of questions, first and foremost: Is there enough snow left to build a *big* snowman?

Savannah and Ennis stepped from the kitchen. Both smiled at their daughters' enthusiasm and Monty's reply.

"Don't worry," Lily's cousin tweaked her nose. "God left plenty of snow for a million huge snowmen."

"And we shoveled enough snow for half of 'em," a weary Tyler said then told Savannah and Ennis, "We're finished – in more ways than one."

The news reenergized the girls, sending them into a dead run toward their parents. Savannah happily prepared to deliver the news – *time to build a snowman* – but the girls ran right past their mama and daddy and into the kitchen. The smile waned. Savannah wasn't sure whether to feel disheartened, indignant or just plain invisible. "They ran past us like we're ghosts."

"I think I know why." Ennis nodded toward the kitchen, "Let's go."

They heard the girls before seeing them, begging Granna for permission to build their snowman. Mama Rutherford corralled the excited children in a great big hug as they used every weapon in their arsenal. Charm, kisses and promises to "be good foe-eveh" as Anna told her grandmother.

Savannah put a hand to her hip, feigning umbrage, "I see you two went over our heads to the highest ranking officer."

Lily and Anna wheeled to their parents, owl-eyed. Ennis and Savannah found it amusing. "So what was Granna's answer?" Ennis asked.

Mama Rutherford huddled her granddaughters close. "I bet if you bundle up in your coats, hats and mittens, your mama and daddy would be happy to see you build that snowman. We all would." She gave them a quick squeeze then sent them on their way.

Georgia trailed behind to help them dress. Minutes later two pink-clad little females charged from the mudroom and down the hall, pom-poms jouncing atop their matching knitted hats. They raced by so fast Savannah stood aside before being T-boned. "Freeze, eager beavers. You forgot something important."

A collective groan rose from both. Lily tried to hide her frustration but not her disappointment, "Wha'd we forget?"

"These," Ennis walked in the living room holding the snowman accessories. "You can't make a snowman without these."

The sight spurred them dashing toward their daddy. "Oh look!" Lily scooped up the buttons and carrot and by that time, Anna claimed the scarf and hat. Both spun toward the door to make a break for it.

Savannah called after them, "Remember, Monty's in charge. Stay right with him and when Daddy or I call you inside, hurry in for a cup of hot chocolate."

They acknowledged their mother's reminder with a *yes, ma'am* then started to the door again.

"One more thing," Savannah said.

Lily's shoulders sagged as she stared out the glass screen door. All that pristine snow just waiting for them and they couldn't get past the front door or their mother. "Yes, Mama?"

"It's very important so listen up." She paused a beat then smiled, "Have fun."

"*Yes, ma'am!*" And then they were gone.

Savannah meandered to the front door. Only a few thick icy patches glazed the porch, steps and sidewalk. Mostly where Eldon Killibrew stood while delivering his goodies. Otherwise Monty and Tyler managed to clean the pavement to a wet but accessible area again. The boys mounded the snow beside the flowerbed. They barely missed Mama Rutherford's prized rose bushes. A small ache pinged in Savannah's back at the sight of the heaped snow and the memory of lifting tons of the loathsome, hateful stuff.

Drifts measured in various heights – from knee to gutter – and circled the house like a miniature mountain range. The tallest stretched to the eaves and extended across the road beside the house. When Lily and Anna saw it, their heads tilted back, mouths agape as if facing a real life giant.

In the near distance, the rumble of a tractor drew Savannah's attention. She watched Cal maneuver the John Deere along the road leading to the ranch. The tire chains and plow blade muscled through the snow with more ease than she expected.

He'd started in the back, clearing trails to the barns and pastures. Now he'd progressed to the front where it took longer to plow since the usual landmarks disappeared. Too far one way and he'd angle into a shallow ravine or run into a fence. Too far the other way and he risked either plowing up part of the yard or knocking down the mailbox (thankfully the box and little red flag protruded from the drift just far enough to see them). The engine strained when Cal tackled a deep, undisturbed drift but he persevered with a shovel, the tractor and his usual patience until making progress. Once that road became passable, not only would it lift her claustrophobia but they could also reschedule their flight.

For the longest the only sounds outside were the tractor's engine and cheerful laughter from five cousins building a snowman. It was the best sound Savannah had heard in ages.

The rest of the adults assembled in the living room, content to watch the kids instead of enduring the TV and its obnoxious commercials and horror stories regarding wrecks and snowfall totals.

Between the girls, Monty, Tyler and Zach, they rolled an impressive bottom for Frosty. At that rate he'd stand about eye level with Savannah.

Tyler busied himself assisting Anna on rolling Frosty's head while Monty and Zach teamed with Lily for the middle section.

The deep throb of Cal's tractor rumbled along the road paralleling the house. Lily waved, shouting, "Hi, Uncle Cal!" He answered with a short *beep beep* on the tractor horn then drove to the stable where he left Jake and Dane tending horses.

Ten minutes later Savannah heard the thump-thump-thump of snow being knocked off boots. The three men chitchatted while shedding their outerwear in the mudroom. Dane and Jake appeared first. Jake's smile stretch a mile wide, "Good news. Heard on the radio that all the highways are finally open. Between that and the airport opening, things'll be running pretty smooth by tomorrow morning and y'all can schedule a flight home."

A stranger might easily take offense to Jake Rutherford's manner and phrasing. Sometimes things slipped out wrong, turning his attempt at conversation into a verbal paper cut. Of course, no one said they had to be a stranger to take offense. Over the years he ticked off plenty of relatives without intending to. Today it was Bobbi who flashed him a dirty look then socked his shoulder big-sister-style, "Nice job, Jacob.

Make 'em think we're tired of havin' 'em here."

By his flinch she'd whacked him good, "That's not what I meant."

Cal stepped in. He shook his head at the squabble. "I think my communication-challenged brother meant to update them, not evict them."

Ennis waved it off, "We'll be using those smooth running highways soon enough." Using his cane he limped to the window to join his wife, "How're they coming along?"

"Looks like they're about finished."

Monty lifted Lily who carefully utilized the carrot and buttons for Frosty's face. Next she wrapped the scarf around his neck. Monty then boosted Anna high enough to place the colorful green and yellow cap atop the large, slightly misproportioned head.

They worked hard on their coveted snowman and that effort deserved commemoration. In later years when the girls flipped through photo albums, they'd remember (she hoped) the day they and their cousins built a snowman after the big blizzard at Granna's.

Savannah retrieved her phone, readied the camera for snapshots. Georgia helped her and Ennis with their coats.

The three ventured out, carefully sidestepping Eldon Killibrew's bootprints encased in ice – a real circus trick with a cane, Savannah lamented – and stood at the porch railing.

Savannah took one look at Frosty and wondered how much money modern art went for these days because their kids could make a small fortune. Frosty's eyes sat a tad too far apart and his smile cocked to one side. They somehow scrounged two twigs for eyebrows that they angled, one higher than the other. That, along with the smile, gave him a rakish Rhett Butler air.

Lily and Anna scrambled to their mama and daddy, kicking up snow behind them as they ran. They pointed to their masterpiece. "Look! We even put buttons on his shirt!"

Yes, and a few accoutrements Granna hadn't sanctioned. Or Uncle Jake, for that matter. A pair of western boots jutted from Frosty's base to represent feet. Savannah admitted the upgrade gave the snowman a certain panache. Only one problem stood between the kids and unanimous glowing praise from everyone. Jake. Though old and worn, those Tony Lamas were still expensive and Savannah doubted he donated them for a snowman.

Ennis's eyes bulged at the sight of his youngest brother's boots. He seemed incapable of speech until, "Where'd you get the boots?"

Lily pointed to Monty who offered a chagrined shrug, "Uncle Jake'll understand. It's for the girls and he doesn't wear 'em much anymore anyway."

Savannah nearly broke into nervous laughter. Uncle Jake will understand? Yeah right, and I'm Marilyn Monroe in high heels. "All the same, let's ditch the footwear and put those back where you found them." *And pray Jake doesn't notice.*

With one sentence her popularity plunged past the Grinch with the girls. She hated to be a buzzkill but they hadn't seen Uncle Jake at his maddest and truthfully she probably hadn't either but if his boots were like his cowboy hat, however old, those babies were sacred.

Lily and Anna pled their case to Daddy but to their great dismay he parroted their Scroogey mama, "Your mother's right. Put 'em back where you found 'em." He looked to Monty, "And put 'em away quick."

Savannah tried to climb from the pit of condemnation, "I love the face. The eyebrows are nice."

Broad smiles beamed again. "We found 'em in the snow," Lily stated as if they'd discovered gold, not two scraggly twigs from a maple tree.

They'd also foraged three small stones from someplace to use as buttons for Frosty's "shirt", aligning them top to bottom right down the middle of the chest – a job done by older children, not Lily and Anna since they leaned toward the Bohemian side. No straight lines. No conformity.

"Frosty's a handsome snowman." Aunt Georgia praised, "You and the boys did a great job."

"His name's not Fwosty," Anna said.

*Not* Fwost, er, Frosty. Okaaay... Savannah wondered how many names there were for snowmen. Olaf? Flake? Snowball? Mr. Freeze? What name booted good old tried-and-true Frosty out the door?

Ennis took the lead, "What *is* his name?"

"Willy," the girls crowed.

Savannah tried wrapping her mind around *that* one. Their girls leaned toward the Bohemian side, sure, but *Willy?*

Zach and Tyler laughed at their puzzled aunts and uncle. "It stands for Willy Melt," Monty explained.

Willy Melt. She smelled Mr. Montgomery all over that name but he gave the credit to Lily and Anna who giggled at the moniker. Their laughter inspired the others to join in. Savannah loved the name. Who knew a Bohemian snowman with a funny name and jaunty Rhett Butler grin would bring levity and joy back to the Rutherford Ranch?

The five cousins proudly stood beside their work of art so Savannah took advantage of the pose. "Time for pictures then y'all go inside for hot chocolate."

Georgia reached for the phone, "I'll take the pictures. You and Ennis stay here."

After the photos, Cal's boys and the two girls raced for the porch. Savannah, Ennis and Georgia flattened against the railing allowing the excited youngsters to pass.

The second Lily reached for the door latch, Savannah stopped her, "Everyone's shoes come off in the entry. Granna doesn't need wet carpet."

"Yes, ma'am," her daughters happily acknowledged as they stepped in.

The delight in their laughter played like a sweet song to Savannah and judging by their own grins, also Ennis and Georgia.

Monty followed behind Lily. He smiled as he passed saying *yes, Aunt Savannah.* Tyler stepped past her offering his own *yes, Aunt Savannah* then Zach, ever-so-polite, parroted the girls' *yes ma'am.*

Ennis waved Georgia ahead. Stepping past her sister she paused, teasing, "Yes, Aunt Savannah."

## 29

The noon news updated viewers on road conditions, the four killers who'd been apprehended at a ranch outside Vega. Bundled up in a parka and gloves, a perky female reporter stood outside Amarillo's courthouse and added one additional detail. The FBI apprehended the Gatesville escapees at the Rutherford Ranch. The family groaned in unison. They knew what it meant. Reporters wanting interviews. Since the phone was out of order, there was only one other way to get one. In person.

"Now the place'll crawl with reporters," Dane bemoaned.

Ennis stared daggers at the newscaster on the screen, "We'll take care of 'em."

"Now boys, don't do anything you'll regret," Mama cautioned.

"We won't regret a thing, Ma," Jake vowed. He pointed to the TV, "They might but we won't."

"Let me rephrase." Their mother made eye contact with each son, "Don't do anything that gets you hauled off to jail. Clear enough?"

"Yes, Ma," they said.

The scene on TV switched to four familiar faces in orange

jumpsuits, waist chains, leg irons and handcuffs. They baby-stepped from two black SUVs then past the newscaster. As Muñoz shuffled behind Brozek, his deadly gaze turned to the camera. Savannah's eyes squeezed shut to block his image. She gritted her teeth, pushing away the flashback of his .45 firing at her.

"Someone's coming!"

The boisterous announcement nearly jerked Savannah into a back spasm.

"Lily," Ennis scolded mildly, "pipe down, sweetheart. Mama has a headache." Last summer he devised that little lie to explain Savannah's jumpy nature and cross moods. The girls understood headache, not PTSD, so his clever fib seemed to work. At least it kept them quieter and Savannah retainer a sliver of sanity.

For the last thirty minutes life verged on dull for Lily. Earlier she stood at the window fascinated by a wrecker pulling Gina's Chevy from the ditch on the main road. The truck soon lumbered away with the sedan in tow. The lack of activity bored Lily to the point she adopted a new hobby. Standing watch over Willy. The sight amused Savannah. *Where could Willy go?* she was tempted to ask. *We stole his boots.*

Lily's enthusiasm returned full force, pointing out the window in case everyone missed the green and yellow tractor motoring up the freshly plowed road. Eldon was back. "Looks like Mr. Killibrew's tractor," Savannah told Lily.

Cal squinted in the distance, "It's Eldon alright, and Jackie's with him."

Eldon toted in two gallons of milk much to Lily's delight and

Jackie uncovered a pot of chicken and dumplings.  Savannah's stomach rumbled louder than Eldon's idling tractor.

That afternoon green and yellow tractors and one or two red ones rumbled up the road at various times, delivering precious and welcome gifts of food.  Christmas morning came to Savannah's mind, only instead of sleighs and reindeer, the benevolent Santas steered big, lumbering John Deere or Case tractors.

By mid-afternoon, mouthwatering meals in pots and disposable cake pans lined the counters.  The haul included chicken soup, spaghetti casserole, beef stew, macaroni and cheese, brownies, cookies and cakes.  It reminded Savannah of the potluck suppers at their church.  Between word of mouth and TV coverage, it seemed everyone in the county heard what happened.  Unfortunately the same proved true for the nation's press...

After the Killibrew's visit, a columnist from the Amarillo newspaper arrived then an hour later another from Dallas popped by. Thanks to Lily's position at the window (Willy still hadn't moved), she gave the family ample warning of any approaching visitors.  Cal, Ennis, Dane, Savannah and Jake crowded the door, armed with deadly frowns and a couple of weapons (the latter against Mama's wishes).  At the back of the group, Jake cradled a double-barrel shotgun across his arm.

Standing in the middle row with Dane (Cal and Ennis were in front), Savannah wore her .38 but kept it holstered.  If questioned about the weapons, she'd tell the reporter they were ambushed once by unwanted visitors and it was *not* happening twice.

The five Rutherfords heard each reporter out – the fella from

Amarillo tried infusing his account with sympathetic commiseration. *Took me a coupla hours just to shovel my car out!* When that failed to impress the stone-faced individuals he groused *And with the schools closed, being locked up with my kids about drove me nuts!*

The brothers scoffed. Savannah stewed. He wanted to complain? She was grateful her children were still *alive* and unharmed. She didn't give a crap about school closings and, by the way, had he not noticed the literal mountains of snow drifts surrounding him? *Try being forced to shovel that, buddy, especially while suffering symptoms of a heart attack.*

Dane saw her tense. He stepped past Cal and issued a terse, "We're not interested in giving interviews. Go back to Amarillo."

"But–"

"There's a sign on that fence out there," he pointed to the ranch entrance, "and you blew right past it. It specifically says *No Trespassing.* I don't want to be rude but we want peace and quiet. Now go."

The reporter did. Unfortunately persuading the fella from Dallas to beat feet became a challenge. Cal and Dane faced this guy, Ennis and Savannah stood behind them which left a grumbling Jake still at the back.

Their refusal to give an interview confused their unwelcome visitor who tried his best to change their minds. When that failed, he changed tactics to recounting his harrowing tale of inching along icy side roads, zig-zagging between abandoned cars and jackknifed trucks. He embellished his efforts with such perilous details it made the Lewis and Clark Expedition sound like a trip to the beach.

Authorities worked overtime to clear roads since the storm ended.

Savannah figured a few cars and trucks still littered the highway but not the perilous minefield the reporter described.

Ennis bristled at the guy's melodrama. Savannah put a hand to her hubby's arm. He ignored it, opting instead to shoulder past his brothers to the door. The reporter retreated a step from the formidable man crowding the doorway – and probably his expression.

Ennis thumbed the latch, swung the door wide to meet him face to face, "Scram."

Savannah worked her way between Cal and Dane as the reporter walked back to his car.

Ennis stood rigid, his muscles flexed and jaw set. His temper toed a thin line but she couldn't exactly blame him. She considered reporters outright intruders. The family's story – as the reporters labeled it – served as a paycheck and a stepping stone for their careers, but the Rutherfords had to live the nightmare the rest of their lives. The mental and physical wounds were still fresh and raw. The healing process took time and left indelible scars. For years to come the smallest, most benign sight or sound would spark painful memories. It was the family's private burden to bear so no, the world didn't need details. Only a few choice people might hear what happened but no one deserved to know everything.

Four o'clock brought another alert from Lily. Another scribe from afar ignored the No Trespassing sign. A figure adequately winterized in a puffy blue parka and matching pants climbed from a black SUV. He stood a minute, surveying the property like he owned it – until he spied Willy Melt.

He took time to retrieve his phone and snap a picture of Willy then a couple of the magnanimous drifts hugging the corner and side of the house. When he plowed, Cal broke through the massive drift stretching high and wide across the road. His efforts left the drift intact, save for its gap-toothed middle wide enough for his tractor. One side still rose to the house's gutter, the other angled down to a respectable yet impressive five feet high.

Dane shook his head, "Here we go again."

"This one's mine," Savannah wanted a piece of someone, *anyone*, with press credentials. The Michelin Man waddling up the porch sufficed just fine.

The bold reporter rapped six times on the door with his fist. Savannah opened the door prepared to school him on common courtesy and ask him if he wanted her to knock six times on his nose with *her* fist. She credited her daughters who sat in Granna's lap for curbing the urge. Nothing taught a person restraint of tongue faster than raising children.

She came face to face with a man matching her height. He had brown, nearly black eyes, short dark hair and a nose perfect for knocking on. The arrogance in his eyes reminded her of Muñoz and only encouraged her to deviate his septum. "What?" she asked in a not so nice manner.

"Good afternoon, ma'am," the smiling interloper introduced himself as Mr. Javi Langer "at your service", straight from the Big Apple's New York Times. "When my article hits the paper, it will be so real the readers will live every moment the way you did."

So he was not only an arrogant pest but a dimwitted one too.

"They don't want to live every moment the way we did." It seemed the safest thing to say. Safest and cleanest. Someone in the Mighty Manhattan must have told him to heap the bullshit on these Texas bumpkins (*Make 'em understand you're doing them a favor by writing this, Javi, or they won't catch on. You know how Texans are. They need oiling before they open up*). Savannah got tired of the South getting a bum rap. They weren't the mental Sunday drivers the Yankees thought they were.

She saw dollar signs and awards gleaming in his eyes. He expected to rake in both on the backs of the family's pain and suffering. She could almost hear him tell his colleagues: *What's an hour listening to these hicks whine and cry about being held at gunpoint? They live in Texas, for God's sake, the most backward state in the Union where guns are more available than candy. What did they expect to happen?*

She intended to realign his thinking one way or another. "Go away." *And that, Harvey, Havi, Whoever-You-Are, is as nice as I get.*

According to Langer's brow, she'd spoken in some foreign dialect he'd never heard before. "But everyone wants their fifteen minutes of fame–"

"We don't. Leave." Ennis put a hand to Savannah's shoulder, gave it a gentle squeeze.

Like the others, Javi (or *was* it Harvey?) related his struggles getting to "this place". "I barely got out of Laguardia before the storm hit and had to sleep on the floor at DFW because that hick town," he jerked his thumb toward Amarillo, "closed their airport. I'm stiff as a board, my rental smells like a wet dog, and I skated on ice to get here.

Now you're refusing an interview? Really?"

"That about sums it up," she said. *Except the part where we tell you to go to hell. I hope you framed that diploma from the Barbed Wire School of Charm, mister, because in two sentences, you've alienated us all. Plus, had Amarillo known such a prestigious New York reporter was flying in, they'd have probably closed the airport sooner.* She physically ached to say it but again, there was that role model aspect to parenting holding her back. She settled for, "We told you to leave so hustle back to that *hick town*, hop a plane and go home."

Langer's mouth dropped open. She noticed many Northerners mistook their Southern counterparts as dense because of their accent and considered their courtesy a weakness. Southerners had limits and Southern women were sweet until they weren't. They possessed sharp tongues and only exercised them with the most deserving people – and did it with a Bless Your Heart and a smile.

The reporter glanced over the cold, white landscape, "Yeah, sure. I don't know what all the fuss is anyway. This snow is impressive for Texas but it's nothing compared to our Nor'easters. When JFK and Laguardia shut down, now *that's* a storm."

The brash remark hit a nerve. She tensed beneath Ennis's touch. His other hand firmly clasped her elbow in case she cut loose on the Big Apple. With her frame of mind lately, she didn't blame him because after that comment, feeding New York a knuckle sandwich grew ever more enticing. *The storm sure didn't feel trivial when I scooped shovels of heavy, wet snow as penance for being a cop,* she fumed silently. She scowled at the bastard who suddenly seemed to realize he'd overstepped.

Ennis urged her to step back but she stayed rooted to the spot, seething. *And this storm certainly didn't feel paltry when I lay bleeding and freezing as the wind drifted snow around me. And it sure hadn't felt small-time when watching Joe Bob's hands plunge past his elbows to dig for the basement doors – so we could try and save our families.*

Ennis tugged again. She slung his hand away to square off with the Yankee cuss, "Listen, you. When you survive what we went through, *then* you can school us about how insignificant this storm was. That *No Trespassing* sign at the entrance warned you to stay off the ranch. You ignored it. You either leave or wait for the sheriff to escort you off the property or *we* will escort you. If we do it, we'll make the trip as unpleasant as you choose it to be."

Ennis's hands returned to her shoulders. This time she didn't shrug away from him. But she stopped long enough to realize she shook with rage. Her fingers blanched around the cane's handle. For one insane moment she entertained using it to beat the shit out of Harvey Wallbanger, Javi Haranguer, or whatever the hell his name was. The family wanted peace. Peace and quiet.

Cal maneuvered to the front, closing ranks around her. "The lady told you to leave. You'd best listen." He shut the door a little too hard. "That's the last straw. I'm posting a second sign at the ranch entrance."

Dane blew him off, "They're already ignoring the No Trespassing sign that's been there for years. Why would they observe another sign saying 'Stay Out or Else'?"

Cal walked away vowing, "I'll make it so crystal clear even a New

Yorker can understand it."

A car door slammed. She and Ennis glanced out the window. Big Apple cranked the engine, turned the SUV around then raced along the road spraying snow the whole way.

Savannah dared not move. Her heart pounded, her fingers still gripped the cane hard enough her hand hurt as she watched the reporter's "wet dog" rental fishtail and swerve down the road. He'd be a casualty of his own temper if he didn't calm down. *A bit like you*, her brain warned. *So try to relax.*

Ennis curled a strand of hair behind her ear, "Are you okay yet?"

Uh, well, not really. Not if fantasies of playing duck hunt with her .38 and a certain ballsy reporter counted as okay. And wouldn't young Monty wonder about her now? Aunt Savannah, the woman he'd written regularly last summer to lift her spirits – a woman he respected, joked around with and considered her (according to his parents) more an older sister than an aunt – this woman salivated to rub out a reporter Gambino-style. Yeah, she scoffed, some role model I am.

Cal stepped in the living room, shrugging on his Sherpa coat. His mouth screwed to the side (a classic Rutherford sign of frustration) while he yanked his gloves on, "You won't believe this. Bobbi saw the Yankee blizzard expert slide off the road. So this Texas hayseed's on his way to pull him out of the ditch." A grim smile crossed his features, "I suggested making him thumb it back to Amarillo but Ma said no."

30

Cal made good on his promise to post a sign below the older, weathered *No Trespassing* one already nailed to the fence. Written in bold black permanent marker, the new sign read "No reporters. Enter at your own risk".

The family approved so carrying the sign, a hammer, nails and the family's blessing, Cal struck out in his trusty Dodge to put the world on notice.

At five-thirty they discovered the world couldn't read. Another SUV. Another journalist from God-Knew-Where.

Cal, Dane, Jake, Savannah and Ennis came to their feet with tired, annoyed groans. After so many years in law enforcement, she considered reporters oversized bedbugs. The bloodsucking beasts invaded and attacked innocent human beings and basically required an exorcism to get rid of them.

Apparently Jake and Dane felt the same since they headed to the gun cabinet. Savannah hoped they meant to use the shotguns for effect, not to shoot holes in their unwelcome arrival (although the notion did sound appealing).

Mama asked for Cal's cell phone.  He stopped and gave her a look.

Charlene gave Savannah the same look after her youngest asked to borrow the Caprice mere hours after passing her driver test.  You want to drive *my* car? she'd asked as if handing her firstborn over for sacrifice.  No, Savannah wanted to drive Georgia's sleek Grand Prix but her sister only allowed her to use it for the test – and that was only because a Georgia State Trooper sat beside her the whole time.

Cal put a protective hand over the phone on his belt, "You've never used a cell phone in your life."  His tone insinuated she might, without trying, find a self-destruct button and accidentally press it.

Mama motioned to hand it over, "Georgia, honey, help me work this contraption.  I'm calling the sheriff.  We'll let him convince this knucklehead to leave us alone."

Cal happily relinquished the phone to Georgia, not his mother.

Meanwhile the dark blue Beemer SUV leisurely traversed the snowpack's bumps and valleys.

Cal and Ennis nudged by Savannah, making themselves the first line of defense against their guest.  That left her and Jake standing behind them and Dane behind her.  She glanced down at the double-barrel shotgun gripped tight in Jake's hand.  Her brow dipped, "You plannin' on using that thing?"

He made no bones about it.  "More than you plan on using yours."

Uh-oh...  His candor sent Lily and Anna to Granna who

struggled to talk on the phone while the two tried to climb in her lap. Georgia and Bobbi claimed a girl apiece and cuddled them close, reassuring them everything was fine but the girls' vision never strayed from that shotgun.

The Beemer's door slammed. Savannah glimpsed between Ennis and Cal's broad shoulders. The fresh-from-college journalist, wrapped up Macaulay-Culkin-style in Home Alone, stopped upon sight of the snowman festooned in its John Deere cap and green scarf. His head cocked a degree. A hint of smile curved his mouth. He shoved a hand in his coat pocket. Out came a phone. He pulled off a glove with his teeth, left it dangling in his grinning mouth and aimed the phone at the snowman. He snapped a couple of pictures then one of the drift beside the house just like the last reporter.

He pocketed his phone and gloves then climbed the porch stairs where he stamped the snow from his boots, clearly expecting an invitation inside. The only invitation he'd receive would be an offer to vacate the property or risk being a moving target for a small army.

Cal opened the door. Dark circles shadowed their visitor's eyes and a sparse preteen-like crop of whiskers lined his jaw. Good God, she thought, this guy's newspaper sent a lamb to slaughter.

No one said a word. The reporter's smile withered slightly. His hand, poised to knock before Cal jerked the door open, waggled its fingers in a little wave instead, "Uh, hi."

Silence. Dane readjusted the shotgun in a non threatening manner but made sure the fella saw it. The guy already zeroed in on the one Jake held.

Home Alone swallowed hard, "I'm Jerrod Heard of the L.A. Times. Could you, um, spare some time for a brief interview?"

Jake racked the shotgun slide.

"I believe that's a no," a terse Ennis replied.

Jerrod looked to Savannah, probably under the misconception that a woman might lend a sympathetic ear, "Ma'am, I finally got out of Albuquerque after two days. I spent the whole time in a fleabag motel and just landed in Amarillo…"

Her hard glare conveyed that the road to Vega may have opened but the road to sympathy closed around three reporters and nine phone calls ago.

He smiled uneasily now, "And… you… don't… want to hear about it. Point is, I've worked really hard to get here just for an interview. How about twenty minutes?"

Silence.

"Ten minutes?"

More silence. The group's collective expression darkened. Jake's hand strangled the shotgun slide.

"Would you consider a brief comment?" Jerrod pushed.

"No," they said in unison.

"We're not talking to reporters," mild-mannered Cal said in a not-so-mild-mannered way. "The sheriff's on his way so unless you want to spend tonight in his jail, you'd best head back to Amarillo before the roads ice up."

"But you don't understand. My boss–"

"Ennis, step aside," Jake hefted the shotgun without actually aiming it at Jerrod. "I'll talk to this fella in twelve gauge. He'll understand that for sure."

The reporter's jaw plummeted, "I only want an interview."

By then Jake and Savannah maneuvered their way to the forefront. She jabbed a finger toward the ranch entrance, "You had fair warning to stay off this land. Either leave before the sheriff arrives or take your chances," she jerked her thumb to Jake, "with him."

"Don't forget me." Dane piped up from the back. "I ain't shot anyone all day." He racked the shotgun slide for effect (she hoped). "How fast are you, buddy?" he asked. "'Cause I get more points for distance shooting."

"Not gonna get many points for him, brother," Ennis joined the conversation. "He looks kinda puny."

Dane tried muscling in, "Lemme out there in case he's faster than we think."

"No," Ennis held him back, "but if he doesn't leave in one minute, *then* we might take drastic measures."

The brothers closed in, squeezing Savannah safely behind them. That suited her fine. She'd had her fill of confrontations the last week. Ennis, though, spoiled for a fight. All the brothers did except Cal. They'd been pushed around long enough Jake declared that morning and as the song said, they weren't gonna take it anymore. Especially from meddlesome reporters.

Savannah put a hand to Ennis's back. Bunched, rigid muscle met her touch. His last statement left no doubt he'd reached his limit. The doorbell and cell phones rang for days. They spent their time answering calls from concerned family and friends and receiving the generous community's food gifts and assistance. There had been precious little peace and even less time to reflect and begin coping with the trauma. Savannah squirreled out alone time once. She spent twenty minutes in the bathroom (amazingly without the girls) crying until exhausting her tears. To her knowledge Ennis hadn't sat down to process what happened. In the meantime anger and guilt (guilt for being unable to rescue his family, he said) – compounded like a volcano about to blow. Every interruption that day pushed him closer to the breaking point and if Savannah didn't step in, she feared he'd go outside and take a swing at Jerrod Heard. Then her hubby, not the reporter, would share the pleasure of Sheriff Guthrie's company (and feast on stale bologna sandwiches).

She stroked the tense muscles, whispering, "Ennis, calm down."

"What'll it be?" Ennis asked the deer-in-the-headlights reporter.

Savannah couldn't believe their role reversal. Usually Ennis kept the cool, level head and talked *her* out of bloodying her knuckles on nitwits. "Those cots are mighty small in that jail," she reminded him. "And Joe Bob said the food sucks."

Jerrod's wide eyes never strayed from Ennis as he backward toward the porch steps, "Take it easy, mister. I'm leaving."

"Dang," Dane said, disappointed. "Are you sure? 'Cause there ain't much to do around here lately but shoot things. I'll give you a head start since you're so peaked from traveling."

"Dane, don't." Georgia cautioned from the couch. She hugged Lily closer, "The girls are scared and Ennis is already on edge."

It was a fun thought, though.  Watching Dane take potshots at the nosy reporter – just to keep him moving.  However Georgia was right.  Why toss gasoline on the flames?

Jerrod's right foot slipped from under him.  Both feet scrambled for purchase on the patch of ice as he clutched for the railing.  His flailing pitched him further off balance until he landed on his butt with a jarring *whump.*

Cal smirked, "You need help?"

Jerrod interpreted Cal's offer as a threat which it wasn't.  "No, no, I'll be okay.  I'm still leaving so don't shoot."

He struggled to his feet, navigated the icy spots dotting the porch and dashed – with a pained limp – to the SUV as if Dane *had* fired at him.  Savannah timed it.  Considering the distance between the porch and car, he clocked an impressive eight seconds.  In rodeo terms he beat the clock and the bull.  In Rutherford terms he avoided Ennis's temper and dancing to a little ditty called Dane and Jake's Dueling Shotguns.

After fumbling with the key fob to unlock the door (Joe Bob would have called him a suspicious City Boy for taking the precaution), he climbed in the car and started the engine in fifteen seconds flat.  She never imagined a Beemer could drive so fast, particularly backwards.

## 31

"I don't wanna get up," Lily whined the next morning. She threw the covers over her head to cocoon herself away from her mother.

Meanwhile on the other side of the bed, Ennis coaxed Anna awake. She protested by giving her daddy the cold shoulder. The night before, both girls relegated their parents to the doghouse the second they heard "the news": *We're going home tomorrow.* They might as well have told their daughters Santa retired.

Neither child wanted to leave Granna, their cousins or the ranch and began a relentless campaign to stay because, as Lily reminded, "Granna said we're her sunshine. We *can't* leave."

Savannah dreaded leaving the family too. She also dreaded the trip home. The crowds, layovers, and long flights with fussy, depressed children. Trying to hurry from terminal to terminal on an ailing leg also presented a challenge. She'd grit her teeth and bear it as long as possible rather than cave to Ennis's bright idea to steer a wheelchair for her. Only in an emergency, she begrudgingly conceded. As in missing-the-connecting-flight type emergency.

Savannah tugged Lily's blanket down to reveal her eyes, "You have to get up or you'll be late for breakfast."

"I'm not hungry," the dejected child mumbled. Anna echoed the sentiment.

Not hungry, hmm? Savannah and Ennis swapped furtive, sidelong glances. They knew one word from Granna and it would be the shortest hunger strike on record. Anything to please their grandmother. Not so much their mama and daddy, at least not today.

Ennis appraised the young, gloomy faces staring back, "I don't want to tell Granna that her two best girls aren't hungry. Do you, Mama?"

Savannah feigned shock that he even suggested it, "*I'm* not tellin' her. It'll break her heart. She's downstairs working hard on a yummy meal for us. I don't like to see Granna cry so you two will have to eat or tell her yourselves that you're skipping her breakfast."

Anna's eyes bulged, "She'll cwy?"

Savannah and Ennis nodded. Here's our first strikebreaker, she thought. Just a teensy-weensie nudge is all it'll take.

Ennis provided it, "I wouldn't want to go home knowing I made her cry, would you?"

The two bailed out of bed. That's as far as their enthusiasm went. They took their time getting dressed. They seemed to realize hurrying expedited seeing Granna but also hastened their departure for home. They didn't want to make Granna cry – they had their pride, after all – and too much gumption might give their party-pooper parents the wrong impression about leaving. So Savannah and Ennis waited patiently for them to change clothes. Lily dutifully collected the clothes her mama laid out the night before and began dressing like a condemned prisoner headed to the gallows.

Little Anna managed to pull on jeans. Period. She left her pajama top on, grabbed her teddy bear off the bed and scampered for the door. Ennis caught her, "No way, little girl. Mama picked your favorite sweater for today so put that and your shoes on then you can go."

Anna frowned as Ennis sat her on the bed. He picked up the sweater. Anna stared at it like a cat about to be bathed.

Savannah waited at the antique vanity to brush Lily's hair. Their oldest trudged over and plopped on the seat with a disgusted *hmmph* then brooded with head bowed.

Savannah lifted Lily's chin until their vision met in the mirror. The child used the moment to hone her pouting. She'd let her mama brush her hair – under silent protest.

Savannah resisted the urge to say *your face will freeze that way*. She'd let the girl sulk a minute longer to feel like she'd accomplished something.

Lily changed tactics to pleading. "Can't we stay longer? Please?"

Ah, so the statue *did* speak...

"We wanna stay," Anna chimed in with Lily.

"So do we but we have to leave today," Ennis said. Mild frustration took over when their baby girl stripped off her pajama top then quit. He held the sweater for her, "Are you gonna put this on?"

She vehemently shook her head. He slipped it over her head, "The faster you dress, the faster you can go downstairs and see Granna."

Anna shoved her arms through the sleeves, clutched her teddy bear close then squirmed to leave. Ennis stopped her with three words. *Shoes are next.* But first he smoothed her flyaway hair. "Daddy," she whined, "stop." She ducked from his touch with another fierce scowl. Or fierce for Anna.

Savannah curtailed a smile. Little Anna's "mad" expression was as intimidating as a basket of mewling kittens.

"Be still," Ennis told her.

Mad Anna surrendered but expelled a sigh two sizes too big for a kid her size.

Savannah couldn't help but smile now, especially when Anna argued, "We hafta go home? I don't fink we hafta."

"Well, we hafta." Mama brushed the wild sleep-inspired tangles from Lily's hair, "Daddy and I hafta go to work and you two hafta go to school."

Lily stared at her mother in the mirror. Accessing her entire arsenal, she went straight to the heart with a parent's kryptonite – sad puppy dog eyes. She focused on the cane leaned against the vanity, "But you're not well yet. Can't we wait till you're well?"

It touched Savannah that her daughter cared about her wellbeing, even if she used it as a ploy to stay longer. She bent to kiss Lily's cheek, "You're a sweetheart to think of my health but going home with a bad leg isn't dangerous. 'Fraid we still gotta go."

She crossed her arms with a huff of displeasure. Foiled again.

Savannah and Ennis exchanged glances. Visits to Texas always ended the same way. Twenty-four hours before liftoff, the girls began campaigning for an extra "day" then "a week" and it always left Mama and Daddy dashing their hopes. Ennis grabbed a comb from the vanity for Anna's tousled locks, "We're coming back. Hopefully before Halloween. If not, then at Christmas."

Lily harrumphed louder. Halloween, Shmalloween. And phooey on Christmas too. She stared at her mama in the mirror. "But we're here *now*," she reiterated as if her parents suffered from Stupid Syndrome.

Savannah continued brushing her daughter's long, silky tresses. "Both of you listen. Granna's coming to see us when the baby's born. Uncle Cal, Aunt Bobbi and the boys are coming with her. We'll see them again soon."

Lily threw a baleful scowl at her suitcase. Such a stark difference from when she skipped through Hartsfield-Jackson and DFW, and then dashed into Uncle Cal's arms for a hug at the Amarillo airport. Now Lily – and Anna – stared daggers at their luggage like they were headed to a deserted island to live forever. Savannah figured if the kids found rope, they'd tie themselves to Granna in protest and chant a preschool version of *hell no, we won't go.*

"Cheer up, girls," Savannah tried again. "Next time you see Granna, Monty and Zach, you'll have a little brother to show off."

Lily heaved a dejected sigh, "Whatever."

## 32

Almost ten years ago Savannah hit the big Three-Oh. With no husband or kids, she delved into her job and set her sights on a promotion to sergeant by thirty-five. The sky was the limit if she stayed on track.

With no distractions (i.e. home life) she felt free to go and do as she pleased. Sure she got lonely but she'd never tell her nosy sister because of Georgia's penchant for arranging blind dates for her. Interfering in a sibling's social life oughta be a felony, she told her sis, then reminded (for the millionth time) that she'd rather be dragged through a briar patch naked than get married. A husband would get in the way. A husband always expects kids and kids take time and too much effort to raise, she said, just ask Daddy who nicknamed me The Insurrection.

Besides, there wasn't a man alive that understood her love for the job. They disapproved or were uncomfortable with a woman who carried a gun. Every single one of them stared at her throughout the evening like they tried to mentally solve the Rubik's Cube sitting across from them.

She'd had enough "romance" between Georgia's picks and her

own lousy choices, especially Toby Jackson, a man who used his hands not to caress but inflict pain. Dating Toby was like growing up with R.J., never knowing what might set him off and trying to survive his wrath. So thanks but no thanks. Her life, though imperfect, suited her fine and if she got lonely for companionship at home, she'd get an orange and white tabby cat and name it Dalai Clawma.

Georgia called her logic "silly" but what did you expect from someone who drank the Kool-Aid and sentenced herself to life with one guy? Georgia bet Savannah before her thirty-fifth birthday she would meet a man who changed her outlook on love and marriage. She actually plunked a hundred dollar bill on the table and said it. Financially Savannah couldn't afford the bet but matched it anyway. After all, by thirty-five she'd be a sergeant and have a very sweet pay raise. She'd laughed when she slapped the bill beside Georgia's with a defiant, "You're on, sis."

She stopped laughing the day her boss marched a tall, strappin' handsome fella into her office. Her new partner, he called him.

God help her, the instant she laid eyes on Ennis her heart sped up, her face grew uncomfortably hot and her mind flashed an enticing fantasy of him taking her in his arms and planting one hell of a kiss on her. The slight accent in his voice replaced images of sharing a bed with an orange and white fuzzball with snuggling up to Big Tex.

One problem though. She and Big Tex were partners on the job, not lovers. It would never work, she told herself in an effort to right her emotional ship (and tame her sudden ravenous libido). "Behave yourself, Savannah," she could almost hear her mama scold. "Ladies do not drool over men."

*I don't feel very ladylike at the moment, Mama. No "lady" should ever have these ideas.* She dreaded spending day after day with this man because she foresaw a constant state of arousal in her future.

Ennis wasn't only handsome. He was kind and genteel. He had a great sense of humor. He was the polar opposite of Toby Jackson and the other clowns she'd known. Ennis was the whole package, damn it, and fending off his requests for a date were killing her. Twice a week he asked her out. Any kind of date, he said, anything she wanted just name it (*that* offer practically finished her off). How about dinner, a movie, stargazing, riding a trail on horseback? "I know just the place an hour outside the city," he told her. "We can spend the day together."

Yay. Just what she needed. More temptation. Eventually she caved on dinner. Everyone had to eat, right? And it was a *safe* date since restaurants frowned on necking in their establishments.

From that day forward "behaving herself" became a twenty-four hour job that distracted her from her paying one. "Keep your head up, knees closed, and eyes open," her mama instructed way back when. "If Cinderella can get her Prince Charming without taking her dress off then so can you."

Savannah didn't want Prince Charming or marriage. Ennis entertained delusions of grandeur though. He mentioned marriage usually in a joking fashion but not always.

"I'll break your stubborn streak," he vowed. "We'll get married, have 2.3 kids and grow old in rocking chairs and fuss over the TV remote."

Yeah sure, anything you say, crazy man, she shot back. Was he crazy – or was she the nut? Night after night she ran those marriage scenarios through her mind and test drove her "married" name for kicks (she felt so adolescent, like a girl scribbling her "married" name on her school notebook). Savannah Rutherford. It sounded nice. Very nice. Oh grow up, she berated herself. *You're thirty, not thirteen. What happened to no jeopardizing your career? No "I Do's", no pledging yourself to a man, no 2.3 kids, no unreasonable expectations of happily ever after – because those belong to Walt Disney, another sadly deluded fool. Remember?* She had strong feelings for Ennis, yes, but strong enough to walk down the aisle? Nuh-uh.

She did, however, agree to spend her vacation in Texas with him and his family. It was either that or spend it painting her living room and bedroom. Riding horses with Ennis, eating BBQ with Ennis and relaxing in the quiet country (with Ennis of course) sounded better.

Her decision delighted him so much he brought her into his arms and kissed her. A kiss that should have warned her to buy paint, not plane tickets, because anything *that* intimate was a red flag for trouble. She seriously considered staying home because she didn't trust herself around him now.

"You'll regret backing out," Georgia told her while helping her pack her suitcase. "Ennis is perfect for you. You need him and meeting his family is a good idea." She winked, "Just in case."

*Thanks for using that phrasing, sis. Needing him is the whole damn problem.*

Georgia's enthusiasm for the trip tweaked her suspicions. Her sister and Ennis were known to confer on certain subjects called "Savannah". Had the two cooked up this trip? Georgia must really want that hundred bucks, Savannah frowned while watching her sister refold clothes "her way" and place them "her way" in the Samsonite. It was no secret Georgia liked Ennis for her poor single sister. Savannah liked him a lot too but, she hated to tell Nosy Rosy, she didn't like him enough to slip a ball and chain on the third finger of her left hand.

Georgia kept packing. Savannah kept smelling a conspiracy. "My place really needs painting," she reminded. "Maybe I should–"

"When you get back I'm sure Ennis will help you paint. Savannah, you'll have a blast and you'll never forgive yourself if you back out now."

Five minutes after stepping off the plane in Amarillo, she regretted not staying home instead.

"I hate to tell you this," Ennis said as they made their way to baggage claim, "but my family is under the impression we're, um…"

*Here we go.* "They think we're getting married, don't they?" Well, it made sense. Why else would a guy invite a woman halfway across the country to spend a week with him and his family? Why else would the woman agree to it? *No doubt about it. I'm an idiot. A trapped idiot now.*

His nod confirmed her worst fear. He offered a not-so-convincing apology but conveniently seized the carry-on from her, probably to prevent her from swinging it at him.

Instead she stopped in mid-stride, not caring that she held up foot traffic behind her, "Ennis, I can't go through with this. I can't lie to your family."

"You will if you like me.  Just play along for a while, see how it goes."

*Like to watch train wrecks, do you?*  She waggled her left hand at him, "So where's my engagement ring, Don Juan?"

At a loss, he shrugged, "Getting sized?"

"M-hmm," she mumbled.  "Tomorrow they'll be sizing us for coffins 'cause your family'll kill us when they find out."

"Maybe they won't find out."

"I'm here for a week.  Someone will find out.  Any questions are yours to answer.  I wanted a vacation, not a wedding dress."

Once the truth came out his family would understandably hate her and she'd never see them again.  Not so for her uneasy partner chattering up a storm as he drove to the ranch.  *He* had a lifetime of embarrassment ahead of him because she knew from experience siblings never let you live anything down.

Before arriving at the ranch they agreed to avoid or skirt the subject whenever possible.  No confirming there was an actual engagement.  Uh-huh, the cynic in her said.  That'll work.  Just like the Titanic.

With the exception of Jake (who seemed to already hold a grudge against her) his family welcomed her so warmly that her conscience needled her.  How could she lie to Ennis's mother and live with herself?  Mama Rutherford was sweet and trusting and reminded Savannah too much of her own mother (and lying to Charlene never, ever worked).  Mama truly cared about Ennis's happiness and treated Savannah like a long lost daughter and the answer to a mother's prayers. Ennis finally found The One.

Savannah doubted she could sink any lower but she tried gently nudging the family toward the truth by offering reasons why a marriage might not be immediately forthcoming.

Mama blamed the excuses on cold feet. She grabbed Savannah in a hug, "Oh honey, you both love each other so why wait? The sooner you get married, the sooner I get grandchildren to spoil and those babies will be darlin'."

*Well, so much for that idea...*

The farce kicked into high gear when Mama Rutherford made a few calls the next day. People flocked to the ranch once Mama put the word out. *Ennis is engaged! Come meet his fiancée and celebrate with some BBQ!* Savannah warned Ennis lying to the family was bad enough but to the whole damn town? Forget it.

Then she met Jenny Lee Crawford. The brazen broad brought blood the instant she saw Savannah. Jenny scowled at her while asking Ennis, "Where'd you find *her?*"

Jenny dominated Ennis during the BBQ, smooched and pawed on him then spirited him away for privacy – until Savannah's jealousy hit the red zone. He was *her* fiancé, not Jenny Lee Craw– *Good God,* Savannah couldn't believe it. *He's got me doing it now.* Fiancé or not, he wasn't interested in Jenny (*he's interested in me, ya bimbo, so back off!*) and Savannah intended to show her that fact up close and personal if need be.

Once seeing the fire in his partner's eyes, Ennis took care of

Jenny. It was the only time Savannah approved of the engagement lie. The news crushed Jenny Lee. She stared at Ennis, heartbroken and accusing him of forsaking her and falling for "that woman's manipulative charms".

"That woman" (Jenny's new pet name for Savannah) remained quiet but prepared for a catfight if Crawford kept disparaging her femininity, paternity, occupation (that's a man's job!) and overall existence.

After Jenny Lee left, the day returned to a bright, happy occasion, at least for the folks not lying about their relationships. Friends and neighbors resumed throwing around phrases like "made for each other" and "perfect couple". Savannah sensed hives starting to sprout.

Men shook Ennis's hand and clapped him on the back with congratulations. Her "fiancé" proudly lapped it up. Throughout the afternoon women squeezed Savannah in hugs and drowned her in conversation and questions. The swarming inquisitive ladies meant no harm of course but it gave her a fair idea what she put suspects through during interrogations.

Growing up in Augusta, her family exchanged hellos with neighbors but aside from family or a boyfriend braving her daddy's unpredictable behavior, no one really visited the Prince house. Meanwhile, a thousand miles away at the Rutherford Ranch, dozens of relatives and close friends crowded the backyard in summer where mesquite smoked BBQ and drinks were as plentiful as smiles and laughter. Young Ennis grew up in a large, loving family and supportive community. Savannah grew up in a smaller, tumultuous family and had a handful of friends (and aforementioned brave boyfriends) so on her first visit at the ranch, being in the spotlight with the large crowd really loosened her screws.

Complete strangers called her darlin' and sweetie. They treated her like an old friend and insisted she join them in a game of Forty-Two. Forty-two what, she'd asked. They just chuckled and pointed to Ennis, "He'll explain it to you, darlin'." She learned Forty-Two was a domino game. "The National Game of Texas" they called it. She further learned she sucked at playing "The National Game of Texas" too.

She still didn't play Forty-Two but had long since "earned her spurs" (as Doc Garrett once said) at poker. She decided not to tell everyone she'd been playing and winning since eighth grade.

By day's end mental and physical exhaustion prevented her from ramming her head in a wall for aiding and abetting such an egregious lie. It grew from a spark to a raging wildfire in one afternoon. The entire community expected invites to a wedding she neither planned nor had a say in.

Why did Ennis joke about marrying her in the first place? Or *was* he joking? That gleam in his eye that afternoon concerned her. Did he honestly believe they'd eventually stand at the alter, exchange "I Do's" and have those 2.3 kids? Couldn't he see she'd make a lousy wife and mother?

*While we're questioning sanity here, what jump-started your jealousy today, dearie? You wanted to haul Jenny to the barn by the ears and teach her a hard lesson about moving in on your man.* Savannah never "claimed" a man in her life or wanted to. However watching Jenny

Lee basically climb Ennis like a tree made her fist ache to dent the woman's nose. Watching the octopus in skintight blouse and jeans attack her partner left Savannah in mute shock – and planning where to hide Jenny's body once she killed her.

It physically pained her to see his arms wrapped around Ms. Crawford's over-ample figure for a simple platonic hug. The night before, he'd held Savannah in those arms (in an anything-but-platonic manner) while he kissed her until her knees went soft.

Ennis finally pried free of Jenny's greedy, apparently bruising grasp and held her firmly at arm's length to avoid her smothering kisses. Seventeen hours earlier he drew Savannah close with those hands and his tender touch roamed and explored her body in a prelude that had her reconsidering her mama's "knees closed" advice.

But she wanted something more than a roll in the hay and had for a while – she just never took time to analyze her feelings. Hours after watching Ennis wrest himself from Jenny Lee's clutches, she took the opportunity to think it through while Ennis showered.

Lately her hormones raged and sex drive broke the speed limit. *That* part of her body worked better than a Swiss clock on steroids. It was her heart that concerned her. It ached for Ennis. Hearing his voice, thinking about him, just saying his name sent it tripping into a livelier, happier cadence. Every time his gaze met hers, a strange tugging in her heart urged her to do rash, unimaginable things like say "I love you". When they were together everything felt right. Perfect even. When they were apart, cold, dark loneliness crept in as if her joy resided in him. Until she saw him again she felt restless, empty and incomplete.

Ennis stepped from the bathroom barefoot, shirtless and in jeans. Her heart launched into its happy dance. She realized the reaction wasn't only physical attraction. This went deeper, to her soul. *I love him. I'm hopelessly, desperately in love with Ennis.*

Savannah coasted on love for days, smiling wider, laughing longer, and truly enjoying life – until days later when the world crashed in.

Little six-year-old Monty discovered their lie by accident. He'd overheard a tense discussion between Savannah and Ennis about telling the family there was no engagement.

Her heart, so light and happy, dropped to a dull, heavy thud. Six stern faces greeted them. Correction. Five stern faces and a devastated one – Monty's. Savannah wanted to crawl in a hole. All she could do was apologize and did so. She centered on Mama but quickly looked away, ashamed. One question lingered in his mother's eyes and it twisted Savannah's gut. *Why did you lie?* But Mama Rutherford never asked. The woman let guilt do the job for her, saying only, "I just wish you'd told us."

A red-faced Monty reluctantly confessed, "I heard you and Uncle Ennis say you weren't 'gaged. I told everyone. I'm sorry."

*You. Are. Kidding.* Her mouth dropped open. *He feels guilty for telling the truth?* "Monty, it's not your fault. It's ours."

"No, it's mine," Ennis said.

"I went along with the charade," Savannah argued.

"I asked you to as a favor to me." He scanned the faces around the table, "I don't want Savannah blamed for any of this."

"Why not?" she asked.  "We both deceived them."

Ennis ignored the comment, "She warned me it would backfire but this family is so relentless about marriage.  No one can be single or it's a sin."

Gee, sounds just like Georgia, she grumbled.

"Really, little brother?" Dane's sarcastic side emerged.  "I hadn't noticed since I'm sooo happily married myself."

His remark didn't set well with Mama or Bobbi, the two biggest cheerleaders for holy matrimony.

Dane crossed his arms, "Ennis, I was content sharing the misery with you and Jake, you know, kinda spread it a tad thinner among us single fellas then you supposedly got engaged and brother, Mama and Bobbi took aim on me.  They know every available female in the county."

"You weren't alone," Jake told Dane.  "They even mentioned that bigmouth Jenny Lee Crawford.  Why, she'd drive me crazy."  He glared at Bobbi, "You really hate me, don't you?  Trying to fix me up with her."  He sounded almost spiteful when he told Savannah, "Personally I'm glad you're not engaged.  It takes the heat off me."

Well, that explained his bristly attitude toward her.  By marrying Ennis, it reduced the single Rutherford population to "endangered" status.  Jake's rude behavior got her dander up in a big way.  Who was he to begrudge her and Ennis happiness together?  Maybe she *wanted* to marry Ennis.  Someday she might.  If he planned to stand in their way if they decided to exchange vows, he'd have a hard lesson to learn about Savannah Charlene Prince.  Her daddy hadn't nicknamed her The

Insurrection for nothing.

Ennis sighed, "If y'all remember I never said we were engaged. You assumed it when I invited her here for a vacation. I said I'd marry her, yes, I didn't say I'd marry her the second she stepped off the plane. I love Savannah and I was hoping she'd eventually change her mind about marriage but now I doubt she ever will."

Monty climbed from the dining chair, circled around to Savannah. He peered up at her as if he'd lost his last friend, "You mean you're not gonna marry Uncle Ennis?"

She hated when kids used that look on her. That mopey, thanks-for-ripping-out-my-heart pout. She could handle Jake's mood much easier but between Mama and Monty, she never stood a chance. She bent to one knee to face Monty. The child deserved the truth. They all did. "Not right now, kiddo. I know that's not what you want to hear and I'm sorry."

The boy hung his head, toed the carpet, dejected.

She tipped his chin up, "But you know what? Uncle Ennis and I love each other. We may not get married real soon but give us time and we'll see how it goes."

His face brightened with the beginnings of a smile, "That means I *can* call you Aunt Savannah? Really?"

"I was sure hoping you would."

Monty beamed, threw his arms around her and hugged her tight. She gladly returned the embrace. She loved that adorable kid with a Rutherford cowlick and twang bigger than Dallas. Hell, who was she kidding? She fell for the whole family shortly after she met them so the "official" name "Aunt Savannah" might come to fruition sooner than she thought.

That week in Texas proved three things. One, she could make a complete, shameful fool of herself. Two, she was madly in love with Ennis – and his family was pretty darn special too and three, some bets were worth losing. Georgia was right. Ennis was perfect for her. Now she owed Georgia a hundred bucks.

## 33

The family sat at the breakfast table that overflowed with food yet no one seemed overly interested in eating. Adults stole quick glimpses at the clock ticking its way closer to time to leave. In less than two hours the marathon began, driving to Amarillo, traversing busy airports all day, waiting to board planes and waiting to land. But first they had to eat breakfast, pack their luggage and get ready to go.

Departure day breakfasts always began subdued and on the sentimental side. After a week of fun and laughter, no one ever wanted to say goodbye but today the atmosphere felt somber. Their time together meant more now and goodbyes seemed harder to say. The last few days hugs felt tighter and held on a little longer. Now a fine meal sat before them – the last step before they said their farewells and parted ways again – and no one appeared in the mood.

Savannah scanned the gloomy faces around her. Dane and Jake seemed to call a truce to their usual banter. Monty and his brothers normally livened up the meals with their upbeat spirits. Today they waited to eat with the same hangdog expressions as Lily and Anna when they dressed that morning.

Savannah sympathized. Home sounded this side of heaven – the familiarity, family, friends and love. Except this place, a ranch built in the windiest, most unpredictable area on the planet also held a special place in her heart and for the very same reasons.

After Mama's poignant prayer, a silent procession of bowls, pans and platters began around the table. Surprisingly Jenny Lee seemed to have mastered her directionally-challenged tendencies and set a proper table again. She'd shown up with Jake that morning and taken time to set the tables before leaving to tend livestock with him and the other men. Savannah heard rumors among the ladies that Jenny agreed to muck the horse stalls that morning, and in Savannah's opinion that equated to another "giant leap for mankind" when Jenny Lee Crawford agreed to shovel horse pucky.

"We hafta go?" Anna stared at her plate as if it were her last meal – ever.

Ennis sighed.

Savannah's shoulders slumped. For the hundredth time, "Yes, honey, we hafta." Since Uncles Cal and Jake, Aunt Bobbi and the boys walked through the door, both girls blitzed their parents with the same tiresome question with a strongly emphasized "hafta". One more mention of it and they'd hafta peel Savannah off the ceiling. "But like we said," she added, "we'll see everyone again soon. You'd both better eat. Granna wants us going home with full tummies." She left off the unspoken implication. *Don't make Granna cry.*

She glanced across at Georgia and Dane in the drag-out-the-straightjacket hopeless way parents did when their tolerance ran on rims. They both offered sympathetic smiles.

"You get everything done this morning?" Ennis asked Cal.

"Yep. We even enlisted Jenny Lee to help with the horses."

Jake proudly put his arm around her, "And she didn't run away once. I got a photo of her dressed in boots and overalls if anyone wants to see it. Looks like a regular ol' stable hand holding that manure fork."

"You better not show that ugly picture, Jake Rutherford," Jenny threatened good-naturedly. "I don't mind helpin' but showin' that picture is the limit." Nose wrinkled, Jenny shivered, "I'd sure rather ride horses than clean up after them."

Savannah chuckled, "I felt the same way the first time I cleaned the stalls too. You never get used to the smell but the horses appreciate your work."

Mucking the stalls still tested her big city constitution. Horses were great to ride but, like cows, they were the poopiest critters she'd ever seen – including her kids. Her babies made her eyes water lots of times but to their credit she never fought the smell *and* squadrons of flies at the same time. Cleaning out horse stalls while shooing those persistent winged devils should have been a rodeo event.

Then there was feeding and milking cows – those smelly old things a person grabbed in the privates (so to speak) for one of the tastiest refreshments known to man. And the beef cattle representing the heart of the Rutherford's business had their own maintenance needs. While she preferred to see her steaks at the store, caring for the cattle before they were Porterhouses or T-bones was quite a change of pace.

Feeding the big ol' bovines dropping smelly patties and caring for the horses swishing their tails at flies (and sometimes accidentally slapping her nose) became oddly cathartic. Yes, farm animals tested a greenhorn's olfactory senses. They crapped a mess but so did her babies once upon a time. Fact was brushing a horse and other ranch duties pushed her day job to the background. No investigations or interrogations required, no handcuffs or reading a suspect their rights. Just the repeated stroke, stroke, stroke of a brush along a horse's back – and their thanks given as a soft nickering. For a city girl she adapted pretty well to ranch life.

Savannah reached for her orange juice then thought better of it, just in case Georgia struck again with the salt shaker. Just because her sister *appeared* down in the dumps did not mean her mischievous side took a powder. Plus, Georgia had poured the juice while Jenny filled the milk glasses. Since Savannah felt confident Jenny wasn't feeling suicidal that morning, she opted for the glass of milk and tilted it to her lips. She got nothing.

She resisted the urge to glare Jenny's way. *She wouldn't pull a prank on me, not after this week, right?*

The boys giggled. One by one chuckles supplanted the group's glum spirits until coming full circle with Jake and Jenny Lee (the latter hid her humor behind a strategically placed napkin). "I didn't do it, I swear," she promised.

Savannah angled the glass to and fro, amazed that the liquid remained firmly in place. *It's fake. It has to be.* So she sniffed it. It sure *smelled* real so she poked the contents with a fork. The perplexing white stuff jiggled like Jell-O.

She frowned at Georgia but noticed Tyler elbowing Monty. *She thinks it was Aunt Georgia,* he whispered.

A shrewd smile eased across Savannah's lips. *So I underestimated my young nephew, did I?*

She zeroed in on the culprit, "Monty, you evil genius. How'd you do this?" She had an idea but considering he sat there so pleased that he tricked Aunt Savannah, she gave him the opportunity to brag.

Tyler and Zach high-fived their older brother who unfurled a Cheshire Cat grin, "I boiled gelatin, added the milk, and put it in the fridge. Aunt Georgia thought of it."

Georgia leaned back with her own smug delight – a little *too* much delight, "That's for murdering my Hardy Boys years ago."

"Can't turn my back on any of you, can I?" Savannah joked. "Between putting food coloring on toothbrushes – and Ennis, don't you dare try that at home – and my sister and nephew in cahoots, a soul isn't safe in any situation."

Tyler belly laughed, "Aunt Georgia spiked your orange juice too, remember?"

"How kind of you to remind me," Savannah aimed the sly expression across to Georgia. "My Machiavellian sister will get hers later, don't worry."

"Good luck," Georgia challenged. "I don't read Hardy Boys anymore."

"Probably not, but it *is* difficult to write a book without a computer."

"I can write longhand in a notebook."

"If you can find it," Savannah teased.

"Macky-what?" Zach was a few steps behind.

Savannah replied, "It means don't mess with Georgia. She holds a grudge forever."

Georgia winked at Monty, "If she swipes my writing tools, you and I will conspire against her this summer. Between the two of us, we'll find some lulus to pull on Aunt Savannah, won't we?"

Bobbi perked up at the mention of their summer trip. She greedily rubbed her hands together, "Oh, I can't wait for July." She counted on her fingers, reciting an inventory of places she planned to visit, "The aquarium, Underground Atlanta, Lenox Square, Phipps Plaza…" When she exhausted her list (that took all ten fingers plus one she didn't have), she'd left precious little time for eating or sleeping.

Everyone's jaws slung open – except Cal who continued eating as if the conversation revolved around weather.

"Miss the big city much?" Ennis asked his sister-in-law.

Dane managed to string together a few words, these to Cal who casually ladled more gravy on his biscuit, "I hope you booked a second flight for all the stuff she buys."

"And build another house to hold it all," Ennis added.

"Better make it that mansion in 'Gone With the Wind'," Jake said. "What was its name? Farrah, Sarah–"

"*Tara*, you big galoot," Bobbi rolled her eyes. "Where'd your culture go? That's a classic like 'Pride & Prejudice' or 'Wuthering Heights'."

His brow puckered, "Withering what?"

"Bobbi, you know ol' Jake reads a different sort of classic," Dane prodded. "The ones written in mostly one syllable words like *see Spot run.*"

The family laughed until Jake came to his feet, shoulders squared. Savannah guessed Dane overstepped with his ribbing because his brother seemed prepared to drag him outside by the nose and refresh his math skills by counting punches. If he takes such offense to Dane's playfulness, imagine the joys of marrying the Queen of Drama, Savannah thought ruefully.

Cal started laughing. Bobbi's husband put a voice to Savannah's thoughts, "Jake, if something that simple riles you up, you don't stand a chance at marriage."

Bobbi stared at her husband as if he'd suddenly gone daffy, "And what's *that* supposed to mean?"

Amused, Cal passed a knowing glance to the others, "Nothing, sweetheart. Nothing at all."

"I'd like Bobbi, Georgia and Savannah to be my bridesmaids," Jenny Lee blurted.

Ennis's fork clattered to his plate. Cal's hand retreated from the bowl of biscuits.

Only Zach, Tyler and the girls were left eating. Soon the stillness and sudden deafening silence brought their consumption to a gradual halt.

The unexpected announcement deflated Jake's discontent enough he sat down, stunned at his fiancée.

Jenny met each woman's gaze, including Savannah's with nervous hope as if anticipating refusals. Apparently vehement refusals.

Savannah debated whether Jenny pulled her own prank by mentioning her. A bridesmaid? For years Jenny hated her full-time with no vacations, no holidays or snow days. She felt obligated to include her. That explained it. Since she mentioned Georgia and Bobbi it would look funny if she left Savannah out. Otherwise it was either a joke or a parallel universe.

Georgia and Bobbi shifted their attention to Savannah who stared ahead as stunned as Jake. Eventually she pieced together one word, "Really?"

Jenny Lee swallowed hard, "That is, if y'all want to."

*Okay, that didn't sound forced or resentful. She wants me, the bane of her existence – the brazen intruder who supposedly "stole" her beloved Ennis from her arms – to be a bridesmaid? Somewhere pigs are flying...*

"I'd love to, Jenny Lee," Bobbi gushed. "Thank you."

Georgia smiled a mile wide, "Count me in."

The family focused on the pregnant lady sitting beside her husband who'd yet to retrieve his wayward fork or close his mouth.

It was obvious Jake also struggled to wrap his mind around the announcement too. "Jenny, you *do* realize who you mentioned, right?"

"Yes," was the soft reply. "Savannah, I understand if you refuse. I've never treated you kindly but it would mean a lot to me if you accepted."

Jenny had promised to change her perspective, to *try* and treat

Savannah "kindly" from now on. Leopards weren't apt to change their spots but hey, Savannah was willing to chance it. Jenny's promise and bridesmaid request took courage and for that Savannah gave her credit. "I'd be honored, Jenny Lee. Thank you."

That *wasn't* disappointment dawning on Jenny. Savannah thought it might be cautious hope.

"You said yes?" Jenny turned to Jake, "She said yes, right?"

Jake smiled beneath the bushy mustache, "She said yes, darlin'. You can breathe now."

Jenny sagged as she expelled a long, loud *whew*. Her face relaxed into a smile, "I'm so relieved you said yes."

A little faith goes a long way, Savannah's mama always said. Savannah prayed she was right because once those vows were exchanged and Jake kissed his bride, the Rutherford family future was cast in stone.

She also prayed the orange juice wasn't spiked with salt because she raised her glass to make a toast, "To Jake and Jenny. Here's to love and laughter and happily ever after."

O   O   O

Grimy, gray snow walled I-40 on both sides of the highway, obscuring views of pastures and livestock that several days before roamed within sight. It had delighted Lily and Anna to see the cattle the day they arrived. Today the girls slumped in their seats, bored with the lack of scenery and pouting that they'd left Granna behind.

The brothers and Georgia chatted as Cal drove. They were

oblivious to the unnatural, ugly, gray barrier to their right. Savannah wasn't. The plows cleared enough road for two lanes and a narrow emergency lane. The imposing wall tickled her claustrophobia at times but that wasn't what occupied her thoughts.

Despite her best efforts, memories of Muñoz and Brozek crept in. The misery of shoveling the back porch. Waiting out the fear of a heart attack. Muñoz's black hatred when he fired at her, the shot barely missing her head. The .45 shoved in her mouth and the march outside to what should have been her death.

Her mind drifted to the miracle of Joe Bob Crawford, of waking up cocooned in warm blankets and a hot water bottle on her belly to warm her baby boy. The man who dropped by to check on his sister and stumbled onto a pregnant woman left to die in the storm. He'd saved two lives that day and humbly denied what he was. A hero.

In the following days, people would return to their routines and bemoan the snow and when it might melt. In another week, the storm would mostly be a memory, save for the shrinking mounds of grungy, plowed snow still lingering as reminders of the blizzard good ol' Windbag Willy and other forecasters grossly misjudged.

Inconvenienced travelers, delayed from their destinations for days were already on the move again, taking with them an experience the people back home might not believe about Texas. Yes, it snowed there and in the Panhandle it occasionally snowed *a lot*.

For the Rutherfords, its effects and resulting encounter with four escaped murderers, the effects would last forever. Only Daniel Joseph Rutherford would live vicariously through his relatives' accounts. The story of a brave family that refused to give up or give in and for their efforts they triumphed over evil.    There would be no shortage of viewpoints of that day's events.    Savannah expected little Daniel would hear them all eventually but she and Ennis would make sure he learned how he came by the middle name Joseph.

J.L. Lemon lives in Texas surrounded by a loving and supportive family, two adorable and devoted puppies, and hordes of garden gnomes.

Before 2002, J.L. Lemon wrote opinions and product reviews for an online consumer guide. When fellow reviewers cited the author's knack for humor, she decided to return to writing fiction. Along with the standalone title Second Chances, she's published 13 books in the Savannah Stories Series.